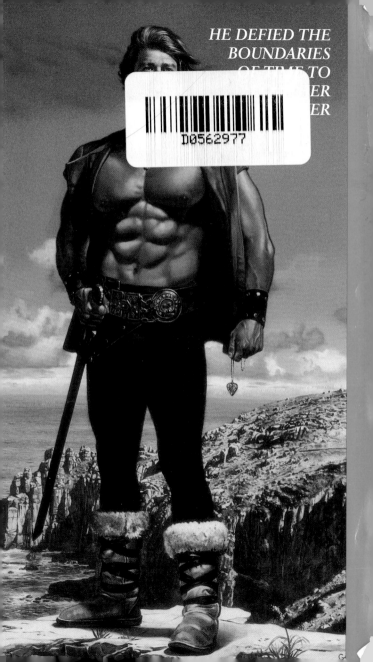

HE DEFIED THE
BOUNDARIES
OF TIME TO
ER
ER

SHE STRUCK OUT WITH HER FISTS. "LET ME GO!" SHE SCREAMED. "LET ME—"

His arms tightened around her until she could not break free.

He wrapped his hand through her hair, forcing her to look at him. "If I had meant you any harm," he said tightly, "if I had intended to kill you, or . . . " His gaze flicked over her body again, and he clenched his jaw and looked away, shifting his attention to the open window. "I already had ample opportunity. Do you not understand? There is nowhere to run, *demoiselle*. You are on an *island*. If you try that again, you will fling yourself over a cliff in the darkness and fall to your death!"

She could feel every inch of his body pressed against hers. Unable to struggle, feeling trapped and helpless and hating him for it, she spat in his face.

He let her go, wiping the back of his hand across his cheek. "Heed me well, milady," he grated out. "Whoever and whatever you were before, it no longer matters. You have a new life now." His eyes semed to glitter unnaturally in the moonlight. "And you will never leave this place . . ."

SHELLY THACKER

Timeless

A DELL BOOK

Published by
Dell Publishing
a division of
Bantam Doubleday Dell Publishing Group, Inc.
1540 Broadway
New York, New York 10036

ISBN: 0-440-22514-0

Printed in the United States of America

Published simultaneously in Canada

March 1998

10 9 8 7 6 5 4 3 2 1

OPM

To Mark,
Christine Zika, Laura Cifelli, and Rob Cohen.
Thank you for believing in me.

And to my sisters of the Clork & Toach,
Beth, LaVerne, and Linda.
Thank you for supplying me with chocolate,
finding me trees, and supporting me
even during super-killer-deadline-crunch.
You truly are the sisters I never had.

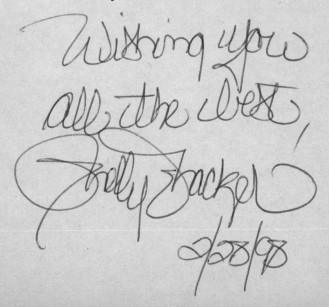

 In a time long ago, when kings and princes ruled the land, when the world's unexplored corners and uncharted seas tempted men of bold heart to explore, a small band of daring Norsemen set out in search of a fabled, fertile domain to the west.

But like a mischievous dragon, the rough northern seas carried their longship to a hidden island instead, a place cloaked in mists and mystery, set apart from the world for centuries, untouched by time.

There they found bountiful fields and deep, cool forests, vast meadows, cascading waterfalls, and midsummer warmth that knew no season. Enchanted, the twenty Norsemen decided to claim the island as their home, naming this newfound paradise Asgard, after the legendary realm of the gods said to float above the earth, invisible to the eyes of men.

True to the daring spirit of their age, the warriors went a-viking, raiding, to seek brides to share their new home—and they soon discovered that Asgard offered much more than natural beauty. The island held a special magic unknown elsewhere in the world, a gift that has been enjoyed by their sons and daughters generation after generation.

Over the centuries, the people of Asgard have kept the island's secret, protecting it from those who would wage war to possess it. Yet the gift also carries a price . . .

I

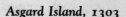

'Twas a dangerous task, stealing women.

A man needed guile, strength, blade-skill, and boldness to find a fair maiden, pluck her from the bosom of her family like ripe fruit from a bough, carry her off—and live long enough to enjoy his prize.

Hauk Valbrand frowned, seated in the stern of the longboat as it pierced the fog and glided across the glassy, night-black sea. Studying the twelve warriors straining at the oars, their sweaty, angular faces illuminated by an oil lantern dangling from the prow, he knew that only seven or eight possessed the qualities needed to survive. The young fools should have listened to him when he argued against taking this risk.

Despite the battle-axes strapped across their backs and the swords at their waists, some of his traveling companions would lose their lives before this voyage was done.

He clenched his jaw and looked back over his shoulder at the distant beach, now a mere ribbon of silver in the moonlight. A brine-scented breeze made the fog shift and dance, while the rhythmic dipping of the oars through the water made the only sound in the stillness. All revelry and bawdy jests had ended when they left shore.

As soon as the young raiders had donned their brown homespun garments and pushed the square-sailed ship into the mist that cloaked their island home, each seemed to realize the seriousness of the dangers ahead.

But neither Hauk's logic nor the threat of facing an outraged father or brother or kinsman had been enough to sway them from their purpose. The ancient drives were too strong, the temptation too powerful.

Had he not felt the same fire in his blood years ago, his first time? Had he not lived to enjoy his pretty prize?

Ja, and he had also lived to regret ever setting eyes on her.

"Still having doubts, old friend?"

Hauk glanced at the man beside him, who had one arm slung across the tiller. "*Nei.* Nay," he replied tightly. "Merely wondering which of us will not survive to return home, Kel."

"I am certain we will all return home." Keldan pushed back the hood of his cloak, revealing thick dark hair, a confident smile, and a face that always made females swoon at his feet in annoying numbers. "You have trained us well, Hauk. Nils is now better with a blade than any man on Asgard—other than you, of course. And Bjarn has become an expert with that odd weapon that fires short arrows—"

"A crossbow."

"A crossbow." Keldan shrugged as if the name did

not matter. "And we have spent six months planning every detail of this journey—"

"And most of you have never left the island before. Even the best among you is little better than a green lad."

Keldan wrinkled his nose in offense. "Inexperienced we may be, but the Claiming voyage is an honored tradition—and even *you* cannot fight tradition, Hauk."

"Stolen fruit tastes the sweetest," one of the other would-be warriors said, quoting the centuries-old saying among the inhabitants of Asgard Island.

Hauk slanted the eager young whelp a quelling look. "If we are to survive, we must *change* some of the old traditions." It seemed he had been saying that every day of late. He sighed, rubbing at his eyes, running a weary hand through his tangled blond hair. "The Claiming voyage was necessary for survival in the early days, but that is no longer true. In these times it is dangerous not only to us but to everyone we leave behind. There are seven hundred lives on that island, and I am responsible for keeping them safe—"

"Mayhap you should have stayed behind with them, Valbrand," another raider commented, his voice laced with undisguised hostility. "We do not need you hovering over us like some overgrown nursemaid."

Hauk sliced his old nemesis with a glare. "I am here by order of the elders, Thorolf. Someone had to ensure that you hot-blooded raiders remember our laws and do not bring a world of trouble down upon us."

Leaning back against the bulwark, he rested one arm along the boat's railing, letting his cloak fall open to display the longsword gleaming at his waist. Won in battle by his grandfather, it was named *Forsvar*. Defender. "I will be keeping watch over *you* most of all."

Staring at the weapon, with its silver hilt and mystical runes inscribed on the blade, Thorolf fell silent, broad shoulders bulging as he hauled on his oar. Hauk still did not understand why the hulking knave had insisted on taking part in this voyage. Older than the others, older than Hauk himself, Thorolf had a heart as black as ocean depths at midnight—and a habit of making trouble purely for his own amusement. He was not the sort to pine away for female companionship or a family.

And that was the true purpose of this voyage; like their ancestors, those men of Asgard who wished to have families had to risk venturing forth into the outside world in search of brides—for the women of Asgard could not bear children.

Thorolf's thick lips curled in a sneer. "I have as much right to be here as any man. The ancient law—"

"During this journey, I *am* the law," Hauk warned silkily. "You will either follow my commands or pay the price." He shifted to a tone that some women had told him was even icier than his blue eyes. "You know from experience that I do not make idle threats."

Thorolf held his stare, gaze glittering with a lifetime of hatred, before he looked away uncomfortably.

"All will be well," Keldan said in a soft voice, trying to make peace, as usual. "We will follow your orders, Hauk, as we promised. But even if one of us *is* captured or killed, there is no chance that our secret could be discovered."

Hauk fingered the rough fabric of his cloak, hoping that was true. They had taken pains to appear unremarkable. Uninteresting. Unworthy of attention. They had removed their gold armbands and jeweled torques, shaved their beards, donned the tunics and leggings favored by common European traders. Hauk had left all mark of his rank and office behind—except for his sword.

Even their ancient ship had been carefully disguised, its name sanded away, the carved dragon's head removed from the prow. Stripped of its finery, the weathered longboat looked like a derelict left over from another age, battered but still fierce.

The thought made Hauk's lips curve in a rueful half smile. The same could be said about him.

Shaking his head, he stared off into the fog. "Every time we set foot in their world," he said quietly, "we risk exposing our secret."

"But we have taken every precaution. Looking at us, no one could tell us apart from ordinary men—"

"Keldan, we are *not* ordinary men."

His young friend fell silent for a moment. "In every way that matters, we are," he insisted stubbornly. "We feel joy and pain, we eat and sleep and laugh and bleed. We *want* what any man wants, to have a wife and a family—"

"But we are not ordinary men," Hauk repeated, fixing him with a hard stare. "We are different, Kel. Someday you will learn to accept that."

Keldan's brown eyes held a hint of sadness. But then he waved a hand as if to brush the subject away, grinning. "Well, I for one intend to enjoy every second of this journey. And if aught goes awry . . ." His smile widened. "Who wants to live forever?"

Hauk arched one brow. "You may not find that so funny two days hence when we land at Antwerp."

"I expect I shall have far more pleasant things to think about in Antwerp. This trade fair should offer a great variety of women from all over the continent." He looked as excited as a boy choosing among a shiny array of new playthings. "I want an exotic beauty—a Moorish girl, or a dark-eyed firebrand from Tuscany, or a Scottish lass with red hair and freckles like Rolf's wife." His smile fading a bit, he lowered his voice, speaking for Hauk's ears alone. "You might find a new bride for yourself, my friend . . . have you considered that?"

Hauk swallowed hard and glanced away. *Nei,* he had not considered it. Not for a moment. He had lost his first wife in childbirth, and his second . . .

He had outlived his second.

"Never again, Kel," he said bitterly. "Never. I am here to watch over you and the others, that is all." Under his breath, he added, "A man can get used to living alone."

Even as he whispered those words, the last of the fog parted before the ship's prow, a west-born wind filled the sail, and the longboat swept into the open sea.

2

Avril parted her lips for her husband's kiss, welcoming him to their bed. *Gerard,* mon coeur, *thank God you have returned at last . . .*

His weight pressed her down into the sheets, his hard body covering and claiming hers, and she twined her arms around his neck, pulling him closer, filled with surprise and joy. He nuzzled her cheek, her hair, whispered words she had not heard in such a long time. Words of love.

You are here. She sighed, all the months of longing and loneliness pouring out. *I thought you were gone forever,* mon amour, *but you are here. Never leave me again. Please never leave me again. I missed you so.*

He tenderly kissed her tears away. She held him tighter, his skin warm and smooth beneath her fingers, her lips. Their mouths met in deep, lingering kisses. His strong hands touched her intimately, each caress slower than the last as he gently aroused her.

Moaning softly, she lifted her hips, wanting to take him inside her. *Please,* mon coeur, *it has been so long. I need . . . I need . . .*

He nudged her thighs apart, positioning himself there at the silky core of her body. Then he raised his head, and in the firelight she could see the passion in—

This was not her husband!

Lady Avril de Varennes jerked awake with a startled cry, eyes wide, heart pounding. She lurched upright, uncertain where she was for a dizzying moment.

A dream. It had only been a dream.

The same one that had tormented her for months now . . . growing more vivid, more sensual each time.

She pushed aside the blankets and stumbled out of bed, her silk kirtle tangling around her legs. Rushes crunched beneath her bare feet. A few embers still glowed on the hearth, helping her eyes adjust to the darkness. With every rapid breath, she inhaled the scent of the lavender oil she had burned earlier to calm her. Of course, she was in Gaston and Celine's château, in one of the guest bedchambers. She had arrived here yestereve. She was quite safe.

And alone. As she had been for three years, four months, a handful of days.

Yet her body tingled in the most sensitive places, and perspiration made her kirtle cling to her back, her thighs, her breasts. Lifting an unsteady hand to her lips, she swore she could feel the lingering heat of a kiss there. And on her cheeks, a trace of dampness, like . . .

Like tears that had been kissed away.

She covered her face with both hands, her wedding ring cold against her flushed skin. The sensations had all felt so real, so intense, so . . .

Mortifying. *How could she dream of making love to any man but her husband?*

"Nay," she whispered fiercely, raking her long brown hair out of her eyes, lifting her chin. "It was only a dream." She was getting upset over naught. Crossing the chamber, she opened the door that connected to the next room.

Inside, bathed in moonlight that poured through a tall, arched window fitted with glass, Giselle lay asleep—her thumb in her mouth, her plump arm curled around the carved toy horse her uncle Gaston had given her.

Avril sank down beside the small bed, resting her cheek on the covers, reaching out to touch her three-year-old daughter's raven curls. Many times these past weeks she had spent sleepless nights this way, disturbed not only by that troubling dream—but by the decision she had made.

"We will be all right, *ma petite*," she murmured. "You will love your new home in Brittany, I promise. And your uncle Gaston is wrong. We do not need a man to take care of us."

She closed her eyes, hoping that was true, praying she was not making a mistake. Not acting like a "stubborn little firebrand," as Gerard used to chide her with a teasing, handsome smile.

Her throat dry and tight, Avril stood, moving to the window, gazing down at the forest that surrounded the château. She looked for the chapel Gaston had built there. Normally she could see a great deal from here, but tonight, despite the full moon, she could make out only the uppermost branches of the trees.

A mist enveloped all else, a silvery fog that wound through the woods to surround the castle.

Strange, she thought, frowning in puzzlement, to see fog on such high ground. Especially at this time of year. The last days of summer had only just given way to the first bite of autumn.

Yet the veil of white was so thick she could see only the spire of the small chapel, there where she and Gaston had agreed it should be . . . built of the finest marble and the most exquisite stained glass, by artisans brought from the East, as befitted a knight who had fought in the Crusades. Gerard always loved Moorish architecture, as he loved those woods where he had spent many happy days as a boy.

They had buried him there.

Three years, four months, and a handful of days ago.

"Forgive me, *mon coeur.*" She rested her forehead against the window, blinking hard. "Forgive me."

Even as the words slipped out, she was not certain whether she was asking forgiveness for the bold step she was about to take.

Or for her dream about the passionate stranger.

"Avril, I do not care how skilled you are with a crossbow—and pray do *not* remind me that you took up arms last month and stood shoulder to shoulder with your retainers to defend your keep against the Flemish. You are a noblewoman, you are but two and twenty, and when you travel such a distance—"

"I do not need half a dozen guards." Avril stopped trying to elude her brother-in-law, turning to stare up at Duc Gaston de Varennes in the blinding morning sunlight. Servants dodged around them, carrying bundles of food and flasks of water needed for her journey north. As she crossed her arms over her chest, the wind tugged at her honey-colored traveling cloak and velvet skirts. "I am going to a friend's wedding, not into battle. I still do not understand why you insist on being so cautious."

"I insist on ensuring your safety." Gaston glowered down at her, looking very much like the name he had earned in battle: the Black Lion. The fact that he carried his two-year-old son, Soren, on his broad shoulders did little to soften the impression. "The northern roads are a haven for outlaws of every ilk. Six men riding under my banner will make any knave who would harm you think twice. You are still under my care, and I mean to protect you, just as I will protect your daughter while you are gone—nay, I will brook no further argument."

"I was not going to argue," Avril said softly, glancing away. With his black hair and brown eyes, Gaston so resembled his elder brother that at times, it hurt to look at him. "I was going to thank you for caring so much."

All around them, the castle's outer bailey hummed with activity as servants continued loading the cart that would carry her north, adding gifts for the bride and for friends Avril had not seen in years. Her dearest companion from childhood, Lady Josette de la Valentin, stood chatting with Gaston's wife, Celine, while groomsmen strapped horses into the traces. Josette had arrived from Brittany yesterday to accompany Avril on the journey.

And after the wedding of their mutual friend, Avril would accompany Josette on her journey home. To Brittany.

"I still wish you would reconsider your decision," Gaston said more gently. "As far as I am concerned, Gerard's castle and holdings are yours for as long as you live. You know that you and Giselle are welcome to stay there. My brother *built* that château for you."

"Aye, he did. And there are reminders of him in every room. I cannot keep living in the past, Gaston. I cannot stay there anymore." She met his gaze again. "I thought you would be happy, *beau-frère*. I have finally admitted that you are right. My recent experience with the Flemish proved that what you have been saying is true—the château *is* too close to the border, too tempting a prize without a man to protect it. And your keep here is too distant to send help quickly enough."

"I never meant that you should leave and return to your dower lands in Brittany." Gaston set his restless son down. The little boy scampered over to a nearby grove of apricot trees, where Giselle was playing with a litter of black-and-white kittens. "Celine and I are happy to take care of you and Giselle."

"And I am grateful to you for being so good to us." She sighed, tucking a wind-blown strand of hair back behind her ear. "But Gerard's château and lands belong to you by right of inheritance, Gaston, and it is time I gave them back—"

"You could stay here."

"Nay, I could not." She nodded toward the spire just visible beyond the castle walls, struggling to keep her voice steady. "The memories here are just as strong."

She started to turn away, but he caught her arm. "Why is it so impossible for you to let anyone take care of you?"

Avril was spared having to reply as Josette and Celine joined them.

"It looks as if all is ready for us to depart." Josette's blue eyes sparkled with excitement as she wrestled the wind for control of her hooded traveling cloak, which was made of lovely—but somewhat impractical—violet brocade and white silk. "Though I fear this weather may prove more troublesome than any forest bandits we might encounter." Giving up her battle, she let the wind blow her unruly curls into a tangled sable-brown mass.

Avril smiled. She and Josette shared a spirit of adventure that had made them best friends since birth, even though petite Josette tended to be sweet and amiable while she herself was more outspoken and headstrong.

"Have you explained to Giselle how long you'll be away?" Celine's cheeks almost matched her red tresses in the chilly morning breeze. Gaston slipped an arm around his wife's shoulders and brushed a kiss through her burnished hair.

"I have tried." Avril glanced to where the children were playing. "But I am not sure she understands what ten days means. So I have made ten raisin sweetcakes for her, and said to eat one each day, and when the last one is gone, *Maman* will be home."

"What a lovely idea."

"Thank you, Celine. I hope it will help. She always loves our visits here, and I think she believes this is simply another holiday. I considered taking her with me, but . . ."

"You made the right decision, Avril. She'll be safe here, and she and Soren always have such fun. We'll take good care of her."

"I know." Avril smiled at her *belle-soeur*. "She loves you both very much. But even with those she loves, she can be rather willful at times."

"I cannot imagine where she inherited that trait," Gaston commented dryly. After giving his wife a last hug, he released her. "If you ladies will excuse me, I would have a word with the guards before this merry caravan departs."

As he walked over to his men, Celine linked one arm through Avril's and the other through Josette's. "And I would like to sit down, if it's all right with the two of you. I didn't want to worry Gaston—because he'll spend the rest of the day hovering over me like a big butterfly—but I'm feeling a little light-headed this morning."

"Oh, Celine, I am sorry. I should have thought of that when we decided to leave at first light." Avril steered her *belle-soeur* toward the grove of apricot trees, still feeling a pang of envy over the joyous news Celine had shared last night: She was expecting her second child. "How are you faring?"

They settled on the grass a few paces from the chil-

dren. "Much better, really, than when I was carrying
Soren. I feel wonderful most of the time." Celine's
expression was blissfully happy as she watched her son
chasing his cousin through the trees. "A little woozy
in the mornings, but that just gives me an excuse to
stay in bed. I lie there looking at the new cradle Gaston is making, and I feel so blessed . . ."

She stopped short and met Avril's gaze. "Oh, Avril,
I'm sorry. I didn't mean to—"

"Nay, it is all right." Avril blinked away the burning in her eyes, surprised by the intensity of the envy
she felt. "It is only that, sometimes, I wish . . ." She
looked up at Giselle, at the small miracle she and
Gerard had created, so full of love and laughter and
mischief.

"You wish that Giselle were not growing up an only
child, as you did," Josette finished quietly.

Avril nodded, dropping her gaze. The wind blowing
through the leaves overhead made the only sound for
a moment.

"It doesn't have to be that way," Celine whispered.
"You are still young." She leaned closer and took
Avril's hand. "You once told me that if I found love, I
should catch it close and hold it tight." She looked
across the bailey at her husband, her expression
tender. "And it was very good advice."

"I remember." Avril paused, squeezing Celine's
hand. "But I-I do not think anyone could replace
Gerard in my heart. For a long time, I thought I
would be happy if I simply stayed in that château, if I
kept everything as it was. That I . . . could keep
him with me somehow. I have always believed that

there is *one* special man for every woman . . . and God granted me mine. For a brief, perfect time, I knew a love some never know. I would not be so selfish and greedy as to expect Him to send me another love like that in my lifetime."

"I am the only maiden here," Josette commented, "so I cannot claim to be an expert, but I do not think God is so miserly with love."

Avril reached out her free hand to Josette, smiling at her sweet nature. "You are both so kind to be concerned about me. I am fortunate indeed to have friends like you. Truly, I *am* happy. I have all of you, and Giselle, and when we return to Brittany, I will be reunited with my cousins and kinsmen. What more could any woman ask? What more love could I need? I . . ."

A sudden, unbidden image of her dream last night flitted through her mind.

She had spoken to no one of the heated images that had disturbed her sleep of late, not even Celine or Josette.

"I . . . think it is time for us to go," she finished awkwardly. "Look how high the sun has gotten."

Gaston came striding across the bailey to join them, apparently finished giving instructions to his men. Both children ran to meet him, Giselle racing ahead of little Soren. Gaston scooped her up with both hands and swung her high over his head, making her squeal with delight. "And who is your favorite uncle today, *ma petite*?" He tucked her close.

She locked her chubby arms around his neck. "Uncle Gaston!"

"Soren up now!" her black-haired cousin demanded, arms extended over his head, his face awash in two-year-old indignation at the attention his cousin was receiving.

"I keep hoping he'll grow out of this." Celine sighed. "He's become an absolute little tyrant."

"I cannot imagine where he inherited that trait." Avril grinned. Rising, she decided to rescue her *beau-frère* from having to choose between the children.

"Soren up now!" the boy repeated, stamping his tiny foot.

Avril took her daughter as Gaston bent to pick up his son.

Giggling, Giselle played with a lock of Avril's hair. "*Maman* bring me a pretty spinny?"

"Aye, my little love." Avril hugged her daughter fiercely. "Oh, how I will miss you."

"A pretty spinny?" Josette asked with a puzzled look.

Avril smiled. "That is her word for a spinning top." She rubbed her nose against her daughter's. "Aye, *Maman* will bring you a pretty spinny, Giselle. Do you remember where *Maman* is going?"

"Lady friend!"

"Aye. I am going to visit a lady friend, who is getting married in a very large city by the sea. Do you remember?"

Giselle nodded vigorously.

"And in ten days—after you have eaten the last of your raisin sweetcakes—I will be back. And then we will go to our new home in Brittany."

"Where *Maman* was a little girl."

"That is right. Where *Maman* was a little girl. But until I return, can you make a promise for me? Can you promise to be very, very good for Aunt Celine and Uncle Gaston?"

"Promise!" Giselle rained kisses over her cheeks and nose.

They all walked over to the cart, but Avril was unprepared for the pain in her heart as she gave her daughter one last kiss, held her just a few seconds longer . . . and handed her to Celine.

"I will be back soon, *ma petite*. I love you."

"I love you, *Maman*." The little girl wiggled her fingers in farewell as Gaston helped Avril and Josette up into the cart.

With a slap of the harness, their driver set off. Wheels creaked and hooves clattered as the cart rolled through the castle gate and over the drawbridge, while everyone they left behind called out farewells and good wishes.

"And off we go," Josette whispered.

"You sound uneasy, Josette. Are you worried by the presence of so many guards?"

"Nay, I . . . mayhap it is because I did not sleep well. Did you . . ." She paused. "Did you notice that strange mist around the castle last night?"

Avril felt a tingle down the back of her neck. She looked away, her gaze falling on the chapel in the woods, rimmed by morning sunlight. "Aye."

"You did? No one else seemed to know what I was talking about when I asked this morn. I thought mayhap it was common here in the Artois. That mist came right through the shutters of my window and . . ." She cleared her throat. "Awakened me. I could not get back to sleep after that."

"I am sure it was merely a strange trick of the weather." Avril turned to face her friend. "There is naught to be uneasy about, Josette. We will be in no danger. It is not as if we are going to Barcelona or Marseilles or some other uncivilized place." She smiled reassuringly. "We are going to Antwerp."

3

 "**M**orvan," Avril said lightly, summoning the leader of the six guardsmen who had accompanied her and Josette into Antwerp, "I believe it may be time to make another delivery to our rooms at Baron Ponthieu's château."

"Aye, milady." The brawny man-at-arms came forward to take the miniature Noah's ark from her, trying not to drop any of the dolls, ribbons, pastel bead necklaces, or the fluffy toy lamb he already carried. With a long-suffering sigh, he handed this latest purchase to one of his men.

Avril swallowed a smile, afraid that she and Josette might dissolve into a fit of giggles at the men's expressions. The six battle-hardened guards Gaston had assigned to protect them during their journey north had been pressed into service of a different sort today.

The guards had done such excellent work escorting them to Antwerp safely and swiftly, they had arrived at their destination earlier than most of the other wedding guests. And when Josette heard that the city was playing host to a trade fair, she had coaxed Avril into spending a day strolling among the market stalls and enjoying the sights.

As they walked along streets crowded with merchants, the late-afternoon air buzzed with voices speaking French and Italian, Arabic and Russian, Antwerp's native Flemish, and a half-dozen languages Avril could not even name. Castle stewards bargained with traders over the price of cook pots or lemons or Persian silks. Servants cursed at the dogs that ran loose in the streets. Richly dressed guild members and sea captains discussed the dancing bears, wrestling matches, fortune-tellers, or pickpockets they had just seen.

Josette almost had to shout to be heard over the din. "You are having a good time," she commented happily, linking her arm through Avril's.

"Oh, aye. Aye, indeed I am." Avril returned her smile in full measure. She could not remember the last time she had spent a day like this, perusing displays of hats and scented soaps, nibbling mince pies purchased from strolling vendors, dabbing on exotic perfumes. They had even indulged in having their hair curled with hot irons and treated with a blend of rare frankincense and ginger. Every time she inhaled, the scent made her smile.

Glancing up at the rose-streaked sky, she found herself regretting that the sun would set in another hour or so.

When they stopped at yet another booth selling shoes, she heard poor Morvan sigh behind her and realized he did not share her sentiments. Avril glanced over her shoulder with a grin. She could not resist teasing the captain of the guards, for he always seemed to be in one of two moods: gloomy or dour. "I believe I have a new assignment for you, Morvan."

"Aye, milady?" he asked warily, mustache twitching as he awaited whatever new indignity might be heaped upon his men's broad shoulders. "We are at your command."

"Well, then, after you return those packages to Baron Ponthieu's château . . . mayhap you and your men should take the rest of the evening to enjoy the fair. You have done us loyal service this day, and you deserve a reward."

She succeeded in bringing a smile to his craggy face. "The men would be most grateful, milady."

Avril opened the velvet purse fastened to her belt and started counting out silver coins. "Then each of you take ten *livres* and have a most pleasant evening."

"You are more than generous, Lady Avril."

Morvan passed the coins to his men, instructing one to stay behind with her and Josette until they were ready to return to the château.

As the five guards departed, a passing merchant caught Avril's eye.

"Oh, Josette, look at that!" She pointed out a man tooting on a pipe and carrying a T-shaped pole festooned with small wooden toys. "I wonder if he has any spinning tops. I promised Giselle I would bring her one."

"Run and ask him, Avril."

"You would not mind if I abandoned you for a moment?"

Josette nodded toward the bright rows of silk slippers in the booth. "There is enough here to keep me happily occupied for, oh, at least an hour or two," she teased. "Go."

"Shall I accompany you, milady?" the guard asked.

"Nay, there is no need. Stay here with Lady Josette until I return." Trying to see where the toymaker had gone, she hurried into the throng.

"Kel, if you cannot keep your mind on the task at hand," Hauk said as he pulled his friend out of the path of an onrushing horse, "at least try not to get yourself killed."

"*Ja*, I will," Keldan replied absently, speaking around a mouthful of pickled pheasant eggs, which was his eleventh or twelfth meal of the day. Hauk had lost count.

Keldan struggled to balance three bulging sacks of souvenirs as they made their way through Antwerp's bustling streets, his head swiveling left and right, dark eyes wide as he took it all in—every foreign sight and taste and scent and sound. He stopped to stare at a passing group of men dressed in flowing black robes and odd, squarish hats. "What sort of people are those?"

"Lecturers from the local university. And those"— Hauk answered the next question before Keldan could ask it—"are Christian pilgrims, the ones in brown homespun wearing large crosses. They travel from city to city visiting cathedrals and the tombs of local saints."

"What is a saint? And what is a university?"

"It will take too long to explain." Hauk pushed him

forward down the street. "Kel, you are supposed to be—"

"How much do you think these cost?" Keldan asked, moving forward only a few paces before he stopped at a booth selling exotic wooden sculptures. He finished the last of his eggs and licked his fingers.

"Never mind how much they cost. If you eat one more thing or buy one more souvenir, our ship will sink long before we reach home. You already have more boots, books, flasks, and food than you can carry. What you do *not* yet have is a woman. And may I point out, " Hauk added dryly, "you might find it difficult to carry one off with your arms full."

"I cannot help it. I have never seen such . . . such . . ." Keldan paused, watching a troupe of acrobats go tumbling past.

"You have seen only the best of the city the past two days, Kel. Most of these people live in filth, packed one atop the other. Fighting to survive. Killing each other on a whim." As they walked on, he nodded to the many peasants and nobles around them who had missing limbs, blackened teeth, pox marks upon their skin. "Violence and illness are part of life in this place you are so busy admiring."

Keldan stopped in his tracks and turned to face him, his expression suddenly serious. The crowd parted to flow around them in a noisy, jostling river. "We could help them."

A pained grin curved Hauk's mouth. Keldan sounded so earnest, as if he were the first man of Asgard to ever have that idea.

"*Nei*, my young friend, we could not." Hauk shook

his head. Keldan was still rather naive and soft-hearted. "We cannot take all of them with us. There are thousands of people in this city alone. And this is but one city. There are hundreds more like it scattered around the world."

Keldan shook his head, as if he could not grasp even the *idea* of such a vast number of people. "But—"

"And we have a more pressing task before us, if you recall." Hauk clapped a hand on Kel's shoulder, pushing him forward once more. "You and the others are to steal the women at twilight. We are supposed to rendezvous back at the ship in little more than an hour." He directed Keldan's attention upward, to where the sun dipped low in the sky. "Everyone but you is ready. If you do not choose a female quickly, you will be returning home with naught more than boots and books to warm your bed."

Keldan sighed, his gaze flitting from a pretty dairymaid to a blond silversmith's daughter. "That is the problem. Choosing only *one*. I do not understand how the others could make their selections so easily. If only I could stay another day, or two or three . . ."

"*Nei*, we have been here two days already. We must leave tonight, under cover of darkness so that no one can follow. That is the law."

"But, Hauk, are you not always saying that some of our laws should be changed?" Kel asked hopefully as he traded a smile with a passing gypsy girl.

"None of us can change *that* particular law," Hauk replied with soft bitterness. They could not be away from Asgard for more than six days. "Now choose a female and be quick about it. What about the wench selling apples you spoke to near the wharf? She held your interest longer than most of the others."

"*Ja*, she was fetching enough, but there was a dullness about her, no spark in her eyes."

Hauk sidestepped around a waddling flock of squawking geese. "Then why not the one who served our midday meal in that tavern? You could hardly take your eyes from her, and she was lively enough."

"Pleasing to the eye," Keldan said thoughtfully, "but with the intelligence of a sheep."

"Sparks, liveliness, intelligence," Hauk grated out impatiently. "What does it matter? One woman is more or less like the next in bed. *Choose* one."

"It matters to *me*," Keldan snapped. "I want a woman who will stir my *heart* as well as my *loins*. Mayhap if I were more like you, if I did not care about anything but . . ." He stopped himself, clearing his throat uncomfortably. "I am sorry, Hauk. I did not mean that."

"*Nei*, it is true." Hauk shrugged, his voice low. "And I regret to tell you it is a lesson you will learn yourself eventually. When you are older. We all do." He turned a corner into an adjoining street. "The less a man feels, the better off he—*oof!*"

An unexpected impact knocked the breath from him as he collided with someone coming around the corner in the opposite direction. The blow knocked him backward a pace and knocked the woman—for the rushing whirl of skirts and soft curves that had hit him was clearly a woman—on her derriere in the dirt.

He bent to assist her, unnerved by an odd, dizzying

sensation, as if the earth itself were tilting beneath his boots. She declined his offered hand and got to her feet without help. His head spinning, he scooped up a small object she had dropped.

"My apologies," she sputtered, brushing filth from her skirts. "The fault was mine. I should have been watching where I was going, but it took so long to find the toymaker and . . ."

As she glanced up at him, she seemed to forget the rest of her sentence.

Hauk could not draw a breath, could not tell whether it was from the collision, the unfamiliar sensation wreaking havoc with his mind and body—or the fact that he was gazing down at the most strikingly lovely and utterly unkempt lady he had seen in . . .

In his entire memory. A silky riot of curls the color of ginger and nutmeg almost concealed a flawless, heart-shaped face, cheeks flushed with excitement, eyes a bright, vivid green. She looked as if she had just tumbled from a man's bed. His heart missed a beat, then started to pound.

The direct way she stared up at him was not in the least ladylike, though her fine velvet garments clearly marked her as a noblewoman. And though it seemed impossible, she even smelled of those same precious spices; he distinctly caught the scent of ginger.

He could not reclaim his balance *Nei*, the unnerving, breathless feeling only became more intense as she returned his gaze.

Even the air around him—between them—seemed to shimmer with a heat, a brightness, as if the sun suddenly blazed hotter in this place where they stood so close together.

She held out one slender hand, her eyes never leaving his. "I . . . I will need that back."

Her voice matched her face and figure, infinitely soft and feminine, yet strong at the same time. Hauk could not coax his tongue to form words.

Keldan—curse him—offered no help at all.

The lady tilted her head to the side and a single spice-colored lock of hair dipped engagingly over one eye. "*Sprechken sie Deutsch?*" she asked him in German. "*Parla l 'italiano? Spreekt u flamande—*"

"I do indeed speak those languages, *demoiselle,*" he replied at last in fluent French. "But I speak yours as well."

For some reason, his voice seemed to render her mute. Her lips parted soundlessly and she reached out to her right, as if expecting to find something solid to steady her rather than empty air.

Hauk took her hand in his, surprised by his own gallantry, even more surprised by the unexpected heat that sizzled straight through him, a feeling like desire yet far more powerful. Consuming. It startled him like a bolt from above.

She withdrew her hand quickly, lips forming an O of shock, as if she too had felt something startling. She stepped back from him a pace, her gaze moving over his features, his eyes . . . almost as if she recognized him. "A-are you one of the wedding guests at Baron Ponthieu's château, sirrah?"

"Wedding?" Hauk could not persuade his brain to supply aught more than that one word.

"I feel as if we have met before," she said breathlessly.

"Nay, that is"—he willed his heart to slow down—"impossible. I would—"

"Remember you," they both said at the same time.

The lady shook her head abruptly, as if awakening from a dream. Looking down, she held out her palm once more. "I-I would like that back, please."

When he did not comply, she shifted her other hand in a subtle movement, resting it on the lush curve of her hip—near a knife she wore sheathed at her waist.

Hauk blinked down at her, bemusement cutting through the other feelings crowding his senses. Did she actually think to threaten him? The idea that this slip of a female, who barely came to his chin, who could be no more than two and twenty, thought to pose any danger to a man of his size . . . What a bold little wench!

Opening his fingers, he glanced down at the object in his hand: a small toy. A brightly colored spinning top.

His brow knit in puzzlement, he held it out toward her. She plucked it from his palm, her fingertips just grazing his skin this time.

"Th-thank you," she said uneasily, stepping back another pace, her eyes searching his once more. "I am sorry for the trouble." Tucking the little toy into the coin purse on her belt, she hurried past him into the crowd.

Keldan, who had remained silent through the entire exchange, started to chuckle. "I believe we have room in the longboat for her, Hauk. For that one, we could most assuredly make room—"

"*Nei.*" Surprised to find himself speaking in a hoarse whisper, Hauk repeated the word more firmly. "*Nei.* I have no need . . . I do not want . . ." Someone brushing past them dropped a coin in his upturned palm, and he abruptly realized he was still holding his hand out in front of him.

Annoyed with himself, he tossed the coin aside and clenched his fist. "I told you before, I am only here to watch over you and the others—"

"*Ja,* that is what you said. But a man does not trip over a lady like that every day. Sparks, liveliness, intelligence . . . I think she merits a second look. Hurry, before she gets away from you."

Before Hauk could gather his scattered wits, Keldan was running off in the direction the green-eyed *demoiselle* had gone.

Spitting curses, Hauk chased after him, catching up at the end of a broad lane full of merchants. The crowds were thinning as the tradesmen closed their stalls for the day, folding down awnings and fastening shutters while the sun's light began fading in a blaze of twilight.

His friend stood staring at a booth on the opposite side of the street, an awestruck smile on his face. "Look at her, Hauk. Just look at her."

"I have already seen her close enough. I have the bruises to prove it. You—"

"*Nei,* not that one. *That* one."

Hauk turned to see what had so captivated his friend: a petite brunette standing at one of the merchant's stalls, her hands moving animatedly as she chatted with the proprietor and her fellow customers. The girl's sparkling laugh carried over the noise of the crowd.

"A voice like music and the body of a goddess," Keldan whispered as if barely daring to say the words aloud for fear she would vanish. "And her laughter . . . her sweet face. She is charming. She is perfect."

"She is well protected. Or did you not notice the armed guard beside her? Trying to carry that lady off would only win you a blade in the belly."

Keldan blinked at the guard as if he truly had not noticed before. Frowning, he set his many souvenirs at his feet. "There must be a way . . . but wait. What is this?"

He elbowed Hauk in the ribs as the green-eyed *demoiselle* came into view, appearing beside the brunette.

"Look! It appears that my lady and yours are friends." Keldan's smile returned. "Do you not agree now that we must have them? Surely Odin himself has guided us here." He glanced up at the deepening sky. "The sun is almost down. We could take them both and—"

"*I* do not want that *demoiselle* or any other. Have you not heard a word I have said? You have never seen what a sword can do to a man—I have. It is too dangerous, Kel. Forget her."

"*Nei*, you told me to choose and I have chosen. That is the woman I want."

Hauk caught him by the shoulder, tried to turn him away. "You will find another."

"*Nei*, Hauk, I—by Thor's hammer!"

The alarm in his voice made Hauk look over at the stall just in time to see a familiar, hulking figure heading straight for the girl Keldan admired.

Keldan swore vividly. "Thorolf!"

Josette felt a shadow fall over her, blocking what little daylight was left. She had been listening intently to Avril, who was upset about some misadventure she had had in the street—but they both turned, gasping, as a towering, dark-haired man appeared suddenly from behind them.

Josette guessed him to be a trader of some sort from his simple clothes. But his eyes, the blackest she had ever seen, fastened on her in a way that chilled her blood.

"Sirrah?" She cringed away, trying to step out of his path only to come up against the hard wooden counter of the booth.

"What is it you want?" Avril demanded.

Their guard stepped forward, his tone challenging. "Be off with you—"

Josette screamed in fear as the stranger shoved the guardsman aside and grabbed her.

He tossed her over his shoulder, the impact and his rough hold knocking the breath from her. Panic seized her. She heard Avril cry out in alarm. Saw the guard leaping forward to defend her—but the stranger drew a sword and dispatched him with a single thrust. The crowd in the street shouted in terror and scrambled for safety.

A scream of shrill terror rose in Josette's throat as

the man brandished his sword at any who would dare challenge him and started to carry her away.

Shocked and furious, Avril snatched her knife from its sheath. Barely even aware of what she was doing, she launched herself forward to help her friend.

"Let her go!" she cried, attacking the black-haired knave, dodging beneath the blow he aimed at her head. Slashing out, she wounded his sword arm.

With a sharp curse of pain and surprise, he lost his grip on his weapon. It clattered to the ground. He let go of Josette to fend off Avril, snarling at her in a language she did not know.

"Run, Josette! Run!" Avril danced backward, trying to hold his attention but stay out of reach, her little knife raised in front of her.

Suddenly a second dark-haired man appeared—the companion of the blond trader she had run into only moments ago. Her heart leaped that this good Samaritan would rush to their aid.

But in that second that she was distracted, the hulking stranger smashed her across the face with his fist. Pain exploded through her jaw as she spun and fell to the ground, her weapon flying from her hand. Dazed with pain, her ears ringing, she could not believe what she saw as she lay sprawled in the dirt, blood in her mouth.

The "good Samaritan" was not rushing to their aid. He was carrying Josette away over his shoulder!

The knave who had attacked them roared something in that odd language, clearly furious at losing his prize. Then he turned on her, fury blazing in his black eyes as he grabbed his sword from the ground, the blade dripping scarlet.

Numb with terror, Avril tried to scramble backward but her limbs would not obey her. The world turned hazy in her vision. The ringing in her ears became a buzz that blocked out all else.

She was defenseless, her knife gone. He lifted his blade to slice her in two. She shut her eyes, a single word filling her mind and heart. *Giselle*.

But before he could touch her, someone grabbed her from behind, yanking her to her feet. A muscular arm circled her waist. She felt herself pulled backward against a hard, male chest. Her rescuer shouted something in that guttural language—the same words twice, his tone clearly threatening as he brandished a sword at her attacker.

Then the pain in her jaw pulled her down into a fog that darkened her vision, and she went limp in his arms.

Silence hung over the longboat as they left Antwerp and its violence behind. The coast was naught more than a slim, dark line in the distance now, a strong wind carrying them swiftly out to sea, beyond the reach of those who had tried to stop them. The only sound came from the lapping of the waves.

And the last, labored breaths of the man who lay dying.

"It could have been worse," Thorolf said with a growl, sitting amidships.

"Worse?" Hauk pierced him with an icy glare. "Worse than almost starting a riot? Worse than a dozen men chasing us all the way to the wharf? Worse than having one of our companions killed and another mortally wounded?"

Thorolf fell into a sullen silence. Hauk looked down at Bjarn, frustrated that the young man's life was slipping away and he could do naught to stop it. He offered what comfort he could but knew words would not be enough to ease the wounded man's suffering—or that of the young raiders gathered around their fallen comrades in the ship's bow, their faces grim and etched with disbelief.

"Will we reach Asgard in time?" Keldan asked desperately, glancing from Bjarn to the other man's still form, covered by a blanket. "Will he recover?"

"*Nei*, Kel," Hauk said quietly.

Keldan's expression became stricken.

Coughing, Bjarn opened his eyes, gripping Hauk's forearm. "She is . . . beautiful, *ja*?"

"*Ja*, that she is," Hauk replied, knowing the young man was referring to the red-haired English girl he had chosen; even wounded, Bjarn had managed to carry her safely aboard.

"Would have made . . . a fine . . . wife." His mouth curving in a peaceful smile, the young raider breathed his last, his eyes on the stars.

"*Nei*," Keldan whispered. "*Nei*, this cannot be!"

Jaw clenched, Hauk gently closed Bjarn's eyes and pulled a blanket over him. "It will not help to keep watch," he said gruffly, addressing Keldan and the others who remained huddled around the two friends they had lost. "They will not awaken again. See to your women."

For a long moment, the raiders seemed unable to move. One whispered a prayer to Tyr, the god of war. Another cursed. Then, one by one, the silent, anguished men of Asgard moved to starboard and port and into the stern, returning to the brides they had won at such great cost.

The women, who had been sobbing or cursing when they were carried aboard, had all quieted after the men gently covered their faces with cloths soaked in the juice of the *sommer* root. They would sleep throughout the journey; it was a necessary precaution, so the captives would never be able to reveal the island's location.

They would awake to a new life, in a new world.

"I begin to understand what you said earlier," Keldan choked out as he and Hauk reclaimed their places near the tiller. "I do not like the outside world so well after all."

Hauk nodded and said naught, his throat dry and tight. He had not wanted Kel and the others to learn the lessons of loss and grief—lessons he himself had learned so well.

Keldan fell silent, his earlier, jovial mood gone. Not even the petite brunette asleep beside him could chase away his somber expression. He eased her into his arms.

Thorolf still looked utterly unrepentant. "Had the two of you not interfered with me, none of this would have happened. No one would have noticed—"

"It is hard not to notice you hacking up a guardsman in the middle of a crowded street," Hauk shot back. "You violated our laws—"

"I was defending myself. Keldan is the one who violated the laws. That woman was to have been mine." His gaze settled on the little brunette. "I saw her first. Since she was stolen from me, I will take Bjarn's female—"

"After what you have done, you do not deserve either of them." Keldan's arm tightened protectively around the girl he had claimed.

"That will be for the council of elders to decide," Thorolf said smugly.

"If I were you," Hauk warned him, "I would not be so quick to speak to the council concerning this night's events."

Thorolf fell silent, rubbing at his blood-soaked, bandaged arm, dividing a glare equally between Hauk and Keldan . . . and the unconscious woman next to Hauk.

Keldan glanced at the sleeping *demoiselle* curled up on Hauk's cloak, his eyes full of concern. "How is she?"

Hauk looked down at his captive, gently brushing a strand of spice-colored hair back from her bruised cheek. "I believe Thorolf may have broken her jaw, but she will recover."

"I am glad, my friend. She is perfect for you. Not only beautiful, but brave enough to take on a man twice her size, armed only with a knife."

Hauk lifted his gaze, giving Keldan a pained look. "I have you to thank for this. I did not want a new bride. Especially some mad Valkyrie who is as quick with a blade as a man."

"But like it or not, she is yours."

Hauk swore under his breath, studying his unwanted prize. After all the commotion in Antwerp, she had a black smudge on her cheek, its shape like a teardrop.

He reached into a bucket of drinking water, wet his hand, and brushed the mark away with his thumb, leaving a trail of dampness behind.

"*Ja*," he agreed at last. He could not deny the truth of Keldan's words. Nor could he disobey the law. He had spoken the words twice, in the presence of another Asgard islander. *I claim her*, he had shouted in the midst of that insanity in the street. *I claim her*.

At the time, it had been the only way to keep Thorolf from killing her. But with those words, this fiery, green-eyed *demoiselle* had become his.

Now and for the rest of her life, she was his.

4

The gentle crackling of a fire drew Avril slowly to awareness, the sound pleasant, familiar. Soothing. She tried to open her eyes but could not summon the strength. Her entire body felt so heavy, drowsy. So . . . strange. She could feel soft, smooth sheets against her skin and a plump, downy pillow beneath her cheek. The scent of woodsmoke tickled her nose.

Struggling to awaken, she managed to lift her lashes, just long enough to catch a glimpse of a stone hearth a few feet away, a fire dancing merrily in the darkness, before her eyes closed again.

She groaned, her mind as befuddled and sleepy as the rest of her. Where was she? She could not remember. It seemed odd, though, that Giselle would allow her to remain abed this way, without scampering about and demanding that her *maman* wake up . . .

But nay, her sweet girl was not with her. She had left Giselle with Gaston and Celine. Left her in their care when she—

Went to Antwerp.

Avril's heart lurched in her chest. Her eyes snapped open as it all came crashing back: the fair, the marketplace, the giant of a man who had attacked her and Josette.

Josette! Where was Josette?

With a choked cry, Avril pushed herself up on one elbow, trembling with the effort, forcing her limbs to obey. Blinking, she looked around her. And felt as if a lead weight had dropped through the pit of her stomach.

She was in an unfamiliar chamber, one unlike any she had seen before. The hearth provided a scant circle of light around the bed she was in, just enough for her to make out walls paneled in glossy, dark wood, square rafters high overhead, a ceiling that looked like it was made of tree bark. The tops of the bed's four curving posts had been carved to look like dragon's heads—complete with jeweled eyes that reflected the fire's glow.

Her heart thudding, Avril peered into the darkness beyond the footboard. "Is . . . is anyone there?" Her voice sounded like a dry croak. Her throat felt parched. "Where am I?"

There was no reply but the echo of her own words; the room sounded as if it were the size of a great hall, and seemed to be much longer than it was wide. She could not tell, could not begin to see the opposite end.

She pushed back the blankets that covered her and stumbled to her feet, strength returning as her heart pumped fear and outrage through her veins. What had happened? Who had brought her here?

And why had they left her alone?

She took a few shaky steps away from the bed, feeling a cool, stone floor beneath her feet.

"Is anyone there?" she repeated, trying to sound bold and challenging rather than frightened out of her wits.

Still there was no reply.

She rubbed her eyes, trying to still her trembling hands, trying to think. She remembered attacking the knave who had first grabbed Josette. Remembered wounding his arm. And then he had struck her to the ground.

The rest was a blur. A haze of pain. She had only a vague memory of shouted words she could not understand. Then darkness.

But she realized her jaw no longer hurt. Touching her cheek, she felt no tenderness at all. How long had she been asleep? Mayhap someone had gallantly carried her to a place of safety and taken care of her.

That hope vanished as she glanced down at the garment she was wearing. Whoever had brought her here had undressed her—and garbed her in a shimmering white silk kirtle that revealed every curve of her body. The bodice dipped indecently low between her breasts, and though the skirt reached her ankles, it was slit on both sides, baring her legs from ankle to hip with each step she took.

She froze for one stomach-churning second. Clearly it was not a chivalrous rescuer who had carried her to this place but someone who did *not* have gallantry on his mind.

With a frightened oath, she ran to the wall, searching for a sconce, a torch, some light she could use to hunt for a door. She found none. Cursing, she kept moving anyway, into the darkened half of the room, feeling her way along the paneling in hope of discovering a way out.

Her fingertips encountered strange scrollwork and carvings in the paneling and odd items displayed on the wall—stone sculptures, a cool piece of ivory, a dented metal great helm. And the furry head of some sort of horned animal. She yelped in alarm and jumped backward a step. Breathing hard, she turned away from the wall, half afraid of what her fingers might brush across next. Panic began bubbling up inside her. *God's mercy, there must be a way out of here!*

She had moved several yards beyond the hearth, but her eyes had adjusted to the dark now. The blackness no longer seemed quite so thick. She could just make out several pairs of tall, flat wooden rectangles lining the opposite wall, a few feet above the floor. It took her befuddled mind a moment to identify them.

Shutters.

Windows!

She rushed across to the nearest one. Fumbled for the latch in the darkness. Found it. Yanked the shutters open wide.

A warm, salty breeze blew against her face and tangled her hair. She blinked in the brightness of a full moon and dazzling starlight, heard surf pounding the shoreline. When her eyes adjusted again, she could see the ocean far below, and a heavy mist that seemed to glow silver in the moonlight. The keep—or whatever this place was—sat perched on a cliff high above the sea.

Mayhap she was not very far from Antwerp!

Then she realized there were no trading ships in view. No sounds of the bustling wharf. No sign of the merchants who had thronged into the city for the trade fair. This coastline was deserted.

And the breeze that caressed her cheeks was not frosty with autumn's chill but warm with the heat of midsummer.

Avril's fingers bit into the edge of the window as she fought a sudden wave of dizziness. How far *had* she traveled? She remembered Gerard telling her of places he had visited in the East and the South, where it was always warm.

Glancing up at the night sky, she realized that the stars were not arranged in the familiar patterns she and Giselle liked to give names and fanciful stories.

Where in the name of all the saints was she?

She looked down, thinking she might jump to freedom, but saw naught but a scant fringe of grass beneath the window. The earth fell away in a sheer drop so high she could only glimpse the shore below—a slender white froth of waves slashed into foam by jagged rocks.

But not far from shore, just for a moment, she thought she saw a glow. Was it a fire of some kind? A ship's lantern?

"Help!" she shouted in desperation, leaning out the window as far as she dared. "Someone help me! I have been abducted! Help me, please!"

She repeated her plea in Flemish, German, a half-dozen languages one after another.

But the glow vanished as if swallowed up by the

sea, and the rhythmic crashing of the waves smothered the sound of her voice. No one replied. She was alone here. Alone and isolated.

No one would be coming to her aid.

Fear slid down her back like melting ice. She whirled away from the window. There *must* be an exit. She had to escape. Return home to her child.

And she had to help Josette, if she was anywhere near here.

If Josette was still alive.

Forcing that frightening thought to the back of her mind, Avril strode into the center of the chamber, able to see better with rays of moonlight spilling through the open window.

The glitter of steel on the wall caught her attention. Along with hunting trophies and strange sculptures and artifacts, the owner—or owners—of this place had a number of weapons on display.

How foolish, she thought with a grim smile of satisfaction, to leave them within easy reach. She walked over and selected a double-edged blade that was long enough to use as a sword yet light enough to throw, if the need arose.

When her abductors returned, they would find themselves with more trouble than they had bargained for.

Gripping the weapon in one hand, she was about to renew her search for an exit when a sound from the dark, distant corner of the chamber startled her—the sound of a key turning in a lock.

Her pulse racing, she retreated a few steps, away from the hearth and the open window, trying to conceal herself in the shadows. She kept the sword raised in front of her and peered into the blackness.

A door creaked open. A massive, heavy portal from the sound of it. It closed an instant later with the clatter of an iron latch. Avril heard a footfall. Another. Then naught more.

Naught but the pounding of her heart.

"Milady?" a quiet male voice called after a moment, speaking French. "There is no need to hide from me. I mean you no harm."

She did not reply, edging silently along the wall. Now that she knew the general location of the door, if she could tiptoe her way around him . . .

"You cannot hide forever." He walked farther into the room, his tone becoming impatient. "And there is nowhere to run."

Ha, she thought, moving faster. That was his opinion. Once she reached the door, he would discover why she had always won footraces when she was a girl—

Her next step carried her straight into a small table and sent both her and whatever had been on it crashing to the floor.

She landed hard and yelped in pain as she bruised her hip on the hard stone and cut her hand on a shard of glass. Cups and platters and a shattered goblet littered the floor around her.

Uttering what sounded like an oath, her abductor closed in on her, a massive shadow looming out of the darkness.

"Stay back!" she shouted, grabbing the sword she

had dropped. "I have a weapon. And I am skilled enough to use it!"

The threat stopped him, at least for the moment. "A blade will avail you naught more than shouting yourself hoarse at the window did." He sounded annoyed rather than concerned about his safety. "You cannot harm me, milady."

What arrogance! Shaking her head, Avril got to her feet, careful of the broken glass. "Come any closer and you will discover precisely how wrong you are." She tried to judge the distance to the door, took a cautious step.

And felt surprised when he moved away from her, toward the window.

"I do not doubt your skill," he said dryly. "I saw you demonstrate it in the marketplace."

He stepped into the pool of moonlight that poured through the open shutters.

Avril gasped, staring at him in open-mouthed astonishment. *"You!"* she choked out. "You are the trader who ran into me at the streetcorner."

Her pounding heart seemed to fill her throat as she gaped at him. It was unmistakably the same tall, heavily muscled rogue who had collided with her. The same fierce, rugged face. The same bronzed skin and sun-colored hair, utterly at odds with the moonlight all around him.

"As I recall," he said sardonically, one corner of his mouth curving, "it was you who ran into me."

Avril felt a rush of dizziness, just as she had in Antwerp—mayhap because he seemed *familiar*, in a way she could not explain. There was something about his deep, quiet voice. Something in his gaze.

He had eyes of the palest blue, like a clear, cool lake reflecting a summer sky.

And as he regarded her silently, the unnerving sensation she had felt upon first meeting him shimmered through her once more—a dazzling heat, as if the sun had tumbled from the heavens to fill every fiber of her being. The impact swept over her so suddenly, so powerfully, it robbed her of breath, voice, of her very senses.

Even as she struggled to give the feeling a name, she sensed, somehow, that he felt it, too. Which only mystified and unsettled her all the more.

Shaken, she managed to tear her gaze from his, and realized that he no longer wore the homespun tunic and cloak of a trader. He was garbed in naught but a pair of close-fitting brown leggings, leather boots, and a gold armband encircling one thick bicep. A sheathed sword and knife hung from his belt.

Every hard plane and angle of his shoulders and chest and powerful arms was exposed to view. From his unyielding stance to the blunt tips of his fingers, he looked as strong and solid as the rocks that sliced up the sea below his keep.

He moved away from the window, and a moment later the center of the room flared with the glow of fire, as he used flint and steel to light the candles in an iron candle-stand. The golden warmth flickered over his back and arms, casting every muscle and sinew in sharp relief.

"Put the weapon down," he said without looking at her.

Avril shivered. It was not a suggestion but a command. He spoke in the same way he moved—with an air of authority. As if he owned not only this place but everything in it.

She felt renewed fear curl in her belly. But she did not comply. She tightened her hand around the blade's hilt, ignoring the sting in her injured palm.

Carrying one of the candles, he moved even closer to light a second candelabra. Avril held her ground— and, in the growing brightness, felt surprised to see that she was not in a bedchamber after all.

There were cook pots, copper utensils, and a cauldron beside the hearth. A table for eating in one corner. Shelves that held linens and soaps for washing, next to a rain barrel. This odd dwelling seemed to be some sort of long, one-room home.

Finished with his task, her abductor glanced toward her, mouth open as if he meant to issue another command. But then his gaze fastened on the revealing silk kirtle and skimmed down her body, taking in every inch of skin illuminated by the light.

Those pale azure eyes suddenly darkened in a blaze of heat. Avril inhaled sharply, filled with feminine alarm at the obvious direction of his thoughts. Every instinct urged her to flee, yet she could not move. And could not understand the tingle that coursed through her limbs, holding her fast.

"I left a tunic for you." His voice sounded even deeper than before. A muscle flexed in his lean jaw. "Did you not see it?" He nodded toward the foot of the bed, where a garment of black velvet lay draped over a trunk.

"I-I was more interested in finding a way out!" She tried to keep her voice from wavering, looked at the distant door. Wondered if she dared try to run past him. "Where am I?" she demanded, deciding boldness was her only choice at the moment. "Who the devil are you and what do you—"

"Put down the blade," he repeated with measured patience, "and we will discuss this"—he seemed to search for the appropriate word—"situation calmly."

"Calmly?" She sputtered. "I have been attacked by brigands, kidnapped, carried off to sweet Mary knows where, locked in a room, and now—"

"Milady," he said in soft warning. Without another word, he advanced toward her, his patience apparently at an end. She retreated only a step.

Then she retreated three more.

As he kept coming, she decided that discretion might be better than valor at the moment. She dashed toward the bed, snatching up the black velvet tunic on the way and clutching it in front of her. She tossed the weapon into the center of the rumpled sheets.

"There. There, are you satisfied?" She kept moving, maneuvering around until the huge bed was between them. The sword was still within reach if she chose to lunge for it.

But he seemed placated for now. He kept his distance, reaching out to close his fingers around one of the dragon-headed posts.

"If I had meant you any harm," he grated out, pronouncing each word distinctly, as if she were a slow-witted child, "if I had intended to kill you, or do aught else"—his gaze flicked over her body again—"I already had ample opportunity. You will have to trust me."

Trust him? Trust him! Avril choked back a biting retort and quickly pulled the tunic over her head. It was obviously one of his, the sleeves much too long, the hem falling to her ankles. But at least she no longer felt as exposed as she did wearing only the ridiculous scrap of silk.

"Where am I?" she repeated more calmly once she was dressed, trying not to provoke him again. "How far are we from Antwerp? How long was I asleep?"

"You were asleep . . ." He paused, clearly choosing his words carefully. "A short time. I brought you here early this morn. That gown was the only female garment I had at the time. I have brought you some others, along with some additional female trappings you might require." He nodded toward a pair of sacks he had left on the far side of the room. "As for where you are, this is Asgard Island. I bid you . . ." He paused again, sighing tiredly. "Welcome."

Despite the greeting, his attitude was hardly hospitable. Naught that he was saying made any sense. This man had kidnapped her, yet he did not seem to want her here.

In fact, from the way his fingers gripped the bedpost, she had the distinct impression he wanted to throttle something. Or someone.

"Asgard Island?" she echoed, searching her memory for all the names of places she had read about, all the places Gerard used to describe when he spoke of his travels. "I have never heard of it."

Those blue eyes met hers again. "I know."

Somehow that simple comment was more terrifying than aught else he could have said. "Who are you?" she whispered. "And what do you want with me?"

"My name is Hauk Valbrand." He inclined his head politely. "And I do not want you at all."

Before she could ask him to explain that baffling comment, he continued.

"My only intention in the marketplace was to keep Thorolf from—"

"Who?"

"The man who was about to kill you. Thorolf. You angered him, and he is not a forgiving sort. If I had not stepped in to rescue you, you would have been drawn and quartered."

"Rescue?" She clung to that word, her heart pounding with hope. "If your only intention was to rescue me, does that mean you intend to let me go?"

He stepped away from the bed, turning his back and staring down at the fire. "Nay," he said, his tone one of regret. "That I cannot do."

Avril was becoming more puzzled by the moment. "I-is it ransom you are seeking, then?" she guessed. Taking hostages was a common enough tactic used by men of a certain ilk, to gain riches or power from noble families.

He choked out a laugh, a humorless sound. "Does it look as if I am lacking in wealth, milady?"

She glanced around the room, seeing everything clearly in the wavering light. The long, single chamber was not only the size of a great hall—it was filled with fine goods, tapestries, costly artifacts, furnishings of every description. One nearby trunk, its top wide open, held an overflowing pile of silver and gold coins in many sizes, including some that looked ancient.

Her stomach started churning. Clearly her abductor was not in need of more riches. "Then why have you kidnapped me?"

"Because once I claimed you, I had no choice," he bit out. "Neither of us has a choice any longer, milady."

She shook her head, unable to breathe. "You are not making sense. Naught you have said makes *any* sense! What do you want with me? What happened to my friend—"

"Your friend is safe and well, as you are," he assured her. "Neither of you has come to any harm, and neither of you will. You have my word."

"What good is the word of a knave and a brigand who kidnaps defenseless women?"

"You are hardly defenseless," he said dryly, turning to regard her once again. "And though you may believe me a brigand, I am in fact honor-bound to protect and care for you now. I *know* this is difficult for you to accept, milady." He raked a hand through his tangled blond hair, looking frustrated. "You will understand eventually. But there is no time now to explain further. We are late for the *althing*—"

"The all-what?"

"*Althing*. There is a meeting of our council of elders tonight, and your presence is required." He gestured toward the sacks he had brought in for her. "Change your garments. Let us be on our way."

Avril gaped at him. Simple as that, he expected her to obey him? "Listen, you . . . you . . . overgrown oaf, I do not know who you are—"

"I have told you my name." He frowned. "I suppose I should ask yours."

"Lady Avril de Varennes," she supplied hotly. "Of the family of the Duc Gaston de Varennes of the Artois." She emphasized the word *duc*. "Mayhap you have heard of him. Mayhap you realize now what a mistake you have made. The Varennes family holds favor with King Philippe himself. They will be looking for me—"

"They will not find you."

The confident way he stated that made Avril's breath catch in her throat. "You are wrong! They will not *rest* until they find me. And when the *duc's* men get their hands on you—"

"They will not."

Again he said it as a simple matter of fact. Avril started to tremble. Her mind was spinning. She felt as if she was caught in a nightmare from which she could not awaken.

"Now, milady, we must go to the *althing*. You may leave the weapon." Her abductor gestured at the sword in the middle of the bed, one corner of his mouth curved in a humorless grin. "You will not need it."

Avril remained rooted in place, blinking at him. She did not know what to make of this mysterious, powerfully muscled, *maddening* man. Thus far, he had not tried to hurt or abuse her; he had spoken the truth about that. And his claim that he was honor-bound to protect and care for her sounded almost chivalrous. For a brigand.

Yet she dared not trust a word he said.

Lowering her gaze to the floor, she slowly moved around the bed, trying to appear docile and chastened and obedient. She walked past him, toward the sacks on the opposite side of the room, holding her breath. Judging the distance.

When she was a few steps from the door, she broke into a run, tore the door open, and rushed headlong outside into the night.

A frightened cry escaped her as she heard him giving chase, cursing with every step. Her heart pumping, she hiked up the silk kirtle and long tunic and raced into the darkness.

But though she was fast, she was not fast enough.

He caught her only a few yards beyond the keep, grabbing her arm. Panic made her strike out with her fists as he spun her around and pulled her against his chest.

"Let me go!" she screamed. "Let me—"

His arms tightened around her until she could not break free, could barely even wriggle.

"There is nowhere to run, milady," he said with a growl, threading one hand through her hair, forcing her to meet his gaze. "Do you not understand? You are on an *island*. If you try that again, you will fling yourself over a cliff in the darkness and fall to your death!"

Unable to struggle, Avril was all too vividly aware of the way his hard body engulfed her, the strength of his arm around her waist, the way her breasts flattened against the solid muscle of his chest. Feeling trapped and helpless and terrified, she spat in his face.

He released her but kept one hand around her wrist like a manacle. "Heed me well, milady," he grated out, wiping the back of his other hand across his cheek. "Whoever and whatever you were before, it no longer matters." His eyes seemed to glitter unnaturally in the moonlight. "Now come back inside and garb yourself. We are late. The council awaits us."

5

Avril had already learned three valuable lessons about this formidable rogue who called himself Hauk Valbrand: He answered her every question with a riddle, he brooked no disobedience to his orders—and he was every bit as powerful and unyielding as he looked.

It had been foolish to run from him on the cliff. And even more foolish to fight when he led her back inside his keep, ordering her to change clothes.

He had some fresh scratches near his eyes, courtesy of her fingernails.

She had her hands bound before her, courtesy of his superior physical strength.

And she was now wearing a simple linen gown in a lovely shade of violet with purple embroidery along the bodice and hem.

"Milady, I have given you my word that you will not be harmed in any way. If you would cease causing trouble, you would make this unfortunate situation less difficult for us both."

Avril did not reply, her breathing fast and shallow, her captor's spicy, male scent invading her senses with every gulp of air. None of his many reassurances eased her fear in the least—not with his brawny arm encircling her waist as he carried her into the darkness astride a swift chestnut stallion. They rode through the moonlit night, following a path that led down the hillside away from his home.

She would not make the mistake of arguing or fighting with him further. After taking her inside his keep, he had turned his back and given her to the count of twenty to don one of the gowns he had brought for her. She had obeyed quickly, calling him a few choice names under her breath, refusing his help in tying the laces up the back of the garment.

That she now regretted . . . because she could feel his bare skin pressed against hers, smooth and warm. He was holding her so tight, she half expected the pattern of the gown's open laces to be branded into her shoulders by the hard, flat muscles of his chest. Clearly he was determined not to let her out of his sight or out of his grasp again.

Suppressing a shiver, she forced herself to ignore the uncomfortable sensation—and the equally disturbing heat that shimmered between them, growing more intense with each moment she remained in his company.

Mayhap it was only the island's humid, sultry air that caused the strange feeling. It could be simply the hot weather making her light-headed, making perspiration trickle down her skin until the fabric of her gown clung to her body.

Or it could be the way her captor held her so close, her every curve fitted to the hard planes of his body.

She banished that thought furiously. Her stomach

knotting with anxiety, she fastened her attention on her surroundings, thinking of what he had said on the cliff. *Whoever and whatever you were before, it no longer matters.* Arrogant oaf! He could take his threats and be damned. Whatever Valbrand's intentions, she did not intend to be here long enough for him to make good on them. Gaston and his men would soon find her. Or she would find some way to escape.

A way to return home to her little Giselle.

Peering into the darkness ahead, she could barely make out the path they followed, but both her captor and his destrier seemed familiar with it. They galloped along the cliffs that soared at such dizzying height above the sea, until the trail widened into a road that veered inland. Off to the north, she glimpsed what looked like flickering lights in the distance, near the ocean.

A *town*, she thought, a spark of hope flaring inside her. If she managed to escape from Valbrand, mayhap she would find help there.

She kept that hope burning inside her as the road forked and they left the coast far behind, riding toward distant hills that rose like dark sentinels along the horizon. A short time later, Valbrand reined his horse to a canter as they entered a forest.

The air was cooler here, rich with the pungent scent of pine needles. Bushes laden with ripe berries sprawled across the path; crushed under the stallion's hooves, the fruit gave off a tangy, pungent aroma. Avril heard owls hooting and animals scurrying through the underbrush.

She tried to keep her thoughts on escape, and

home. And Giselle's sweet, smiling face. And the hope of finding Josette safe and well.

But as evergreen branches blotted out most of the moonlight, renewed fear closed in on her, like a hand tightening around her neck, squeezing off her air.

"Wh-where *are* we going?" she choked out.

"To the *althing-vellir*," he said tightly. "The place of the *althing*."

A few moments later the trees thinned and the forest gave way to an open meadow where a throng of men awaited—at least two score, gathered at the base of a rocky outcropping so tall that its upper reaches could not be seen in the darkness; a waterfall spilled over one edge, splashing down from the night sky in a glistening cascade, ending at the bottom in a clear pool and a moonlit cloud of mist.

Avril's mouth went dry with shock and fear as she stared at the brawny warriors, most clad only in leggings, as Valbrand was. The crowd was a veritable sea of sun-bronzed muscle.

And at the foot of the wall of stone, apart from the others, stood a line of men—each holding a sobbing, hysterical woman by his side.

She had not realized that there were *more* captives here. "God's breath, what *is* this?" Icy dread seized her and she struggled against her abductor's steely hold. "What do you intend to—"

"Do not be afraid," Valbrand said in a low tone. "No one is going to hurt you."

She was no doubt supposed to find that soothing. But she could feel his voice rumbling through his broad chest, and it only sharpened her panic. "Nay, I do not believe you! I—"

"Avril, cease," he commanded, holding her still as he reined his destrier to a halt, at a place just beyond the trees where dozens of other horses were picketed. "Your questions will be answered and all will be well. And I will stay by your side—"

"That is not reassuring!"

Muttering an oath, he swung his leg over the stallion's back and leaped to the ground in one smooth motion. "We are late, milady. Hurry."

He reached up to help her down, but just then she spotted a familiar figure in the middle of the line of men and women. "*Josette.*" Avril slipped from the horse's back without help, despite her bound hands.

Before she could take one step, Valbrand caught her by the shoulder and pulled her back.

She tried to twist free, could not tell if Josette had heard her over the noise of the crowd and the waterfall. "Please, let me go to her—"

"You cannot stand before the men of Asgard with your gown falling off," he said impatiently. His fingers working quickly, he tied the laces, brooking no protest this time. Avril did her best to endure in silence without flinching away.

But the feathery brushes of his fingertips along her bare spine made something inside her clench tight and sent a ticklish heat dancing along her limbs, the feeling almost like—

Nay. She stiffened in shock and savagely cut off the thought before she could complete it. Nay, she was confused! This tension that had been sizzling between herself and Valbrand all night came from fear. Nervousness. Outrage. The island's warm weather. The sensation had naught to do with any kind of . . . of . . .

She had not known feelings of that sort since Gerard's death. Had not experienced so much as one flicker of awareness of another man in more than three years. How could she *possibly* be feeling that now, for a stranger who held her hostage?

"Are you finished?" she asked, the tension making her tone sharp.

"Aye," Valbrand replied, a similar edge in his voice as he knotted the laces securely at the top.

The rogue seemed most familiar with the way of lacing a lady's gown.

"Move." He nudged her forward, keeping one hand firmly on her shoulder as he strode into the crowd. The men parted to let him pass, offering what sounded like warm welcomes. He returned their greetings with curt nods; apparently he was not in the best humor at the moment.

"Take a place there, at the far end," he said gruffly, guiding her toward the line of couples. "And speak only if you are spoken—"

"Josette!" Avril cried, trying to break free of his hold as they came within sight of her friend.

Josette whirled with a look of relief. "Avril!" Her face was pale and tearstained, but otherwise she appeared unharmed. The dark-haired young man next to her—the one who had carried her off in Antwerp—would not let her leave his side.

And Valbrand took a firm grasp on Avril's arm.

"Milady, we have kept everyone waiting long enough." He tugged her away, heading for their place at the end of the line. "The elders are assembling."

Avril kept fighting—until Valbrand tightened his grip enough to make her blood-starved arm tingle. She decided it would be wiser to obey, for now.

At least Josette seemed to be faring better than the other captives. A petite Moorish girl sobbed uncontrollably. A voluptuous Italian with curly blond hair cursed in her native tongue at her captor—who had to struggle to keep his hold on her. Next to her stood a tall, red-haired maiden who for some reason had no warrior by her side; she kept her eyes squeezed shut and recited prayers in English.

The five other women were all babbling or wailing or wide-eyed in numb shock. Avril noticed she was not the only one who had her hands tied.

Her gaze darted to the brawny men gathered around, their straight, white teeth gleaming in the moonlight as they smiled. All the air seemed to vanish from her lungs.

Were the captives meant to be shared with this horde? Raped here in the forest in the dead of night—far from the eyes of those in the town?

Or sacrificed in some kind of midnight, pagan religious ceremony?

All the blood drained from her face. For a moment, only Valbrand's firm grip on her arm kept her standing. Her mind reeling, she clung madly to the promise he had made earlier. *No one is going to hurt you,* he had said. *No one is going to hurt you.*

Even the Italian girl fell silent as the elders arrayed

themselves in an impressive, solemn line at the base of the wall of rock. There were fourteen of them. All garbed in richly embroidered, silk-lined mantles fastened by huge gold brooches. Oddly enough, none looked particularly old.

In fact, most appeared to be as young as Valbrand, whom she guessed was no more than thirty.

When the last of the fourteen took his place, every man present bowed to them, almost as one. Silence reigned, broken only by the splashing of the waterfall a few yards away.

Then one of the elders stepped forward and addressed the gathering. From his tone, it sounded like a most serious, solemn speech. Avril's pulse slowed a bit. She even managed to take a deep breath.

All of this formality and ceremony seemed a bit excessive—not to mention unnecessary—if it was truly rape they intended. And none of the elders carried weapons of any kind.

She struggled to make sense of his words, frustrated that she could not understand what was being said and what it had to do with her and the other captives. This language was so foreign to her ear, she could not begin to even guess its roots. It was rough, guttural, yet it had a regular, almost musical cadence. Was it Germanic? Slavic?

The first man finished his address and stepped back, and another came forward, this one holding a sparkling silver chalice. Lifting his arms, he spoke in an impassioned tone, his voice booming up to the night sky. He used the cup to gesture to the waterfall, to the moon, then to each woman in turn. Reaching into his cloak with his free hand, he withdrew a handful of grain that he sprinkled across the ground.

Avril's heart kept skipping beats. "What is—"

"*Silence*," Valbrand whispered harshly.

The man with the chalice returned to his place and a third elder came forward, from the center of the fourteen. This one had cropped blond hair and a full beard, and carried himself with the assured, dignified air of a lord, mayhap even a king. A chain of gold encircled his neck, its massive links supporting a huge jewel of midnight blue.

Not saying a word, he strode to the far end of the line of captors and women, studying each pair in turn, his face set in harsh lines. The men in the clearing fell so silent that Avril could hear the beating wings of a bird taking flight in the forest.

He paused only briefly, before the English girl, then continued down the row—until he reached her and Valbrand. His gaze fastened on her for a moment, his eyes a clear, pale blue that made Avril gasp. With his sky-colored eyes, chiseled features, and golden hair, this man bore a striking resemblance to her captor.

She returned his probing stare in full measure, not glancing away or even blinking. She did not care *who* he was; she would not bow down to him or any man here. Lifting her chin, she steeled herself to face whatever might come.

But to her surprise, one corner of his mouth curved upward—so slightly that if she had not been standing only inches away, she would not have noticed—and the look in his eyes softened almost imperceptibly.

For an instant, his mien could only be described as . . . approving.

Almost kindly.

The impression lasted but a heartbeat, for he glanced at Hauk and the two regarded each other with cool expressions, the air between them all but freezing with iciness. Then Hauk lowered his gaze and bowed his head. A muscle flexed in his tanned cheek. His entire body seemed rigid, with some emotion Avril could not puzzle out.

If the two men were indeed related, she thought, it seemed there was little love lost between them.

Turning on his heel, the blue-eyed elder motioned for one of the other fourteen to join him. A second elder came forth carrying a small, ancient-looking chest, and the two walked to the far end of the line of couples.

Standing before the first pair—a flaxen-haired young warrior and the frightened Moorish girl, who was still crying—the leader intoned what sounded like yet another serious, solemn speech. Someone from the crowd stepped up behind the pair, bending to speak to the girl in low tones.

After a moment, she stopped crying.

Avril's brow furrowed. Was he translating for her? What had been said that could stop the girl's tears? From her place midway down the line, Josette leaned over and glanced back at Avril with a bewildered look. Avril could only shrug and shake her head.

As the speech continued, the Moorish girl's face brightened considerably—and Avril's confusion deepened. With everyone's attention focused on the pair, she seized the opportunity to look at the men gathered around, studying the inhabitants of this island in detail for the first time, struggling to discern who and what—and, more important, *where*—they were.

Their spare, simple garments offered few clues. And though many were fair-haired, others looked as dark as Spaniards. Most left their hair long and unbound, and several had beards, some so full they wore them forked or braided. They also seemed fond of jewelry, though it was simple as well. Arm rings. Brooches. Neck rings. Dangling pendants.

Those caught her eye, for many of the men wore the same device: a pendant in the shape of an upside-down ax or hammer.

Her heart started to pound. By all the saints, it looked almost like . . . but nay, that could not be. Not Thor's hammer. That symbol had not been seen in the world for centuries.

With a gasp of disbelief, she returned her gaze to her captor, studying his profile. Suddenly it all started to make sense, as she remembered the frightening tales passed down from the time before her grandmother's grandmother.

Tales of fierce raiders who came by sea.

Blond, bearded warriors who attacked with speed and daring, pillaging towns large and small. Ransacking churches. Burning homes. By the thousands, they had swept across the continent. They had even conquered Paris by sailing up the Seine.

In their dragon-headed longships.

An image of the dragon-headed posts on Hauk's bed seared Avril's memory. All at once the forest and night sky whirled in her vision. The words the elder was speaking struck her like icy hail. Little wonder she had not recognized their strange language.

The tongue they were speaking was Norse. Old Norse. This band must have been hiding here for centuries. Since the time when their kind had been driven from the continent. An uncharted island would make the perfect place of concealment for a hated, hunted people. They built their longhouses in the old way. Wore the sort of clothing favored by their ancestors. Worshipped the old gods.

And lived as pirates of the seas, raiding along the coasts.

Stealing women to warm their beds.

"By sweet, Holy Mary. You are Vikings," she choked out, trying to wrest her arm from Valbrand's grasp. "You are Vikings!"

"You have discovered our secret," Hauk said in a hushed whisper.

He tried to sound convincing.

"Did you think I would not?" The surprisingly strong little *demoiselle* tried unsuccessfully to wrench free of his grasp. "I will not be made some kind of bond slave to warm your bed, Norseman—"

"Indeed you will not," he agreed readily. "That is not our purpose here." He wondered again whether he should have taken the time to explain the truth earlier, regardless of the fact that they were late. But she had been convinced her stay on Asgard would be short; telling her she would spend the rest of her life here—as his bride—would have made her utterly impossible to manage.

At the moment, all he wanted was for her to be silent. They stood last in line. Once the ceremony was finished, he could scoop her up and make a swift retreat before she caused too much trouble.

She continued to struggle, cursing him. His uncle—Erik Valbrand, highest of all the *eldrer*—shot him a disapproving look from where he stood addressing young Svein and his Moorish captive.

Hauk tugged Avril closer, pressing his lips to her ear. "Mayhap I should have gagged and blindfolded you as well as tying your hands. I will remedy the oversight at once, if you wish."

He had no patience left to deal with the *demoiselle*'s unruly temper. Not after the day he had endured. But the threat and a slight shifting of his grip on her arm were sufficient to quiet her for the moment—though she looked furious enough to murder him and every man here, even unarmed and with her hands tied.

By great Thor's bearded goats, he thought with a rueful glance up at the night sky, what had he done to merit such a female in his life? Never had he met a woman so headstrong and spirited and reckless . . . and bewitching.

Whoever had named her had chosen well. *Avril*. French for April. Springtime. She was every bit as fair and tempestuous as that most unpredictable of all seasons.

Unfortunately for him, she was also intelligent. It usually took newly arrived captives days or even weeks to guess that their abductors were Norsemen;

Avril had unraveled the mystery in less than two hours.

Odin help him if she proved equally quick at discovering the true nature of Asgard Island and its people. If he thought she was difficult to control now, he did not wish to imagine . . .

His uncle's deep growl of a voice reclaimed his attention. The elders and their translator had finished their explanations to the Moorish girl.

Svein took his bride's hand while Erik intoned the traditional closing words of the ritual.

"Svein, you have risked all to bring this woman to Asgard, and we now recognize her as yours. On your oath of honor, do you accept her life and her safety as your responsibility? Will you see to her needs and her happiness, and protect and care for her all the days of her life?"

"*Ja,*" the young groom replied solemnly. "*Jeg gjør.* I will."

The second elder, Storr, opened the ancient *horde* that he cradled in his hands, reaching inside to withdraw a silver brooch encrusted with pearls. He lifted it toward the night sky and then toward the waterfall. As it glittered in the moonlight, it drew soft sounds of wonder from a few of the women—those who were not still crying, or cursing like the unruly Italian wench.

After accepting the brooch, Svein pinned it to his bride's gown, his movements gentle, almost tentative, as if he feared that his delicate, fawn-eyed beauty might break. "Let it be known to all that this is Fadilah," he announced, smiling at her, "wife of Svein."

A cheer went up from the crowd. Erik and Storr moved on to the second man in line, who eagerly stepped forward to take his vows.

"What is happening?" Avril asked in an impatient whisper, watching as the ritual was repeated, clearly not understanding a word of what was being said. "What sort of ceremony is this? I do not—"

"*Silence.*"

His tone was enough to make her bite her lip and hold back whatever reply she wanted to make. She returned her attention to the ritual, brow furrowed.

Hauk only wished *he* did not understand what was happening.

He glanced away into the darkness, wishing he could escape the sound of his uncle's voice. Wishing he were anywhere but here.

Here in this sacred grove that he hated so much.

His every nerve felt raw. And he knew that the uncommon heat smoldering between him and the lady at his side was only partly to blame. By all the earth goddesses, she seemed to burn his very fingers, even through the fabric of her sleeve.

If only he had been able to steal a few hours' sleep, this place and this woman and this ceremony would not affect him so strongly. But he had rested only fitfully during the voyage home and not at all since depositing Avril in his bed this morn. While she had dozed peacefully within the walls of his *vaningshus*, and the other raiders slept after their long absence from Asgard, he had gone to face his uncle. To report the events of the journey. And the loss of two men.

Two men who had been under his command. Under his protection. The eager would-be warriors had known the risks when they left Asgard, but their safety had been entrusted to him.

As his uncle had been swift to point out.

Erik Valbrand had ordered him to arrange their funeral, since few on Asgard were familiar with the ancient rites anymore. Hauk had spent the day preparing the bodies, with their families' help, then set them out to sea after nightfall, in the very longship that had carried them to their fate, set ablaze.

He had had no time to mourn—and less than an hour to gather necessities for this bride he did not want, return to his *vaningshus* and collect her without getting a blade in his gullet, and bring her here to the *althing*.

Hauk stared up at the towering wall of stone before him. He had not attended an *althing*, had not even set foot in this part of the forest, in years. Everyone believed his absence was due to his well-known opinion that this custom, like so many others, should be changed. That it was a waste of breath to gather here at midnight on the night of the raiders' return, offering toasts to the gods and listening to the elders' endless speeches about the old ways and ancestral traditions.

No one knew the true reason he stayed away.

He resisted the tightening in his throat, the ache that filled his chest. But as he listened to the men in line taking their vows, one after another, he felt something inside him wrench open. Felt the memories clawing at him, trying to break free of the deep, black place inside him where he kept them caged.

Tonight—here—he could not hold them back. The memories that were at once sweeter than honey and more bitter than the last dregs of spoiled wine spilled through him.

Karolina. He swallowed hard. Lovely, gentle Karolina. How excited he had been, standing here beside her. How proud and pleased with himself—just as young Svein and the others were now. Grinning like a witless fool, as eager as a stag in rut.

Utterly unaware of how soon it would all end.

He could still hear her screams as she died. Calling out his name with her last breath.

Taking his unborn son with her.

Struggling for breath, he shut his eyes, trying to force the memory back. In command of himself after only a moment, he glanced up at the waterfall.

Only to be assaulted by memories of the second time he had stood here, years later. Beside Maeve.

Maeve, whose laughter had brightened his life like the sun. She had been so entranced by the moonlit waterfall, she barely uttered a sound during the ceremony. His cheerful Celtic lass had been happy to leave behind her life of poverty in Ireland, had quickly fallen in love with Asgard's beauty . . . and with him.

And for a time, he had known hope. Had allowed himself to believe that this time, it would be different. That she could heal the emptiness inside that had been with him since he was a boy.

He could still see the look on her face when she found the first gray hair in her ebony tresses, how she had made a jest over it . . .

And when he lost her, as well, the emptiness inside him had widened and deepened, and his life was all the darker for having known even a brief touch of the sun.

Hauk dropped his gaze to the trampled earth beneath his boots, trying to shrug off the memories as Avril had tried to shrug off his hand earlier. None of it mattered any longer. He had learned his lesson: It was best not to hope, not to dream of a life different from the one the gods had given him. Most of the time it was not even a struggle anymore.

Except here, in this place.

"*Ja,*" another young groom was saying happily. "*Jeg gjør.* I will."

Nei, Hauk wanted to say. *Nay, I will not.* He had vowed never to allow another *utlending* woman—an outsider—into his life, his home. His heart. They were too fragile. Too rare and precious, like delicate blooms he could hold in his hands for only an instant of time. He preferred the occasional liaisons he enjoyed with Asgard women, which lasted however long he and the lady might wish.

Women like his last mistress, Nina, who had kept him company and shared his nights and asked naught more. She had shed no tears when they parted a few months ago. Mayhap because she understood that the only thing that endured in this world was time itself.

Understood that he must devote his attention to what mattered most: his duty. To protect this island and its people.

And its secret.

The elders came to the sixth place in line, where

the red-haired English girl stood alone, and Hauk raised his head, bracing himself.

Thorolf stepped forward from the crowd.

He heard Avril's small gasp of recognition and fear as Thorolf turned an icy glance their way before shifting his attention to the elders.

"Mine eldrer," he said, addressing the council in a determined, purposeful tone, "I wish to claim this female, taken by Bjarn. She will replace the woman who *was* to have been mine." He pointed to Keldan's lady. "That woman was in my possession before Keldan interfered and stole her from me."

Exclamations of shock rippled through the crowd. Even to touch another man's claimed female was a serious offense.

Hauk swore under his breath, but he had been expecting this. *"Nei, mine eldrer.* Thorolf does not tell the full truth."

He was speaking out of turn, before the elders could talk to Thorolf—and his impertinence earned him an annoyed glance from his uncle.

But Hauk would not be silenced. Not even by that look, well remembered from boyhood, from this man who had raised him.

"It was Thorolf who first broke our laws," he continued, directing his words to the full council. "He did not wait until the brunette was alone. He attacked a guard who was protecting her and killed him in the street. In full view of dozens of people."

A louder ripple of surprise and discussion went through the crowd.

"Stille! Peace. Let there be peace," one of the elders

said calmly, quieting the throng. "Is this true, Thorolf? Did you use violence apurpose?"

The knave shook his head, managing to look offended at the very idea. "The guard came at me with sword drawn. I merely defended myself—"

"*Nei*, he attacked first, without warning," Keldan corrected, stepping forward to join the fray. "And he only chose the lady out of spite, because he saw that Hauk and I had stopped to admire her and her friend."

Hauk briefly thought to protest that he had not been admiring Avril, but decided it would be better not to dispute any part of Keldan's explanation.

He heard knowing whispers going through the crowd behind him; all were well aware of the old animosity between himself and Thorolf. It occurred to him that he had in truth been staring at the little brunette just before Thorolf moved in to take her.

No doubt the knave had chosen her for that reason alone.

"Lies," Thorolf insisted. "*I* obeyed our laws. I first saw the wench earlier in the day, long before Valbrand or Keldan ever noticed her. I waited until sunset, as we had all agreed, and I claimed her. I used violence only to defend myself against those who tried to stop me—"

"You used violence because you have a taste for it," Hauk said in disgust. "It pleases you the way drink pleases some men. You even used violence against a female—"

This brought so many gasps and exclamations from the crowd, the noise drowned him out.

"*Stille!*" another of the elders commanded. "Let there be peace!"

"It is true," Hauk insisted, gesturing to Avril. "When she tried to rescue her friend, Thorolf struck her so hard he broke her jaw."

The crowd erupted in noise again. Avril, who had been glancing worriedly from one speaker to the next, seemed to realize the conversation had taken a sudden turn in her direction.

"What are you saying?" she demanded of Hauk with wide, frightened eyes. "What is going—"

"It is my word or theirs." Thorolf spoke over her. "And Keldan has just admitted that the brunette was in my hands before he interfered. I have been wronged. I ask that either my claim to this woman be recognized"—he indicated the English girl, who stood whispering prayers and trembling—"or that Keldan be required to return the female he stole from me."

Keldan looked thunder-struck, devastated at the possibility that his charming little brunette might be taken from him.

Hauk quickly came to his friend's assistance. "*Mine eldrer*, you have more than *our* word. There were two other witnesses." He nodded to Avril and her friend. "Ask the women themselves. They cannot understand what has been said, and they have no reason to lie about Thorolf's actions."

The elders gathered for a moment to discuss this suggestion among themselves. One of them who spoke French came over to stand before Keldan's lady. Keldan immediately returned to hover possessively at her side.

"We have need of your help, *ma demoiselle*," the elder said with a bow, his voice gentle and his expression warm. "Tell me, if you would be so kind, what is your name?"

The girl looked astonished to find herself suddenly addressed in her native tongue. She glanced over at Avril, seeking guidance.

Avril shook her head, clearly opposed to offering help of any kind. Hauk frowned at her.

But the brunette seemed to see no harm in revealing her name. "J-Josette."

"*Merci*, Josette. And could you also tell me, when did you first see this man in Antwerp?" He pointed to Thorolf.

She cringed away from the black-haired giant who stared at her—only to bump into Keldan. But she did not protest the protective arm Kel draped around her shoulders.

"When . . . when he grabbed me." She shuddered visibly. "At the fair."

"You had not seen him before that?"

She shook her head. "Nay."

"We would have noticed a man of his size," Avril put in. "He does not blend easily into a crowd."

"Do not interrupt," Hauk chided, though it occurred to him that he had just done the same thing, speaking out of turn to help a friend.

"Nay, Valbrand, I would hear from her, as well," the elder said easily. "Tell me, *ma demoiselle*, did Thorolf hurt you?"

"Aye, he . . ." Avril paused, lifting a hand to her

cheek, her gaze on Thorolf's massive fists. "He struck me so hard, I fell to the ground. The pain was so great that I thought my jaw was—"

"Fortunately, the injury has healed," Hauk finished for her.

"*Merci, mes demoiselles.*" Bowing to each, the elder returned to translate the women's answers to the other thirteen, while Thorolf stood waiting impatiently.

Avril remained very still, her fingers on her cheek. "But my jaw *was* broken," she whispered. "I am sure of it. He hit me after I wounded him." Blinking, she stared at Thorolf's right arm. "With my knife."

Hauk shifted uncomfortably, trying to think of how he was going to explain *that* away. Thorolf was close enough that she could see clearly there was no injury to his arm.

His skin was unmarred. There was no scar. No mark at all.

"The wound must not have been as serious as you thought," Hauk said casually.

"But it *was*," she insisted. "His blood was all over my gown—"

"It was twilight." Hauk had burned the garment this morn, hoping she would forget that particular detail of the incident. "The shadows play odd tricks at that time of day."

"But—"

"Silence. The elders have reached their decision."

Avril quieted—more out of shock, Hauk guessed, than any newfound obedience. By all the gods, the fiery little *demoiselle* was adding up the evidence before her eyes much too quickly.

As the elders reclaimed their places, she even thought to look at her palm, which she had cut on a shard of glass in his *vaningshus* not an hour ago.

Already it was completely healed. There was no mark of the injury. No blood, no scar, not even a scratch.

Her mouth dropped open in a round O of disbelief.

If she thought to notice, he thought sourly, she might see that the scratches her nails had inflicted on his face were gone as well.

'Twas something she would have to grow accustomed to in her new life here on Asgard.

One of many things.

"We have reached our decision," Erik announced. "*Stille*. Let there be peace."

A tense hush fell over the crowd. For once, his uncle did not indulge in a long-winded oration, simply stating the judgment flatly.

"Keldan was indeed wrong to take the woman Josette when Thorolf already had her in his hold."

Keldan uttered a strangled sound. Hauk bit back a curse.

"But Thorolf committed the more serious offense," Erik continued, "by killing the guard instead of waiting until the girl was alone. He engaged in wanton violence, endangered the lives of others in his traveling party, and risked bringing unwanted, dangerous attention to the peaceful people of Asgard."

Thorolf shot a simmering glare at Hauk and Avril,

looking wrathful enough to kill them both for having thwarted him again.

Without even thinking, Hauk stepped in front of her, obeying an instinct to protect her.

"Keldan may keep the woman Josette," Erik announced, "and Thorolf is also denied any right to the female that Bjarn had claimed."

"Nei!" Thorolf shouted, his face awash in disbelief. "I risked as much in the voyage as the others. Am I to have naught to show for it?"

"Be grateful the punishment is so light," one of the other elders said, his voice and his gaze cool. "And do not risk our ire further. Using violence against a female proves you unfit to be a husband. Bjarn's woman shall be free to choose a mate from among those men of Asgard who are unmarried. She will not be given to you, Thorolf."

Glowering at them, Thorolf started to say more, then apparently thought the better of it. With a curse, he turned on his heel and stalked away, shoving a path through the crowd.

Keldan looked like he would melt from relief.

The English girl opened her eyes, blinking in wonderment at Thorolf's abrupt departure. She stopped muttering prayers, as if they had just been answered.

But as Hauk watched Thorolf stalk away into the night, he had the gut-churning feeling that the most troublesome malcontent among them had just been rendered even more dangerous.

The elders resumed the interrupted ceremony, Storr bringing over the chest of brooches, Erik moving to stand before the next man in line, while another elder came to lead the English girl away, quietly speaking to her in her native tongue.

The seventh bride, the Italian firebrand, was not nearly as accepting of her new status as the others had been. Once told in her language what was happening, she became even angrier, kicking and screaming. Her unfortunate groom had to take his vows quickly, then carry her off over his shoulder, his new wife pounding on his back.

Hauk sighed wearily, afraid he had just gotten an advance look at his own evening.

And then it was Keldan's turn. Beaming, he took Josette's hand and lifted it to his lips, brushing a kiss over her fingers.

Poor fool. He already looked to be half in love.

The elder who spoke French returned to tell the little brunette what was to happen—and though he spoke softly, Avril picked out just enough words to understand at last.

Eyes wide with shock, she turned to Hauk. "This is some sort of *wedding* ceremony?"

That, apparently, was the last guess she would have made.

"Aye, milady. I am surprised you did not deduce it sooner." He arched one brow. "Did you think we savage Norsemen meant to devour you in some heathen sacrifice here under the moon?"

Color rose in her cheeks as she gaped at him—and astonishment seemed to have stolen her voice.

Her friend burst into tears, evidently less than

pleased to hear that she would be spending her future here with Keldan.

But naught could dampen Kel's spirits as he fulfilled his part of the ritual.

"*Ja,*" he said eagerly when it came to the traditional questions. "*Jeg gjor.* I will."

With a broad smile, he pinned the silver brooch to Josette's gown, though she tried to bat his hands away, sobbing.

"Let it be known to all that this is Josette," he said gently, "wife of Keldan."

Avril's numb shock had given way to panic by the time Erik and Storr reached them. Hauk had to hold her with both hands to keep her from bolting.

"Nay! Let go of me!" She shook her head wildly, not even listening as the French-speaking elder explained.

"*Ma demoiselle,* you have been brought here to be this man's wife, and will live here with him the rest of your days—"

"*Nay.*" She kept twisting, trying to break free. "I cannot. I will not! You cannot mean to keep me here forever. You cannot—"

"Avril, you will not be harmed." Hauk tried to subdue her as gently as he could, her terrified words striking him like darts. "You have a new life here."

". . . Though you will never see your homeland again, you will know no hunger, no illness, no want—"

"*Nay!*" she shouted, clenching her fists. "You have no right to do this! You—" As if an idea had struck, she suddenly raised her bound hands, showing them the gold band that gleamed on her left ring finger. "I-I am already married!"

Hauk had noticed the ring this morn, when he undressed her.

But the fact that she already had a husband changed nothing.

He turned her to face him, holding her by the shoulders. "It matters not, milady. You are mine now."

Defiance blazed in her eyes, so hot he felt it sear through him like a torch. "Never," she spat. "I will never be yours! I will not stay here!"

His uncle Erik began the traditional questions. "Hauk, you have risked all to bring this woman to Asgard, and we now recognize her as yours . . ."

He forced away the memories that slashed him deep inside.

". . . On your oath of honor, do you accept her life and her safety as your responsibility?"

Avril bared her teeth, as if she longed to fasten them on his throat.

"Will you see to her needs and her happiness, and protect and care for her all the days of her life?"

"*Ja,*" he grated out reluctantly. "*Jeg gjor.* I will."

His uncle handed him the pearl-encrusted silver brooch, adding an unexpected phrase he had not said to any of the others. "May she bear you many fine sons and bring you happiness."

Hauk did not reveal the surprise he felt at his uncle's good wishes. Nor did he correct his error.

Hauk did not want this defiant *demoiselle* to bring him happiness. Or any other emotion.

And she would bear him neither sons nor daughters—for he had no intention of bedding her.

"Let it be known to all that this is Avril." He pinned the brooch to her gown as she glared up at him with green eyes full of fury. "Wife of Hauk."

6

Avril stood in the entrance of Valbrand's darkened keep, her blood seething with outrage, her rapid breaths unnaturally loud in the silence. Flickering points of fire began to illuminate the long chamber, one by one. Her captor was slowly lighting candles, his boot steps echoing on the stone floor.

The gag in her mouth prevented her from voicing any more of the choice words she had shouted when he carried her away from the *althing*. By nails and blood, if this arrogant Norseman thought he was actually her *husband* now, if he was under the delusion that he was about to enjoy a wedding night . . .

She twisted her hands, trying to loosen the leather thongs that bound her. He only bothered to light a few candles before returning to her side—the silver flash of a dagger in his hand.

The gag muffled her cry. But she stood her ground, summoned all her courage, and glared up at him. Curling her fingers into fists, she prepared to defend her virtue to her last breath.

His jaw was clenched, his pale-blue eyes unreadable. And he towered over her at a height that suddenly seemed as great as the cliffs above the ocean.

Yet when he lifted the knife toward her, he only sliced through the bindings that tied her hands, setting her free.

Avril choked out a muted, wordless exclamation of disbelief.

When he raised the blade again, her gaze snapped up to meet his.

But he merely reached for the gag—then paused, as if reconsidering.

"Milady," he said, his voice low and rough, "let us strike a bargain. I am damnably tired and I would prefer not to spend any more time arguing this night. I want naught but to go to bed—"

With a muffled squeak of fear, she kicked him in the shin.

He dropped the knife, hobbling back a step. "Alone," he added with an annoyed scowl, scooping up the dagger before she could grab for it. "I meant alone. I want only *sleep*. In truth, you may take the bed. I will make a place on the floor."

Avril could not believe her ears. She flinched away when he reached for her again. Inhaled sharply when the cold edge of the blade pressed against her cheek.

Yet he surprised her a second time, cutting through the cloth that had rendered her mute. Before she could even exhale, he returned the dagger to its sheath on his belt and walked away from her.

"What I am asking is that we declare a truce between us," he said in that same gruff voice. "At least for the rest of the night."

Avril blinked at him, reaching up with tingling fingers to remove the bits of cloth from her mouth. She spat out a mouthful of fuzz, not taking her eyes from his broad, muscled back as he strode toward the bed.

He took a pillow and blanket and returned to this side of the chamber, dropping them in the far corner. Avril felt so confused she could not coax her tongue to form words.

Gallantry was the last thing she had expected from him.

"In the morn," he continued, opening a nearby trunk and taking out another pillow, "I will explain more to you about the island and our ways. You will fare well here, Avril. Now that you have been recognized as my wife, everyone will—"

"Norseman," she choked out, finally gathering her wits enough to interrupt him. "Allow me to make something clear to you. I am *not* your wife and I am *not* staying here."

He sighed, letting the chest's lid fall with a solid *thwack*. "Aye, unfortunately for me," he said, "you are, and you will be."

Avril glared at him across the firelit darkness. She could throttle the man. Happily. Surely God would forgive her.

Taking a deep breath, she tried to make him see reason. "Listen to me, Hauk Valbrand," she said as politely as she could manage. "It is obvious that you do not want me here. And we both know that *I* do not want to be here. There is a simple solution to our problems. Let me go home."

His fingers clenched around the pillow. With a whispered oath, he tossed it into the corner, hanging his head. He raked one hand through his hair, the strands pale gold against the darker skin of his tanned shoulders in the candlelight. For a moment, despite all his size and sinew, he looked . . .

Worn out. Weary. Spent.

"I cannot."

"Why not?" she demanded in frustration. "It should be a simple enough matter to return me to Antwerp the way we came—"

"The matter is out of my hands." He shook his head.

"Are you afraid I will reveal your secret? Is that why you refuse to let me leave?" She moved closer. "I *swear* to you I will not tell anyone."

He glanced at her over one brawny shoulder. "Our secret?"

"That you are Vikings. Hidden away here all these years from a world that hates you. I will not tell anyone about this island. You have my word."

He turned to face her. "And I am to trust your word? I am to trust that you would not have a change of heart once you were free? That you would not return here with men-at-arms to take vengeance and ensure we never go raiding again?"

She lifted her hands helplessly. "All I can give you is my word of honor."

He shook his head. "That is why we have the laws. Once a woman is brought to Asgard, she may never leave. Regardless of how convincingly she promises to keep our secret."

"And the woman has no choice in the matter?" Her temper flared. "That is barbaric! It is unspeakably cruel—"

"It may seem cruel, but it is the only way to ensure the safety and peace of this island and its people. There is naught to be done, Avril. Least of all by me. I am the *vokter* here. The peace-keeper. The man charged with *enforcing* our laws—"

"Well, you will not force *me* to obey them!" She stalked closer until they were almost face to face. "You had no right to bring me here and you have no right to keep me against my will! The devil take you and your laws! I will not sit tamely by while you destroy my life—"

He touched her cheek and her breath caught.

It was a gentle, startling contact of his palm, his fingertips, barely grazing her skin. The unexpected sensation of his hand—so strong, so warm—lightly stroking her face rendered her mute and held her still far more effectively than any force could have.

He touched her as if she were the most fragile, delicate woman he had ever met.

"I was trying to *save* your life," he said roughly, his eyes dark, his voice somehow both quiet and forceful at the same time. "If I had not stopped Thorolf . . ."

He left the sentence unfinished. His words held an edge of tension, yet Avril also heard genuine concern, for her safety. For her. Which only confused her even more.

All at once, she was aware of how their breathing sounded together, rapid and shallow. How dark the room was. How his gaze traced over her features, the color of his eyes deepening to a midnight blue.

His attention settled on her mouth. Her heart fluttered, then began pounding hard. A muscle flexed in his tanned, beard-stubbled cheek.

Abruptly he withdrew his hand and turned away from her. "There is no point in discussing this further," he grated out, stalking over to the cold hearth on the opposite side of the chamber. "You will not be leaving Asgard. You should not torment yourself by holding out hope of rescue, and you cannot escape. There is no way off this island."

"I-I will *make* a way," she insisted, wishing her legs would stop trembling.

"You misunderstand, wife. What I am telling you is that *no one* leaves Asgard Island."

Gasping, she spun toward him. "That is a lie. You left. You and the others who came to Antwerp—"

"Such voyages are rare. We do not even keep boats. The longship we used to sail to Antwerp has already been destroyed. Unless you are skilled at shipbuilding, you will not be leaving." He braced one arm against the carved paneling above the hearth. "Neither of us may like it, but this is your home now. And we are husband and wife—"

"We are *not* husband and wife! There was no church, no priest. *I* spoke no vows—"

"You will adjust. All the women do. It is but a matter of time." He glanced up at the wall, at the display of weapons and artifacts. "And time is something we have in abundance here."

Those words—or mayhap his hollow tone as he said them—sent a chill down her back.

"If I were here a hundred years, I would never stop trying to gain my freedom," she replied hotly. "You do not understand. I have a *daughter* at home in France. A three-year-old daughter. She needs me. I must return to her!"

For a moment, he did not reply, remained utterly still.

Then he gave her a heated glance over his shoulder. "And to your husband as well? Does he not need you?"

"Aye," she amended quickly. "I must return to my daughter and to my husband."

She cursed herself for forgetting; he would never believe her word of honor if he caught her in a lie.

He turned around, leaning back against the hearth, his eyes narrowed. "Why did you not mention him before?"

"Because . . ." *Because I had no idea you meant to keep me here forever. Because he has been dead for more than three years. Because* . . . "Why would I disclose anything to the brigand who abducted me? I *told* you I come from a powerful and influential family. And I wear a wedding band. You must have noticed it."

"Aye, I did." His gaze dropped to her hand and his voice dropped to a deep, almost predatory growl. "This morn when I undressed you."

She gasped, partly from the bold way he said it— and partly from the heat that sizzled through her midsection as a shocking, unbidden image filled her mind.

Valbrand's dark, callused hands on her body . . . sliding cloth downward to reveal bare flesh . . . gently lowering her to the sheets . . .

She clenched her left hand, as if the ring Gerard

had given her were a talisman that could right her wayward thoughts and ward off this daring Norseman.

But the wedding band felt cold against her damp palm. Powerless.

And strangely, she swore she could feel heat radiating from the silver brooch that rested above her heart, where Hauk had pinned it to her bodice.

His gaze lifted to hers, slowly. "Odd that I noticed no husband with you in Antwerp," he said when she did not speak. "What kind of husband allows his wife to go running about the streets unescorted?"

"He . . ." She fervently bade her jumbled thoughts to untangle themselves. When she fixed her mind on Gerard, the words came. "He is generous and kind and loving and the best sort of man." Her voice strengthened. She added a bit more for good measure. "And I am his wife and I belong to him body and heart and soul."

Hauk did not move. Not one steely muscle.

But the look in his eyes became hot. Intimate. Challenging.

"I am not interested in your heart or your soul," he said in that quiet, predatory growl, pausing before he added, "or your body."

Trembling, Avril wrapped her arms around her middle, caught in a storm of confusing, conflicting emotions that drenched her like hot rain. The silver brooch almost seemed to burn her skin. She tried to unfasten it, but could not work the clasp.

Frustrated, she ripped it from her gown and threw it aside. "Then you have no reason to keep me here!"

His attention suddenly fastened on her bodice.

Avril looked down and gasped. In tearing off the symbol of his claim over her, she had ripped her linen gown. The violet fabric gaped at the top, revealing the pale upper curve of her breast. She grabbed the torn material, covering herself.

And glanced up to find Hauk watching her with potent male hunger etched on his chiseled features. He straightened, took one step toward her. Then he started to advance slowly.

Avril felt that unnerving, unwelcome heat spilling through her. She stumbled backward a pace. Struggled to find her voice. *"Nay."*

She did not know which she was denying: his intentions or her own bewildering feelings. But he halted. For a moment he remained frozen, his hands clenching and unclenching.

Then he turned sharply and stalked to a chest beneath one of the shuttered windows. "All that you have need of, you will find in the town." He opened the trunk, took out a leather sack, and began stuffing clothes into it. "Food. Drink. New garments, if you do not like the ones I chose for you. Ask the shopkeepers for whatever you wish and it will be given you. We use barter rather than coin here."

Avril could only stare at him, trembling, her thoughts tangled like a dozen strands of yarn all knotted together.

He let the chest's lid fall and moved on to another. "A few people in the village speak French. If you cannot make yourself understood, one of them can translate for you. I will leave Ildfast, my horse, here for you. He can be unmanageable at times"—he slanted her a quick glance—"but I do not think you will have any trouble with him."

She shook her head, surprise and disbelief battering her senses. "You . . . you are leaving?"

"One of my duties is to patrol the shoreline and see that our border remains secure. I am often away." He took a pair of gloves and a length of rope from the next trunk and added them to his pack. "While I am gone, you are free to go where you wish—"

"Norseman—"

"See your friend. Visit the town. Explore the island." Carrying the sack, he stalked toward the weapons displayed above the hearth. "But stay away from the cliffs. People fall now and then. And keep out of the western part of the forest. There are wolves there—"

"What makes you believe I will *be* here when you get back?"

He did not look at her as he selected a battle-ax and lashed it to his pack. "Do not hope that my absence will make it easier for you to escape from Asgard," he said quietly. "It will not."

He slung the pack over his shoulder and headed for the door.

Shaking with desperation, with astonishment, Avril followed him. "You cannot mean to keep me here! You must let me return to my child!"

He turned to face her. "Avril—"

"You are not a barbarian. If you were, you would have let me die in Antwerp. You seem to have some code of honor or chivalry by which you live."

He did not reply.

She lowered her gaze to the stone floor, willing to humble herself, willing to do anything to get home to her little girl.

"Hauk," she pleaded quietly. "Do you want me to beg? Then I am begging you. *Please*, in the name of whatever gods you believe in, show mercy. My little Giselle is only three. When I left for Antwerp, I told her I would be gone but ten days, no more." Dampness burned in Avril's eyes. "She did not understand, so I gave her ten raisin sweetcakes and told her to eat one each day, and when the last one was gone, her *maman* would be home—"

Her voice choked out. *Had Giselle eaten the last cake yet? Had she looked at Celine and Gaston with tear-filled eyes and asked why Maman had not returned, why Maman had broken her promise?*

"She . . . she is barely more than a baby. She likes pink flowers and mud puddles and spinning tops." Avril lifted her head to find him looking at her intently, and she could not stop the tear that slid down her cheek. "The toy I had in my hand in Antwerp, the one I dropped when you and I collided—I bought it for her. I promised I would bring her a spinning top from the fair. She calls them 'pretty spinnys.'" Another tear slipped past her lashes. "Would you do this to an innocent child? Would you take a baby's mother from her?"

He said naught for a moment, remained frozen.

Then he looked off into the darkness and answered her, his voice flat, emotionless.

"I already have."

"Damn you!" She slapped him hard enough to

leave the red imprint of her hand on his face. "Damn you, Norseman! If you try to keep me here, I swear I will—"

"Kill me?" An odd, self-mocking expression curved his mouth. "I doubt that."

Turning on his heel, he strode away from her. "Heed what I have told you and do not make things more difficult, Avril. I will return in two or three days. Until then, I bid you farewell."

With that, he walked out and slammed the door behind him.

She could only stare in open-mouthed disbelief at the spot where he had last stood. Robbed of a target for her outrage, she could not even move for a moment. Turning her head, she looked around the vast, empty chamber with its guttering candles and silent shadows.

Then she rushed over to the door and tried the latch.

It was open. He had not bothered to lock her in.

Which meant he was entirely confident of what he said: There was no way to escape from this island.

Avril sagged against the door, despair closing in on her, black and overpowering. She pounded one fist against the wood, but the futile gesture only hurt her hand. Her throat tightened until she could not draw breath.

She shut her eyes, remembering the last time she had seen her baby, with her ruddy cheeks, her raven curls shining in the sun, her chubby fingers waving farewell.

"Giselle." The cherished name came out as a sob. "My sweet Giselle."

Shaking her head, Avril pushed herself away from the door, refusing to accept what Hauk had told her. If she could not hope to be rescued, then she would rescue herself.

It was too dark to venture out, but as soon as dawn broke, her escape efforts would begin.

"I will return to you, my little one," she vowed. "Even if I must build a boat with my own two hands!"

Hauk strode down the moonlit path, the sound of his pulse competing with the distant roar of the surf in the darkness. His fingers gripped the leather sash of his pack, but he was only distantly aware of its familiar weight on his shoulder, the jagged stones beneath his boots, the night wind cooling the sweat from his body.

He could hardly see or even *think* past the fatigue and sexual need and frustration that clouded his brain. By Odin's black ravens, all he wanted was for this accursed night to end before some new torment presented itself.

You are not a barbarian, she had said. Hel, he had never felt *more* like a barbarian. Had he remained in her company any longer, he would have had his lovely bride on her back in his bed, proving her wrong, ravishing her as thoroughly as any lawless brigand.

How could she affect him so powerfully in so short a time? Had he not sworn only an hour ago, at the *althing,* never to bed her, never to allow her into his heart? He could not even seem to make the vow last one night. Could not resist touching her. Was beginning to admire the way she stood up to him, all courage and boldness and curses.

And he had been utterly unprepared for the impact of her tears.

Hauk shifted the pack to his other shoulder and kept walking, trying to forget those two glistening droplets, gliding down her cheek one after the other. For one horrible moment, he had felt as if he were drowning in them.

In that instant, he had glimpsed a completely different Avril—not defiant and tempestuous, but tender and soft-hearted, utterly devoted to those she loved . . . and utterly vulnerable.

He could not banish the uncomfortable feeling that stabbed at his belly as if he had eaten a bowlful of thorns.

Guilt.

I have a daughter. A three-year-old daughter.

His cheek still stung from Avril's slap—but he felt as if she had punched him in the gut with those words. By all the gods, he had never suspected she had a young child awaiting her in France along with her husband.

But she would not be returning home to them.

Not now, not ever.

He glanced up into the black, star-strewn sky and spat an oath, cursing the fates for throwing her into his path on that crowded streetcorner in Antwerp. If she had been a few moments earlier or he a few moments later, if Keldan had not insisted on chasing after her, if she had not attacked Thorolf . . .

Nei, it was too late for regrets now. What was done could not be undone. He could not risk the lives of everyone on Asgard for the sake of one woman.

Or even one child.

He fastened his attention on the trail before him. At least the child still had her father. At least she would not be alone.

That was more than he had had growing up.

Forcing those thoughts to the back of his mind, he focused on the familiar curve of the path beneath his boots, the brine-scented wind in his face, the journey that lay ahead. His life had been wrenched out of his control on that ill-fated voyage to Antwerp, and he felt an urgent need to put it back in order. What he needed was routine. Habit. A good night's sleep and some hard, physical work.

He needed some distance from the mesmerizing little beauty who had just become his wife. Enough to keep him from thinking of her spice-scented hair and her body soft against his and her shamelessly ripe, ruby lips that begged him to . . .

He cut the image short, thoroughly annoyed. He would *not* do this to himself. He would drown these heated thoughts in sweat. Remind himself of what was truly important—his people and his duty.

When he returned, he would be able to deal with her presence in his life coolly and rationally.

It took half an hour to reach Keldan's *vaningshus*. The young groom had spent the better part of the past year building it in a meadow west of town, in antici-

pation of enjoying a secluded and happy sojourn here
with his new bride.

Hauk pounded on the door, a single blow of his fist.
Since Keldan was mostly to blame for his predica-
ment, Keldan could grant him a favor.

The polished pine door opened quickly—and the
young groom in question looked surprisingly glad to
see him. "Hauk! Why are you not with your lady?
Nei, never mind. Thank the gods you are here!" Kel
grabbed his arm and hauled him inside, his expression
matching his agitated voice. "You must teach me to
speak French. It is accursed difficult to woo a woman
when she cannot even understand what you are saying."

He gestured to the far side of the chamber, where
pretty Josette stood in a corner, her face damp with
furious tears, what looked like wreckage strewn about
her feet—upturned jewel chests, ripped garments,
shredded velvet pillows with their goose-feather stuffing spilled everywhere, and the remains of what had
been a gracefully carved chair.

"The gifts did not work," Keldan explained, dodging a flagon of perfume she flung at him. It sailed past
him to shatter against the wall.

Hauk realized that Josette must have been hurling
bits and pieces of debris at her new husband's head for
some time, for the wall behind Keldan had been
newly decorated in disgusting shades of dripping wine
and precious oils, with a few goose feathers stuck to
the goo here and there.

"By Tyr's blade, Kel." He waved a hand in front of

his nose. "It smells like a bawd's bedchamber in here."

"Do you have any *helpful* comments to make?"

"I was the one who warned you that language differences could be a problem."

"That is not the kind of help I was hoping for."

With a shrug, Hauk bowed in the lady's direction and tried addressing her in French. "Good eventide, milady. How fare you?"

She only shouted curses and threats in reply. And reached for a piece of the chair.

Hauk stepped out of the way as it came flying at Keldan, grateful that he was not her target. "I fear I cannot help you, Kel. I would say this wooing may take months. Mayhap years. Thor's hammer, I did not realize before that your bride had a sailor's vocabulary." A silk slipper smacked Keldan right between the eyes. "Or such excellent aim."

"I do not understand," Keldan said miserably, rubbing his forehead and frowning at her. "I have followed all the advice given in the *Havamal*."

"Which shows how useful that ancient text is," Hauk replied scornfully. Every young man of Asgard studied the *Havamal* before taking a bride, to learn how to be a good husband, how to please a wife. "The so-called wisdom of past generations is mostly poetic nonsense."

"So you have said before."

"Mayhap we had better speak outside, where the air is not so full of"—Hauk dodged the silk slipper's mate—"projectiles."

Keldan hastily led the retreat, closing the door

firmly behind them once they had escaped to the relative safety of the outdoors. "You are enjoying this," he accused with a scowl.

"Not at all," Hauk lied, feeling one corner of his mouth curve. "I am afflicted with sorrow that your wife is not fawning at your feet as the women of Asgard have always done."

"*Ja, ja,* I can tell," Keldan drawled. Folding his arms, he nodded toward Hauk's pack. "And how have you fared? It would appear you have declared defeat and deserted your new bride already. Have you come seeking a place to sleep for the night?"

"*Nei.* Nor am I deserting her." Hauk looked to the south, where he could just make out his *vaningshus* in the distance.

How strange it felt, to see lights burning in his home when he was not there. To have someone else living in that place, waiting for him.

Waiting to bury a blade in his heart, he corrected himself.

"I thought it best to allow time for our blood to cool," he explained. "I am going out on sentry duty."

"But, Hauk, you took a vow—"

"*Ja,* and I will keep it. At the moment, we are like fire and tinder. If I stay with her, there is going to be an explosion and one of us might get damaged by the blast. I vowed to protect her, and for now the best way to protect her is to stay *away* from her."

"But who will care for her and see to her needs?"

"Believe me, Keldan, there has never been a woman *less* in need of a man to take care of her."

An unwanted memory struck him: those two tears

gliding down her face, how she had looked so vulnerable, so . . .

He shook it off. "Avril is more than capable of looking after herself. I only came here to ask you to check on her now and then while I am away. See that she stays out of trouble."

"You want me to watch over the *two* of them?" Keldan looked like he might choke. "When I do not even speak their language?"

"You were the one who insisted that these women and no others would do, if you recall. You insisted that we have them; well, now we have them." He arched one brow. "Or more accurately," he said lightly, "now *you* have them."

He turned to leave.

Keldan caught him by the shoulder. "But, Hauk, you go on sentry only once a month. Surely it could wait. It will take you a week to travel all the way around the island. You cannot mean to leave her   "

"*Nei*, trust me, it is better that I go now. And I am not setting out on a full patrol. I will be gone only two or three days." Hauk returned the younger man's disapproving regard with a hard stare. "Cease looking at me that way. I am not breaking my vows. I *am* seeing to her needs. She is safe and well. She is intelligent enough to stay away from the cliffs and out of the western part of the forest, as I have warned her. She has shelter, food, clothing—"

"But that is not all a woman needs," Keldan said with the all-knowing confidence of a groom on his wedding night. "According to the *Havamal*—"

"Do not quote that accursed book to me," Hauk

snapped, shaking off his friend's restraining hand. "It tells you only how a marriage is to begin. It does not reveal how it ends. But I *know* how it ends—in a black pit of misery and torment. And I may not believe in the *Havamal* or tradition or the justness of the gods anymore, but I do believe in one thing. I believe in sparing myself misery and torment." He nodded toward Keldan's home. "Your little cottage in a meadow by the sea is idyllic now, but it will change, Kel. *She* will change. Everything and everyone around us changes—"

"Mayhap someday when I am as old as you," Keldan interrupted, "I will feel the same. But I hope not. And I think you are making a mistake, leaving your bride on your wedding night."

"Well, it is my mistake to make." Hauk turned again to leave.

Only to find Josette peeking out the door with wide eyes, watching the two of them argue.

"Milord?" she asked tentatively, opening the door a bit wider. "Please, what . . . what have you done with Avril? Is she all right? You have not—"

"Nay, milady, she is unharmed." Hauk shook his head. Keldan's little brunette seemed to fear they had been discussing some dire fate that had befallen her friend. "You may see her in the morn if you wish."

She stepped outside when he started to walk away. "Please, milord, you cannot keep us here." She gave Keldan a glare, as if she had been trying to explain that idea to him as well. "You must set Avril free."

Hauk sighed, feeling the full weight of this endless

day pressing down on him. "That I cannot do, milady. You ask for what is impossible."

"But I am not sure you understand. She has a little daughter, at home in France—"

"I know. She told me. But there is naught that can be done." As he looked down into a woman's tear-filled eyes for the second time that night, regret tore at him with fresh, sharp claws. "I am sorry."

Black lashes shaded her blue eyes as she glanced down at the ground. "But I . . ." Josette chewed at her lower lip, seemed to fight some inner battle. "I am not sure she has told you the *full* truth."

"About what?"

"About her husband." Still biting her lip, Josette lifted her gaze.

Hauk almost told her he did not care. It did not matter. He did not want to know aught more about this man in France who had claimed Avril heart and body and soul. Why should he?

"What of him?"

"I tell you only because it will make you understand *why* Avril must be set free." Josette took a breath and spoke quickly. "Avril's husband Gerard was killed three years ago. She is a widow."

Hauk felt as if he had just been struck by a shower of cold hail. He could not speak.

She was a widow. She belonged to no other man.

Belonged to no man but . . .

He sliced off the last word of that thought. Resisted the quick, hot surge of male possessiveness that shot through him. "It matters not."

"But do you not see?" Josette asked plaintively.

"Little Giselle lost her father before she was even born. You cannot take her mother from her as well. You must let Avril return to her daughter. You *must*. If you do not, the poor child will be an orphan."

Hauk turned away from her, feeling the thorns return to his belly. He thought for a moment he was going to be sick.

Had he truly believed this day could get no worse?

"It matters not." He heard himself repeat the words. Numbly. Like a chant that he might believe if he only said it enough times.

"How can you say that?" Josette gasped. "How can you be so heartless?"

"Keldan, take her inside," Hauk ground out. He had had enough of everyone pointing out his flaws for one day.

Without another word to either of them, he strode away into the darkness, barely even aware of the direction he took.

He had made a child an orphan.

7

The warm touch of the sun against her cheek made Josette stir. She yawned sleepily, listening to birds twittering somewhere outside her window. Oh, but this would not do at all. Her brothers were forever calling her a lazy little feather-wit, and here she was proving them right. Opening her eyes, she blinked in confusion at the scent of warm bread and cinnamon. Who had brought food to her bedchamber?

With a gasp of alarm, she remembered abruptly that she was not in Brittany. She sat up, wondering *how* she had come to be in the bed.

Bright sunlight poured through the open shutters, along with the summery-green smell of the meadow and the birds' noisy songs. Brushing her tangled hair out of her eyes, she saw *him* there: her dark-haired captor, Keldan. Seated at a trestle table on the opposite side of his long, strange dwelling, he was peacefully eating his morning meal.

"Good morn," he said in broken French, regarding her with a tentative smile. "Sleep well?"

Josette scrambled backward until she came up against the headboard, clutching the blankets to her chin. But he did not move, did not look as if he intended to pounce on her. Yet. She quickly glanced around. He had cleaned away the mess she had created last night, even washed the paneled walls that had been dripping with perfume and wine.

She frowned, trying to remember what had happened after his burly blond friend left them. She had planted herself in the corner, clutching a broken arm of the chair as a weapon, determined to protect her virginity. But she must have eventually fallen asleep.

Blushing, she realized *he* must have carried her to bed and covered her with the blanket. She gave him an accusing, suspicious stare.

But she was still fully clothed, except for her boots, which sat on the floor beside the bed. And judging by the rumpled bedding on the floor near the table, it appeared he had spent the night over on that side of the room.

He held out a basket filled with bread toward her, as if it were a peace offering. "Hungry?"

"Nay." Her stomach growled at the tantalizing scent of cinnamon, declaring her a liar. "Nay, I do not want food, I do not want gifts, I do not want to be married to you, and I will *not* stay here with you for the rest of my life."

He only shook his head and shrugged, clearly unable to follow her.

"On my oath, this is maddening!" Josette dropped the blankets. "Can you not understand even a word of what I am saying?"

He cocked his head to one side, still smiling at her.

She folded her arms. "I wager I could say anything I want to you. I could even call you a . . ." She returned his smile and spoke softly, sweetly. "An ugly, swaggering, bug-eyed beef-wit who has the manners of a toad and smells like old socks."

His grin widened and those dark eyes warmed with what looked like hope.

His reaction to her insults almost made her laugh.

Instead, she sighed. "But none of that would be true," she admitted reluctantly. "The truth is that you have behaved most chivalrously so far."

She studied him for a moment, perplexed by this gentle warrior who had abducted her. The lean, muscled width of his shoulders and chest left her no doubt he was strong enough to impose his will by force if he chose. Yet he had not tried to so much as kiss her.

And his angular features, ready smile, and thick, glossy black hair made it impossible to call him ugly.

On the contrary, he was one of the handsomest men she had ever seen. It brought an unfamiliar, fluttery feeling to her stomach to think of him lifting her in his arms last night, carrying her to bed.

"I want to go *home*," she said plaintively. "Do you not understand that much? I want to go home."

"Josette." He pointed to the floor, his voice gentle. "Home now."

She understood his meaning—this was her home now. "That is *your* opinion, beef-wit."

"Keldan," he corrected, grinning as if he understood that she was calling him a different, less complimentary name. Again he held out the basket of bread toward her. "Hungry?"

Josette caught her lower lip between her teeth; thus far, she had refused to cooperate with him in any way.

However, if she starved herself, she would not have the strength to fight him off, if and when he decided to pounce on her.

"Mayhap just one piece," she said slowly, walking over to the table. She gingerly plucked a small loaf from the basket in his hand. The bread was studded with raisins, soft and warm to the touch, and tasted as heavenly as it smelled.

"Mmmmm." She closed her eyes, barely even aware of the low sound of pleasure that escaped her.

Keldan uttered a single, tense word in reply, but she was too busy looking down at the array of foods on the table to pay him heed. Biting off another mouthful of the delicious bread, she stared at bowls of bright raspberries and dewy plums. A platter piled high with thinly sliced, roasted meats. A jug of milk with the froth of cream still on top. And *oranges*.

"Saints' breath, the last time I saw food such as this . . ." Josette took a handful of sugared nuts. And a plum, just to keep her strength up. "I do not think any but *kings* enjoy food such as this for breakfast where I come from."

A moment later, her hands were so full, she doubted she could carry her booty away without dropping something.

"Josette." Keldan chuckled.

She glanced up to find him regarding her with amusement sparkling in his brown eyes. He gestured to the empty bench opposite him.

She hesitated. "I do not think I should. Eating breakfast at your table would almost certainly qualify as cooperating."

Keldan calmly picked up an orange, made short work of the peel, split it, then held half out to her.

The juice dripped through his long, dark fingers. Josette swallowed hard, wariness battling longing as she contemplated that rare, sweet fruit.

Slowly, cautiously, never taking her eyes from his, she sat down on the empty bench.

"Do not think this means I am giving in," she informed him, hesitantly taking the orange. "Avril and I will be leaving at the first opportunity. I am . . ." She paused, unable to wait a second longer, and bit into the treat, transported to heaven by its ripe taste. "I am certain she is planning our escape even now."

Escape was going to be impossible.

Avril reined the stallion to a halt on one of the hills to the west of Hauk's keep, telling herself it was only the salty wind and loose strands of her hair that made her eyes water. Tree branches and the ocean breeze had tugged her braid into disarray hours ago.

She was right back where she had started from at dawn, when she had set out to explore with high hopes—under the mistaken impression that she could circle the coast in a matter of hours.

All morning she had ridden along the shoreline, to the east and then back to the west, stunned by the vast size of the island. And as the sun had risen, her hopes had fallen.

She had not seen a single ship. Or a harbor.

Or so much as one leaky rowboat.

Hauk had told her the truth. It truly seemed as if *no one* left Asgard Island. And she could guess why: to describe the coastline as inhospitable would be generous. Everywhere, towering cliffs gave way to the sea in a sheer drop, creating a series of narrow inlets. Even in those places where she *could* see a beach, it was little more than a thin ribbon of sand.

And all around, sharp, massive rocks protruded from the waters like the fangs of some giant, mythical beast, ready to crush in its jaws any passing ship.

Or anyone who dared try to leave here.

She lifted one hand to shade her eyes against the afternoon glare, looking out to sea. If the cliffs and rocks were not daunting enough, a silvery-white fog surrounded the island, hovering above the waves within a few miles of the shore. At first, she had thought it would dissipate when the sun rose, but the accursed stuff lingered, a mist that apparently remained unchanged no matter the time of day.

If it was a permanent feature of the weather here, she now understood how these Vikings had been able to remain hidden in this place so long. A ship could sail right past the island and never know it was here. Even if some sharp-eyed sea captain did notice Asgard, she doubted any but the most expert sailors would risk navigating such treacherous rocks. Especially in a fog like that.

She wiped at her eyes and nudged the stallion forward, the midday sun beating down on her, making her shoulders droop even lower. Though the air felt almost sultry, she shivered at the thought of that fog. It seemed unnatural somehow, reminded her of the mist she had seen around Gaston's castle on the night before she left for Antwerp.

Shaking her head, she told herself not to be foolish. It was only fog. Harmless. A mere trick of the weather.

She turned the stallion inland, away from the sea and its silvery cloak. She had to find Josette. Avril had not intended to be gone all morning, had hoped to bring good news and a plan for escape back from her ride—and now she felt like both a terrible failure and a terrible friend. Her heart thudding with worry, she prayed that Josette was still safe and well.

She tapped her heels against the stallion's flanks, galloping down the grassy hillside, heading for the town. Mayhap someone there would help her find her friend. Hauk had said she could visit but had neglected to mention where Josette would be.

The thought of her captor brought an unexpected knot to her stomach. She had been trying all morn not to think about the rough-hewn, perplexing Viking warrior who had brought her to this place. His words and actions last night still mystified her. What kind of man could kidnap her, marry her against her will, keep her from her child—yet also be capable of honor and gallantry, gentleness and concern for her?

And how was it possible that his every glance, his lightest touch, could rob her of reason and kindle unbidden heat within her?

Blushing, she banished Hauk Valbrand from her thoughts. She was supposed to be thinking of escape, not of her captor. For now he was gone, and for that she was grateful.

At least his destrier had proven to be more manageable than its owner. Ildfast responded well to her firm hand on his reins, carrying her swiftly down into the vale and across a rolling meadow. The wind caught at her braid and her skirts as she rode, the air thick with the scents of foliage and flowers in bloom. All around her, the sun blazed over tall grasses that danced in the wind.

The village that lay ahead had been built on a green, fertile plain, between the ocean on one side and a small range of mountains on the other; she could just discern the outline of the craggy peaks in the distance.

She might have called this place beautiful, Avril thought grudgingly, were she a *willing* visitor.

She slowed the destrier to a trot as she drew near the town, which was much larger than it had seemed from a distance last night; from here she could see scores of rooftops, large and small, of wood or thatch or stone. One odd fact made her brow furrow in puzzlement: She did not see a gate. There were no walls around this village, no towers, no defensive barriers of any kind. Not so much as a single sentry on patrol.

Her heart thudded. These people would not leave their homes so vulnerable to attack—unless they trusted that the cliffs and the rocky coast and the fog truly made it impossible for anyone to invade their island.

Or for anyone to escape.

The destrier's hooves clattered on flat, smooth cobbles that paved a wide street as she entered the town's outskirts. The air buzzed with dozens of conversations in that incomprehensible Norse tongue. People bustled about their daily tasks—men, women, children.

Two boys of about fifteen walked by with fishing poles over their shoulders. A blacksmith's hammer rang out on an anvil. Housewives leaned on windowsills, chatting with friends. A dog yapped at a squawking gaggle of geese.

Glancing around, Avril felt astonished. After being surrounded by a brawny sea of muscular Vikings last night, she had not expected to find the town so peaceful, so . . . normal. One by one, every head turned her way, and people slowly set aside their baskets and bundles and tools and pitchforks and stared at her.

Avril's pounding heart seemed to fill her throat. For an instant, she regretted leaving behind the brooch Hauk had pinned to her last night. She refused to wear a badge of ownership that marked her as his.

But how would these people receive a strange woman in their midst? Especially when she looked a sight, as Avril knew she must, with her hair all askew and her gown stained with perspiration and dirt from her long ride. Might they be unpleasant, mayhap even hostile?

Several in the crowd started animated conversations with their fellows, gesturing at her and speaking quickly. Everyone gazed up at her with expressions of amazement and avid curiosity.

Then a few began to smile. Some called out what sounded like greetings.

And they all quickly left their work behind to gather around her, bowing or inclining their heads. Avril's hand tightened on the reins and she drew the stallion up short, startled by the gestures of respect.

Ildfast tossed his head and she abruptly remembered that she was riding *Hauk's* stallion. And from what little he had told her, he held a position of some importance among these people.

Apparently his wife—or rather, the woman they *believed* to be his wife—was due a certain amount of honor.

"Good . . . good day to you," she said uncertainly, wishing more than ever that she knew a word or two of their tongue. Her whole life, she had been enamored of languages; words in all their vivid colors fascinated her the way that spices in a kitchen fascinated other women. But now when she needed the skill most, it availed her naught. "Do any of you speak French?"

She doubted they could even hear her over the din; her arrival had created quite a commotion. Dozens more people came out of their dwellings to take a look at her. Before she knew what was happening, someone thrust a bouquet of flowers into her hands. Then a basket full of fruit.

"Wait . . . nay . . . I do not want any gifts. I need to find my friend. I—"

Ildfast snorted and reared skittishly. One of the men took hold of the reins to calm him. Someone else tucked a flower into his bridle. Before Avril or her horse could protest further, they were being led farther into town in the midst of a festive procession. Someone started to sing a song.

"Wait, wait," Avril cried, baffled at the way these people seemed so overjoyed to meet her. "I do not have time for this. You must let me find my friend Josette—"

"Avril!"

Avril turned to see Josette pushing her way through the throng. "Oh, thank God!" She slipped from Ildfast's back, thrust her armful of goods toward the nearest happy villager, and rushed into her friend's embrace.

Josette wrapped her in a fierce hug. "Avril—"

"Josette, sweet mercy, are you all right?" Avril stepped back to hold her at arm's length, breathless with relief to find her safe. "Hauk told me that you would not be harmed, but I was not certain I could believe—"

"Do not worry over me, Avril. I am fine. It was you I was concerned about. After breakfast this morn, Keldan and I stopped by your *vaningshus*—"

"Who? My what?"

"*Vaningshus*. That is their word for these odd dwellings of theirs." She indicated the homes along the street, most built in the same style as Hauk's: long structures made of stone, with roofs covered in thatch or overlapping squares of tree bark.

"And who is Keldan?"

"That is his name." She indicated the tall, dark-haired man who elbowed his way through the crowd until he stood at her side—the man who had "married" her in last night's ceremony.

"He speaks only a few words of French," Josette continued, hooking an arm through Avril's and leading her down the street. Some of the festive crowd followed along, one of them bringing Ildfast. "I cannot understand most of what he says, but he has been quite kind."

"Josette, he abducted you." Avril bestowed a frown upon her friend's grinning captor. "That is hardly kind."

"Aye, of course, you are right," Josette corrected herself, a hint of color in her cheeks. "But . . . he has been most chivalrous. And today Keldan has been showing me the town."

"Keldan has been showing you the town," Avril echoed, surprised and a little concerned at the way her friend seemed so charmed by her handsome companion.

"Aye, and when we stopped by your *vaningshus*—he has also been teaching me a few words—you were not there."

"I was out riding."

Josette nodded. "I thought you might be exploring." She glanced at the man beside her, then lowered her voice to a whisper. "Have you found a way for us to escape?"

Avril hesitated. She had worried about frightening her friend with this news—but Josette seemed anything but frightened. And she needed to understand the situation. "Josette, from what I saw of the island, I do not think Gaston and his men will be able to help us. I think . . . I think we must depend on ourselves."

"Well, you will think of something. I know you will."

Before Avril could explain about Asgard's lack of boats, Keldan interrupted.

"Come see," he said in heavily accented French, taking Josette's elbow and gesturing down a side street. "Good place. Come see."

"He wants to show us something." Avril regarded him warily.

"Aye." Josette exchanged a look with her, then shrugged. "I do not think any harm will come of it, do you? This truly is the prettiest town I have ever seen. It rather reminds me of some of the villages in Brittany."

"It does that," Avril admitted reluctantly, thinking of the rugged coast and lush, green land dotted with sleepy villages. "Except that Brittany is not this warm."

"True." Josette turned her face up to the sun, closing her eyes and sighing in a way that made Avril feel decidedly uneasy. "Nor is it this wealthy."

Avril kept a firm hold on her friend's arm as Keldan led them down the side street. She noted that this was indeed a most prosperous hamlet—the cobbled streets neatly swept, the people dressed in fine, embroidered garments with gold and silver fastenings. Some of the dwellings had their shutters open to the ocean breeze, and she could see families at work and play within, amid polished furnishings and vivid tapestries.

The merry revelers following at their heels attracted a great deal of attention, and at every turn, more inhabitants came out to greet them with what seemed like genuine warmth, their eyes curious and their gifts plentiful—especially those they presented to Avril.

She finally gave up trying to decline. What had

started with a bouquet of flowers and some fruit soon turned into a flood of foodstuffs, necklaces of sparkling beads, clothes, perfumes, lace, jewelry. When it all became too much for poor Ildfast to carry, someone fetched a cart.

As they walked on, Avril noted that hunger did not seem to be any problem here. They passed by many animals in pens: flocks of chickens and ducks, shaggy-looking brown sheep that sported huge, curling horns, and a herd of . . .

She blinked as they walked by that particular pen, staring at the creatures with placid faces and broad, felted horns. "Josette, is the sun playing tricks on my eyes, or are those—"

"Reindeer." Josette nodded. "Apparently they raise them for both meat and milk. I had some of the milk at breakfast, and it is very sweet—"

"But reindeer are usually found only in the *North*." Avril's heart thudded. "Judging by the weather, I thought this island was located in the South or East."

"Mayhap you guessed wrong."

"Oh, Josette," Avril said mournfully. "I do not have the first idea *where* we are."

"Do not despair. After walking about today, I have guessed something that might be useful to us." Josette lowered her voice again. "I think these people may be Vikings."

"Aye, indeed they are." Avril tried to keep the frustration from her voice. "I guessed as much last night, and Hauk admitted it. They have been living here for centuries in hiding—and they are determined to keep this place secret. That is why they will not let us leave."

"Oh."

They fell silent as they followed Keldan into another part of town, one that played host to many flourishing craftsmen. As they walked along the rows of shops, Avril could recognize some from the implements hanging outside or the goods displayed in windows fitted with glass: jewelers, goldsmiths, a baker, a tanner, a wood carver.

Keldan opened the door to one of the shops, and they left their flock of jolly followers behind. One of the townspeople tied Ildfast's reins to a tall post carved in the shape of some sort of mythical wood sprite.

"Like here?" Keldan asked in mangled French as he ushered them both inside and closed the door. "People nice here," he said with an enthusiastic, hopeful smile.

"Aye, they are," Avril admitted, plucking a stray flower from her hair. She sneezed on sawdust. Keldan had found them refuge in an unoccupied carpenter's shop.

The scents of oil and fresh-cut pine stacked along the walls filled the air. Pieces of furniture in various stages of completion sat on counters and tabletops, and woodworking tools hung from the ceiling, glinting in the afternoon sun that poured through windows fitted with glass.

"Indeed, your people seem very nice," Josette said politely. "But you must let us go home. We cannot stay here. Do you understand? We must return to France."

"France, France, France." He sighed as if tired of hearing that word, nodded to indicate he understood what she meant when she said it. "Why?"

Josette frowned. "What an odd question. Because it is our home, of course—"

"Because you cannot simply go about kidnapping people and expect them to be happy about it," Avril grumbled.

"And because Avril has a daughter at home," Josette continued, "and as I told your friend last night, the poor child will be an orphan if—"

"What?" Avril sputtered. "*What* did you say to Hauk?"

"I . . ." Josette coughed nervously and glanced away. "I was going to mention this to you. But I was not sure whether you—"

"What did you tell him?"

"Oh, Avril, you must forgive me. I was only trying to help! I told him the truth about Gerard. I thought if he knew that Giselle's father was dead, it might soften his heart and persuade him to set you free—"

"Josette, how *could* you?" Avril cried. "Now he knows that I was lying to him. I already *tried* to soften his heart and I failed."

"I am sorry." Josette dusted off a chair and sank down on it.

"Saints' breath, Josette, we have to *help* each other, not . . ." Avril lifted both hands and let them drop back to her sides, feeling even more frustrated and helpless than before. Turning away, she stared out the window. "I do not suppose it matters now. I had hoped he might trust me enough to set me free, but he will never trust me." She shut her eyes. "And these men have no intention of setting us free."

An uncomfortable silence descended. Keldan disappeared into the back of the shop and came back a moment later. Avril turned just in time to watch him place a delicate, beautifully carved chair in front of Josette, with obvious pride. Josette gasped.

"What?" Avril muttered in confusion. "What is it?"

"Did you *make* this?" Josette asked him. "You are a carpenter?"

He pointed from himself, to the shop, and then to the chair, nodding.

"Oh, my oath." Josette glanced at Avril. "This matches a chair he gave me last night. I . . . I smashed it against the wall."

"*You* smashed a chair against a wall?"

"I was terribly angry. And I had no idea he had made it for me. Oh, now I feel terrible."

"You have no reason to feel terrible," Avril pointed out. "This man abducted you. He brought you here against your will. He is your captor. He is . . ."

Her friend was not listening; she was looking up at Keldan, smiling shyly. "Thank you."

"Josette," Avril said in exasperation. "Do you hear what you are saying? You cannot accept that. We do not *want* food or gifts from these people. We want our *freedom*. We want to escape."

Josette glanced from her to Keldan and back again. "I am sorry. You are right. It is just . . . it is rather hard for me to remember to be angry with people who are so kind." She dropped her gaze to the sawdust-covered floor. "And this place is so lovely. The weather is perfect, the food abundant. And it seems so peaceful. Have you noticed?"

"Aye." Avril turned to look out the window again, studying the people gathered in the street. "Everyone seems happy and healthy—" Another quality they all seemed to have in common caught her attention. "And young. Josette, I do not see anyone beyond . . . two score years, at the most. Even the elders we saw last night did not look especially old." She turned to study Keldan.

He stood watching them with that hopeful, warm expression, his attention on Josette.

Avril guessed him to be about thirty. The same age as Hauk.

"Something is not right here," she said uneasily, glancing out at the street again. She could see people of her own age, and younger, and a few women who seemed to be in their middle years, with wrinkles etched by time and gray in their hair. But most of Asgard's inhabitants were surprisingly youthful. "What do they *do* with all their older people? And if everyone is so healthy and happy on this island, why abduct us? Why have they brought us here?"

Josette shrugged. "Mayhap they simply want to share this lovely place with others."

Avril gave her a pained look. "Josette, that is a most charitable thought. But if that were true, kidnapping would not be necessary. An invitation would suffice. And no matter how 'nice' this place is, *I* will never meekly accept being held captive." Facing the window, she folded her arms. "I have a daughter I must return to, and I will not let anyone or anything keep me from her."

"I am sorry, Avril. Of course you are right." Josette rose to stand beside her. "But how are we to escape? We are in the middle of the ocean somewhere. We do not even know in which direction home lies—"

"We are not going to let that stop us. We grew up in Brittany, after all. On the seashore. And I still know a brace from a bowline and a cog from a clinker. I might even . . ." Avril hesitated, looking over at Keldan, but he clearly could not follow what they were saying. "I might even be able to build a seaworthy craft, somewhere in secret." She glanced at the ceiling. "With the right tools."

"Mayhap some of the other captives will want to help," Josette said uncertainly.

"Aye. That is a good idea. If we work together, we can succeed." She touched Josette's arm. "I will need your help, Josette. I cannot do it alone."

Josette looked from her to Keldan and back again before she said, softly, "Of course I will help."

"Thank you." Avril hugged her. "I believe I have the ideal task for you. We will need information about where this island is located. How far it is back to the continent, and in which direction we must sail to get home. Since you and he"—she gave Keldan a smile—"are on somewhat cordial terms, you may have the best chance of finding out what we need to know."

"I will try."

"Good. I know you can do it, Josette." Avril felt her spirits lift for the first time all day. "Now, I think I will go try to find some of the other captives. You stay here with your carpenter and seek information. Try to be subtle."

"That should be easy, since we each hardly understand a word the other is saying."

"Just be careful, Josette." Avril waved farewell to Keldan and headed for the door, leaving her friend to consort with the enemy.

Hoping Josette would not forget that he was, in fact, the enemy.

8

Rain pattered against the shutters of Hauk's keep, a steady downpour that had started before daybreak and only strengthened as the hours slipped past. Sighing in frustration, Avril stood at an open window, gazing up at the gray clouds that blotted out the afternoon sun. Thunder rumbled overhead. Another slash of lightning stabbed at the roiling sea. The storm showed no sign of abating.

She drummed her fingers against the wooden sill of the window. Her successful, stealthy meetings with the other captives yesterday made her impatient to put her plan of escape into action—but tromping about in the rain would only earn her a good soaking and make her ill.

If she intended to lead a half-dozen women on a dangerous sea voyage, she would need all her health and strength.

Only the Moorish girl had been too timid even to consider trying to escape. And Avril had not yet been able to speak to the English girl alone, for she had been under the escort and watchful eye of the chief elder, the one who looked like he was Hauk's relative.

And then there was the worrisome matter of the Italian girl.

Closing her eyes, Avril offered another prayer that the sharp-tongued *signorina* was all right. The Italian would no doubt prove to be the most daring and strong-hearted sister-in-arms . . . but she had not been seen since her captor forcibly dragged her away from the *althing* ceremony kicking and screaming.

The two of them had disappeared somewhere.

Avril shivered as cold raindrops spattered against her face, not wanting to imagine what the woman might be enduring even now.

Her stomach in knots, she turned away from the window, closing the shutters against the gathering wind. She would have to wait until the morrow to venture out and look for a suitable, secret place to begin building their boat. Mayhap by then the *signorina* would be found safe and well.

Holding fast to that hope, she tiptoed around the piles of goods bestowed upon her by the people in town, and reclaimed her place on the floor, amid a stack of dusty books. She lit another candle to ward off the gloom and huddled over the text she had been studying since midday.

To her surprise, she had discovered scores of ancient volumes while searching through the trunks and chests that cluttered Hauk's chamber. While the Norse runes were little more than tangled squiggles to her eyes, some of the cracked, yellowed pages contained drawings—a night sky, trees, the island's rocky shoreline. If she could make sense of the writing, find a description of this place or a map of some kind, it might help in the escape.

She kept turning pages, listening to the rain pounding on the tree-bark roof, trying not to feel guilty for having rifled through Hauk's belongings.

Belongings that were clearly personal. And most unexpected.

The things on display in his keep—or *vaningshus*, or whatever they called these odd, long houses— suited a Viking warrior, from the weapons and hunting trophies on the walls, to the dark paneling with its runic carving, to the massive bed topped by those ferocious, dragon-headed posts.

But in the trunks, she had found possessions that bespoke a much softer side to the man: a delicate length of Damascus silk, carefully folded around an ivory hair comb. A pair of ice skates made of bone. Board games. A wooden statue of what might have been a Christian saint, its paint chipped away by time. A small velvet bag filled with seashells.

And most unexpected of all, the large number of books. Aristotle's philosophies in Greek, painstakingly copied and illuminated by some long-dead monk. Texts on hunting and astronomy in Latin. An entertaining rendition of the Arthurian legends in French.

If given only the contents of the trunks to judge by, she might have guessed Hauk to be a man of gentle, even scholarly inclinations.

For some reason, that brought a lump to her throat. She swallowed hard and tried to ignore the troubling feeling. Turning another page, she kept her mind on returning to Giselle as quickly as possible.

A soft, solid object bumped against her back, interrupting her concentration—and almost knocking her over.

"Not again," she complained lightly, glancing over her shoulder. "Do you wish to find yourself outside in the rain?"

The reindeer calf bleated at her, its voice somewhere between the honking of a goose and the bawl of a sheep.

"Oh, by all the saints." She gave in reluctantly and scratched behind the animal's oversized ears, undone by the forlorn look in its large, liquid brown eyes. "You should not be in here at all, you know."

The gangly newborn made happy, snuffling sounds. All legs and downy gray fur, it was too small to be away from its mother—which was how it had come to be in her care.

Since her appearance in the village yesterday, a steady stream of townspeople had arrived at the door, offering her greetings and gifts. Every table and trunk in Hauk's *vaningshus* now groaned under piles of foodstuffs and furs, blankets and baskets, clothing and cookpots, goods of every description.

This morn, in the rain, a girl of about ten had shown up with the baby reindeer in her arms, a drooping red bow around the animal's neck. Her elder brother had accompanied her, a lad of about sixteen who spoke just enough French to make the gift understood: Apparently, the calf had been born a sickly runt, its mother had rejected it, and the girl's father planned to put the animal out of its misery.

But if Avril would accept the little reindeer as a gift, the girl promised to visit often enough to take care of him. She had already named him: Floyel. Which meant "velvet," the boy said.

Looking down into the girl's hopeful face and teary eyes, Avril had not been able to refuse. And when the child had hugged her with gratitude and joy, she had felt her heart torn open.

Sweet Mary, how she longed to feel Giselle's arms around her so tight.

Blinking hard, she reached out now and stroked Floyel's velvety nose. "Do not grow accustomed to being in my care," she advised him, her voice wavering. "I will not be here for long. My little girl needs me, and no ocean, no Viking warrior, and no helpless reindeer will keep me from her."

The animal nibbled at the wide sleeve of Avril's garnet-colored gown—another pretty gift—before clopping off to the corner. Avril had used straw from Ildfast's stall and a few of her new blankets to make a bed for him near the hearth.

"Hauk would certainly not like having you in his keep," she said as she returned to her reading. "Which is why I am allowing you to stay," she added, a mischievous curve tugging at her mouth. "Imagine the havoc you will wreak when you grow large enough to have horns. I wonder how long that might take."

For another hour, she sat poring over the Norse books, until she was forced to admit that they would be of no help, though the drawings were lovely. Apparently, some Vikings were of more poetic than warlike spirit. Whoever had written these volumes long ago possessed an artist's eye and a deft touch with pen and ink. In addition to the drawings of the island, there were sketches of European cities, castles and cathedrals, the ruins of Roman aqueducts, sailing ships, a snowy mountainside.

And one sketch that was particularly striking: a beautiful young woman caught in a moment of laughter, her long black hair blowing in the wind.

Avril closed the book with care, for some of the pages were so old and fragile, they crumbled at her touch.

She stood and returned the texts to the trunks where she had found them, hoping Josette and the others were having better luck in discovering the island's location. They had all agreed to share word of their progress tomorrow night; the townspeople were planning some sort of grand celebration to welcome the new brides formally to Asgard.

A knock sounded at the door. Startled, Avril turned. Who would venture out in this drenching downpour to pay a visit, other than a child with a homeless reindeer?

Whoever it was knocked again. Sharply. Impatiently.

"Saints' breath." Avril crossed toward the entrance. "Have I not been greeted by the entire town yet?" She glanced at Floyel sleeping in the corner. Mayhap little Marta could not wait to see him again.

She lifted the latch, opened the door, and stepped

back, letting in gray afternoon light and a chilly breeze wet with rain.

And a tall, cloaked figure who was definitely not Marta.

Her visitor hurried in out of the storm, reaching up with slender hands to lower the cloak's hood—revealing an elegant, feminine face framed by a wealth of auburn tresses. The lady's movements were so graceful, her bearing so regal, that Avril almost felt as if she should drop in a curtsy.

Was this the wife of one of the elders, or one of the prosperous merchants, come to offer even more presents?

"No more gifts," Avril pleaded, pointing to the overflowing tables. "Too many now. No need."

"My, what a charming way of speaking you have," the woman replied in fluent French, shaking out her damp hair and running her fingers through it. Her voice was as cool as the gray eyes that skimmed Avril from head to slippers in a quick, assessing glance. "And you are even lovelier than everyone said. But I am afraid I brought no gift." She smiled.

It was not one of the warm, welcoming smiles that Avril had become accustomed to.

The woman made a disapproving *tch, tch* sound with her tongue. "Well, do not simply stand there staring at me like a sheep." She swept off her cloak and tossed the sodden garment toward Avril, scattering water all over her. "Show a bit of hospitality."

Avril could not catch the cloak, recover from her confusion, and summon a reply all at the same time.

"Imagine my surprise upon hearing that Hauk Valbrand had returned from the voyage with a new bride." The woman brushed past her, looking around the chamber. "I simply had to come and see for my— by all the gods, is that a *reindeer?*" she asked with distaste.

Floyel bleated at her, then buried his head in his blankets.

"Indeed it is," Avril said at last, dropping the cloak over a chair, brushing raindrops from her face and gown. "If you are looking for Hauk, he is not here. And I have had—"

"Oh, I know he is not here, my dear," her visitor replied with cool amusement, glancing at the gifts piled everywhere, pausing to run her hand over a white fur. Ruby and sapphire rings glittered on her long, tapered fingers. "I heard that he left on sentry duty. You poor, poor child, to be deserted already. So soon after the wedding. The man is *so* accursedly devoted to duty."

"Is he indeed?" Avril frowned, watching as the woman moved from one heap of presents to the next, unable to guess her purpose. Had she come all this way in the rain in hopes of procuring a few unwanted wedding gifts? "If you will pardon me, I have had rather a large number of visitors since—"

"You must not let it hurt you, you know. The way Hauk abandons you in favor of his work. You must not take it personally." The lady glanced at Avril over her shoulder, her white teeth gleaming in the candlelight, her voice low. "I never do."

Avril inhaled sharply, feeling foolish for not having guessed sooner that this stunning, coolly regal woman was his . . . his . . . "How interesting," she said woodenly, her cheeks burning. "But it matters not to me what he—"

"Nay, my dear, do not protest to *me* that you do not care that he has abandoned you. And so *soon* after the wedding night," the woman repeated, her smile widening as if that fact pleased her immeasurably. "Once a woman has had a taste of Hauk Valbrand, she is never quite the same. Of all the men of Asgard, he is the most . . ." She paused, stroking a tasseled pillow someone had brought, sighing dreamily. "Gifted."

Avril felt a strange, cold sensation lance through her, as if she had been stabbed with an icicle. "How kind of you to come and keep me company," she choked out. "But I am truly not interested in hearing any more of this. Now if you would—"

"Nina." Pushing gifts off a large, carved oak chair, the lady helped herself to a seat, curling up comfortably and tossing her russet tresses. "You may call me Nina. And I have not come here to keep you company, or to pay court as everyone else has. I came here to reclaim something that belongs to me."

She pierced Avril with a chilly glare, and for a moment, the noise of rain drumming on the roof made the only sound.

"My white silk kirtle," Nina continued lightly, her lips curving upward at one corner. "I left it here some time ago, but I suppose I must retrieve it now. Mayhap you have seen it? It is cut low here"—she trailed a fingertip between her breasts—"and high here." She traced a line up her thigh.

Avril gritted her teeth, not certain for a moment which of them vexed her more: Hauk, who had dressed her in a garment that belonged to his paramour, or the wench who sat here waiting for her to erupt in outrage or crumple in tears.

"If I happen across it," she said smoothly, "I will have it returned to you."

"You are so kind," Nina drawled. "I cannot understand why Hauk left you so soon. I would think someone as young and charming as you would hold his interest." She arched one slim, red-gold brow. "How old *are* you, my dear? Eighteen? Nineteen?"

Avril folded her arms. "Two and twenty."

"Two and twenty!" Nina laughed—a deep, throaty laugh that had poor Floyel burrowing for cover—as if this were the most amusing jest she had heard in a long time. "Oh, the way you say it! As if you are far too sophisticated and mature to be mistaken for eighteen." Her shoulders shook. "My dear, you are barely out of swaddling clothes."

"But you cannot be more than . . . five or six years older than I," Avril replied, not understanding the woman's amusement.

Nina kept chuckling. "You flatter me, silly child. But then, I do adore flattery. And I *have* aged well, haven't I?"

Avril sighed, gesturing toward the door. "You have also worn out your welcome. It has been a *pleasure* making your acquaintance, milady, but now you must allow me to bid you—"

"Oh, by Frigga's mother." Nina waved a hand dismissively and made no move to rise. "Your kind are always so sensitive, so delicate, so fragile." Her voice was laced with disdain, and her eyes as she regarded Avril suddenly burned with resentment. "But the men seem to find that attractive for some reason. When Hauk and I last parted, I assumed he would return to *me* anon. I never suspected he was secretly longing for one of your kind."

"My kind?" Avril demanded. "What do you mean, my kind? Captives? Women who have been forced here against their will?"

"*Utlending*," Nina spat. "You are *utlending*. A foreigner. I am *innfodt*," she informed her loftily, rising gracefully from the chair, crossing to a mirror that hung over the washbasin. "A native-born woman of Asgard." She studied her reflection, running her fingertips over her flawless ivory skin.

"I see. Well, mayhap I should correct a mistaken impression you seem to have—it was not *my* idea to come here. I would like naught better than to leave this island and let you claim Hauk and his clifftop dwelling and whatever *gifts* you say he has."

Nina turned to stare at her, eyes wide with surprise. "He has not bedded you yet, has he?"

Startled by such a question, Avril opened her mouth but no sound came out.

"Nay, clearly he has not." Nina brightened, looking even more pleased than before. "If he had, you would not be so eager to leave."

"Hauk Valbrand is a . . . a brigand. A rogue. He is keeping me here against my will. I would never let him take me to his bed!"

Nina laughed, softly this time, glancing down at

the toes of her embroidered slippers. "Oh, I do not think that is true. But if you are indeed unhappy here, if you truly wish to leave Asgard—"

"I *must* leave Asgard. I have a three-year-old daughter awaiting my return home."

Nina's head came up. "A daughter?" She paused, something shifting in that icy, gray gaze. "You are a mother?"

Avril could not reply, astonished by the change in Nina's tone and expression. For once, the woman was not mocking her.

"Aye, and I am"—she swallowed hard—"I am all my little Giselle has left. I was widowed three years ago."

"Then of course you must return home." Nina's long lashes swept downward, concealing her eyes, and she turned away. A moment later, she glanced over her shoulder. "And I am willing to offer my help," she said, her voice cool and regal once more.

Avril regarded her warily, still trying to puzzle out what emotion she had seen in Nina's eyes for that brief instant. Whatever it had been, it was gone, replaced by that remote, faintly superior air.

Which made Avril reluctant to trust Nina's offer of help. The woman clearly viewed her—however mistakenly—as a rival for Hauk's affections. Avril could too well imagine what kind of help Nina might offer.

She might happily help her fall off a cliff.

"Would you not be breaking the laws?"

"It *would* involve a certain amount of risk," Nina admitted. "But we cannot think of that, with our happiness at stake—both yours and mine."

"Hauk told me no one ever leaves Asgard."

"Did he?" Nina shook her head, smiling ruefully. "That is not entirely true. Hauk himself leaves, now and then. It is part of his duty as *vokter*."

Avril turned away, biting back an oath. *He had lied to her. That son of a cur—*

"He keeps a *knorr*—a small sailing ship—in a sheltered cove on the western side of the island. It is only a few hours' journey through the western part of the forest."

"I see." Avril felt angry enough to spit. No wonder he had told her to avoid that part of the woods.

Unless . . .

She turned again, studying Nina, cautious. "I thought the western part of the forest was dangerous. Someone mentioned there were wolves there."

"Aye, there are. But there is a safe way to reach the cove. How do you think Hauk goes there and returns safely?" Nina rested her hands on her slender waist. "I would be happy to show you where to find it, little *utlending*. I will escort you myself."

She looked sincere.

Or was *trying* to look sincere.

Avril held her tongue and listened to the rain, uncertain what to do or whom to believe.

Which one had lied to her? Was there in truth a boat in a sheltered cove—or was Nina making up the tale, thinking to lure her into danger? Finding a boat *would* be faster, and safer, than building one of her own.

Avril glanced away, and the glitter of steel above the hearth caught her eye.

Which gave her an idea. "Thank you for the offer," she said lightly, picking up Nina's wet cloak from the chair, "but I am afraid I must decline." She went to the entrance and opened the door, holding it for her guest.

Nina sighed. "As you wish." She walked over and plucked the cloak from Avril's hands. "But if you change your mind, you will find me in town. And it might be best if you did not tell Hauk we have met— else he will suspect that you now know about his ship." She donned the cloak, lifting the hood as she stepped past Avril, into the rain.

Then she paused and turned, her expression concealed within the depths of the hood as the storm spattered them both with wind-driven water. "I truly *am* willing to help you, little *utlending*, in any way I can."

Before Avril could respond, Nina turned and walked away into the storm.

Watching her go, Avril wondered again if she should accept the woman's offer. But with so much at stake, she dared not take the risk. And she did not need to: She had more trustworthy allies in her fellow captives.

And a wall full of weapons at her disposal.

In the morn, she and her sisters-in-arms could go and search for the boat on their own.

9

He tenderly kissed her tears away, whispering words she had not heard in such a long time. Words of love. His strong hands touched her intimately, each caress slower than the last as he gently aroused her.

Moaning softly, she lifted her hips, wanting to take him inside her. *Please, mon coeur, it has been so long, I need . . . I need . . .*

He nudged her thighs apart, positioning himself there at the silky core of her body. Then he raised his head, and in the firelight she could see the passion in his eyes—those pale-blue eyes, like the sky lit by the sun's hottest rays, his hair like strands of gold between her fingers—

Avril jerked awake with a sharp cry, eyes wide, heart thundering.

The night sky tilted dizzily in her vision. She thrust out a hand to steady herself. Felt the sand beneath her, a warm sea wind blowing through her hair. Waves swept rhythmically onto the shore a few paces away. The torch she had staked into the sand flickered beside her. She had been dreaming. Only dreaming. She had come down to sleep on the beach after the storm abated. Hauk was not here. He was . . .

God's mercy, he was the man in her dream.

"Nay!" She stumbled to her feet. The ocean breeze billowed her emerald cloak out behind her and cut through her linen shift, cooling the perspiration from her body, her breasts. Her limbs still tingled with arousal.

Hauk Valbrand could *not* be the man in the sensual dream that had tormented her for months. How could he be? She had not even met him until a few days—

The roar of the surf seemed deafening as she remembered their first meeting in Antwerp. That jarring moment of time when he had seemed familiar. His face. His eyes. His voice. So hauntingly familiar.

Only now did she understand why.

Because he was the man she had been making love to in her dreams.

Stunned, breathless, she touched her mouth, aware of the lingering heat of a kiss there. Nay, it was impossible! She was confused. Tired. Overwrought by Nina's visit and her talk of Hauk's "gifts."

That was the reason Avril had fled his *vaningshus*. But it was not enough that she had avoided sleeping in his bed. Not enough to banish him from her thoughts.

From her dreams.

With a wordless sound of confusion and denial, she grabbed the torch and hurried blindly down the shore, gulping mouthfuls of air that still held the lingering scent of rain. The damp sand gave way softly beneath her bare feet. The storm had ended hours ago, yet the moon barely glimmered through the clouds hanging overhead.

Waves rushed up to bubble around her ankles and

dampen the hem of her shift and the embroidered cloak, one of the wedding gifts she had received from the kind people of Asgard. Her steps gradually slowed but she kept walking, too restless, too agitated to stop.

Oddly, the water felt cold. Icy cold—in stark contrast to the island's summery weather and lush greenery and air that, even down here, was warm and scented with the fragrance of exotic blooms.

Avril tucked the water's temperature away in her mind with all the other troublesome, conflicting bits and pieces of information she had been gathering about Asgard Island.

And the man who had brought her here.

Even now she could not chase him from her thoughts. Could not keep herself from wondering where he was. If he had found shelter in the storm. Had he been gone two days now? Or was it longer?

She halted, chastising herself. It was ridiculous to feel worried about her captor. And if she found it difficult to count the days since she had seen him last, mayhap it was because the pace of life seemed so slow on Asgard.

Almost as if time itself moved more slowly here.

Frowning, she continued down the shore, wondering if God had purposely designed this place to confuse and confound any poor mortal who set foot here.

She would try to make sense of it all tomorrow. Tomorrow, when she had the chance to meet with her fellow captives and discuss whatever answers they had found. Tonight, she was too exhausted to think anymore.

A short distance down the beach, looming out of

the darkness, she noticed a massive tangle of broken trees, lodged among rocks at the base of the cliff. Driftwood, washed ashore by some long-ago storm. The jagged trunks created a sheltered place away from the wind and waves.

She walked over and staked her torch into the sand, then took off her cloak, spreading the garment out. Sinking down onto the silk-lined fabric, she lay on her back within the driftwood's shadow and gazed up at the gray clouds high overhead.

The clouds concealed the stars as well as the moon, but one silvery pinprick managed to pierce the murk, just for an instant, winking at her. Avril's heart pulled tight.

Whenever Giselle saw a star wink like that, she said it was her father, smiling down on her from Heaven—watching over her and winking at her. Though Giselle had never known him, she stated with a three-year-old's certainty that she felt him close to her sometimes, especially when she was afraid. That she could reach up to the stars and he would hold her hand.

Avril closed her eyes against the hot dampness that filled them. "Stay close to her, Gerard," she whispered. "Watch over her, until I can return." She lifted her lashes, searching the sky for another star. "Hold her hand."

Just as she said that, another star winked through the clouds. And though it was ridiculous, utterly nonsensical and ridiculous, a sense of peace stole over her.

A feeling that, here in this sanctuary of driftwood

and sand, she was a little closer to the daughter she loved.

She rolled onto her side, drawing the cloak with her, resting her cheek on her bent arm. Blinking drowsily, she tried to stay awake, for she was reluctant to let herself drift off, to let herself dream . . .

It was a shout that awoke her—a high-pitched, feminine cry. Startled, Avril pushed herself up on one hand, not certain how long she had been asleep. The torch had almost burned out, offering naught but a dull glow that did little to help her see into the darkness.

The shout came again, a squeal that rose and just as quickly tumbled an octave or two, dissolving into a laugh. Sitting up, Avril saw the source a moment later: two dark silhouettes near the water. A man and woman, playfully splashing each other as they wandered down the beach.

The woman gave her companion a thorough dousing, laughing and running from him. He gave chase and caught her by the edge of her cloak, and the two wrapped around each other in a heated embrace, filling the night air with sighs and hungry moans.

Cheeks flaming, Avril grabbed her torch and scooted back into the shadows beneath the driftwood trees, embarrassed at being privy to such intimacy. But she need not have bothered, for the pair had eyes only for each other. Untangling themselves at last, they strolled past her hiding place, hand in hand, oblivious to her presence.

Avril's jaw dropped when she recognized them.

It was the Italian girl!

And her companion was the very man who had hoisted the poor *signorina* over his shoulder and carried her kicking and screaming from the *althing* two nights ago.

But the poor *signorina* had clearly not spent the past days suffering the sort of torments Avril had imagined. Peeking over the tree trunk, Avril caught them in another kiss, heard the woman whisper an endearment in Italian when they finally came up for breath.

As they walked on, the *signorina* rested her head on his shoulder, and he draped an arm gently around her waist.

Avril clutched the tree trunk, fighting the urge to chase the pair down the beach and slap some sense into the woman.

"He is your *captor*," she whispered, half tempted to shout it. "Have you taken leave of your reason?"

When they were a few yards farther away, she stood up, gripping her torch and watching in amazement as the couple continued down the beach, looking for all the world like a happy, newly wed husband and wife. Avril shook her head.

How could this have happened? How could the man have so changed the Italian's feelings toward him? What sorcery had he used? What potion? What . . .

Nina's voice suddenly flitted through her head, sighing dreamily that the men of Asgard were exceptionally gifted at lovemaking.

And Hauk the most gifted of all.

"Not possible," Avril said aloud. No man could be *that* skilled. "Not possible."

"What is not possible?"

Gasping, Avril whirled at the soft question—to find another brawny male silhouette looming out of the darkness behind her.

For a moment, she had the dizzying sensation that she must still be asleep.

That she was dreaming.

It was Hauk.

Her heart filled her throat as he appeared out of the night shadows, as silently as if he were made of fog and sea air. He carried no torch; not until he drew near could she see him by the sputtering glow of the one in her hand.

He looked tired and worn from his journey, a stubbly beard of burnished gold darkening his jaw, not thick enough to obscure the hard angles of his face. He still wore his pack and a traveling cloak tossed back over his broad, tanned shoulders, fluttering in the wind, held in place by a thick chain across his muscled neck.

His gaze met and held hers with an intensity that stole her breath. She lowered her lashes, trying not to notice the way her heart skipped a beat. "You . . . you are back."

"Are you all right?"

She looked up, curious at the unexpected question and the edge of tension in his voice. "Aye, I am well enough—"

"What are you doing down here?"

"You said I was free to go wherever I wished," she said defensively.

"I also warned you to stay away from the cliffs. Yet I return home past midnight to find my *vaningshus* unoccupied and the bed not slept in. Until I saw your torch, I thought you—" He cut himself off, glanced away. "Never mind. It matters not." He dropped his heavy pack, running one hand over his grizzled face. "Why is there a reindeer calf in my home?"

"He was a gift."

"That gift relieved himself all over several other gifts."

Avril suppressed a grin at that news. "Do not blame me. The fault is entirely yours."

"I do not remember asking anyone to give me a reindeer." He released a low sound that might have been a sigh. "Any more than I remember asking the gods to give me a wife."

"I am not your wife," she said lightly. "And if you had left well enough alone in Antwerp, you would not now be in possession of me *or* a reindeer."

He looked at her with a dour expression, started to say something in reply, then apparently changed his mind. For a moment, the noise of the surf rushing ashore and the faint crackling of the torch in her hand made the only sound.

And at that very instant, Avril abruptly remembered what she was wearing.

Or rather, what she was not.

She was standing there garbed only in a thin linen shift, holding a torch that no doubt cast enough light for him to see through the fabric.

As if he had read her thoughts, those pale-blue eyes left hers to trace downward, slowly. Avril felt her cheeks flush with warmth. Her pulse quickened, her body tingling in response to the hungry, possessive way he looked at her. Her breasts drew taut.

By the time his gaze reached her bare feet, she could hear his breathing, deep and unsteady—matching hers. That familiar, dazzling heat that always seemed to shimmer between them unfurled within her, flowing to the very core of her being.

Shocked at her body's response, she could not move. Could not understand this unsettling bond they seemed to share. Could not fathom how, without even touching her, this quiet, enigmatic Norseman could rouse her in such a way.

She forced her limbs to move, reaching down with all the grace she could muster—when she wanted to make a mad dive—to pick up the cloak she had left on the ground. But she could not don the cloak and hold the torch at the same time.

"Allow me, milady." His voice sounded deep, husky.

She felt the torch plucked from her grasp before she could decline his assistance. His other hand felt warm and strong on her shoulders as he helped settle the heavy cloak around her. A little frisson of awareness and anxiety tingled down her back.

But his touch was surprisingly gentle, and as soon as she covered herself, he gave her back the torch and moved away a few paces.

She wrapped the garment snugly around her, surprised once again at his gallantry. "Thank you."

"Are you certain you are well, Avril?" He glanced over his shoulder at her. "You seem pale." His eyes searched her face once more. "And tired."

The concern in his gaze, in his voice, brought an uncomfortable, ticklish sensation to her stomach. "Not all women thrive in captivity," she said quietly. "You need not trouble yourself over my well-being."

"I am bound by my word of honor to trouble myself over your well-being."

She looked away. "If I am tired, it is because the hour is late and I have had bad—" She caught herself. "Trouble sleeping," she finished awkwardly.

He did not reply.

Avril felt her cheeks turning red. "The storm kept me awake," she added quickly. "After being inside all day, I found your keep rather stuffy, and while riding yesterday, I had noticed a path down to the shore. So after the rain abated, I decided to spend the night on the beach. I often did so when I was a child, in the summer, on the shore at home in Brittany."

She was babbling. God's breath, why was she babbling?

And why did the man not *say* something? No doubt he expected her to return to his *vaningshus* with him now.

All at once, a rush of heated images flashed through her mind like lightning: she and Hauk in his bed, his mouth on hers, his hard body pressing her down into the sheets, his hands in her hair, her fingers caressing his back, their voices blending in sighs and whispers.

Shocked, Avril wrestled her thoughts under control, her heart thumping. She sat down, deciding she would spend the rest of the night right here, where she had planned. She staked her torch into the sand again. He could have his *vaningshus* all to himself.

A moment later, his cloak hit the ground beside her.

Startled, she glanced up. "What are you doing?"

"If you wish to spend the night out here, we will spend the night out here—together."

Together. Avril forced herself to remain still as he went to retrieve his pack. He was only being chivalrous again, conceding to her wishes.

Was he not?

The possibility that he might have a moonlight tryst in mind almost made her jump up and run. But she did not want him to know he had an overwhelming sensual impact on her. Her feminine instincts warned her that would be a most serious mistake.

At least sharing a night in the open, she reasoned, was better than sharing the privacy of his keep.

"By all means," she said lightly as he returned to her side. "Help yourself to a patch of sand." She shrugged as if his actions did not matter to her in the least, then looked at the sea, as if she found the waves far more interesting than him.

He sat on his cloak, opening the pack and fishing through it until he produced a wooden trencher, which he tossed onto the sand.

Then he began untying the thongs that molded his boots to his legs.

"Now what are you doing?" she tried to keep her voice light, casual. Steady.

"I have not had supper yet. I keep a few nets and traps out there among the rocks." He nodded toward the water, then slanted her a curious glance. "I often come here to enjoy the night air and some fresh shellfish. Must I change my habits now that I have a wife?"

She shrugged again, trying to hide her chagrin that the driftwood sanctuary she found appealing also happened to be a favorite place of his.

"You do not have a wife," she reminded him. "And pray do not change any of your habits on my account. If you wish to douse yourself in that freezing water, by all means do so." She smiled prettily at him. "Mayhap you will develop a cramp and drown."

"There is always hope." He returned her smile with a slow, wry grin, a flash of white teeth that revealed dimples in his bearded cheeks. "But unfortunately for you, I am a strong swimmer."

Avril could not summon a clever reply. Or tear her gaze from his. She had never seen him smile before, at least not with genuine amusement. The expression brought a warmth, an appealing gentleness to his rugged face that had a strange effect on her heartbeat.

"Milady?" Taking off his boots, he reached for his belt. "Am I offending your sense of modesty?"

"Nay, why would you think so?"

"You are staring."

She glanced away, managed to laugh. "Fear not. I am hardly some blushing maiden who will faint at the sight of a man disrobing."

"Indeed?" He stood.

She hoped it was too dark for him to tell that she was blushing as furiously as any maiden.

His weapons hit the sand—his sheathed knife and sword. His belt followed. Avril kept her gaze fastened on a distant rock in the darkness, wondering whether he meant to remove *all* his garments. Tensing, she poised to flee if he reached for the waist of his leggings.

"Would you care to help me, milady?"

"What?" Her voice came out as a squeak.

She heard him searching through his pack, and a moment later, something heavy hit the sand beside her.

A flat cooking pan.

"Start a fire and have that hot when I return," he suggested.

Avril picked up the pan as he headed for the water, half tempted to fling it at him for teasing her. He had indeed left the leggings on, she realized. *Thank the saints.*

As she watched his tall, broad-shouldered silhouette moving through the moonlit darkness, she thought she might not need to start a fire.

The pan was already hot from being held in her palm.

10

Not even a cold midnight swim had been enough to cool his blood.

Hauk watched the firelight caress his wife's skin and deepen the tempting shadow of the cleft between her breasts. Sitting next to Avril, before a crackling fire, he had barely touched the shellfish on his trencher. Though his hair and beard still dripped with icy seawater, he felt painfully aware of the heat simmering in his gut, his arousal straining against the leggings he wore.

He had dreamed of her like this.

While on patrol, he had barely slept, tormented by a fevered vision of Avril looking just as she did now—her eyes languid and drowsy, her hair mussed from sleep, her body veiled by a thin shift, rumpled in just the right way to reveal an enticing glimpse of pale, feminine secrets.

A shift so delicate, he could slip it from her shoulders with a single brush of his fingertips.

His breathing deepened. His blood seemed to flow hot and thick in his veins. In his dream, she had not been sitting on a moonlit beach, daintily nibbling seafood, her kirtle half concealed beneath a green cloak.

Nei, she had been in his bed, her lips parted for his kiss, her hands drawing him near, her whispers filled with wanting and welcome. And he had pressed her back into the sheets, poised to join his body to hers, to thrust deeply inside and feel her tight and hot and wet—

The snap of a burning driftwood log wrenched him back to the present. His heart thundering, he tore his gaze from Avril, unnerved by the power of the images that fogged his senses. By Odin, when he left two days ago, he had thought he would regain his reason, be able to deal with her presence in his life calmly and rationally upon his return.

Instead, his new bride wreaked havoc with his senses and ruled his thoughts all the more.

And if that were not annoying enough, she seemed oblivious to his suffering.

At the moment, she was ignoring him, her gaze on the flat rock she had found to serve as a trencher. She was using his knife to crack open a lobster shell.

"By all means," he commented, his voice taut with a different kind of hunger, "enjoy my supper."

"You are not eating much." She broke a claw in half and fished out the steaming meat.

Words failed him as he watched her lift the morsel to her lips, watched the juices glisten on her fingers, on her soft, pink tongue as she drew the tidbit into her mouth. Her appreciative sigh of pleasure flooded his entire body with throbbing need.

It was a shame, he thought ruefully, that she could not plunge the knife into his heart and put him out of his misery.

She merely swallowed and continued eating, still blithely unaware of his plight. "I see no reason to waste all of this. It has been years since I—"

"Purloined a man's meal from under his nose?"

An amused smile tugged at one corner of her mouth. "Since I have enjoyed fresh seafood. It is almost impossible to obtain inland." Her voice became wistful. "When I was growing up in Brittany, my parents used to love to cook on the beach like this. Before my mother took ill."

Her smile fading, she continued eating in silence.

Hauk toyed with a crab claw on his trencher, ignoring the curiosity that buzzed through his thoughts like a pestering fly. He was not going to question her about what had happened to her mother. Did not want to learn aught about her past, her family, her home—the life he had taken her from forever.

He already knew more than he wanted to know.

Studying her pale cheeks, the shadows beneath her sable lashes, he realized there was something different about Avril tonight, though he could not discern what it was. She spoke little, avoided looking at him . . . yet she remained by his side. As if she were a curious sparrow that had hopped near enough to steal a few crumbs from him.

He wondered if she would take flight if he made any move toward her.

He lifted the crab claw to his mouth, gnawing at it as he turned that thought over in his mind. Mayhap she seemed different tonight because this was, in truth, the first time he had seen her sitting still. The Avril he had grown used to was a vivid bundle of conflicting emotions, constantly changing, endlessly provoking him, always in motion.

He had never seen her like this: quiet, at rest, almost . . .

Nay, not tame. That word would never apply. But there was a certain sweetness about the way she sat there, enjoying her lobster, her hair in tangles, her lashes dipping sleepily low over her emerald eyes, her bare toes peeking out from the hem of her rumpled nightclothes. She looked like she needed to be scooped up and carried to bed.

Hauk tore his gaze from her, not liking the unexpected, unwelcome feelings that stole through him, softer and warmer than the desire that stirred his loins.

By all the gods, she was so young. So much younger than him. And she did not even begin to guess.

He crushed the piece of crab shell in his fingers and flicked it away, annoyed. Seeing her this way—so vulnerable and sweet—only reminded him of how delicate his lovely *utlending* bride was. How different from him.

How fragile.

Reminded him too vividly of the fear he had felt earlier today when he cut his journey short.

When he had discovered Thorolf missing from his enclave on the eastern shore.

The place had been deserted. Abandoned. Thorolf might have gone off somewhere to sulk, as he often did, but he was also vicious enough to seek vengeance against those he blamed for his punishment by the *eldrer*.

Including Avril.

For one moment, standing in the doorway of Thorolf's empty dwelling, Hauk had felt a stab of cold fear—not for his people, or for his friend Keldan, but for the bride he had left alone and unprotected.

He had run all afternoon, through the rain, not even stopping to eat, pausing at Keldan's just long enough to warn him. Then he had finally reached his own *vaningshus*. And found Avril missing.

Hauk raked a hand through his hair and forced the memory away, not wanting to relive the dread he had experienced. Or the relief and gratitude to the gods he had felt upon finding her safe and well. He could not allow her to stir his heart this way.

Misery and torment, he reminded himself. *She can only bring you misery and torment in the end.*

Avril sighed in enjoyment as she finished her meal—and Hauk realized he had unintentionally fulfilled one of the commands set forth in the *Havamal*: A new husband was to discover his bride's favorite foods and provide them for her.

Just as he was to discover all of her favorite, secret pleasures.

"Did you eat naught while I was away?" he asked, chagrined.

"What?"

"You eat as if you had been starving, and you are"—despite himself, he found his gaze drawn back to her—"unusually quiet."

They regarded each other across the scant distance that separated them, the cookfire making the night air crackle with flames and heat.

As before, she held his gaze only a moment before she glanced away, color rising in her cheeks. "If I seem quiet, it is simply because I am tired. As I told you earlier, the storm kept me awake."

Her blush deepened.

Hauk frowned at her in confusion, unable to fathom why she would turn scarlet because a storm had kept her awake.

Unless it was not, in truth, the weather that had disturbed her sleep . . . but something else.

He almost choked on his own breath, remembering the unfinished explanation she had offered earlier, just before she began babbling on about the storm.

I have had bad . . .

Dreams? Was it her dreams that left her blushing and breathless?

Had she been unable to sleep for the same reason as him?

His heart thudded a single, violent stroke then began hammering against his ribs. He had heard legends of Asgard men and their mates who shared a bond so deep that they did not need words to communicate, even when distance separated them—a bond so strong they even shared the same dreams.

He had always dismissed such tales as fanciful nonsense.

But he could not dismiss the way Avril was reacting to him tonight. How different she seemed. His brain rioted with questions.

Had she been dreaming of him? Was it desire that made her blush? Was that why she remained by his side—because she was drawn to him in the same powerful, inescapable way he was drawn to her?

How she might respond if he closed the distance between them now, if he drew her near and kissed her? Would it win him a slap? A knife in his gullet?

Or the kind of response he had dreamed of?

Her gaze still lowered, she wiped his knife in the sand and tossed it aside. It landed next to his discarded sword. "Sword, knife, battle-ax," she mused. "You travel heavily armed, Hauk. Was your journey dangerous?"

"Were you worried for me, wife?" His voice sounded deep, husky, even to his own ears.

"Do not call me that," she chided.

He noticed she had not answered his question.

He also noted that at some point, she had started calling him by his first name rather than "Norseman" or "Valbrand."

How would she taste? Would her mouth be hot and hungry beneath his, or sweet and soft?

"Fear not," he managed to say, "I am unharmed. I suffered naught but a small gash." Lifting his right hand, he revealed an angry red mark that ran up his arm from wrist to elbow, earned when he slipped on a jagged outcropping of stone while running home through the rain.

She gasped. "Sweet Mary." Lips parted, she started to say more, then stopped herself, regarding him with a look that held . . .

By all the gods, it was concern he saw in her gaze. Concern for his pain. For him. She *had* been worried about him.

Just as he had been worried about her.

He turned away abruptly, shaking off the feelings, unable to look into his wife's sparkling emerald eyes a moment longer. He would not *do* this to himself! It was bad enough that she trespassed on his thoughts waking and sleeping. Bad enough that she made him *want,* in a way he had not wanted in half a lifetime.

He had to accept her presence in his life, had to protect her and see to her needs—but he could *not* allow her to stir the ashes of feelings he had forgotten how to feel. For the sake of his sanity, he had to leave them buried. Buried, like the volumes of notes and sketches he kept shut away in trunks because he could not bear to look at them and could not bring himself to destroy them.

He stretched out on the sand, on his side, giving her his back. Then he reached for his cloak, pounding it into the shape of a pillow and jamming it under his head. Avril was merely a woman, like any other. He could control the desire he felt for her, and the other feelings as well.

It was only fatigue that made the task *seem* unusually difficult.

"You are going to sleep?" she asked curiously.

"It is what I normally do when I am tired after a long journey," he grated out.

"Oh." She remained quiet a moment. "I thought we might . . ."

He clenched his teeth to resist the suggestive replies that sprang to mind: *Kiss? Slowly undress one another? Discover how your body would feel against mine? Make hot, passionate love under the moon?*

"Talk," she said.

He released a harsh breath. "We can talk on the morrow." Horn of Odin, if he had to look at her again, he was not sure he could keep himself from pulling her into his arms, pressing her down beside the fire, lifting the hem of her shift until her naked bottom met warm sand and his fingers found soft, damp silk.

He wrestled his unruly thoughts under control, thwacked his pillow for good measure. "Go to sleep, Avril."

After a moment, he heard her move away a few paces, then stretch out on the sand. Grateful, he shut his eyes and prayed to all the gods to grant him sleep.

Dreamless sleep.

But apparently the gods were busy elsewhere this night.

"I am certain your wounded arm will heal," she said quietly. "No doubt within the hour."

"That does not make it hurt any less," he muttered. The ocean breeze felt cool against his chest, the fire's warmth hot against the bare skin of his back. The soothing, familiar sound of the wind and waves might have lulled him to sleep eventually.

If he had not been blessed with a talkative bride.

"How can that be?" she prodded. "How is it that wounds heal so quickly here? My jaw *was* broken in Antwerp, I am certain of it. And the other night, when I cut my hand, it healed almost at once. And *everyone* in the town seems to be in perfect health."

He did not reply.

"Hauk?"

He glared into the night, annoyed with himself for having leaped to half-witted conclusions earlier like some naive, first-time groom. He had been wrong, of course. He and Avril did not share dreams or desire or any gentler sort of feelings.

This was why she had remained near him: because she hoped to glean information about Asgard, while he was tired enough to be careless. Information that might help her in whatever escape attempt she was no doubt planning.

"Hauk? Are you awake?"

He could pretend to be asleep, but he had known from the beginning that he would have to answer her questions about the island sooner or later. Revealing part of the truth—a small part—might satisfy her curiosity for now.

And keep her from asking questions he truly did not wish to answer.

"Asgard has certain natural healing qualities," he said simply, remaining on his side with his back to her. "Injuries heal swiftly and illness is unknown among us."

He could hear her sitting up. "But how is that possible? Is it some quality of the air? Or the water or the food? Or . . . or some unique herb or root found here and nowhere else?"

"We do not know."

She uttered a scoffing sound. "I do not believe you. You know but you do not wish to tell me."

"I am speaking the truth. Many among us have sought to answer the question you ask." He paused for a moment, an image of his father bright and sharp in his mind. "But no one knows for certain. It may be a combination of several qualities found in nature here, native to Asgard. We do not know."

She fell silent, as if weighing what he had said and trying to decide if he was telling the truth.

"It is a shame that it remains a mystery," she said at last.

"Aye," he agreed, with a bitterness he doubted she could fathom.

"But even if you do not know *how* this place offers such wondrous healing, why do you not share it with the world? Why take such care to keep your island secret? Imagine the good you could do. Imagine the people you could help—"

"Imagine how quickly Asgard would be overrun and destroyed," he said flatly. "We *must* keep it secret. It is the only way to protect our home and those who live here."

A soft note of understanding came into her voice. "And that is why you will not allow any of the captives to leave."

"Aye."

There was more to it than that, but he was not ready to reveal the rest. There was no telling what a woman as unpredictable as Avril might do—especially when she was still bent on escape.

"But why bring captives here at all?" she asked, sounding bewildered. "It seems a terrible risk to take, merely to . . ." She hesitated. "To *what?* What in the name of all the saints *do* you want with us?"

He rolled onto his back, sighing wearily and staring up at the cloud-darkened sky. It seemed he would get no more sleep tonight than he had the last two nights. "I told you before, I do not want you at—"

"Aye, I know. You do not want me at all. You acquired me purely by accident," she said dryly. "But what about the others? Why would men risk so much simply to get a wife?"

"Some young hotheads find risk exciting. And they want what most men want. Companionship. A comely wench to warm their beds." He slanted her a glance.

Avril reddened and lowered her lashes. "But why not marry one of the women who are already here?" she persisted. "Why not marry a . . . an *innfodt* woman?"

Hauk narrowed his eyes, wondering who had told her that word—and how much she had been told about the difference between *utlending* and *innfodt* women. That discussion was supposed to be left for a husband to have with his wife. When he decided the time was right.

"Some do," he said slowly. "But others want . . ." He paused, assaulted by jagged memories, shards of hopes and dreams shattered long ago.

He shrugged, the sand rough against his bare back. There was no need to open that painful subject. Not yet. Not now. "Bringing *utlending* brides here is a tradition."

"It seems a foolish tradition."

"Aye, I have said the same. Many times. But young ears are too often deaf to reason."

If she understood that he included her in that comment, she gave no sign.

Still looking down, she drew a fingertip through the sand. "Then if you agree that it is a foolish tradition, and if I vowed by my child's life that I would keep your secret—"

"I still would not be able to set you free. By Thor's hammer, Avril, save your breath and cease asking." He let his head fall back, flung an arm over his eyes, wished he could shut her out. "And I would be a fool to trust your word of honor, since you have already lied to me once. Your friend told me the truth about your husband. About the fact that you are a widow."

"You cannot blame me for lying about that." Avril's voice sharpened. "Josette should not have . . . she did not mean to . . ." She whispered an oath. "She mistakenly thought she was helping me."

The breeze caught the flames of the dying cookfire, making them snap and hiss.

"I could bring her here to live with you."

"Josette?" Avril asked in confusion.

Hauk let his arm drop to the sand, realizing he had just voiced an idea that had been forming in his mind the past two days.

"Your daughter," he said quietly. "It might be possible for me to bring your daughter here to live with you."

For an instant Avril seemed incapable of speech. "*What?*"

He pushed himself up and met her gaze beyond the dancing fire. "Despite your belief that we Norsemen are half-civilized barbarians, I would not see a child made an orphan."

She gaped at him, blinking, as if the moon had just

fallen through the clouds and landed beside her. "You would go and get Giselle?" she whispered. Her face brightened. "Aye, it is an excellent idea. I will go with you. I will take you there myself—"

"Nay, milady, you will not," he said with a frown, not taken in for a second by that suggestion; she meant to escape the instant she set foot on her home soil. "You will remain here. I would go alone."

She lowered her gaze. "But you will not find her without my help. And Gaston and Celine would not simply hand her over to a stranger. Her uncle will never allow you to take her—"

"The uncle who is a *duc,* who lives in the Artois region?" He had thought the child might be in Brittany or somewhere else.

Somewhere closer.

"Aye, Duc Gaston de Varennes." Her head came up, her eyes widening. "Hauk, he is not a man to be trifled with. You cannot even *think* of going there without me. He would *kill* anyone who tried to take Giselle—"

"The Artois is too far." Hauk shook his head, not sure what bothered him more: the fact that he had actually considered the idea, or that he felt genuine regret because it would not work. "It is impossible."

Avril was silent a moment.

Her voice sounded unsteady when she spoke again. "And I would not see my daughter made a captive along with me," she admitted. "Her life and her freedom mean more to me than my own. It is out of the question." She closed her eyes, her lashes dark against her pale cheeks. "But you are . . . kind to think of her well-being, Hauk." Slowly she looked up, her eyes searching his face. "You are not a barbarian. That is not what I think of you. I think you are not . . . not at all what I expected. I did not know a Viking warrior could be gentle. Or thoughtful."

Hauk could not summon a reply, the warmth in her expression playing havoc with his heartbeat. He did not *want* to be thoughtful or gentle or kind. Did not want this tempestuous, emerald-eyed lady to rouse such tenderness within him, make him remember what it was like to feel concern.

And protectiveness. And caring.

Not only for her, but for a child he had never even met.

"I am not so virtuous," he said roughly, half in denial, half in warning. "I merely want you to accept your new life here."

Shaking her head, Avril rose. "That I can never do." She walked around the fire, toward the water, and stood facing the waves.

The silence stretched out for a long moment before she said, "I thought you told me that no one kept boats on Asgard."

"Aye, that is what I told you." He watched the wind play through her long hair and swirl her cloak and shift around her slender body.

"So you lied to me," she said with soft accusation, looking over her shoulder at him. "And if it is possible for you to leave—"

"I am the only one who leaves," he said firmly, "and I leave only rarely." He had ventured out more often in his youth, but it had become too painful to glimpse the outside world—with all its variety and excitement and constant change—only to be forced to return here. To remain here.

Where even the perfect weather varied little from day to day, season to season, year to year.

Avril turned to face him. "Then what did you mean when you said 'the Artois is too far'?"

"No one can leave the island for more than six days at a time. It is—" *Impossible.* "—the law."

She arched one brow in surprise. "If that is so, then Antwerp must be no more than six days from here. Nay . . ." A hint of satisfaction came into her voice as she looked out over the ocean. "Three."

Hauk growled a curse, annoyed that he had just heedlessly revealed information she might use to try to escape.

He thrust himself to his feet and stalked over to her. "Avril, do not think what you are thinking. You cannot escape Asgard."

She lifted her chin and stared up at him mutinously. "So you have said."

"By Hel, woman, do not act like a reckless little fool." He took her arm, his fingers gripping the soft fabric of her cloak. "If you are drowned or crushed against the rocks, your child *will* be an orphan!"

"Do you care so much?" Her eyes were suddenly bright with tears. "Do I matter to you so much?"

Her tears burned him. Her question froze him.

"I am trying to make you listen to logic," he insisted hoarsely. "Logic and reason."

She struggled to wrench her arm from his grasp.

"Reason does not matter to me. Your laws do not matter to me! You do not . . . y-you do not . . ."

She seemed unable to finish that sentence, looked startled and dismayed that she could not. Her voice dissolved in a thready whisper. *"Hauk."*

The pain in her eyes made his heart thud a hard stroke against his ribs. His hand came up to brush her tears away, as if his will were no longer in command of his movements.

And then all logic and reason vanished.

His fingers threaded into her tangled hair, tilting her head up. His other arm slid around her back and his mouth covered hers. Their lips met in a kiss that was tentative and hot, tender and hungry. A kiss full of longing—and stunning need. Need that should have stopped him. Should have made him let her go.

But her mouth tasted so soft and sweet beneath his, her lips as full and lush as he had imagined from the moment he met her. *As he had dreamed.* Her hands closed on his bare shoulders, but she did not push him away.

Instead she melted against him, the sound in her throat filled with longing and need that matched his. She clung to him as if the world had shifted beneath her feet.

He crushed her closer, heat glittering through him, a rain of sensations that wrenched a groan from deep in his chest. Her cloak had fallen open and he felt her body lithe and soft and warm in his embrace. Felt the fullness of her breasts flattened against his chest, the tips drawn tight beneath the thin fabric of her shift, all that separated his bare skin from hers.

Even as he urged her mouth to open, he struggled for sanity. Control. Her lips parted, letting him deepen the kiss, letting him inside her—and he was lost.

Plummeting downward into a sultry abyss, he touched his tongue to hers, wanting. Needing her breath, her body, her nearness. *Her*. Avril. Wild and tempestuous, delicate and silky, her mouth a tantalizing heat beneath his.

Her nails made passionate marks on his skin. The stubble of his beard abraded her jaw. Thoughts rioted through his mind. Thoughts that were not virtuous in the least.

There were ways to persuade his bride to accept her life here. To accept him. Ways they would both enjoy.

Slowly he sank to his knees in the sand, drawing her down with him. She shivered in his arms, uttered a small sound of uncertainty.

"Shhh," he murmured, trailing feather-light kisses along her jaw. "There is much that you would like about Asgard, Avril." His voice had become a deep, husky entreaty. "Let me show you." He nuzzled a sensitive place just below her ear. "Let me show you."

"Hauk—"

"Tell me you do not want this, and I will stop." He slid one hand beneath her cloak.

"I do n—" She gasped as his fingers caressed her through the thin fabric of her shift. "I do n-n . . ."

"You must be specific, milady," he murmured. "What is it you do not want? Do you not want this?" He nibbled at that sensitive spot below her ear, a quick kiss of tongue and teeth that made her tremble. "Or is it this?" He trailed his fingertips down the graceful curve of her spine.

She caught her lower lip between her teeth, shutting her eyes, her nails digging into his shoulders.

His own body shaking with need, he drew her closer. "There are many exquisitely sensitive places on a woman's body," he whispered. "A wise husband takes the time to find them all. One . . ." He kissed her mouth. "By . . ." He kissed the hollow of her throat. "One."

He eased her down onto the sand, on her back, reaching for the hem of her shift. He sucked in a breath as she moved beneath him, the softness of her thigh pressing against his arousal.

She cried out and stiffened in his embrace, blinking as if suddenly awakened from a dream. *"Nay—"*

"Avril." He groaned, holding her fast, lowering his mouth to hers.

She fought against his hold. "Nay! Let me go!"

Her frightened words cut through him, cold as a steel blade—and though her eyes were still dark with passion, her lips swollen from the shared ardor of their kisses, he did not argue with her.

He let her go. It was all he could do. He would not take her against her will.

She stumbled to her feet and backed away, gathering her cloak around her, trembling visibly. "I *cannot* . . ." She was breathing hard, shook her head wildly. "I cannot stay here!"

The words came out as a choked sob.

Then she turned from him and ran.

Hauk lurched to his feet, almost chased after her, stopped himself. The ocean breeze quickly cooled the sweat from his body and cleared the fog from his senses. *By Loki's dark daughter, what had he been doing?*

How had one kiss led to so much more so quickly?

Nei, he did not want an answer to that question.

He had merely been satisfying a physical need that had become painfully sharp. And trying to show her some of the pleasures Asgard had to offer. It was his responsibility to persuade her to stay willingly, to please her and see to her happiness.

Instead, he had frightened her, gone too far, too soon. That had been a mistake, and he would not repeat it.

He kicked sand over the cookfire to douse it, snatched up his sword and pack and set off to follow her, not relishing the impossible task he faced. With Thorolf missing, he had to watch over his reckless little bride more closely, stay with her every moment.

But he also needed to resist temptation, grant her time to adjust to her new life, to this place, to him.

He would simply have to be strong.

Ja, he thought derisively as he headed down the beach, strong as a starving man trying to deny himself food.

Or a man parched with thirst trying not to sip from the brimming, sweet, beautiful cup so close within his reach.

Thorolf stood in the shadows a safe distance from Valbrand's *vaningshus*, waiting. Patient. Running his thumb along the smooth glass surface of the slender flask in his hand, he reminded himself that he had worked and planned for this a great many years. Another few hours would not matter.

Especially if it meant adding sweet vengeance to sweet freedom.

After his humiliation at the *althing*, he wanted the former almost as much as the latter. The *vokter* had thwarted him for the last time.

And this time he would pay.

At last, the woman returned, garbed in a hooded cloak—but Valbrand was only a few steps behind her.

Thorolf bared his teeth in a frustrated snarl. How like Valbrand to ruin his plans. Again! Just when Thorolf learned that the *vokter* had unexpectedly left his new bride alone, he unexpectedly returned to her.

As if he were purposely foiling Thorolf's plans.

But that could not be. He could not know. No one knew.

Thorolf paced restlessly across the grass, gripping the flask. By Kvasir's blood, if he had to waste one more *day* on this accursed rock, he would go mad. He was not a sheep, like the others, so satisfied with their placid, peaceful, dull little lives. He was meant for more.

An entire *world* of new places and pleasures awaited him beyond the boundaries of Asgard. And he meant to enjoy them all. The elders and the *vokter* and their laws could burn in Hel for all he cared. He had lived too long under their rule.

But he would not have to endure much longer. Freedom was tantalizingly close now.

He literally held it in his hand.

The thought cooled Thorolf's ire as he turned to stare at Hauk's cozy clifftop home.

Valbrand was always saying he wanted change. And his wish was about to be granted.

All Thorolf needed was one of the *utlending* women; that was why he had taken part in the claiming voyage in the first place.

He was not about to test his potion himself. Not after failing in the past. He was reasonably certain that he held in his hand the answer that the men of Asgard had sought for centuries—the elixir would bring him wealth and acclaim throughout the world, make him a king. A god.

Yet there was still a chance, however small, that it might prove to be a deadly poison.

He meant to find out—with the help of Valbrand's pretty bride.

The thought made Thorolf smile. All he had to do was keep his temper in check, and he would succeed. Patience was the key.

Patience.

He could wait one more day. Turning, he walked down the grassy hill. He would move his boat and conceal it better, now while he still had the cover of darkness.

Then he would return here. The *vokter* could not watch over his bride every second. She would be alone at some point.

And Thorolf would be here, lying in wait.

His smile widened. On the morrow, Hauk Valbrand would lose his new wife.

 The sun felt glorious after yester-
day's rain. Josette could not help
but sigh as she relaxed against a
tree, warmed by the shimmering rays, a basket of
fresh-picked berries in her lap. A pair of horses grazed
a few yards away, and Keldan lay stretched out on the
grass beside her, eyes closed, one hand behind his
head. He still had traces of dark juice on his face and
chest.

Their morning ride had ended with the two of
them picking their breakfast fresh from the fields—
and their berry hunt had ended in a laughing berry
battle.

Smiling, Josette popped one of the sweet fruits in
her mouth, its taste as refreshing as the breathtaking
view from this hilltop. From here, she could see the
entire island spread out in an endless, colorful ex-
panse: fields dotted with bright wildflowers, the western forest a rumpled blanket of leafy green; lavender
mountains rising in the distance; streams glinting
here and there, streaks of silver amid the darker, lush
shades of the meadows.

A gentle breeze warmed her face, rustling the

branches overhead. It was so pleasant here. So peaceful.

So difficult to keep her mind on the task she had been assigned. She was *supposed* to be gathering information about the island's location; Avril would be expecting her report tonight, at the celebration in town.

But thus far, Josette had no useful contribution to make to the captives' escape plan.

Feeling guilty, she ate another berry and looked down at Keldan.

Yesterday's drenching rain had kept the two of them inside his *vaningshus*—so it was not actually her fault that she had been unable to carry out her assignment. After all, they could hardly understand each other.

Although that had not kept them from enjoying a most agreeable day. They had played draughts, and chess, and a game he said was called *hneftafl*, which involved colored stones and a decorated board. After a leisurely supper, he had worked at his carving and she had fallen asleep listening to the rain and the sound of his deep voice humming a Norse tune.

When she awoke this morn, she realized he had once again carried her to bed and retreated to spend the night on the floor on the opposite side of the chamber.

Josette chewed at her lower lip, knowing that this friendly companionship growing between them should make her uneasy. He was still a stranger to her, and as powerfully built as any warrior she had met.

Yet, despite their language differences, she already felt as if she knew him somehow.

There was such a playful quality about him. Something so endearing about that hint of a smile that always curved his lips, about his unfailing cheerfulness. He seemed to take such pleasure in making those around him smile, both the people in the town . . . and her.

Watching the wind ruffle his black hair and the sun warm his tanned skin, she felt an unfamiliar sensation inside her, like hot ribbons whirling together, all ticklish and shivery.

Mayhap it had something to do with the fact that she liked him; she had never enjoyed a man's company so much.

As if aware of her gaze on him, he opened his eyes. His crooked grin widened.

Josette felt warmth flood her face, embarrassed to have been caught studying him with such rapt interest. She shifted her attention to the basket of berries in her lap.

Barely stirring, he picked a tall blade of grass and reached up to tickle her cheek with it.

"*Gress,*" he said.

She did not look at him, but smiled as she stared down into her basket. This was a game they had devised, to teach each other their native languages. "*Gress,*" she echoed, before translating the Norse word into French. "Grass."

"Grass," he repeated in his thick accent. "Josette . . ." His voice turned serious as he sat up. "Happy here?"

She glanced at him, sitting there beside her with a hopeful expression and a blade of grass in his fingers, this gentle Viking who liked to make furniture and hunt berries for breakfast and laugh with her beneath a sun-drenched sky.

"*Ja,*" she admitted softly. It was one of the first words he had taught her. "*Ja,* Keldan. I know I should not be, but I *am* happy here with you. No one has ever . . ."

Keldan looked at her earnestly. She did not know why she kept talking, when he could not understand. Mayhap it was *because* he could not understand that she felt she could tell him the rest.

"No one has ever made me feel special the way you do," she continued, blinking away the dampness that suddenly filled her eyes. "In truth, no one ever had much time for me."

She dropped her gaze again, shaking her head. "But I am supposed to be helping Avril. Giselle needs her." Her throat tightened. "I have to find out from you which direction we will have to sail to get . . . to get . . ."

She felt Keldan's hand lightly touch her chin.

"To get home," she finished, her heart beating hard as he tilted her head up.

His dark eyes held as much gentleness as his touch.

"Josette," he murmured, "home here now. Stay." He added another word that she did not realize he had learned yet. "Please."

Her lower lip trembled. She could not find breath to respond.

His fingertips slowly glided along her jaw, down her neck . . . coming to rest over her pounding heart.

"*Hjerte*," he whispered, taking her hand and placing it in the center of his chest.

She could feel his heart pounding as fast as hers. Their gazes met and held.

"*H-hjerte*," she repeated, whispering the word in her language as he leaned closer. "Heart."

He kissed her, a gentle brush of his mouth over hers. It was the first time he had ever kissed her.

The first time any man had kissed her.

And it felt as warm and sweet and tender as the sunlight that dappled the meadow. He tasted of the berries they had shared, his lips a soft, intriguing contrast to the muscles flexing beneath her hand, so hard and solid and male. The shivery-hot ribbons spun tight within her, and when he lifted his head all too soon, the sigh that escaped her carried a longing that was new and confusing to her.

And tantalizing.

The sound he made was a deeper echo of hers; she could feel it rumble through his chest, could feel him breathing fast and shallow. He dusted kisses over her chin, her nose, her forehead.

"Josette, home here," he whispered. "Home. *Hjem*."

Her senses danced like the leaves overhead, warmed by the sun, by his caress, by the yearning in his voice that so matched the feeling inside her.

And all she could think was that the word for home sounded rather like the word for heart.

"*Ja*, Keldan." She sighed, whispering the word

against his mouth as he lay back in the grass, drawing her with him. *"Hjem."*

Avril paced in front of the hearth, examining Hauk's collection of weapons and entertaining thoughts of mayhem. Floyel's small hooves clacked on the stone floor as he followed at her heels.

"Must you do that?" she bit out, halting in her tracks and turning to give him a stern look.

The little reindeer bleated loudly, his brown eyes large and innocent as he gazed up at her.

She sighed. "I am sorry." Bending down, she scratched beneath his furry chin. "Poor little Floyel, I should not snap at you. It is not *your* fault I have been trapped in here all day."

She moved restlessly to the open windows, where late-afternoon sun and warm, fresh air poured in to brighten the chamber. The weather was ideal for exploring, and she had planned to do just that today, to go and find Hauk's ship. But he refused to let her go riding—or anywhere, for that matter—alone.

He had offered to accompany her wherever she might wish, but she had declined. She could hardly take him along as she searched for his boat.

And she thought it best to keep as much distance between them as possible.

She turned away from the window, suddenly awash in memories of last night. His unexpected thoughtfulness. His caring.

His mouth, hot and ravishing on hers. His hands buried in her hair. The way she had parted her lips, trembled with longing, reveled in his embrace for one reckless moment.

She shut her eyes, still shocked by her response, by the way she trembled even now. Since their moonlit encounter on the beach, they had barely spoken more than a few, tense words to each other—and she meant to keep it that way.

She could not allow herself to view Hauk Valbrand as aught but her abductor. An obstacle to be overcome on her way home to Giselle.

No matter how kind or gentle or compassionate he might be.

Or how his touch made her melt.

"Saint's breath," she whispered miserably. "How am I to ignore the man when I cannot stop thinking about him?"

Floyel, ever at her heels, snuffled at her hand as if in sympathy, before ambling off to plop down on his bed in one corner.

"Thank you," she said with a reluctant grin as she wiped her damp palm on her skirt. "At least reindeer kisses do not cause me to take leave of my senses." Under her breath, she added, "Only Hauk's kisses."

Releasing·a frustrated sigh, she returned to the chair she had occupied for the past hour and picked up a book. She had dug out the Norse texts again, hoping she might notice something helpful that she had missed before.

Thumbing through the pages, she tried to think of a way to sneak out without Hauk seeing her.

It would be difficult, since he had been working outside all day, hammering away at some kind of repairs to Ildfast's stall. No doubt he *suspected* she was making plans to escape. He might not even allow her to attend the celebration tonight—and then how would she meet with her fellow captives?

Whispering an oath, she shut the book. This was maddening. She was accustomed to going and doing as she pleased; having a man restrict her every movement was intolerable. It made her blood simmer, made her feel like doing something rash and reckless and—

The door opened and Hauk strode in, his face and chest streaked with sweat, dirt, sawdust. Avril lowered her gaze, partly to conceal her unruly mood . . . and partly because a different kind of heat tingled through her blood and curled in her belly.

Curse the man, how could the merest glimpse of him affect her this way?

"Where did you get those?" he asked with a growl.

She looked up. He was frowning at the books stacked beside her chair.

"I meant no harm," she said defensively. "Since you will not allow me to venture out, I must pass the time in some way, and I enjoy reading—"

"I never said you could not venture out."

"I meant alone." Lifting the book in her hands, she placed it atop the stack. "I am sorry, I should not have gone through your belongings without permission." Her cheeks warmed. He had every right to be angry with her. "I will put them back."

"Nay, it matters not," he said more evenly. Brushing sawdust from his dark-gold hair, he walked over to the rain barrel against the nearby wall. "What is mine is yours now. You are my wife."

Avril bit her tongue. It was pointless to keep correcting him about that.

He reached for a wooden pipe above the rain barrel, releasing a spigot that let fresh water flow in from outside, where it collected in troughs below the eaves. "If you are bored, milady," he said above the splashing of the water as it filled the half-empty barrel, "I am willing to entertain you."

Heat flooded her as she imagined what sort of entertainment he had in mind. "I would prefer to be alone, thank you," she said coolly.

He slanted her a glance. "I only meant that we might go for a walk. Or mayhap play a game. Chess, draughts, tables—"

"Darts?" she suggested innocently. "It has always been my favorite."

He arched one brow. "I am not sure it would be wise of me to supply you with small, pointy objects in my vicinity."

"I might miss the target." She nodded, a sly curve tugging at her mouth. "But probably only once or twice."

A smile dimpled his unshaven cheek. "Or three or four times." He twisted the spigot again to shut the water off. "Why is darts your favorite? 'Tis usually played only by men, by archers."

"Aye, but it is also one of the few games of skill in which women can compete. And win. Even against men."

"Most women do not like to compete against

men." Hauk splashed his face and chest, and washed the back of his neck.

"Only because the men get so churlish when a woman wins." Avril felt her mouth go dry as she watched the play of muscle and sinew across his back and shoulders, the water gliding down his tanned skin. "But I am not like most women."

"Nay." He sighed, and she was not sure whether it was admiration or chagrin she heard in his voice. "You are not." He dunked his head under the surface, quickly, then straightened and ran his hands through his wet hair. "Gods, but the water is cold today."

Avril could not reply, nor tear her gaze from the glistening rivulets cascading down his bearded face, his chest, over the rippling muscles of his stomach. Fire bloomed in her at the too-vivid reminder of how he had looked last night—when he strode ashore like an untamed, golden god risen from the sea.

She glanced away, vexed that she was once again blushing like a maiden.

Mayhap he would believe the constant color in her cheeks had been put there by Asgard's hot sun.

Keeping her gaze averted, she quickly sought a safe topic of conversation. "You have a great many books," she said lightly, running her hand over one leather-bound volume. "I have been in the castles of lords and barons who did not have so many. They must have cost a great deal."

"They did not cost a single coin."

"You stole them?" She glanced at him in surprise.

He frowned. "I wrote them." Turning his back, he

reached for a length of folded linen on a shelf next to the rain barrel.

"Nay, you jest." She shook her head in disbelief. "You wrote these books? These, with the sketches of European cities, castles and cathedrals and sailing ships—"

"Aye."

"But how could that be? You said that no one left Asgard for more than six days."

"True."

"Then if you wrote these," she said dubiously, "you must have barely had time to *glimpse* these places."

He did not answer for a moment, rubbing his face and hair with the linen. "Most of them are from journeys made in my youth." He paused. "Brief journeys."

His voice was quiet, and he seemed entirely serious. Avril felt stunned, remembering what she had thought when she first found the books: that whoever had written them possessed an artist's eye and a poet's spirit.

Never had she guessed that the powerful, hard-muscled Viking warrior who had abducted her could be that man.

Glancing down, she studied the weathered volumes with their yellowed pages, and her brow furrowed. "But you could not have written these," she said softly. "They are all so old."

He tossed the damp cloth aside. "Salt air and sea winds take a merciless toll on paper."

She had not thought of that. "And the other books?" she asked curiously. "The texts on hunting and astronomy, the discussion of Aristotle's philosophies in Greek, the retelling of the Arthurian legends in French—"

"Mine as well."

She blinked at him in astonishment. Not only did he have the eye of an artist and the spirit of a poet, but the mind of a scholar. "But how—when—have you managed to pursue so many different subjects? I thought you said your duties as *vokter* occupied your time."

Shrugging, he rested one lean hip against a table beside the rain barrel. "As I told you before, time is something we have in abundance on Asgard. Illness is unknown here, food is plentiful, poverty unknown among us. So we do not have to spend our lives struggling to eke out an existence, or battling our neighbors." He picked up a small stone sculpture from the table, turning it in his fingers. "We each have time for many interests and pursuits. And every man—or woman—is free to choose a trade according to his talents and skills, whether as shopkeeper or storyteller, merchant or farmer—"

"Or warrior and artist."

He looked up, his gaze and voice gentle. "Avril, do you begin yet to see that Asgard has much to offer? Do you still think your homeland so much better?"

She lowered her gaze, realized her hands were clenched tightly in her lap. He was being kind to her again. Trying to make her feel at home here.

He simply did not understand that this could never possibly be her home.

"My home is with Giselle," she said softly.

He was silent a moment.

Then he set the sculpture down on the table and changed the subject. "It is time to prepare for this evening's celebration, milady. Let us not be late this time."

Avril held back an exclamation of relief. She had been prepared to argue or cajole or sneak away for her rendezvous with her fellow captives.

He hunted through the piles of wedding gifts still heaped on the room's tables and chairs, digging out a gown of pale gold edged with shimmering embroidery. Walking over to her, he held it out. "Wear the gold."

She stood, about to protest that she was not going to allow him to choose her clothes. It was too personal. Too intimate—

Then his fingers brushed hers as he handed her the gown, and she could not speak at all.

"The color will be most becoming on you," he added.

The husky depth of his voice made her heart flutter. She suddenly had to fight an urge to reach up and touch those dimples, to run her fingertips over the whiskers that darkened his strong, square jaw.

A muscle flexed in his cheek, as if he felt her touch there, though she had not moved. She felt his body tense. His sky-colored gaze settled on her mouth and her breath caught. He leaned closer, angling his head.

A voice at the door calling in Norse made them both freeze.

Hauk looked over her shoulder and Avril darted out of his reach, the gown clutched in her shaking fingers. Their visitor was Marta—and from her tone, the little girl seemed impatient about something.

Hauk spoke quietly to the child and sent her on her way before turning to translate to Avril. "Marta reminds me that I have kept her waiting rather a long time. I am supposed to be fetching her troublesome pet."

Her heart beating too hard, Avril nodded and turned away, not trusting herself to speak.

He walked over and scooped up Floyel, who bleated in alarm at being lifted so high above the floor.

"I will leave you to dress, milady," Hauk said as he headed for the door.

Watching him cradle the small bundle of gray fluff in his massive, muscular arms, Avril felt an unexpected knot in her stomach. Curious to know where he was taking the animal—and half afraid he intended to make sweet little Marta take the creature back—she followed him.

Peeking out the door, Avril covered her mouth to stifle a sound of surprise.

He had not spent the day repairing Ildfast's stall; he had been adding a small shelter for Floyel.

Warmth tingled through her. Despite all of Hauk's cursing and bluster about the animal last night, especially as they had cleaned up the mess Floyel made, he was naught but gentle as he carried the bawling reindeer out to its new home. He set Floyel down in the shelter, and Marta looked delighted, hugging her pet.

Then she turned and hugged Hauk with equal enthusiasm.

Avril could only see him from the back, but she

noticed him flinch . . . then he bent down and hugged the little girl close.

Avril's vision suddenly blurred. She felt her heart beating unsteadily.

He was not at all what she had once believed him to be. He was not a fierce, harsh Viking warrior but a man of gentleness and soft heart. She wondered why he tried to keep that side of himself hidden, like the books he kept shut away in the trunks.

Turning, she pulled the door closed and forced the perplexing question aside. She had to get ready for the celebration, for her rendezvous with the other captives. Hauk would have to remain a mystery to her, forever.

Because she and Josette and the others would be leaving at the first opportunity.

12

"I cannot believe three more of our fellow captives would abandon our cause," Avril said mournfully. Walking beside Josette, she struggled to keep her voice low, despite the music of pipes and harps and drums that filled the night, and the noise of men, women, and children all around them, laughing and singing and conversing. Torches brightly lit the clearing on the outskirts of town. "*Three* more, Josette. That leaves only . . . God's breath, it may leave only you and I to make the voyage."

Josette was apparently as troubled as she, for she offered no comment, her attention on the orange she was eating for dessert.

The three women Avril had just referred to moved to the center of the clearing—with their captors— joining a group that had gathered to dance, now that supper was finished and the trestle tables carried away.

"Look at them," Avril lamented. "When I spoke to those women but two days ago, they were all eager to escape—and tonight they tell me they do not wish to leave. All they can do is stare at their *husbands* with absurd grins on their faces, acting like . . . like . . ."

"Happy new brides?" Josette offered meekly.

"Addled feather-wits," Avril said in exasperation. "By the suffering saints, I never expected *all* of them to be so quickly bewitched."

A hearty male cheer went up behind them, and Avril glanced over her shoulder. In addition to dancing and music, the townspeople were being entertained by jugglers and ballad singers and storytellers, and some of the men had formed a group off to one side, challenging each other to tests of strength; they were currently lifting and throwing boulders, huffing and grunting and roaring with the effort.

Hauk stood among those watching the sport, talking to his friend Keldan and to others who came over to bow or shake his hand or slap him on the back, all smiling broadly. People had been greeting him happily all night. From everyone's reactions, it seemed as if many had not seen him in some time.

Avril felt grateful to have finally gained a bit of distance from him. At supper, sitting next to Hauk, she had barely managed to say a word or eat a bite, too aware of the husky sound of his voice, the tangy pine scent of the soap he had used for shaving, the way her stomach knotted every time he leaned near to refill her cup. And every time he looked at her—

Just as the thought entered her mind, Hauk happened to glance her way; he had been keeping a close eye on her since she left his side. Their eyes met across the crowd, and the air around her seemed to shimmer with heat, as if there were no distance between them at all.

Her heart fluttering, she dropped her gaze to her sapphire-blue skirts. She had refused to wear the gown he had chosen for her. Nor had she donned the silver wedding brooch he had given her the night of the *althing*, the one Josette and all the other new brides were wearing.

Avril feared that if she allowed herself to give in to such requests, to please him in such small ways, she would be unable to keep herself from giving in to him, and pleasing him, in far more meaningful ways.

She clasped her hands tightly, until her wedding band left an imprint on her palm. *She had to return home to Giselle.*

Even if she and Josette were the only two left to make the voyage.

"What of the Italian girl?" Josette asked hopefully as they stopped to watch a juggler and his dog perform tricks. "If you could find her, I am certain she would help—"

"I already found her," Avril muttered. "And I am afraid she will not be joining us. I also managed to speak to the English lady before supper was served, and you will not believe what *she* said. It seems she was traveling through Antwerp on her way to join a convent. She feels it is God's will that brought her here, so she wishes to stay and try to convert these people to Christianity."

"Oh?" Josette nibbled at the last bite of her orange. "That seems . . . noble. But . . . but there are still the other two captives, are there not? The other two who said they wished to escape—"

"The ones who did not even attend the feast tonight? They have not been seen all day." Avril sighed. "And unfortunately, I think I know what may be keeping them busy elsewhere. I am afraid we can no longer count on them either." She frowned as they walked on. "It seems rather foolish to hold a celebration to *welcome* the new brides when a third of the new brides do not even attend."

"One of the townspeople told me that this celebration is normally held the night of the *althing*," Josette said, "but it was postponed out of respect for two men who died during the voyage to Antwerp."

Avril shook her head. "So they risk even *death* to kidnap a wife," she said under her breath. "I still do not understand it."

She glanced over her shoulder, to where Hauk stood watching the other men enjoy their competitions, remembering how tense and curt he had been that first night. She wondered if the loss of the two men had grieved him, if that could account for his mood that night.

A tap on her arm made her turn and look down. A boy of about eleven was holding out a folded piece of parchment. Saying something in Norse, he thrust the paper into her hands.

"What is it?" Josette asked.

"I do not know." Brow furrowed, Avril opened the page to find two lines written in French.

I wish to speak with you. The child will show you where. Nina.

She glanced up, wondering what Nina could possibly want with her. Searching the crowd, Avril did not see her—but she did notice Hauk looking this way again.

Keeping her back to him, she folded the note and slid it into the sleeve of her gown. It would be impossible to go anywhere without him following her.

"Thank you," she said to the boy, "but Nina will have to wait."

"Who?" Josette asked curiously.

"No one of importance." After sending the lad away, Avril linked her arm through Josette's and led her onward through the milling townspeople. She stopped near a group gathered around a piper, whose playing was both merry and loud enough to drown out their conversation.

Avril took Josette's hand, giving it an encouraging squeeze; her friend had been uncharacteristically quiet this evening. "Josette, all will be well, I promise. Do not be afraid. We do not need the others. You and I can manage on our own." She smiled. "Think of it as an adventure, the sort we always loved when we were small—the two pirates of Morlaix ride the high seas again."

"The two pirates of Morlaix." Josette's expression was wistful. "We had such fun in those days, Avril. You have always been my closest friend—"

"And I always will be. And I am sure we will reach home safely. Using Hauk's boat will make our journey much easier and less dangerous."

"But . . ." Josette glanced away, chewing at her

lower lip. "You said you do not even know where his boat is."

"True." Avril flicked an irritated glance in Hauk's direction. "He would not let me venture out today, but mayhap on the morrow, when everyone is tired from the festivities, we will be able to slip away and search for it. I was able to find out from Hauk that Antwerp is but three days distant," she whispered. "Were you able to discover any helpful information? Did you learn aught from Keldan about which direction we must sail to reach home?"

"Well, I—" Josette cleared her throat. "Avril, I have been trying to think of a way to tell you this. Today I . . ."

"What, Josette? What did you learn today?"

Josette blushed to the roots of her brown hair.

And Avril felt her heart thud against her ribs, suddenly guessing that her friend had not been quiet and awkward tonight because of fear about their upcoming voyage.

"Josette," she said hollowly, full of dread. "What have you and Keldan been doing since I saw you last?"

"Berries!" her friend blurted. "Today w-we were picking berries."

"All day?"

Josette had turned as red as a berry herself.

"God's breath, Josette, tell me you did not—"

"Nay! I . . . h-he only kissed me. And . . . and . . ." She stared at the ground as if fascinated with the toes of her slippers. "Well, he is a carpenter, you know, and . . ."

Avril regarded her in complete puzzlement.

"He has . . ." A hint of a smile curved Josette's lips—the same blissful smile all the other captives had been wearing. "Very sensitive hands."

Avril felt as if one of the boulders the men were throwing had landed on her. "Josette, you cannot be thinking—nay, we must return to France! I have to get home to Giselle, and you—"

"What?" Josette raised her head. "What do I have waiting for me at home in France?"

Avril frantically searched for a way to make her see reason. "Your brothers! What about your brothers? I am certain they are mad with worry that you are missing."

"Aye, I am certain they are mad." She lowered her lashes, blinking. "Mad that I have caused them such trouble. Mad at the thought that they might be asked to pay a ransom to get me back." Josette shook her head. "My family is not like yours, Avril. They never were."

"I know that. Oh, my friend, I know." Avril took both of Josette's hands in hers, holding tight. "But you cannot be thinking of . . . of . . ."

"Of accepting a sweet and caring and gentle man as my husband?"

"He brought you here against your will!"

"But is that so different from the way women marry in France? If I were at home, my brothers would be choosing a suitor for me. From the day a woman is born, her father or brothers or overlord rules her life. *They* decide what we do and where we live and whom we wed. What woman *ever* lives by her own will?"

"I live by my own will," Avril declared hotly.

Josette pulled her hands free of Avril's. "Your own marriage to Gerard was an arranged match."

"That was different."

"Why? Because you fell in love with him? Because he made you happy? Avril, I remember your letters from the weeks after your wedding—how you spent all your time fighting with him, crying, wanting to come home to Brittany because you thought you had made a mistake."

Avril folded her arms and looked away, uncomfortable at the reminder, barely able to remember that time in her life when she had so disliked Gerard; it seemed as distant as the stars that speckled the night sky overhead.

"And then you grew to love him," Josette continued softly. "I have to confess, I never truly understood how your feelings for him could change so completely." Whispering, she glanced over at Keldan. "Until now."

Avril did not know what more to say. She felt helpless, stunned.

Lost.

"I have been happy here," Josette continued gently. "Happier than I ever was at home. Asgard is such a peaceful place—have you noticed that no one carries weapons?"

"Nay." Avril had not noticed. She glanced at the people milling around, at the men on the other side of the clearing.

Not one was carrying a sword, or even a knife.

Except Hauk, who was armed with both.

"How *odd*." She frowned. "These Vikings do not at all match the savage reputation their kind have earned over the centuries."

"Aye. Apparently fighting is not allowed among these people," Josette said. "There are no wars here, no battles. They take their laws most seriously."

"But, Josette, I still think you are making a mistake. There is too much we do not understand about this place and these people. Such as where all the *older* people might be." She studied the crowd, noticing again that only a handful were beyond their middle years. "They may have some sort of shortened life span. Or mayhap the men die at a young age," she added, seeing a few couples in which the wives seemed older than the husbands.

Then another fact struck her, one she had not noticed before. "And do you see any young children here? Or any babies? I do not think I see anyone younger than . . . than eight or nine."

"The littlest ones would all be abed by this hour, would they not?"

"True," Avril admitted. "But, Josette, do you not see that you cannot—"

"Avril, please. Do not try to change my mind. I have always allowed others to make my choices for me. For once, I . . ." Her voice faltered, then grew stronger. "*I* am making a decision for myself. I want to stay here. With Keldan."

Avril's throat felt dry. Her voice became hoarse. "Josette, you have been my closest friend since I was . . . since I was old enough to know what a friend is. How can I simply leave you behind?"

"I do not want to lose you, either, my beloved fellow pirate of Morlaix." Josette hugged her. "But I cannot go with you."

"And I cannot stay." Avril held on tight.

"I know. I am sorry that you have to do this alone." Josette stepped back, wiping at her eyes. "But I will do whatever I can to help you, Avril. I promise I will find out the information you need and bring it to you as soon as I can."

Avril could only stand mute as her most cherished friend hurried off into the crowd—toward her husband.

The sounds of the festivities were but a muffled hum, here a few streets away from the clearing, in the silent, almost deserted town. Avril kept glancing behind her, but she had chosen her moment carefully, waited until Hauk's attention was elsewhere. He had become embroiled in a lengthy conversation with the elder who looked like his relative, and she had seized the opportunity to slip away.

She edged into the darkened space between two dwellings, following the boy who had led her. "Nina?" she whispered.

"My dear child, what a pleasure to see you again," Nina drawled, stepping out of the shadows. The jewels on her fingers flashed in the moonlight as she waved the boy away. "You certainly took your time. I *do* have better things to do than wait for you all night, you know. And the air is taking on a chill—"

"I am sorry for the delay." Avril darted a nervous look behind her.

"I take it you have decided at last that I am worthy of your trust?"

"Mayhap," Avril replied uneasily, not about to reveal the truth.

I have no one else to turn to. Her throat threatened to close. She prayed that she could trust the woman. That Nina truly meant to help her rather than harm her.

"Do not fear, silly *utlending*." Nina sighed dramatically. "I would not have gone to this trouble, and come all this way to see you, if I meant to do you ill. My friends and I have been enjoying a private gathering in my *vaningshus* this evening—"

"Private gathering? You did not attend the celebration?"

Nina laughed as if the very idea were ridiculous. "Nay. I am playing hostess to some of my fellow *innfodt* women who chose not to attend tonight's celebration." She crossed her arms. "Because we see no reason to celebrate."

"I see," Avril said warily. "And you have left them in order to speak with me."

"I told you when we last parted that I would be willing to help you in any way I can." Nina paused. Her lashes swept downward to conceal her gray eyes, and for a moment, the frost melted from her voice. "I may not be a mother, but I can imagine how you must feel, being separated from your little one."

Avril finally recognized the emotion that tinged Nina's voice, the one she had not been able to identify before.

Envy.

"You do not have children of your own?" she asked gently, her heart filling with sympathy for the older woman.

"Do not pity me, *utlending*." Nina looked up sharply, her gaze once again cool. "I am quite happy with my life. I am an adoring aunt to my nieces and nephews, I have my work as a jeweler, and I may even have a husband one day—if the best men of Asgard would give up this foolish tradition of bringing home foreign brides."

"Do you mean you can only choose among the men of Asgard?" Avril asked in confusion. "The women here are not free to venture out and seek foreign husbands?"

"Women are hardly capable of kidnapping men," Nina scoffed.

"A woman as beautiful as you would hardly need to resort to kidnapping to attract a husband."

Nina's red lips curved in a smile. "I do adore flattery. But unfortunately, there are laws and traditions that prevent such—"

"Laws that apply to the women and not to the men?" Avril shook her head. "That is unfair. Mayhap you and your *innfodt* friends should start a new tradition."

Nina arched one auburn brow. "What bold ideas you have, little *utlending*." She looked away, musing half to herself. "Women going on a claiming voyage. Mayhap . . ." Then she flicked one bejeweled hand in an impatient gesture. "This is all most interesting, but you and I really do not have time—"

"Aye," Avril agreed, glancing over her shoulder

again. "As soon as Hauk realizes I have left the festivities without him, he will begin searching for me." She looked at Nina. "We need to make plans. I want you to take me to Hauk's boat on the morrow—"

"That may no longer be necessary. As I started to explain, before you began asking so many questions, I discussed your plight with my friends this evening. And one of them told a tale you may find of interest." She smiled, looking quite pleased with herself. "I believe I have found you another boat, my dear. One that is much closer at hand than Hauk's."

Avril gasped, overcome with surprise. With hope.

"Well, do not stand their gaping." Nina motioned for Avril to join her and started down the street. "We may have little time to spare. Let us be on our way."

"You mean to take me there now? Tonight?"

"Aye, unless you prefer to take your chances in the western forest." Turning, Nina planted her hands on her hips. "*I* for one have no desire to end my days as a wolf's toothsome tidbit."

Avril moved forward a step, then paused, looking back over her shoulder.

She could still see the glow of the celebration that lit the night sky, could hear the distant strains of music and laughter.

Nina released an exasperated sound. "Do you wish to escape or not?"

"Aye," Avril said, her voice wavering, before she repeated it more firmly. "Aye."

"Then come along, my dear." Nina turned to lead the way through the darkened streets. "If all goes well, you will be leaving Asgard tonight."

*   *   *

"I do not believe I have ever seen you clean-shaven, Valbrand. *Ja,* that is what seems different about you."

"Can a man not change one aspect of his appearance without half of Asgard making comment?" Hauk grumbled, wishing everyone would stop noticing.

Hamar, the ale maker, laughed heartily as he refilled Hauk's cup. "*Nei,* not if he has worn a beard for as long as you have." He scratched at his own thick red whiskers, winking. "But then, a married man must think of his wife, must he not? Ladies are so accursed reluctant to kiss a man with whiskers."

Hauk muttered an oath into his cup while Hamar moved on with his jug of ale. His uncle Erik, standing beside him, chuckled.

Hauk took a long drink and slanted him a glance. "I am so glad I amuse you, Uncle."

"So am I," Erik replied, in an unusually light mood tonight. "I had forgotten how enjoyable a night such as this could be."

Hauk scowled, wishing he were having so pleasant a time. It had been torture to sit beside Avril during supper, burning for her while she remained remote and silent and resisted all his attempts at conversation.

If he had dared think he might persuade her to accept her life here, she had disabused him of that notion today. She would never accept Asgard. Or him.

He had taken her away from her child, an innocent little girl who would grow up an orphan because of what he had done—and for that, she could never forgive him. Not that he could blame her.

"You cannot begrudge everyone being happy for you," Erik commented. "They are pleased you have brought a new bride to Asgard."

Hauk did not reply, seeing no need to discuss the real reason behind his churlish humor tonight with his uncle.

Erik Valbrand was normally aloof, stoic, and a rare visitor to these events; he had explained that he needed to introduce the English girl, Blythe, to the island's unmarried men, so that she might choose a husband.

At the moment, Blythe stood beside Keldan's bride, who was cheering Keldan on in the wrestling matches that had begun after the strength competitions.

Hauk took another swallow from his cup. "My mind has been on *duty* tonight, Uncle. I should think that would please you." All night he had been watching the crowd for Thorolf, concerned that the black-eyed knave might come here to cause trouble. But thus far there had been no sign of him. "As for my new bride, she wants naught to do with me."

His uncle turned to regard him with a more serious expression. "The two of you seemed to be getting along well enough during supper."

"We managed to be civil," Hauk said curtly. "We are not getting along."

"Indeed? And when do you intend to remedy that?"

Hauk held his tongue to bite back an oath, which

only would have been drowned out by the cheers and shouts that rose as Keldan pinned yet another opponent to the ground.

Hauk winced as his bruised and battered friend rose and immediately motioned for the next challenger. Kel was trying to exhaust himself into unconsciousness. Which, as Hauk had tried to point out, would not help at all.

He should know, he thought ruefully; he had tried all day to do the same.

Only Josette would be able to ease poor Keldan's suffering.

"You must give your wife time," Erik advised. "Show her care and gentleness. And affection."

Hauk pierced his uncle with a glare. "That is strange advice, coming from you."

Erik Valbrand had shown precious little care or gentleness or affection while Hauk was growing up; he had always been determined that Hauk should be strong enough and tough enough not to repeat his father's mistakes.

Not to dream his father's dreams.

"Men can change," Erik said, meeting his accusing glare without flinching. "You can change. You must have a son one day. There must be another Valbrand to carry on the tradition—"

"By all the gods," Hauk swore, "*that* word again."

"*Ja.* Tradition. One day you may wish to turn your attention to other pursuits, and there must be another ready to take your place and serve as *vokter.*"

"Are you so dissatisfied with how *I* have carried out my duties, Uncle?"

"*Nei*, that is not what I meant."

"I have no intention of abandoning my post," Hauk said flatly. "I am not my father. And as for my wife—"

He glanced behind him, to where Avril had been standing the last time he saw her, visiting with Marta and her family.

But she was no longer there.

Turning, he looked around, alarm slicing through him.

She was nowhere to be seen.

13

"How am I to know what Thorolf would be doing with a boat?" Nina said in an impatient voice. "Do we really care to pause and ask questions at this moment?"

Avril stood blinking in the moonlight, barely able to believe what lay before her on the rugged strip of shoreline. She stared, speechless, her heart soaring at her good fortune.

Nina continued throwing aside branches and underbrush to reveal a small sailing vessel—single-masted, shallow-keeled, with a curving prow and stern. Mayhap a fishing boat, or a pleasure craft meant for rivers and lakes. It was about twenty paces long, sitting partly in the water. And it looked new.

"Mayhap Thorolf wished to take up fishing. He is always searching for some new way to amuse himself." Nina found a heavy anchor stone that had been used to keep the boat from drifting out with the tide. "My friend sometimes comes to this secluded stretch of beach with her"—she flicked a look at Avril—"favorite companion, and she mentioned that the two of them saw Thorolf here late last night."

As Avril moved closer, Nina started tugging at the

rope knotted around the stone. "My friend said that Thorolf kept looking around nervously, as if afraid someone might see him. She could not think of what a man like him would be doing sneaking about the shore at such an hour, unless he was breaking one of our laws—"

"Such as the one against leaving Asgard." Avril pulled back a length of canvas flung over the stern, uncovering a jumble of supplies. "Look at all of these barrels and chests, and baskets of food and . . ." She opened the lid of one trunk, to find it gleaming with jewels and coins. "He has a king's ransom in riches here."

"Is there drinking water?"

Avril uncorked a flask. "Aye. But what could he—"

"Good. That is all you will need for your voyage." Nina tossed the anchor rope aside and placed both hands on the stern. "You must promise me you will not tell anyone about Asgard, little *utlending*, or ever try to return here. You must keep our secret."

"Aye, of course, you have my word. But I cannot go *tonight*." Avril was paralyzed by fear as she looked out across the black sea, toward the distant fog and those towering rocks that stood ready to block her way. "I will leave in the daylight, on the morrow—"

"The boat could be *gone* by the morrow. There is no telling when Thorolf might move it. Whatever his purpose, he would not risk leaving it here for long—"

"But I would have to be mad to try to sail through those rocks in the dark!"

"The moon and stars are bright enough to guide you. And there is an easy passage at this part of the shoreline—just there." Nina pointed to a towering pair of twin stones that poked up through the mist. "Aim for that spot and you will be free in a trice."

Avril's pulse seemed to roar in her ears, louder than the surf. *Free.* From the moment she had first awakened in Hauk's bed, she had hoped and planned for this moment—but now the ocean and the jagged fangs of rock looked impossibly huge, and the boat so small.

She glanced up at the deserted cliffs high above her. She and Nina had been careful to slip out through the back streets, but their walk from town had taken less than half an hour. And Hauk was no doubt looking for her already. If he came this way—

"*Utlending*, there is no time for second thoughts," Nina said emphatically. "You may never get another chance like this."

Taking a deep breath, Avril turned and planted both hands on the port side of the stern.

"Finally." Nina huffed. "Now push, little *utlending*. Push!"

"Aye aye, *mon capitaine*," Avril muttered under her breath. Every muscle in her arms and shoulders and back hurt as she threw all her weight against the boat. Slowly she felt it sliding across the sand, one inch at a time. Straining with all their might, side by side, she and Nina managed to shove the small craft farther out into the water.

It slid forward, bobbing on the waves. Scrambling to keep her grip on the side, Avril sloshed through the shallows, grabbed the railing, pulled herself up and over. She landed with a wet splat on the flat wooden thwarts that served as seats. "Nina"—she looked back over the railing—"in which direction am I to sail? Which way is it to the continent?"

"Southeast, of course." Nina gave the boat one last shove. "You should reach your homeland in three days."

Avril would have to trust that she was telling the truth about the direction, since she was telling the truth about the distance. "Thank you." Sitting up, Avril took hold of the tiller, her heart thrumming with anxiety and excitement and gratitude and the first real hope she had felt in days. "I know you are breaking your laws by helping me."

"Do not worry for me, *utlending*." Nina almost had to shout to be heard over the crashing waves. "No one will know that I had aught to do with this. My friends are not about to hand me over to the council of elders." Her smile flashed in the moonlight. "And in a few days, after Hauk accepts that you have truly escaped, I will go and console him. Now off with you. Quickly." After a moment, she added, "The gods be with you and carry you safely to your daughter."

Nina picked up her wet, ruined silk skirts with regal grace and hurried back toward shore.

Avril turned her attention forward, shivering from the icy water that soaked her gown, her stomach bobbing as violently as the boat. She had often sailed alone in her youth—but never on a three-day journey across the sea. She had counted on having a crew of other women to help her.

She had counted on Josette.

Swallowing hard, she snatched up a rope and

lashed the tiller to the railing to keep the ship on a steady course. She did not need anyone's help. She would manage alone.

Quickly, one last time, she looked back, anguished that she had not even had a chance to bid her friend farewell. "*Adieu,* Josette," she whispered. "Be happy." Closing her eyes, she offered a quick prayer for her.

And added a plea that she herself would reach home and Giselle safely.

Then she stood and picked her way forward across the thwarts to take up the oars. Sitting amidships, she slid each oar into its pivot and started pulling on the smooth wooden handles.

But the tide was so strong, it felt as if she were trying to move a full-size warship all by herself. Her arms and back ached and her bare hands stung after only a few strokes. She kept at it, hauling on the oars, clenching her teeth, panting for breath.

Yet all her work scarcely moved the boat forward a dozen yards.

Cursing in frustration, she stopped trying to row, hung her head, panting for breath. The boat was too large for a woman to manage alone. Too heavy to make any headway against the surf. She shut her eyes, unwilling to believe she had come this far only to be halted by the very ship that should be carrying her home.

Home to Giselle.

Her sweet, bright-eyed Giselle, who might be crying herself to sleep even now, praying that her *maman* would return to her.

Avril lifted her head, flooded with determination.

She would not let *anything* keep her from reaching her little girl. Raising the oars, she pulled them back into the boat. Then she hurried aft, to the supplies Thorolf had stowed aboard.

He had lashed them in place; she yanked on the ropes and started dumping the chests and sacks and barrels over the side. One after another they hit the surface and sank. She was careful to keep the food and drinking water, but sent his riches and all the rest to the bottom of the bay.

The boat sat higher on the waves by the time she finished. When she reclaimed her place at the oars, she discovered to her relief that the lightened ship moved much faster over the water. Rowing still made her muscles painfully sore, but she began to gain distance from the beach.

With every rhythmic splash of the wooden poles against the water, Asgard faded into the night behind her, the island becoming naught but a dim shadow as she left it behind.

Left him behind.

She would never see Hauk Valbrand again.

Instead of bringing happiness or relief, that thought left her feeling strangely hollow inside. The idea of never again seeing one of Hauk's slow, reluctant smiles, or hearing his husky voice, or being surprised by his gentleness, or knowing his kiss filled her with a confusing tangle of emotions.

She would miss him. It made no sense at all, but she would miss the man who had brought her here against her will and held her captive.

Glancing over her shoulder, she refused to think on

it further. She was halfway between the shore and the fog-enshrouded rocks now. It was time to let out the sail. After taking in the oars, she leaped up and took a firm hold on the leech lines, yanking them free. The rectangular sail unfurled with a smooth snap and caught the wind.

Avril ducked under the foot of the sail as it swung around. The boat heeled hard onto its port beam, the rail dipping toward the sea. Struggling to keep her balance, she grabbed one of the halyards and made her way aft. She untied the rope she had knotted around the tiller and took a seat, using the halyard to hold the sail in place while grasping the tiller with her other hand.

Salty air and splashing, icy spray chilled her face and hands. The wind felt much colder this far out— and stronger. For a moment, she regretted throwing all of Thorolf's belongings overboard; she should have thought to look for a cloak and gloves. She did not want to escape the island only to die of exposure.

It was hard to remember that it was autumn everywhere else, after experiencing the summery warmth of Asgard.

But she could not regret the speed she had gained. In full sail, the lightened boat glided over the waves as fast as a skate over the ice. And it was not as hard as she had expected to control both the sail and the tiller. She guided the boat toward the twin rocks Nina had pointed out.

With the sea breeze tangling her hair and the island now far behind her, Avril felt a rush of confidence.

Then the first tendrils of fog curled around the boat.

And the circle of dark, giant rocks loomed ahead of her all at once—much faster than she had anticipated. With a stab of alarm, she suddenly realized her mistake.

Dumping Thorolf's supplies had helped her escape the pull of the tide, but without the extra ballast, the shallow-keeled boat was moving so fast that she would not have time to plot a safe path through the fog and the rocks, into the open passage.

She lunged for the sheets and leech lines to take up the sail. But before she could reach them, the wind shifted abruptly, sending the ship heeling over onto its opposite beam. Avril cried out, tumbling, the lines torn from her grip. The fog closed in, as swift and thick as a January blizzard. It blotted out the moon and stars. Left her in darkness.

Another gust of wind howled through the rocks and the boat skipped sideways, like a stone tossed over the waves by a mischievous child. She grabbed the rudder and held on with both hands. It fought her grasp like a living thing.

A fierce, cold draft blew in from leeward and she heard the sail rip. Looked up to see a towering wall of stone looming out of the mist off her starboard rail. A terrified oath tore from her. She threw her full weight against the tiller.

But could not change course fast enough.

"Mercy of God, nay!"

The boat's side sheared along the rock. She felt the entire vessel shudder with the impact. Heard wood scraping. Splintering. And still the treacherous winds forced the battered craft onward.

Avril could barely see through the cloak of fog—but she felt water sloshing around her feet.

Water bubbling in through a hole in the boat's side.

Stark terror drenched her. She relinquished her hold on the tiller, ran forward, and tore a flapping section of the sail's canvas free from the snarl of lines. She stuffed it in the breach, desperately trying to staunch the flow of the sea into the boat's wounded side.

For an instant, she thought of shouting for help—but knew she was too far from the island. Knew the shore was deserted. No one would hear her.

And nay, she would not give up! Not while there was even a chance she might escape. She could do this!

For Giselle's sake, she could do—

Before she could even complete the thought, a huge wave snatched the boat up like a toy, tossing it high and letting it fall. Avril felt herself dropping with the boat, heard her own scream fill the darkness.

A rock shattered the hull in two and Avril felt pain explode through her body. She hit the water, plunging into the depths with the broken remains of her ship. Stunned by the impact, she floated downward. Then panic made her fight the icy blackness.

She clawed her way to the surface. Broke above the waves and gasped one breath of salty air and fog and water before the merciless ocean overpowered her and pushed her under again.

Dear God, help me! She grabbed a piece of wood,

bobbed upward, but her muscles felt limp. Her body blazed with agony. She could not hang on. Her gown was too heavy, dragging her downward, the water so cold, her arms too weak from rowing.

From somewhere deep inside her, a panicked, desperate plea filled her mind and heart and soul.

Hauk, help me!

Hauk jerked Ildfast to a halt so suddenly that the startled destrier reared and danced sideways.

By Thor's hammer—*what was that?* It had sounded like Avril's voice.

As clear as if she were riding beside him. Breathing hard, he looked around in the darkness, saw only the silent cliffs, the sea far below. Heard only the wind and the distant sounds of the celebration in the night air.

But he *swore* he had heard Avril calling him.

Calling for help.

The fury and annoyance that had gripped him from the moment he found her missing abruptly shifted. To a far more disturbing, unfamiliar feeling.

Fear.

He dug his heels into the stallion's flanks, set off at a gallop along the cliff's edge, back toward town. He had checked his *vaningshus*, thinking she had simply gone home without him. Josette had suggested that as the most likely possibility when he questioned her.

But Hauk had not found his troublesome bride there. Or on the beach below.

And now another possibility pounded through him: Thorolf.

Hauk had not seen the knave at the celebration. Could not imagine him walking up and snatching Avril from the middle of the crowd. She would have screamed. Someone would have noticed. Everyone would have noticed. *He* would have noticed. He had been keeping close watch over her until he had been drawn into arguing with his uncle.

Avril would *never* have gone with Thorolf willingly. But if the whoreson had gotten his hands on her somehow, if he had hurt—

Hauk, help me.

Choking out a curse, Hauk yanked Ildfast to a halt again, his heart beating violently, his pulse thundering in his ears.

That was no trick of the wind! He had heard her clearly.

Not only heard her but . . . *felt* her. Felt a crashing wave of pain and icy terror and helplessness that washed over him—and vanished just as suddenly.

Shaken, trembling in the grip of those feelings, he could not pause to question where in the name of all the gods the unnerving sensation had come from. Or how it was possible.

Because he felt—*knew*—where she was in that moment.

His gaze was drawn to the fog-cloaked sea, to a distant point off the coast, north of town.

She was not with Thorolf.

She was out *there*. Alone. Helpless. Hurt.

He swore viciously and struck his boots against Ildfast's sides, sending the destrier leaping forward into a headlong, rock-spewing gallop. Hauk did not follow the road back to town, did not veer from the cliffs. Did not take his eyes from that spot offshore.

And did not hear her again.

He felt an icy numbness fill his veins and could not tell if the feeling was hers or his own. Racing along the cliffs at a lethally fast speed, he found an ancient footpath. He pulled hard on Ildfast's reins, threw himself from the saddle, and ran down the steep trail in the darkness until he reached the shore.

In the moonlight, he could see fresh footprints—two pairs. They led him to a jumble of underbrush, tree branches. And an abandoned anchor stone. A boat of some kind had been scraped across the sand.

What boat? How had she—

It did not matter now. She was out there, in trouble.

She might already be dead.

He kicked off his boots, looking out at the distant, fog-enshrouded rocks. It was too far. Too far to swim in the icy water. Especially at night. If fatigue did not finish him, the cold would. If he did not become confused in the darkness and drown first.

He threw his belt and weapons to the sand, ran for the water, and dove in.

With all his strength, he stroked through the waves, heading straight out from the place where the boat had been launched. Ignoring the cold that seeped into his bones, ignoring the powerful pull of the tide, he aimed himself at the rocks like an arrow.

Halfway to the wreath of fog, several hundred yards from shore, he began encountering wreckage. Chunks

of shattered oak planking. A broken oar. The curving
top of the prow.

"Avril!" he shouted, talons of fear sinking into
him. "Avril, where are you?"

There was no answer from the darkness. No way to
know where the ship had foundered.

Or if she had survived.

He forced that possibility to the back of his mind.
Kept swimming. Slashing through the cold depths.
Faster. Stronger. Farther out, where the wind picked
up, the surf became brutal. Waves pushed him back
until he was exhausted from fighting them and cold
air stole every breath he gasped. By the time he
reached the fog, his lungs burned and his strength was
nearly spent.

"Avril!"

He did not hear—or feel—any response. Could not
see her anywhere. Could not see at all as he kept
going, swimming deeper into the fog that choked all
light from the moon and stars. The savage winds here
gave him almost as much trouble as the treacherous
current.

And when he paused to call her name again, a
black wave surged over him from out of the darkness.
Plucked him up like a leaf. And carried him backward, slamming him into a rock. Sharp pain exploded
through his side.

He slid below the surface, awash in agony. But
even as the sea closed over his head, he furiously
clung to life, reaching out to the very rock that had
injured him, using it to drag himself back to the surface.

Lifting his head above water, he gasped for air. Every breath was torture. Broken ribs. He had felt the pain before. But identifying the source of the agony did not ease it. He tried forcing it to a distant corner of his mind but could not even breathe deeply enough to call out again.

Frustration and fear surged through him, colder and sharper than the wind and waves.

Avril! He did not know if it would work, *how* it could work, but he tried reaching out to her with his thoughts, with the riot of feelings inside him. *In the name of whatever god you hold dear, where are—*

Hauk . . .

Her voice this time was a scant, feeble whisper through his mind, like a tendril of mist. But he struck out in the direction it came from, swimming as well as he could across the water, his muscles and broken ribs objecting to every stroke and kick.

Finally he saw her—a small, dark form clinging to one of the rocks, barely visible above the waves.

Relief flooded through him. Relief and another emotion he did not have time to think about.

She was barely conscious, her dress ripped, her skin bloodied and bruised. She had found an outcropping to hold onto, clinging to it in a death grip, her other arm wrapped around a piece of the ship's thick mast. When he touched her, tried to ease her into his arms, she moaned in pain, would not release her grasp on the rock.

"Let go, Avril," he choked out. "I am with you. Let go."

A terrified, helpless sob wracked her—but the wind

and the fog swallowed even that sharp, broken sound. She let him pull her toward him.

Treading water, Hauk grabbed the piece of mast, grateful for any help he could get. Avril was shuddering with cold, as was he. Swimming out this far had been difficult enough; he did not know how they could survive the journey back.

Did not know if he had enough strength left to battle the waves for both of them.

Avril choked on a mouthful of water, gasped and coughed and thought she felt sand beneath her cheek.

Finally she opened her eyes. It was indeed sand. Grainy. Rough. She was on dry land. Dry, solid, blessed land! For a soaring, dizzying moment, all she knew was that she was alive.

And freezing.

It was still dark out. She tried to push herself up, but pain lanced through her body. Her every muscle hurt, her limbs stabbed by agony that wrenched a groan from her lips. She was shaking with bone-deep cold, her gown and hair soaked and dripping.

And somehow she had gotten all tangled up in rigging attached to a large section of the ship's planking. How had she . . .

She did not remember finding the makeshift raft. Or tying herself to it.

Slowly, dizzy with the pain, she managed to sit up and untangle herself from the knotted lines. Turning her head to look behind her, at the moonlit waves gently lapping the shore, she realized all at once that her escape had failed.

But before she could feel more than a single, piercing jolt of defeat and sorrow, she saw Hauk—sprawled in the sand a few yards up the beach.

He lay on his back, one arm flung out to the side.

God's breath. Had *he* saved her? Stumbling to her feet, she staggered over to him. Had he *swum* all that distance in the icy water? Risked his life to save hers?

"Hauk?"

He did not stir, did not respond. Dropping to her knees in the sand beside him, she touched his face.

And realized he did not seem to be breathing.

"Sweet holy Mary." She gasped, shifting her hand to his throat. "Hauk? *Hauk!*"

She could not find a pulse. Her own heart racing, she pressed her ear to his chest. Struggled to listen over the pounding of the surf. She thought she heard a single, faint beat.

But then she could hear naught more.

He was dead.

Shouting a wordless sound of horror, she straightened with a jerk, grasped his shoulders. "Hauk, wake up!" His skin was cold. She tried shaking him. "Damn you, Norseman, wake up! Wake up!" She slapped him. Could not rouse him.

He remained limp.

He had not risked his life to save her—he had lost it.

"Dear God!" she cried, lurching to her feet, shaking her head wildly. "Help! Someone—"

It was no use.

It was too late.

A sob rose from deep in her chest, full of a pain

sharper than the physical hurt that wrenched her body. Dazed, mad with confusion and denial and disbelief, she looked up and saw his horse on the cliff. Heart pumping, she ran toward the footpath, stumbling, her vision blurred by inexplicable tears. She had to get help. This could not be happening! He could not be dead. If she could get help—

"Avril!"

She staggered to a halt, stunned by the sound of that familiar voice behind her. Icy fingers skidded up her spine, lifting the fine hairs on the back of her neck.

Unable to speak, unable to breathe, she slowly turned around.

And saw Hauk sitting up. Slowly, struggling, he got to his feet.

Her mouth opened, but no sound would come out. She felt naught in that moment but the tears running down her face—tears she had shed for him.

Because he had *died*.

His features etched with pain, he walked toward her. "Avril? Are you all right?" He moved slowly, kept one hand pressed to his side—but he was very much alive.

"I-I . . ." She felt dizzy. She felt faint. "I-I am dreaming!" When she started to back away from him, he took her arm.

His grip was as strong as ever. His skin warm against hers. His eyes the same sky blue. His voice deep and steady. "You are not dreaming. You have been through a confusing ordeal—"

"But y-you were—"

"Avril—"

"Nay!" Terrified by what she had seen and heard and felt, she tried to pull away from him. "You were not breathing! I could not hear your heartbeat. You were—"

"Calm yourself—"

"*You were dead!*" Too many impossible facts crashed together all at once, sent the world spinning around her.

And suddenly she was no longer aware of the pain in her limbs or the weakness in her muscles or aught but a sensation of falling into darkness.

And Hauk catching her in his strong arms.

14

Hauk kicked the door shut behind him and carried Avril across his darkened *vaningshus*, pain stabbing his side in sharp bursts that made spots dance before his eyes. Every breath he gulped burned his lungs like fire, and a savage headache pounded between his temples with the force of Odin throwing angry thunderbolts. But he managed to reach the bed, lay her down gently before he sank onto the mattress beside her, gripping one of the bedposts to keep himself from lying down.

Grimacing, he gingerly probed his ribs, could not understand why or how he had awakened from the *langvarig sovn* trance before his injuries were fully healed.

But there was no time to question it; his heart pounding, he rose unsteadily to start a fire on the hearth. He had to care for Avril's wounds before seeing to his own. He would recover.

She might not.

When the flames glowed bright enough for him to see in the night-blackened chamber, he returned to her side.

He could not tell how badly she was hurt, did not

know if she had fainted from her injuries—or from shock. Quickly he worked the soaked, bloodied gown downward from her shoulders, tugging at the sodden laces. In truth, he felt grateful that she was unconscious at the moment. Not only because she would object to his disrobing her.

But because he did not look forward to persuading her that she had not witnessed what she had witnessed.

Anger crowded in on the pain that ravaged his senses. Anger at her—and at himself. He had had no choice, out in that freezing water, had not possessed strength enough to save her *and* himself. But the shock of seeing his miraculous recovery had been too much for her.

It was too soon. Too soon to entrust her with the truth about Asgard and its people. She had been here only a few days and had not yet had time to adjust. She was still determined to escape the island. To escape him.

So determined that she had taken an insane risk and almost gotten herself killed.

For that, he could only blame himself, he thought blackly, pulling her ruined garment down her body and tossing it to the floor. He never should have allowed her to leave his side. Not for a moment.

Seeing her flawless, pale skin in the firelight—now bruised and cut and bloodied—brought a sharp pain to his stomach, far worse than the throbbing in his side and his head. It hit him like a battering ram, this brutal reminder of how fragile, how tenuous her life was.

How inevitable it was that he would lose her.

He turned away, his throat burning. Not only from the seawater he had swallowed, but from unwanted emotions that choked him.

Damn her for putting her life in danger.

And for making him feel what he was feeling.

He moved to a nearby trunk, dug out a thick linen towel, then sat beside her once more. Careful not to wake her, he gently brushed the soft fabric over her chilled skin, trying to dry and warm her while he checked for broken bones.

To his relief, he found none. Some of the scrapes and cuts were deep, and he found several large, angry bruises, but her injuries did not appear life-threatening. She had been fortunate. This time.

Cold fear slid through him at the thought of what *could* have happened when the ship went down.

Forcing aside the gut-churning image, he pulled the bedcovers over her to keep her warm and then stood up—too fast.

Stabs of agony stole his breath. He grabbed the nearest bedpost, swaying on his feet. He pressed one hand to his rib cage and crossed to the far side of the chamber, to a chest near the corner where he kept his foodstuffs. Shoving aside the wedding gifts piled on top, he hunted inside until he found a bag of dried herbs, and some salve for her cuts.

As he made his way back through the darkness, he heard her stir, heard her moan in pain.

The sound cut through him like a blade. He returned to the bed quickly, his own injuries forgotten.

"Lie still," he ordered as he sat next to her, his

voice rough with concern. "You are hurt. Lie still and let me help you."

Still asleep, she kept moving her head restlessly, her wet hair almost black against the pillow. Then her lashes fluttered open.

When she looked up and saw him, her pupils constricted to black pinpricks in the firelight. She started to sit up, only to gasp in pain—then she abruptly seemed to realize she was naked beneath the blankets.

He resisted the urge to hold her still, knowing his touch might upset her further. "Avril, calm yourself. You are all right—"

"W-what happened?" She lay back down, staring at him. "You were—"

"What?" he asked innocently. "Will you please cease looking at me as if I were a ghost?"

"I-I thought you were *dead*."

Hauk uttered a scoffing sound, and at the same time he felt relief. Her voice was clear and steady, which helped reassure him that her injuries were not serious—and she seemed more worried for him than afraid of him.

"Obviously I was not," he said dryly, setting the bandages and herbs on the bedside table and opening the earthen jar of salve, "or I would not be sitting here beside you, would I?"

Her brow furrowed.

For once, he felt grateful that Avril was a woman of keen intelligence; she could not argue with simple logic.

He only wished he knew what she was thinking—and he wondered what in the name of Loki had happened to the connection he had felt between them earlier; when her life had been in danger, he had experienced her thoughts, her emotions.

Now he could not tell what she was feeling.

"I could not find your pulse," she said a bit uncertainly. "I listened for your heartbeat—"

"And you were distraught from your ordeal. And in pain. Mayhap you had seawater in your ears." He shrugged as if it were all nonsense, took her hand, and gently started applying the salve to her cuts and scrapes. "With the surf so loud, I am surprised you could hear at all. Avril, you need to sleep now."

He met her gaze, silently willing her to stop asking questions and get the rest she urgently needed.

Blinking up at him with those keen emerald eyes, she was the picture of abject confusion.

And stubbornness. She kept trying to sort out the conflicting evidence. "I tried shaking you," she said slowly. "I even slapped you."

He glanced away. So *that* was why he had roused too soon. "We both blacked out. You awoke first." He took her other hand, applying the salve lightly, gently to her palm, her arm, her shoulder. "And your manhandling succeeded in waking me."

Setting the salve down, he wove his fingers through hers, entwining their hands. "Could a dead man touch you like this?" he asked in a deep, soft voice.

Spots of bright pink colored her pale cheeks, and a more familiar wariness replaced the bewilderment in her eyes.

She pulled her hand from his, turning her face away, toward the closed shutters.

"I am . . . grateful that you are all right," she said haltingly. "Thank you for saving my life, Hauk." She gathered the covers to her chin. "How did you find me? How did you know where I was, out there in the fog?"

"I heard you calling for help." His heart thudded at the memory, and he quickly changed the subject before either of them could further examine *that* strange facet of their ordeal. "It is not important now. I need you to tell me if this hurts." He lifted the blanket, lightly touched a particularly angry bruise on her stomach.

She flinched away and squeezed her eyes shut.

Her pain at the gentle brush of his fingertips made his gut wrench tight. "I am sorry, Avril. You will be all right, I promise. All you need is to sleep and let yourself heal." He picked up the jar of salve. "I will take care of you."

Her lashes fluttered open, but she kept her face turned away. Her lower lip quivered. "I do not want you to take care of me. I can—"

"Take care of yourself?" he asked tightly. "So you have said. But I believe your ill-advised adventure tonight proves you wrong." His anger simmered again. "What were you *thinking,* woman? What made you believe you could sail through that maze of rocks and fog by yourself? You could have—"

"Escaped," she whispered, her voice wavering.

He swallowed the rest of his rebuke, equally maddened and impressed by her courage. Her determination.

Her unwavering devotion to her plan to leave him.

"You cannot do everything alone," he said gruffly. Looking down at his headstrong bride, snuggled safely in his bed, he felt a wave of protectiveness. She needed someone to take care of her, this tempestuous, bold, vulnerable lady.

She needed him.

Whether she wanted to admit it or not.

Gently, being careful of her modesty, he pulled the blankets aside a bit further, so he could continue applying the healing salve. She flinched, then remained absolutely still. And silent.

He touched her without speaking, not even allowing himself to think as he treated her cuts and scrapes. Working briskly, he finished in a matter of moments.

And felt as if every beautiful inch of her had been branded onto his hands.

After drawing the covers back over her, he set the jar down on the table—a bit too sharply—and stood up, fighting another wave of dizziness. Biting back a pained curse, he stepped toward the hearth and reached for a small copper cookpot.

He filled it with fresh rainwater from the barrel and then suspended it from a hook over the fire.

"Tell me, Avril," he said when he trusted himself to speak evenly, "how did you come to be in possession of a boat?"

For a moment, he did not think she would answer.

"I found it," she said evasively.

Hauk picked up the bag of herbs and took a cup from its place on the shelf. "And how did you happen to *find* a boat?"

She remained silent.

"Avril, I saw two sets of footprints. Who helped you?" He glanced over his shoulder at her.

She regarded him with a familiar, mutinous spark in her eyes. "I am not going to tell you. I do not think the person who helped me deserves to be punished for it."

"I beg to differ," he said with a growl. "Whoever was trying to help the *vokter*'s bride leave Asgard needs to have a few of our laws explained to him. By the *vokter*."

Her gaze shifted to the weapons displayed behind him on the wall. "Now I am definitely not going to tell you."

He muttered an oath but decided not to press her further until she was well. Turning back to the hearth, he used an iron poker to tip the steaming cookpot and pour hot water into the cup. Then he scooped a spoonful of herbs into it and sat on the edge of the bed.

He slid a hand beneath Avril's pillow to support her head, holding the cup to her lips. "Drink this."

Sniffing at it, she made a face and hesitated.

"I hardly intend to poison you," he said dryly, "after spending half this night in freezing water trying to save your life and earning a few broken ribs for my trouble. Drink."

Eyes narrowing at his scolding, she took a sip. She wrinkled her nose at the taste but drained the cup without protest.

He let her head down gently, then moved back to

the hearth, where he made a second cup of the brew for himself, sighing. "Avril, you are my wife—"

"Your captive," she corrected quietly.

"On second thought, poisoning you does possess a certain appeal." He gulped a mouthful of the tea, felt it burn down his throat. "You are the most stubborn, most troublesome female I have ever—"

"If you find me disagreeable," she suggested lightly, "you could let me go."

"Nay. That I can never do." He scowled at her. "Do you understand what that word means? *Never.*" He set the cup on the table with a crack that echoed through the dark chamber.

Stalking away from her, into a far corner, he peeled off his still-damp leggings, toweled dry, and changed into a fresh pair.

Then he returned to the bed.

And lay down on the other side.

It was mayhap a measure of how tired she was or how much pain she was in that she did not object.

Even if she had, he thought in annoyance, he was not going to spend the night on the floor. Not when he had broken ribs. He remained atop the covers. And it was a large bed. There was ample distance between them.

"I have been too lenient with you," he said, half to himself. "It is time to cease this foolishness about escape, once and for all. You are my wife, you will not be leaving, and you must accept that."

"I will never stop trying to get home," she whispered fiercely. "I cannot stay here. And I do not *want* to be your wife."

"Indeed, milady?" he asked mockingly, turning his head to stare at her across the pillows. "Were those not tears I saw in your eyes, tonight on the beach, when you thought I was dead?"

She looked away, toward the hearth. *"Nei."*

He grimaced up at the rafters. "I should have known that would be the first word of Norse you learned to use."

"If you thought you saw tears," she said stiffly, "it must have been seawater. Mayhap it affected my *eyes* as well as my hearing."

Hauk responded only with an irritated grumble, too tired to argue with her any more. Too tired even to feel any stirrings at sharing a bed with his wife for the first time, lying so close to her lush, naked body. Separated from her only by the covers.

Which was a sign of just how badly he needed sleep, he thought blackly. He closed his eyes and lay still, drifting downward into soothing darkness.

Until he heard quiet, snuffling sounds from her side of the bed.

He opened his eyes, glanced toward her. Her whole body was trembling.

"Avril?" Alarm shot through him. "What is wrong?"

She kept her face turned away, lifted a hand to cover her eyes.

And he realized she was not suffering a spasm of pain.

She was crying. Struggling to hold back tears.

"Y-you are . . . right," she said hoarsely, a tortured breath escaping with each word. "I may never

. . . be able to leave here. I may never see my home
or . . . my daughter again."

A single, deep sob slipped out.

Hauk could not move, robbed of his senses. It was
the first time he had heard her admit even the *possibility* of defeat.

But he did not feel relief that she was facing the
facts at last. The sight of her in despair, lying there
alone and hurt and fighting so hard to keep it all
inside, tore at him. Made him hate himself—almost
as much as she must hate him for taking her away
from her little girl.

And suddenly the tears overwhelmed her, wrenching sobs that she could not hold back, though she
buried her face in both hands.

Hauk felt every fiber of his being drawn up tight,
felt as if his limbs were held fast by iron bonds. He did
not know what to do, did not know how he could
comfort her.

But he could not lie there in silence while she
suffered alone.

He reached out, touched her shoulder.

And instead of flinching away or cursing him as he
had expected, she allowed him to pull her close, just
as she had in the water earlier tonight.

He gathered her to him with the blankets, offering
her his strength and his silence, stunned that she
would accept solace from the very man responsible for
her pain.

She cried her tears against his chest, her body shaking with the force of her sorrow, and he shut his eyes,
burned by each salty droplet.

By Odin, he could not allow her to continue suffering this way. Somehow, he had to persuade her to accept what could not be changed.

Even if it meant a bit of yielding on his part. If he wanted her to accept her new life, he had to fulfill the vows he had taken.

For her sake, and her safety, he must do what all the other grooms on Asgard had been doing the past three days.

On the morrow, he would begin wooing his wife . . . with care and gentleness and affection.

With his whole heart.

The pain was gone. That was the first thing Avril became aware of as she slowly awakened. Her last memory was of feeling shattered and hurt, but now she felt rested, whole.

Safe.

Mayhap because she was still lying in Hauk's arms.

That made her open her eyes with a start. The first glimmer of dawn had crept in through cracks in the shutters, forcing its way into the dark *vaningshus* and lightening the room's shadows. She did not move a muscle, realizing he was still asleep. He lay with one arm beneath her pillow, the other a slack, heavy weight over her waist. She could feel his chest rising and falling evenly beneath her cheek, his breath soft in her hair.

His body warm and solid against hers, even with the blankets wrapped around her.

For a moment, she let herself remain there. Just for a moment. It felt so good to be engulfed in his strength and warmth and reassurance; it had been so long since she had allowed herself to be held like this. Allowed a man to soothe and protect her.

To care for her.

She blinked hard as the faint morning light blurred in her vision, remembering how he had risked his life to save hers. Her heartbeat unsteady, she lifted her head, looking at his bronzed, chiseled features, so peaceful in sleep.

A tingling ache filled her as she remembered all that had happened last night, how the terror of almost drowning had left her so disoriented, she had mistakenly thought he was dead.

How she had cried for him.

Then later turned to him for comfort when she felt so alone and full of despair.

And he had offered the solace she sought. Gently, silently. Was he even aware of how tender he could be? She found herself reluctant to leave his arms, to resume their endless battle of wills.

Dear God, what was wrong with her? She was acting like a woman who had lost her wits, like a woman—

She stiffened, remembering Josette's comment about the early days of her marriage to Gerard, how she had fallen in love with him slowly, almost without noticing.

Trembling, she pulled away from Hauk, trying to quickly unwrap herself from his hold and the twisted blankets. He made a sound in his sleep and his arm flexed around her, pulling her closer again. She uttered a whimper of distress and he opened his eyes.

She held her breath, mortifyingly aware that her efforts to get free had only bared her to the waist. Her breasts were flattened against his chest, softness against steely muscle, pale ivory against bronzed darkness.

He blinked, waking rapidly, his eyes uncommonly blue in the scant, gray illumination of morning.

"Are you all right?" His voice was soft, low. Husky with sleep.

"Aye. The pain is gone."

She almost clarified that she meant her physical pain but did not want to remind him of the other, deeper pain that had made her sob in his arms last night.

Instead, she tried to sound calm. Unaffected by his embrace. "You can let me go now."

He did not speak, that azure gaze tracing over her face, her hair, her cheeks.

Her heart started thrumming. She had seen that look before. "Hauk—"

"Nay," he said, his voice deep, slow. "I cannot." His hand moved up her bare back, pressing her closer. "I will not let you go." His lips brushed over her temple.

Her breath caught. "Hauk, please . . ." Instead of sounding calm and cool, as she intended, the words came out wavering. Hot.

"Nay, sweet wife." His voice sounded rough. His other hand twined through her hair, gently pulling her head back until her mouth tilted up to his. "I will not let you go. Not until I have shown you how a proper Asgard husband bids his bride good morning."

"But you are not—"

His lips stole her protest, covering hers in a deep kiss, a mating of their mouths, a slow, hungering penetration of his tongue. She breathed him in, tasted him—spicy and potent and *male*. Even as she flattened her hands against his chest, tried to gain her freedom, she was shocked to realize that the trembling in her body had naught to do with fear or protest.

And he seemed to realize it too. A deep sound of passionate approval rumbled beneath her palms. And when he finally lifted his head, she could feel his body rigid with strain against hers.

"You—" She could not utter more than that one word before he kissed her again, a light, teasing kiss this time. "—are not—" A rain of teasing kisses left her dizzy. "—my h-h—"

"Husband."

Avril could not voice a denial—because what she saw in his eyes robbed her of her ability to speak. Or breathe.

She saw tenderness and yearning that matched her own, saw the same caring and need she felt for him. And passion that had darkened his pale-blue eyes to a color like the sky lit by the sun's hottest rays.

It was the look she had seen in her dreams.

She parted her lips, unable to utter a sound.

"Avril . . ." Still lying on his side, holding her close with one arm, he lifted his other hand to caress her cheek. "There is no shame in needing what you need . . . what I need. And there is no point in being alone when we could be . . ." He slowly drew her mouth toward his.

Still he did not kiss her, pausing, his lips so close to hers that she felt his breath as he completed the sentence.

"Together."

He awaited her reply. She shuddered and closed her eyes, hearing a far different note in his voice than she had ever heard before. Request. Entreaty. As if he were not demanding that she accept him, but asking.

"*Together,*" she whispered, all the longing in her heart spilling into that one word.

She heard a low moan that might have been hers or his or both. He kissed her, rolling onto his back, pulling her atop him in a jumble of blankets and her long hair that fell around them in a cascade. His broad hands cupped her face, holding her still while he sampled and explored her mouth in the most leisurely, arousing way, as if he meant to spend the entire morning learning her taste.

She shivered at the feel of his stubbled, unshaven jaw abrading her skin. Felt herself melting against him, afire with emotions that made her heart pound, enflamed by the intoxicating sensations that each movement of his lips sent coursing through her.

God's mercy, she should feel terrified at the heat of his body against her naked breasts, the fact that the covers were bunched around her hips, the hard shape of his arousal pressed against her thigh. The blankets and the leggings he wore created only the most fragile barrier between them, one he could dispense with in a heartbeat.

Yet she knew no fear. She parted her lips for him, welcomed the velvety, languid probing of his tongue, did not pull away when his hands moved up and down her back, kneading, stroking. She knew it was wrong of her. Wrong for so many reasons.

But she felt alive, in a way she had not felt in so many years. This maddening, gruff, tender Norseman stirred her soul. He breathed *life* into her. She did not understand, uttered a soft, bewildered sound against his mouth, knew only that she did not want the feeling to end.

His touch became stronger, his hands shaping her body with slow, erotic purpose, and fire darted through her.

She felt the backs of his fingers brush the side of her breast, and she gasped. His hands lifted her, urging her upward, and she complied shamelessly, arching her back, raising herself above him so that he could suckle her.

At first he took only a taste, flicking his tongue over one tight peak, then the other. Then suddenly he drew her soft fullness deeply into his mouth.

She cried out, the exquisite sensation like having that sensitive, feminine part of her held captive in hot silk. She had to brace her hands against the mattress, panting as he laved the hard pearl with his tongue, nibbling, pressing it against his teeth. Feasting on her. She trembled above him as he kindled a fire that raced through her blood.

His hard, powerful body shuddered beneath her. His breathing had become ragged. Yet he sought no pleasure for himself, only for her, teasing her nipples

with kisses, with his fingers, brushing his stubbled
cheek against them, dragging sharp sounds of need
from her.

When she tried to move, he wrapped one arm
around her to hold her fast, lavishing attention on her
breasts until the taut, wet crowns felt as aroused, as
sensitive as the throbbing flesh between her thighs.

And then he touched her there, slid his hand between their bodies until his fingers found the damp,
feminine core of her being. White-hot flames of pleasure seared her at every caress of his fingertips. Every
touch of his tongue.

The dual attention soon had her writhing in his
embrace, her hands gripping the sheets, her entire
body strung tight. He caught one peak in his mouth
and drew it in, hard and fast, the suction intense and
startling. Fierce, stabbing pleasure went through her.
He released it slowly, using his tongue to drag her
nipple against his teeth.

She gasped, her body arching into his, wanting
more of the extraordinary sensations. Wanting . . .
needing . . .

He repeated the strangely erotic motion, again and
again—sudden and slow, in and out, while his fingers
stroked the dampness between her thighs. Her eyes
widened in astonishment as whirls of flame gathered
deep within her, spinning tight. Tighter.

"Hold your breath," he ordered hoarsely.

She obeyed his rough command, gulping in air as
he continued the sweet, intense torment, faster.
Harder. Until she could not bear it any more. She
held her breath and felt her whole body rising. Reach-

ing. Felt a shudder begin inside her, from the very depths of her womb.

He caught her nipple between the edges of his teeth.

And a blinding burst of fire exploded within her, shattered the whole world, sent pieces of it blazing through her, inside her. The stunning force of it brought a sharp exclamation from her throat as waves of ecstasy broke over her, cascades of heat that claimed her breath, her body, until she was beyond thought, burned to cinders. Falling.

When she finally returned to awareness, she was draped over him like a blanket, limp. Sheened with sweat and still trembling from tiny sparks of sensation that rippled from her tender, aching breasts, from all her most secret, feminine places. Never had she experienced such a forceful release. Never.

Dear God, never.

Hauk nuzzled her ear. "Good morning," he murmured wickedly.

She could only utter a wordless groan in reply, felt as if her very bones had melted.

He chuckled, a low sound of male satisfaction, arching his hips. She inhaled a ragged breath, aware of the hard length of his arousal through the layers of fabric that separated them.

"Now," he whispered, "allow me to show you—"

A sharp knock at the door interrupted him.

He cursed. Vividly. Avril slid off of him, clutching the blankets to her throat, scarlet heat in her face as the world suddenly collided with the dreamy haze of passion he had woven around her. "It is probably Marta," she whispered, "come to visit Floyel."

The knock sounded again, louder.

Hauk sat up, took a deep breath. "Not unless she has grown larger and stronger since yesterday."

He rose and stalked to the door, looking ready to pound senseless whoever had dared intrude on them at this hour.

Avril could not think of who it might be, too overwhelmed with embarrassment to think at all.

What had she done? Only yesterday she had looked with dismay at the women who had allowed themselves to be bedazzled by their captors.

And now she had done the same. Thrown reason to the winds. Acted as wanton, as hopelessly in love as they had. She did not even know herself anymore.

She heard a male voice at the entrance, babbling in Norse—then she barely had time to gather the covers around her as Keldan rushed in, looking disheveled and wild-eyed, with Hauk right at his heels. Keldan took one quick glance around the room and his expression became even more alarmed.

Avril got up from the bed, clutching the covers around her. "What is it? What has happened?"

Hauk managed to silence Keldan long enough to translate for her, his eyes full of concern as they met hers. "Josette is missing."

15

"*Stille!* Quiet!" Hauk held up both hands, unable to think with both Keldan and Avril filling the air with frantic questions in two different languages. He could barely hear over the pounding of his own heart. "Tell me what happened," he told Keldan in Norse. "Calmly."

"I woke up and she was gone!" The younger man raked his fingers through his hair, his dark eyes wide, his words tumbling out. "She was not in the town. I thought she might be here. I thought—"

"Kel, I told you to keep watch over her. I told you Thorolf might come seeking vengeance for his punishment by the *eldrer*—"

"*Ja,* and I *did* keep watch over her!" Keldan retorted. "I never left her alone for a moment yesterday. I made certain she was safe."

"When did you see her last?" Hauk dared to hope that Thorolf might not have her.

"When we left the celebration last night, not long after you did. She looked distraught after you talked to her, and I was exhausted from the wrestling matches, so I took her home. And I . . ." He paced away and back like a caged animal. "By Tyr's blade, I should not have taken on so many opponents. But you have no idea what it was like, being with her all day without *being* with her—"

"*Ja*, Kel, no idea at all." Hauk glanced at Avril, his body still afire from their interrupted lovemaking.

She was still clothed only in the blankets, her hair falling about her bare shoulders in waves that clung to her perspiration-sheened skin. Her green eyes dark with worry, she kept glancing from one of them to the other. "What is he saying?" she demanded in French.

Hauk held up a hand to quiet her, just as Keldan's gaze skipped from Avril in the blankets to the mussed bed, to her gown discarded on the floor.

"By great Thor's bearded goats," he choked out, giving Hauk a curious, disbelieving look. "Have I—"

"Interrupted a most pleasant morning. *Ja*, but never mind that now. What happened after you and Josette returned to your *vaningshus*?"

"I fell asleep," he moaned. "I was so accursedly tired, I fell asleep—"

"What is he *saying*?" Avril repeated.

"Mayhap she left me." Keldan sank into a chair, holding his head in both hands. "Mayhap I frightened her in the meadow yesterday. It may have been too soon for her. Mayhap she is hiding from me. Mayhap I—"

"What has happened to Josette?" Avril all but shouted.

Hauk turned toward her and translated what Keldan had told him.

Her expression troubled, she shook her head. "She has not left him. Not of her own will."

"How can you be so certain?"

"Because she . . . we had . . . I had . . ." She stopped herself, then muttered an oath and said the rest all at once, her gaze on the floor. "We had an escape plan. I was going to take your ship and lead the other captives in an escape, except that all the other captives decided they did not wish to escape—"

"My ship?" Hauk stared at her, stunned and angry. "And who told you where to find my ship? The same person who helped you try to escape last night?"

"It is not important now! What I am trying to tell you is that Josette did not want to leave. No matter how I tried to reason with her, she would not come with me. She . . ." Avril glanced at Keldan. "She refused to leave him. I think she is in love with him."

Hauk took a deep breath before he turned to translate that quietly for Keldan—who came out of his chair with a start, looking even more agitated and fearful. "If that is true, then Thorolf *must* have taken her."

"But you said she was safely in your *vaningshus* last night when you fell asleep. Why would she have left?"

"I do not know. It makes no sense. Unless . . . she looked worried after you spoke with her at the celebration. After you asked her where Avril had gone."

"*Ja,* and she told me that Avril had probably come back here." He turned to Avril, shifting to French. "Was Josette to help with your escape last night?"

"Nay, she did not *know* that I meant to escape last night." Eyes widening, Avril sank down on the edge of the mattress. "But she *had* pledged to help me," she said unsteadily. "And she felt so guilty for not coming with me, she may have come looking for me—"

"And run into Thorolf instead."

Avril looked stricken. "It is my fault! God's blood, would he hurt her? Would he—"

"I do not know." Hauk kept his back to Keldan, did not want to translate what they were saying.

"Hauk, we have to find her!" Avril rose from the bed, her fingers white on the blankets clutched around her shoulders. "Where would he—" She gasped. "His *boat*. Hauk, it was Thorolf's boat I took last night!"

"What?" Hauk exclaimed in disbelief. "What would Thorolf be doing with—"

"What is it?" Keldan demanded.

Avril rushed on. "The boat was his, loaded with supplies. I threw them over the side and took it." She pressed a shaking hand to her forehead. "God's breath, if only I had told you everything last night—"

"That does not matter now." Hauk clenched his jaw, glancing worriedly at Keldan and trying to think of *what* in the name of Loki's black heart Thorolf was planning. "If Thorolf intends to take Josette and leave Asgard—"

"And his ship is in pieces washing up on shore," Avril said hollowly. "Where would he get another?"

"Mine. He would take mine." Hauk was already moving, hunting for his weapons and his traveling pack. "It is the only ship left on Asgard, unless he has another I do not know about."

"Hauk, we have to stop him! We have to—"

"*You* are not going anywhere, milady." Dismissing

that dangerous idea with a stern look, he quickly, reluctantly translated their conversation for Keldan.

Who immediately headed for the display of weapons on the wall and grabbed a sword.

"Kel, wait—"

"I will *kill* him if he has touched her!" Keldan jerked his arm away when Hauk tried to reclaim the sword.

"*Nei*, you are not going to kill anyone."

Avril cleared her throat. "I wonder if the two of you might grant me a moment's privacy so I can don a few clothes?"

Hauk glanced at her, surprised that she did not argue about the order he had given her. "Of course," he said gratefully. Nodding, he grasped Keldan's shoulder, hauling his friend toward the door.

Outside, the bright sunlight dazzled his eyes, and the sound of the surf and seabirds made it seem deceptively like any other idyllic, tranquil Asgard morning.

Keldan shrugged off his restraining hand. "Take the blade if you will, Hauk. I will tear him apart with my bare hands—"

"And break the most sacred of our laws."

"I do not care!" Keldan was already striding toward his horse.

Hauk caught his shoulder. "Kel, you are a carpenter, not a warrior. *I* will go after Thorolf. You return to town, alert everyone, and have them ride out to search the rest of the island. There is a chance he might have taken her somewhere else—"

"But it is most likely he is heading for the cove where you keep your *knorr*. He might already be there. He might already have . . ." He shut his eyes, lost the rest of the sentence in an agonized oath.

Hauk tightened his hand on his friend's shoulder, his gut knotting. "He would not harm her, Kel," he said more quietly, "not on Asgard soil. His fear of the *eldrer* is too great. And he would not have gone through the forest at night, when the wolves hunt. Thorolf may be a black-hearted knave, but he is not witless. He would have waited until this morn to enter the woods."

"Which means he has been in the woods for more than an hour." Keldan glanced up at the sun. "And it will take us at least an hour to get there."

"*Ja*, but I take a shorter route through the forest than the path everyone else knows. I can reach the cove before he even—"

"*We* can. If we leave now." Keldan stalked toward his horse, jumped nimbly onto the animal's bare back. "I am going with you."

Before Hauk could try to dissuade him, a sound behind them made him turn around to see Avril striding out his front door—dressed in a billowy white linen tunic, tucked into a pair of his leggings cinched at the waist with one of his belts. Leather boots and gloves completed the outrageous outfit. A sheathed knife hung from her belt, and she carried a crossbow in one hand.

Speech eluded him for a full minute. "What in the name of Loki do you think you are you *doing*, woman?"

"I did exactly what I said—I donned a few clothes." She set the crossbow in the grass and reached up to tie a thong around her loosely plaited hair. "The boots and gloves were a wedding gift, and with a few of your garments, I am ready to set out—"

"You will not *be* setting out," Hauk managed to say, though his heart was in his throat. "You will be turning around. Go back inside, take off those outlandish garments, and await my return."

"Hauk, please." She tossed her braid back over her shoulder, her eyes earnest as they held his. "I am not very good at sitting and waiting while everyone around me rides off into danger. And I cannot remain here while my closest friend's life is at stake. Especially when *I* may be responsible for getting her into this situation in the first place—"

Keldan interrupted. "Are we going?"

Hauk turned on him. "*I* am going. I am the *vokter*. The responsibility is mine—"

"And the responsibility for Josette is mine," Keldan retorted. "I am the one who took a vow to protect her. If I had been more careful—"

"You could not have known she would walk out in the middle of the night."

"While we all stand here arguing"—Avril came between them—"Josette is in danger."

Hauk grated out a curse. There was not time for this. He made a decision. "Keldan, ride to town and tell everyone to start searching the island—"

"*Nei.*"

"And while you are there, gather up four or five of the men who went with us to Antwerp, the ones I taught to use weapons. They should still have the blades they carried with them on the voyage. Send one of them back here to watch over Avril, and take the rest with you and follow the common path through the woods. That is the way Thorolf would have gone. If you encounter him . . ."

Looking up at his friend, who was more at home carving or sanding wood than wielding a weapon, he did not know what advice to give.

"Be careful. Keep your heads about you. Capture him and leave his fate for the council to decide, if you can . . . but do what you must to save your lady. I will leave at once and secure the boat before he can reach it. Rendezvous at the cove at midday."

Jaw clenched, Keldan dug his heels into his stallion's sides and set off at a gallop.

"Where is he going?" Avril asked. "What—"

"He is going for help. I am going through the forest by a faster way than the path Thorolf would have taken." Hauk grabbed Avril's elbow. "As for *you*, milady—"

"Alone?" She wrested her arm from his grip, her eyes, her voice full of concern for him. "You are going alone?"

His throat tightened. "Aye." Instead of trying to recapture her, he headed for Ildfast's stall. "The people of Asgard are not accustomed to facing animals more dangerous than the chickens in their cookpots or the reindeer they milk in the mornings. And most have never used a weapon. If I were to take anyone along, they would only slow me down and most likely shoot themselves in the foot with their own crossbow or end up as food for the wolves."

"I will go with you," she insisted, following at his heels.

He grabbed a bridle from its iron hook. "Avril, are you not listening?" he demanded impatiently. "Anyone with a speck of intelligence avoids the western forest—"

"I am an experienced huntress. I know how to use this." She rested the crossbow over her shoulder. "I have taken down wolves before. And wild boar and full-grown stags. You do not have to worry about me."

Hauk's fingers clenched around the leather of the bridle as he slid the bit between Ildfast's teeth. As much as he might admire Avril's courage and loyalty to her friend, he also knew the fragile, vulnerable lady hidden beneath that boldness.

And he *was* worried about her. Her life had become important to him, in a way that had little to do with vows or duty.

She had become important to him.

"Avril," he said tightly, unlatching the stall door and leading his destrier out. "I am grateful for the offer, but I do not need your help. I do not need—"

"Anyone?" Holding his gaze, she planted one gloved hand on her hip. "As someone said to me last night, you cannot do everything alone."

He scowled, sweeping a glance over her masculine garb and her weapons and her intrepid stance.

But instead of being impressed by her strength and fortitude, as she no doubt intended, he only found himself painfully aware of how very soft and feminine she was, the garments accenting her slender waist and lush curves . . . her breasts unbound beneath the tunic, the taut crowns chafed by the fabric, still sensitive from the attentions of his hands and mouth but a few wild, sweet moments ago.

Heat rivered through him. "I had intended to spend the day making love to you," he said with regret.

She blushed furiously and looked down at her boots. "I . . . what we shared this morn was . . ." Closing her eyes, she left the sentence unfinished. "Hauk, we have to go."

Wrenched by conflicting needs, he reached out to tilt her head up. He did not want to take her into the path of danger. And until Thorolf had been captured and brought before the council to answer for breaking the laws, Hauk needed to keep his mind on his duty.

Impulsively he drew her against him and gave her a quick, hard kiss. "You will be safer here. Keldan is sending someone to stay with you." Turning, he tossed the reins over Ildfast's head and leaped up onto the destrier's broad back.

She grabbed a handful of the stallion's mane. "Hauk, if you leave me behind, I will only go into the woods by myself and try to help her!"

"I could tie you up," he threatened, exasperated. "Carry you inside and tie you to the bed—"

"And I would fight you and we would waste more valuable time."

He swore. "Stubborn, reckless, willful—"

"True. All true," she conceded, reaching up to him with one hand. "So you had best keep a close watch on me personally, *ja?*"

He glowered down at her, provoked and astounded

at her audacity. He did not know which he wanted more: to turn her over his knee or pull her into his arms and kiss her senseless.

With an oath, he grabbed her arm and helped her up behind him. "Someday soon, milady—"

"You will come to your senses and realize I am entirely too much trouble and set me free." She gingerly wrapped her arms around his waist. "But for now we need to reach the cove as quickly as possible."

Midmorning sunlight spiraled down to the forest floor, spattering the fallen leaves and grass and gnarled roots with cascades of brightness that whirled past in a blur. Avril kept her arms locked around Hauk as he guided Ildfast at a swift pace through towering oaks and dark evergreens that looked ancient, their massive trunks four and five feet wide, their bark almost black.

They had left the fields behind more than an hour ago, riding into the shadowy depths of the forest, where the thatch of branches high overhead made the air feel cool and damp. They followed no path that Avril could make out, but Hauk clearly knew exactly where he was going, his attention on the trees as if he followed some secret marks that served as guideposts only he could see.

She became only distantly aware of the direction they took, the pungent scent of pine in the air, the rhythmic drumming of the stallion's strides. Her heart beating hard, she kept watch for any wolfish shapes that might appear out of the shadows.

Especially after she heard the first howl—an eerie,

hollow cry rising and then falling, distant but unmistakable, answered by another wolf somewhere unseen.

A large fox darted past and gave her a scare at one point, but after riding half the morning, they had encountered naught more threatening than a few partridges, some curious rabbits, and a herd of small red deer.

Still, she remained tense, ready to grab the crossbow slung over her shoulder by its leather strap. "I do not understand," she said nervously. "If the wolves here are such a threat, why do you not kill them?"

Her mouth was so close to his ear, she did not even have to shout to be heard over the wind that tugged at her plaited hair.

"Because if we killed the wolves, then the smaller animals would increase until they ran riot," Hauk told her without looking back at her. "Then the plants would be destroyed. And there is no way to know what might happen next. We are careful not to tip the scales of nature in one direction or another."

"Because you might destroy the island's healing qualities."

"Aye." He flicked a glance at her over his shoulder. "We care for the island and the island cares for us."

She considered that for a time, as they cantered through the maze of trees. "And why is it that your people do not carry weapons? Does no one ever go hunting?"

For a moment he did not answer.

"Peace is important among us," he said simply, "and it is impossible to have peace if every man is armed, so weapons and violence are outlawed."

"But I had always thought that the Norse were by nature a . . . a . . ."

"A race of savage marauders, bent on pillaging and destruction?"

"That is certainly the reputation you had earned over the centuries," she said defensively.

"That is the reputation our raiding ancestors earned for us," he corrected. "But most of our people lived as peaceful farmers or craftsmen. And for all the Norsemen who went abroad in search of plunder, others went in search of trade and new sea routes and new lands."

"Like this one." Avril fell silent for a moment. She heard a note of wistfulness in his voice; it reminded her that the people of Asgard were the last of their kind.

Reminded her once more of how important it was to them that they remain hidden here, safe from the world.

"I believe you would find Asgard a pleasant place, if you would give it a chance." Hauk glanced back at her over his shoulder, a quick, heated locking of their gazes. "A most pleasant place."

She looked away, suddenly, vividly reminded of what had happened between them this morn—and acutely aware of Hauk's body against hers now, so hard and powerful, his muscles flexing as he guided Ildfast.

Aware of how her arms barely encircled his rib cage; how the horse's canter caused a rhythmic friction between them; how her breasts, pressed against his back, still felt so sensitive and tight from his urgent kisses.

She ducked her head, thankful he could not see her scarlet face. The destrier's hoofbeats made the only sound for a long time, the sunlight splintering through the branches overhead, Avril's mind splintering into a dozen troubling thoughts.

Above all else, worry for Josette tore at her heart. Shutting her eyes, she offered another desperate prayer for her friend's life and safety. If Thorolf had hurt her . . .

But nay, she could not let herself lose hope.

Any more than she could let herself lose hope of escape, of returning home.

That was the only way to explain what had happened this morn in Hauk's bed, she thought, her eyes misting. For a flicker of time, hope had abandoned her, and she had abandoned herself to him. Given in to the yearning and tenderness and other, stronger emotions she dared not feel for him. Allowed herself to want and need in ways she had almost forgotten.

A new fear twisted through her: a fear of *herself*. Now that she had set those feelings free this morn, what if she could not conceal them from him, return them to that place in her heart where she must keep them hidden?

That same deep, secret place, she thought, raising her head, that felt strangely at home in the forest around her, even with all its dangers. Mayhap *because* of all its dangers. Part of her found a fierce excitement in this place of ancient beauty, saturated with darkness and cool, rich colors of emerald and sky blue and a hint of gold. It was made all of shadows and mystery, risk and refuge, and she found it stirring, moving, somewhere in her heart. In her soul.

Much like Hauk himself.

She pulled away from him a bit as they rode on, trying to gain whatever distance from him she could. Last night, what she had realized, what had so filled her with despair, was that she *knew* now that it would be impossible for her to leave Asgard by herself.

So she must try to gain his trust, hope that he would grant her a bit more freedom. And try to find someone to help her reach home.

That would be a difficult enough task if she only had to struggle against the gentle warrior who had made her his captive bride.

But now she had to fight her own heart, as well.

For Giselle's sake, she would.

She *must*.

The sun had passed higher into its arc when they came to the crest of a hill and Hauk reined Ildfast in, the horse prancing and blowing out noisy breaths.

"We are halfway there." Hauk pointed off into the distance.

Through the trees, on the horizon, Avril could just make out the silvery-blue sparkle of the ocean. "Thank God." Hope filled her heart. "How much longer until we reach the cove?"

"Two hours, mayhap less." Hauk swung his leg over the destrier's neck and leaped to the ground.

"Then why are we stopping?" Avril asked when he reached up to help her down.

"To grant Ildfast a needed rest and a drink."

As she landed beside him, her stomach tightened. Hauk held onto her a second longer than was necessary, his gaze on hers, one of his hands lingering at the small of her back in a gesture that was steadying and possessive.

Then he released her and tugged on the reins. "This is where I normally stop to rest him, and I have never ridden him through these woods at such a pace before." He led the horse toward a stream that wound through the trees a few paces away—a quiet brook that trickled over the hillside in a bubbling waterfall.

Avril followed, keeping one hand on the strap of her crossbow and a wary eye out for wolves. "I wish it were not necessary to stop at all. I will not be able to rest until Josette is safe."

"Nor I," he agreed tensely. At the edge of the stream, Hauk dropped the reins to the ground. "But we should reach the ship well ahead of Thorolf. Ildfast is earning his name today." He patted the animal's lathered flank as Ildfast stretched out his neck and guzzled greedily. "Faster than fire."

Avril nodded, trying to feel reassured. After moving a few paces upstream, she knelt on the grassy riverbank and took off her gloves. She cupped her hands in the cool water, drank several handfuls to soothe her parched throat, then splashed her face, washing away dust and grit.

"We will have to go a bit more slowly from here," Hauk told her. "The hills and valleys in this part of the woods are steep, and I cannot risk him breaking a leg."

"But will we still reach the cove in time?" she asked worriedly, glancing toward him.

"Aye." Hauk was rubbing the horse's legs. Ildfast's muscles twitched beneath his glossy, sweat-streaked chestnut coat. "We will continue on just as soon as this poor fellow has a chance to catch his breath."

Avril felt a tingle in the region of her heart as she watched Hauk straighten and scratch the huge animal's forelock with obvious affection.

Picking up her gloves, she stood and paced restlessly, tired from the long ride but too tense to sit down.

"Are you hungry, milady?"

She turned as Hauk tossed her an apple from his pack, which was lashed to Ildfast's saddle. She caught it easily. "Thank you."

Her stomach was in knots, but she took a bite anyway as she walked to the hillside and looked up at the sky, clearly visible over the nearby valley.

"You ride well," Hauk said around a mouthful of apple, coming over to join her, "for a woman."

Avril felt a reluctant smile tug at one corner of her mouth, despite all her anxiety. "I rather enjoyed the hint of surprise on your face, every time you glanced over your shoulder and saw that I had not fallen off."

"I was not certain you could endure the rough pace."

"Have I caused you any trouble thus far?"

"The day is still young."

She took another bite of her apple. "And I believe I will continue to surprise you."

His mouth curved, the look neither frown nor grin. "You usually do."

From the way he said it, she was not sure if that was a complaint or a compliment.

He tossed the core of his apple toward Ildfast, who nickered in pleasure and nibbled it up. "Riding, sailing, hunting. Have you never learned any proper female pursuits, woman?" He cast a dour look over her masculine garb. "Sewing? Gardening?"

"Nay."

It seemed strange, to be having an ordinary conversation with him in the midst of this awful, desperate day. She realized he was being thoughtful again, trying to distract her from her worry about Josette.

Which only made her uneasy for an entirely different reason.

"Not even weaving on a loom," he continued, "singing—"

"A sick cat is more melodious than I," she said honestly.

"Dancing?"

"A sick cat is also a better dancer than I." Unable to eat more than a few bites, she tossed her apple to Ildfast as he had done. The easy closeness growing between her and Hauk made her nervous; she knew she should not allow it to continue.

Did not want him to suspect how much her feelings for him had changed.

She moved away a few paces, along the crest of the hillside. "I have always found such pursuits deadly dull. And since I have no skill at them, I prefer to spend my time elsewhere, at some genuinely useful task." Pulling on her gloves, she slanted him a look. "So now you know the awful truth about me, Hauk. You chose poorly in Antwerp. I cannot sew, I am better at making messes than tidying up—and I am the most hopeless cook you would ever care to meet."

"Ah, well." He shrugged and a quick smile curved his mouth, a flash of straight white teeth. "I suppose it is unreasonable for a man to expect his wife to be well skilled in *all* of her wifely duties."

The huskiness of his voice made her breath catch. "For the last time," she said unsteadily, "I am not your—"

"Must we still argue that, after this morn?"

Her heart fluttered. "What we shared this morn does *not* make me your wife." She turned away from him.

"Nay, the *althing* ceremony made you my wife." He followed her. "What we shared in my bed this morn made you my lover."

She spun to face him. "I do *not* love you! I do not—"

He reached out to caress her cheek. "Do you hate me, then, Avril? Is that what made you cry out so sweetly when you found release in my arms this morn?"

She resisted the entreaty in his gaze, the heat that tingled through her. Forced herself to rebuff him. Pushed his hand away. "I will never let you touch me again!"

"Do not make threats you do not intend to keep, milady," he said roughly. "Do you not see—"

An animal screech made them both whirl toward the stream.

It was Ildfast. Rearing and whinnying in terror as a dark shape appeared from out of nowhere, slinking forward. Avril gasped in panic. *Wolf!* Her mind was so dazed, it took her a moment to remember the crossbow still slung across her back by its strap.

The horse danced sideways, ears flattened, eyes white—then turned blindly and ran.

Straight toward them.

Hauk threw himself into the destrier's path. "Ildfast!"

Unable to stop the panicked stallion, Hauk attempted to grab the reins as the animal charged past them. He caught one and pulled hard—only to be yanked off his feet when Ildfast plunged over the edge of the steep hillside.

Avril screamed as Hauk lost his footing and fell. She did not know which way to turn. Somehow she found the crossbow in her hands and spun to fend off the wolf—but it had turned tail and run. She could see it loping away into the trees.

The weapon still clutched in her hands, she ran to the edge of the hill. "Hauk!"

He lay at the bottom of the valley, cursing viciously. Ildfast, still moving at lightning speed, loose reins flying behind, galloped up the opposite slope and vanished into the trees.

With a frightened oath, Avril scrambled down the hill, slipping on layers of fallen leaves, grabbing saplings to slow her headlong progress. "Hauk, are you all right?"

"Nay, I am not all right!" He pushed himself up to a seated position, jaw clenched. "We have just lost our horse."

"But are you hurt?" she cried as she slid to a halt next to him.

"I am fine. We have to catch him." He started to get to his feet.

Then hissed an oath and remained on the ground.

"Hauk?" She bent over him.

"I do not need help," he insisted. He stood, carefully, favoring his left leg.

"What is wrong with your leg?" Her heart started thrumming. "It is not . . . saints' breath, it is not—"

"Not broken, nay," he said through gritted teeth, taking one hobbling step. "I must have twisted my ankle when I landed." He took another step. Cursed again. "Mayhap you had better help me," he grumbled.

With a cautious look at the top of the hill, she slung the crossbow over her back, then slipped an arm around him, supporting his weight as he leaned on her, one arm across her shoulders.

But they managed to take only a few hobbling steps before he had to sit down again.

She dropped to her knees beside him. "Hauk, we will not get very far at this pace."

"I know that," he bit out in a frustrated voice.

She looked at the broken branches and churned leaves Ildfast had left in his terrified wake. "He will come back, will he not?"

"Mayhap. Eventually. If he can find his way back. If he does not find something interesting to eat. Or break a leg on a hill. Or forget us entirely." Hauk looked up at her, his expression pained. "I value Ildfast for his speed, Avril, not for his intelligence."

She swallowed hard. "But we have to get to the ship. Will your ankle not heal by itself?" she asked hopefully.

"Aye. In a few hours."

Her heart thudded. "But we do not have that much—"

A howl rose through the trees, closer than the ones they had heard earlier.

It skipped up her spine like an icy finger, lifting the fine hairs on the back of her neck.

And Avril suddenly realized they had a more pressing worry than reaching the ship. "Mercy of God. The wolves . . ."

She looked down at Hauk.

Their eyes met and held for a long moment. "Avril, you will have to go on without me."

"What?"

"Do not argue with me—"

"Nay, I cannot leave you here." *She could not leave him to die.*

A movement at the top of the hill made her glance up. It was the wolf they had seen before—a huge, black, shaggy animal. She slid the crossbow from her shoulder, slowly, never taking her eyes from the predator. It might merely be curious.

With a teeth-baring snarl, it sprang down the hill, so fast it was merely a black blur.

She heard Hauk shout at her to run. But she was

already on one knee, bringing up the crossbow in a smooth arc. She fired.

The steel-tipped bolt struck the wolf in the chest. It howled in pain, tripped and tumbled in a yelping ball, sliding through the leaves.

And fell dead at her feet.

She was shaking, staring down at it, barely even aware of what had happened.

"Avril!" Hauk said sharply, bringing her gaze around to him. "I want you to get out of here," he ordered. "They travel in packs. He will have companions."

"I will not leave you."

He muttered what sounded like a string of curses in Norse. "All this time you have wanted naught *but* to escape me, and now that I *want* you to leave, you will not go. Contrary, stubborn—"

"I believe we have already established that." Still shaking, she snapped another bolt into place on her crossbow, lifting her eyes to his. "Now what do you suggest we do?"

16

"Of all the trees in the forest, you had to choose a pine," Hauk grumbled, trying to ignore the throbbing pain in his ankle, wincing at dozens of tiny stings as he plucked evergreen needles from his bare chest and arms.

"This was your idea."

"You could have taken the time to select a more comfortable refuge," he called down to her.

"Aye, and left you alone at the bottom of the hill even longer."

The branches swayed as Avril pulled herself up the last few inches, breathing hard. She claimed a perch on a thick tree limb just above and to the right of the one he occupied.

Brushing needles from her tunic, she looked at him with an annoyed expression. "This was the tallest tree I could find that had branches low enough to climb and strong enough to hold us. And at the time, I was concerned with avoiding fangs—not with providing us luxurious accommodations." Grabbing a bough to steady herself, she glanced at the ground more than twenty feet below them. "If you are unhappy here, mayhap you would prefer to go play with our new friends down there."

Hauk subdued any further complaint, wiping sweat from his brow, the tree bark rubbing his back raw. It was almost impossible to find a comfortable position on the branch, though it was as wide as the span of two hands. He settled for straddling it as if he were on horseback, resting one foot on another nearby bough.

They were likely to be here awhile, he thought with a grimace, following Avril's gaze to the dark shapes milling around the trunk. He counted nine, their shaggy coats dappled by the sunlight.

Drawn by the dying howls of the first wolf, the rest of the pack had quickly found its way to the clearing—and followed his and Avril's scent straight to their chosen place of refuge: at the top of the next hill in one of the rugged, ancient black pines common on Asgard.

They would be safe here, if not comfortable; the trunk had to be at least four feet wide, the limbs more than sturdy enough to support them. All they had to do was avoid the annoying clusters of sharp-pointed needles.

"Go away," Avril called down to the wolves. "Begone. We are not good to eat."

"I do not think reasoning with them is going to help," Hauk said dryly.

One of the wolves leaped up the trunk, claws scrabbling at the bark, jaws closing on air with a powerful snap.

Avril flinched and had to grab her bough with both

hands to keep from tumbling. "They . . . they do not look very pleased with us."

"You," he corrected lightly. "They do not look very pleased with you. I did not kill the wolf."

"Pardon me for saving your life." She frowned at him. "And by the way, you are welcome."

Hauk could not hide the grin that played around his lips. Not only was he enjoying Avril's company, he was actually teasing her.

He, Hauk Valbrand, the *vokter*, renowned for his reserved and solitary ways, was teasing his wife.

While she worriedly observed the predators below, he studied her in the glimmering sunlight that managed to pierce the evergreen. She had indeed saved his life, placed herself between him and that onrushing wolf, and left him stunned.

She had been pale with terror—still looked pale with terror—but instead of running as most women would have done, as he had told her to do, she had stood her ground. Kept her wits about her. And brought down a charging, snarling wolf with one well-aimed shot.

And instead of feeling angry with her for disobeying him, he found himself fighting the strange, unbidden grin that curled one corner of his mouth. Avril was like no other woman he had known: bold, fiercely independent, indifferent to what anyone else wanted her to do or be. And while those qualities exasperated him, they also fascinated him in some inexplicable way.

He had to disagree with what she said earlier: Though it had happened entirely by accident, or by some mischievous trick of the gods, he *had* chosen well in Antwerp.

"Mayhap if you shot two or three more, little Valkyrie, our new friends would leave us in peace."

Avril glanced at him with a raised eyebrow. "Little what?"

"Valkyrie. The fierce warrior-women of our religion, who swoop down from the sky to rescue fallen warriors and escort them to Valhalla—what you would call heaven."

Her lips curved downward. "I suppose that is better than 'wife.'" Her expression tense, she slid the crossbow from her shoulder and counted the small, steel-tipped arrows lashed to its stock. "But I do not have many bolts left, and I am not sure it is wise to waste what I have." She whispered an oath.

Hauk sighed in frustration, as anxious as she was to reach the cove and help Josette and Keldan. "Then we shall have to wait until the wolves give up and leave. My ankle will heal in a few hours, and we can walk the rest of the way." He let himself rest back against the tree trunk. Turning his head, he looked west, toward the sea. "Mayhap we will even find Ildfast somewhere along the—" He sat up straighter. "Avril, I can see it from here."

"Your witless horse?"

"Nay—"

"The cove?"

"The ship. My ship. We are so high in this tree, I can see the top of the mast."

"Thanks be to God," Avril exclaimed, her voice full of relief and hope. "If it is still there, that means—sweet Mary, mayhap Josette is already safe. Mayhap Keldan and the others captured Thorolf and prevented him from reaching it."

"Aye." Hauk tried to sound confident.

For a moment, they both fell silent, the yapping and growling of the wolves filling the warm air, the wind making the upper branches sway and clatter.

"Or," Avril said more quietly, "Thorolf simply has not reached it yet. Or he has taken Josette elsewhere, they are not even in these woods, and we have been going in the wrong direction all day."

Hauk settled back against the tree trunk, forcing himself to meet her gaze. "There is no way to know, Avril. But even if he has taken her elsewhere, he will be found. Everyone on Asgard is searching, and they will not rest until Josette is safe."

She shut her eyes as if in pain, her hands clenching around the crossbow. "But what if he . . . if he has already . . ."

"Thorolf knows we will be hunting him," Hauk said gently. "And I do not believe he would harm her, not until he was safely beyond the reach of Asgard."

He still wondered *what* Thorolf could possibly be planning; leaving the island even for a short time meant risking the ire of the elders, and he doubted Thorolf would do that on a whim or a quest for trade goods.

Avril blinked hard, then met his gaze, looking grateful for his reassurance. "I hope you are right—"

A bird flew out of the branches behind her, startling her. She whirled, lost her hold on the crossbow, and instinctively lunged for the weapon as it fell.

The sudden movement sent her tumbling from her perch.

For one horrified second, Hauk saw her falling, heard her scream, heard the wolves snarling below. Her hands grasped wildly, her fingers closing on empty air.

He lunged down and grabbed her, caught her forearm, fastened his hand around it. The crossbow clattered through the branches and hit the ground, the pack yelping and snarling as they attacked it.

A panicked cry escaped her. She clung to him with both hands, dangling, kicking with her feet.

"*Avril!*" Holding onto the branch with one hand, Hauk started to haul her up—but felt her slipping from his grasp, the sleeve of her linen tunic so smooth it slid through his fingers. Clenching his jaw, he locked his hand around her wrist.

The wolves became frenzied, howling and leaping up the trunk.

"*Mercy of God!*" she cried, eyes white with fear. "God, nay, *please.*"

Her panic tore at his heart. With brute force and sheer will, Hauk pulled her up, one agonizing inch at a time, until she could reach for the branch, for him. He caught her close and she fell forward into his embrace, clinging to him, trembling.

His back flattened against the rough bark, he locked both arms around her, shaking almost as hard as she was. "You are all right," he choked out between rapid, unsteady breaths. "I have you."

The wolves continued growling and jumping at the

tree, as if frustrated that he had snatched their prize from their jaws.

He shut his eyes and held on to her, his heart beating hard and fast. He could have lost her. Quickly, suddenly. Forever.

"Avril, do you think you could stay out of danger for mayhap five minutes at a time?" he demanded gruffly.

"It was not my fault!" She lifted her head. "The bird—"

A gust of wind made the branches sway and she buried her face against his neck, her hands digging into his shoulders.

Hauk did not chastise her further; he simply held her tight. They would have to get her back to her own branch safely, but at the moment, she did not seem willing to go anywhere, shivering as if the combined dangers she had faced today had all become too much for her. Breathing rapidly, she remained pressed against him tightly.

And he could feel each breath, warm against his neck.

Could feel her breasts pillowed against his chest through her soft linen tunic. The belt she wore dug into his waist. And the way she was sitting, with her legs across his lap, her soft thigh rested against a most sensitive part of his anatomy. The fact that she was wearing masculine leggings only made it feel more provocative.

"Avril?" His own breathing deepened, his heart thudding as she wriggled against him. "What are you doing?"

She did it again, a shifting motion of her hips before she glanced over her shoulder with a small sound of distress. "I think when I slid from that branch, I must have—I have either splinters or pine needles in my . . ."

He looked down the curve of her back to see a half-dozen pine needles piercing her shapely derriere. She could not reach them without letting go of him and twisting around.

"Hold still," he ordered.

"Ouch!" She flinched in his arms. "That—*ouch*—"

He plucked out the offending needles for her, one by one, quickly.

"—stings!"

"My apologies." He rubbed his hand over the injured spot, gently.

She went still, her head still turned away from him. Which meant that she was watching what he was doing.

"Would you please stop that?" Her voice sounded strained.

"I am trying to make you feel better."

"That is *not* making me feel better." She turned an accusing gaze on him.

"Indeed?" he asked innocently. "How does it make you feel?"

"Like pushing you out of this tree!"

He lifted his hand from her bottom.

"Men!" Whispering an oath, she tried to peel herself away from him, but could not get far without risking another fall; their bodies still touched. Intimately. She planted one hand in the middle of his chest as if to hold him at bay. "How can you even think of *that* at a time like this?"

"A brush with death tends to have a stimulating effect." He kept his arms looped around her waist. Purely for safety. "And it has been almost a hundred years since I—"

"What?" She blinked at him.

"It feels like it has been almost a hundred years," he amended smoothly, "since I have shared—" *My time, my life, anything with an* utlending *woman* "—a bed with a woman of your considerable charms."

Her face reddened and she glanced away. "This is not a bed, it is a branch."

"It has been even longer since I shared a branch with a woman." He arched one brow. "In fact, I do not think I have ever shared a branch with a woman."

"Well, you mere mortals simply never know where we Valkyries might take you."

His heart thudded a single, hard stroke.

When he did not speak, she looked at him again. "Since we go swooping about," she clarified, "rescuing stray, wounded warriors and the like. One is bound to get stuck in a tree on his way to heaven, eventually."

"Aye," he managed to choke out. She was only teasing him, had no idea that her words held any other meaning, that what she had just said was incorrect. "Avril, stop moving like that."

Her efforts to wriggle her lower body away from his were having the opposite effect from what she intended.

And they both felt the result at the same moment.

She went still, shut her eyes with an embarrassed oath. "Now look what you have done."

"On the contrary, little Valkyrie. It is what you do to me."

She shifted her weight uncomfortably.

"Misery and torment." He groaned under his breath. "Avril, if you insist on wriggling like that, we will be sharing more than a branch. At the moment, my desire to stay alive is matched by my desire to be inside you."

She froze. "Would you please stop saying things like that?"

They stared at each other, listening to the wolves growling and circling the tree below.

"I think I had better return to my own branch," she said uneasily.

"Mayhap that would be safer."

He released his arms from around her waist, then helped steady her as she stretched both arms toward a bough above them.

"Careful," he said.

She grabbed onto the tree limb, and he lifted her as she pulled herself up, managing a somewhat graceful jump back to the perch she had occupied earlier.

"Thank you." She settled securely against the trunk, holding onto the branch with both hands. She glanced up at the sun, now directly overhead. "I suppose we will have to spend the afternoon up here."

"Unfortunately, I do not think the wolves intend to offer us a choice. Just be certain that you stay on guard for stray birds this time," he said sternly.

"I had planned on it." She sighed. "Wherever would I be without a man to tell me what to do?"

"In endless trouble and danger, evidently." He slanted her a glance. "You may not wish to believe it, milady, but you are a woman who needs a firm hand, someone to protect you. Watch over you."

"Ha!" she scoffed. "I have managed quite well on my own for three years."

"I am amazed you have *managed* to reach the age of two and twenty in one piece."

"God's breath, you sound almost like"—her words started out as an annoyed complaint, but ended on a note of soft surprise—"Gerard."

Hauk looked away. He did not have to ask who Gerard was.

He remembered the name quite clearly, from his conversation with Josette, the night of the *althing* ceremony. When she had revealed that Avril was not a wife but a widow, that she had lost her husband three years ago.

"He did not approve of your habit of getting into trouble?"

Hauk had asked the question almost before he completed the thought.

To his surprise, she answered him—slowly, quietly, after a long pause filled only with the sound of the wind.

"He found it . . . difficult to accept my independent ways. At first. I was accustomed to doing as I pleased, and he was . . ." She hesitated, her voice almost a whisper. "He was a knight, accustomed to issuing orders and having them followed."

Hauk still did not look at her, oddly found himself sympathizing with the man. He sounded like an entirely reasonable sort.

Hauk wondered how she had come to find this Gerard worthy of her love and devotion.

But he did not ask that. "I do not understand how you came to be accustomed to doing as you please—wielding a crossbow and sailing a ship and the rest. Your parents must have indulged you shamelessly."

"I was an only child."

So was he. That did not explain it. He glanced toward her curiously. "And your father wished you to be the son he did not have?"

"Nay." A hint of a smile curved her mouth. "My parents wished me to be proper and ladylike, but *I* was always conscious that I needed to be both daughter and son to them. I was born late in their marriage, long after they thought they could not have children, and I always knew that one day the responsibility for our lands and people would fall to me."

"Or rather, to your husband," he corrected gently.

"Aye." Her smile faded. "But I was so close to my parents, I was reluctant to marry and leave them and our home on the seashore in Brittany. Only when my mother became ill did my father decide he must give thought to my future, when I was seventeen. He was well along in years, and wanted to see me . . ." Her voice became a whisper again. "Settled. Happy."

Hauk did not speak, his own throat burning at the sorrow and love and wistfulness in her voice, in her expression. Avril had lost much for one so young.

Too much.

"And for some reason," she continued after a moment, a trace of a frown tugging at one corner of her mouth, "my father *also* felt that I needed 'a firm hand.'" She glanced up through the tree branches, at the bright sun. "So he chose for my husband a knight recently returned from the Crusades, the son of one of his closest friends." She swallowed, blinking hard. "Sir Gerard de Varennes, of the Artois."

The hurt in her voice struck such a chord inside Hauk, he almost reached out to her; they were close enough that if they both stretched out their hands—

Then he noticed the band of gold she still wore, the wedding ring gleaming dully in the shifting light.

And he remained still. Did not ask how she had lost her beloved knight, her first husband, the father of her child. This man who possessed her heart so completely, she still wore the ring he had given her.

"And what of your father?" he asked instead, fearing he already knew the answer. "Does he still live in your home on the seashore in Brittany?"

"Nay." She dropped her gaze to her fingers, so pale clutched against the dark wood of the tree. "My father died earlier this year. I was planning to return home to Brittany after my visit to Antwerp."

Home. The word and the sadness in her expression tore at him.

She had lost them both, he thought, unable to tear his gaze from her face. Both of the men in her life. Strong men who protected her, cared for her . . . and then left her alone.

Little wonder she was loathe to surrender her independence, to let herself depend on a man again. To allow a man to hold her close and keep her safe.

She was afraid. His bold, daring little Valkyrie was afraid.

Hauk turned his head, not liking the thick, hot feeling that filled his throat. By all the gods, he had not wanted this; had not wanted to set foot on this same, dangerous ground he had covered in the past. With Karolina. With Maeve.

He had been willing to give and receive pleasure, even to enjoy Avril's company. That was simply a matter of two solitary people satisfying a need. A need for companionship and physical contact. Like hunger. Or thirst.

But he did not want to feel more. Because no matter what they shared between them, it would last but a brief wink of time. And it would not ease his pain; *nei*, it would only bring him more when it ended.

But even as he reminded himself of that, he could not stop himself from trying to ease her pain.

He reached out with his right hand, his gaze still lowered.

And a moment later, he felt the touch of her fingertips against his.

Closing his eyes, he intertwined their fingers, felt the cool metal of her wedding band.

But for once, she did not pull away.

"Hauk?"

He heard an unexpected softness in her voice as she said his name.

"What?"

"Do you think Josette is safe yet?"

He turned his head to look toward the cove. "I can still see the ship."

"I hope that means she is all right."

"Aye," he agreed. "And Keldan as well."

The sky blazed with sunlight. Dazzling, blinding sunlight.

Josette blinked up into the brightness of midday, frightened and confused. What had happened? It seemed like only an instant ago, she had been outside of Avril and Hauk's *vaningshus*, in moonlit darkness.

But now she was lying on a beach, and there were treetops nearby. And her heart was hammering. And a strange, tingling sensation coursed through her limbs. The gag Thorolf had tied around her mouth still muffled any sound she might try to make. Her hands were still tied behind her back, her arms sore and cramped as if she had been lying there a long while.

Yet it seemed to her mind that no more than a second had passed—when obviously at least half a day had passed. It felt as if . . . as if she had somehow lost several hours of time.

The jarring sensation made her feel dizzy, sick. Her pulse racing, she tried to lift her head. She could not see Thorolf anywhere.

But she saw a boat. A large sailing vessel, with a curving prow and stern, moored a short distance out in a . . . an elongated bay or channel of some kind. She could see land on the other side.

She was in a deserted cove, at the edge of a forest. Suddenly she remembered what Avril had told her:

that Hauk had a boat hidden beyond the western woods.

But why had Thorolf brought her here only to leave her alone?

Josette let her head sink back onto the sand, felt tears threaten, tried to remember what had happened. She had gone to find Avril, only to have Thorolf seize her in the darkness. Her mind had gone blank with terror when he yanked back the hood of her cloak and snarled something at her with a furious, surprised expression.

Then he had forced a liquid of some kind down her throat. The strong-smelling, thick drink had almost choked her, it was so bitter and sweet and tangy. It seemed to be made of dozens of different tastes. And it had the most frightening effect on her.

She had thought he was poisoning her. Or trying to render her unconscious. But the drink had made her feel strangely hot; not as she would with a fever, but as if her very blood burned her veins. Then all at once every muscle in her body had cramped into knots. A sudden, monstrous headache pounded between her temples. Her very bones seemed to hurt. The pain had made her cry.

All the while, Thorolf had watched her with cool detachment, a slow grin spreading across his blunt features. Then he had fastened a hand around her throat, squeezing off her breath until she lost consciousness . . .

Only to awaken here. Several hours later. Hours that felt to her like an instant.

It was all so strange. Confusing. Terrifying. She

tried to sit up, pushing her numb, aching arms into the sand.

And then she saw Thorolf—in the water, striding toward her through the shallows, coming from the boat.

He stopped when he saw her. Froze in place, the waves lapping about his knees. Stared at her as she sat up.

Then he abruptly broke into laughter. Loud, overjoyed laughter. He looked up to the sky, raised both arms in the air, shook his fists as if he were laughing at the heavens, at God Himself.

Josette whimpered in fear, certain that Thorolf must be mad—and utterly perplexed about what he wanted with her. He hurried through the water toward her.

She struggled against her bonds, kicked sand at him when he came to tower over her. He snarled something in Norse, raising his fist. Flinching, Josette cowered at his feet, the gag muffling her small sob of terror.

But he did not strike her. Instead he leaned down and grabbed her chin with one hand, squeezing her face between his fingers with bruising force. He turned her head left and right, studying her, and murmured something in a low voice.

Then he released her and stepped back, looking down at her with a strange, malevolent grin that sent a chill to her heart.

"Thorolf!"

The shout came from the forest. Even as Thorolf

spun, Josette felt her heart skip a beat at the sound of
that deep, strong voice.

Keldan!

Relief and fear both flooded her at once. A half-
dozen men came riding out of the woods, charging
across the shore, Keldan in the lead.

Thorolf growled what sounded like a curse and
hauled her to her feet, jerking her in front of him.
Josette struggled and kicked, tried to twist from his
hold. But he was too strong.

He shouted at the men, his tone sharp, and moved
backward toward the surf. Toward the boat. Water
splashed her gown as he reached the water's edge.

Nay! She kept fighting him, her gaze on Keldan's
dark, worried eyes—until the cold edge of a knife
against her throat made her go still.

Thorolf backed farther into the water, away from
the men, snarling at them in Norse.

Keldan and the others dismounted. She saw that
they all carried weapons. One even had a crossbow.
But Thorolf kept her in front of him as a shield, moving toward the ship, carrying her deeper into the
waves.

She could not fight him. Could not strike him with
her hands tied. Could barely even breathe with the
gag in her mouth and the knife at her throat.

So she did the only thing she could think of.

Pretending to faint, she went limp in his hold.

Her sudden lassitude startled him. Enough that the
blade came away from her neck, just for an instant—
and Josette lunged down with her bound hands and
used another trick. One Avril had taught her when

they were younger, in case a boy ever became overly friendly. She reached between his legs, grabbed, and twisted.

Thorolf howled in pain and Josette dove sideways, into the knee-deep water.

She went under, felt a moment of panic as the icy surface closed over her head. Then a pair of hands caught her, strong arms lifted her. She saw Keldan and the rest descending upon Thorolf, while one of the men carried her to safety.

Shouts and curses filled the air, Thorolf bellowing in fury. The man who had plucked her from the waves set her down in the sand, took the gag from her mouth, worked at the ropes around her wrists.

But Josette no longer cared about her bonds, her eyes on Keldan, her heart in her throat.

It was a brutal struggle. They were trying to subdue Thorolf, not to kill him. But he knew no such restraint, slashing and stabbing at them with the long knife, trying to break free.

Then it all became a tangle of arms and bronzed backs and splashing water. She heard a sharp cry, saw the battle end at last, and they were dragging Thorolf back to shore. One of the men ran to fetch ropes from his saddle.

Her hands freed, she rose and ran down the beach to throw herself into Keldan's arms.

She melted into his strong embrace, sobbing. "Keldan! God's mercy, I was so afraid! I was so afraid!"

"Josette . . ." He held her tight, breathing hard, his voice strained.

Then he began to sink to his knees.

"Keldan?" she cried, pulling back, falling with him as he went down. "What—" Only then did she notice the blood.

The deep wound in his back. Just above his waist. Thorolf had stabbed him.

Her heart seemed to stop. "Nay! Oh, sweet, holy Mary, nay!"

His eyes were bright with pain. Still holding her, he met her gaze for a long, silent moment, then looked toward the others.

Then he started giving what sounded like orders.

Thorolf was still bellowing in rage as they tied him securely and lifted him onto one of the horses. Keldan lay down on the sand, groaning in agony.

The sound struck at Josette, made her heart clench tight. She looked back at the men, stunned that they were getting on their horses. "What are you doing? Someone help him! He may be dying!"

"Josette . . ." Keldan muttered a few breathless words in Norse; he seemed frustrated that he could not make her understand. "Will be . . . right. Stay." He looked fiercely into her eyes and squeezed her hand, hard.

She shook her head in disbelief. "They cannot simply leave you. They cannot—"

Even as she said it, one of the men called out to Keldan, but he waved them away. Keeping Thorolf in their midst, lashed securely across one saddle, they all turned and galloped up the shoreline, disappearing into the forest.

"Nay!" Josette cried. "How can they ride off and abandon you?"

She started to rise, but Keldan's grasp on her hand tightened. "Safe . . . here. Stay."

"Nay, I have to help you! I have to—"

"*Nei*, Josette," he said sharply—the first time he had ever used such a tone with her. "*Ulv*. Wolf. Stay here. Hauk . . . come."

Tears filled her eyes. She felt like shouting at him. How could he be so calm? How could he be concerned about her safety when his life was ebbing from him? "But he may be too late! Even if Hauk comes, it may be too late!"

He shook his head, his eyes becoming glassy. "Sleep . . . now."

"Nay, do not go to sleep." She smoothed his dark hair back from his forehead, panic rising. "Keldan, I am afraid if you go to sleep you may never awaken."

"Stay." It was unmistakably an order, his hand gripping hers, his dark eyes worried. "*Jeg elsker deg.*"

Her vision blurred. He had first said those words to her in the meadow. Only yesterday. But she had been unable to bring herself to repeat them, unsure she could truly mean them.

"*Jeg elsker deg*, Keldan. I love you."

Her declaration did not seem to ease the anguish in his expression. A spasm of pain wracked him.

Then his lashes drifted closed. He went still.

"*Nay!*" The wail of denial rose from the depths of her heart. "Keldan, do not leave me!"

17

Ildfast, curse him, did not turn up until Hauk and Avril had almost reached the edge of the forest on foot. Finding his stallion happily munching clover in a clearing, Hauk was sorely tempted to feed the bird-witted beast to the wolves, which had finally vanished into the woods in search of easier prey.

As the fading light of sunset sifted down through the forest canopy, he tried to take some comfort from the fact that they now had a horse—a well-rested horse—to carry them the rest of the way to the cove. But after spending all afternoon in the tree, he felt as snappish and restless as a wolf himself, impatient to reach their destination, concerned about whether Keldan and the others had intercepted Thorolf.

About whether the young men had managed to keep the confrontation from turning violent.

Avril also seemed unusually tense and quiet, mayhap because of her worry for Josette.

Or mayhap because she did not know what to say about what had happened between the two of them in the tree this afternoon, any more than he did. That long, silent linking of their hands had felt as intimate, somehow, as the lovemaking they had shared in his bed this morn.

Except that it had left him feeling more awkward and out of sorts than lovemaking ever did.

He told himself he had simply been fulfilling the vow he had made: wooing his wife. Getting to know her better. It was necessary, if he was to see to her needs and her happiness.

And as soon as Josette was out of danger and Thorolf hauled before the council, he meant to carry his little Valkyrie back to his *vaningshus*, to keep her safe and protected, to spend a great deal of time getting to know her better . . . and seeing to her happiness in ways that would leave them both so utterly spent, they would not be able to speak, much less walk.

Ildfast's smooth gait carried them swiftly toward the cove—but when they broke through the trees at last, the sight that greeted them told Hauk his day was not about to get better, but worse.

Much worse.

"Avril!" Josette cried, jumping to her feet and running toward them across the sand. She had been huddled beside Keldan—who lay stretched out near the water, unmoving.

Hauk felt his gut clench.

"Josette, thank God!" Avril leaped down from Ildfast's back and rushed to meet her friend. "Are you all right?"

Josette almost collapsed in her arms. "Oh, Avril, he is dead!" She sobbed. "Thorolf killed him. I barely had the chance to tell him I love him and now he is dead."

"Nay," Avril cried. "Josette, I am so sorry. If only we had gotten here sooner!"

"He is gone." Her friend wailed. "He is *gone*."

Holding his tongue, Hauk dismounted, tying Ildfast's reins to a tree branch before stalking toward them across the shore, choked by the emotions pulsing through him: anger at Thorolf for breaking the most sacred of Asgard's laws.

And frustration that he had not been here when Keldan and the others had been forced to fight. They were too young. Too inexperienced with weapons. He should have been here when they needed him.

"Keldan and some other men came to rescue me," Josette was babbling, "and there was a terrible struggle and they captured Thorolf but he stabbed Keldan first and—"

"Shh, Josette." Avril pressed Josette's head against her shoulder, trying to comfort the hysterical girl.

"When?" Hauk asked as he drew near. "When did it happen?"

Avril looked at him strangely, but Josette seemed too upset to wonder at the question.

"Hours ago, at midday. And the other five men rode off and *left* him." She sobbed. "The heartless wretches, they tied Thorolf up and took him away, but left Keldan to *die*!"

Hauk scowled at that news, annoyance crowding in on his anger and frustration.

Annoyance at Keldan, who apparently lacked any sense at all.

He strode over to where his young friend lay. Keeping his back to the women—who continued talking and sobbing and making all manner of loud, mournful noise—Hauk crouched down next to him.

"Kel," he whispered.

The younger man did not stir.

Hauk tapped his face lightly with one hand. "Kel, wake up."

Another, stronger slap roused him. Gasping a deep breath, Keldan opened his eyes.

"Welcome back," Hauk said under his breath in Norse. "And welcome to the trouble you have created. Josette tells me Thorolf is in custody. Why did you not send her away with the others?"

Keldan shut his eyes against the sun. "Tyr's blade, what a headache." He groaned quietly. "Thorolf, that whoreson, he stabbed me. By all the gods, did it hurt—"

"Try drowning some time," Hauk muttered dryly. "You have my thanks for capturing Thorolf—but you should have sent Josette away with the others."

"I did not want her near Thorolf." Smiling, Keldan sighed dreamily. "Hauk, she told me she loves me."

"Wonderful. I am overjoyed for you. Now how do you intend to explain to her that you were not, in fact, dead all afternoon?"

The younger man's eyes snapped open wide, his smile vanishing. "All afternoon?"

"It is evening, Kel. Your poor, hysterical bride has been sitting here grieving for you half the day."

Keldan blinked up into the red- and orange-streaked sky, abruptly realizing that it was sunset.

"But I thought you would arrive within a few moments! We agreed to rendezvous at midday. I thought you would explain—"

"Unfortunately, I met some wolves with other plans. And it is too *soon* to tell them, Kel! It is customary to wait a few weeks—"

"Josette is ready to know the truth."

"Avril is not."

"Avril is with you?" Keldan sat up. "I thought you meant to leave her in your *vaningshus*."

Hauk suddenly realized that the women, who had been chattering and sobbing, had fallen into silence.

An astounded, breathless silence.

He muttered a curse. Slowly, reluctantly, he and Keldan turned and looked up the beach—to see their two brides clinging to each other, staring at Keldan with expressions of shock and disbelief. And terror.

"A-are you going to tell me I am merely *confused* this time?" Avril exclaimed. "Or that Josette could not hear his heartbeat because she had seawater in her ears?"

"Hauk?" Keldan stood, placing one hand on Hauk's shoulder to steady himself. "You are going to have to explain this to them." He lifted a hand in gentle entreaty toward his wife. "Josette—"

"Nay!" She flinched back, clutching at Avril.

With an anguished oath, Keldan looked down. "Hauk, you have to tell her. I do not know enough of her words to make her understand. You must explain it to them. Now. There is no other choice."

"*Ja*, so it seems," Hauk grated. "By all the gods, Kel, *I* am not ready for this."

He had come here prepared to do battle with Thorolf. Would almost *prefer* to face an armed foe than this discussion. He had done this twice before, knew it was never easy for a bride to accept. And how could he make them understand Asgard's secret when they had been here only days, when it was so far beyond the realm of their experience?

"Hauk"—Keldan moaned—"I cannot bear the way she is looking at me."

"Then brace yourself, Kel, because it may not improve once she hears what we are about to tell her." He waved the women over, shifting to French. "Avril, Josette, my young friend here has decided it is time you knew the truth." He sighed, trying to think of the best way to begin. "And you may wish to sit down. It is rather a long story."

"I do not want to sit down! I do not want to listen!" Josette exclaimed, hanging back. "This is impossible! It is madness. He was dead—"

"I am not so certain of that, Josette." Avril's heart had lodged in her throat and her senses were spinning; she could not believe her voice sounded so calm.

But she could not deny evidence she had just seen with her own eyes. For the second time. "I . . . I think mayhap we should listen to what they have to say."

"What are you talking about?" Josette looked at her as if she thought Avril, too, had lost her mind.

"Josette, we have known from the beginning that there was something strange about this island. At least *I* have known. If you want to stay here, do you not want to know what it is?"

"I do not want to stay here! I have changed my mind! I have—"

"Josette," Keldan called to her, his expression desolate. "*Vaer snill.* Please."

Josette ceased babbling and looked at him, then stopped trying to bolt and run. She studied his face for a long moment. "He did rescue me," she said softly, chewing at her lower lip. "I . . . I thought he *gave* his life for me."

Avril remained silent, her gaze on Hauk; she knew exactly how Josette was feeling. Confused and frightened and touched and wary of these unpredictable, perplexing men.

"V-very well," Josette said unsteadily, still clinging to Avril. "I will listen."

Together they walked down the beach toward the men, close enough to converse—but not too close.

"So, Norsemen," Avril said, trying to keep her voice steady, "what is this truth you wish to tell us?"

"Keldan was not dead," Hauk said quietly, tugging his friend down to sit beside him. "He cannot die, *we* cannot die—"

"We?" Avril thought she had better sit down; her knees had begun trembling so hard, her legs would no longer hold her.

"The native-born of Asgard. The *innfodt.*" He met her gaze as she sat opposite him, a few paces away. "We cannot die, not on Asgard soil. Not from a blade or injury or drowning or . . . most of the usual ways."

Josette sank down—or rather, collapsed—next to Avril. "But he *was* dead. He—"

"Nay, milady, he was not. Had you listened very carefully, over a long time, you would have heard his heart beat lightly, once every few minutes. His skin was cool to the touch because the flow of his blood had slowed. And his pulse and breathing were too faint for most people to detect. We call it *langvarig sovn.*" He glanced from Josette to Avril. "The deepest sleep. It can last a short time or many hours, depending on how long the body requires to heal whatever injury has occurred."

"That was what happened in the bay," Avril said breathlessly, "when you swam out to me—"

"I did not have strength enough to save us both," he told her simply. "But I knew that as long as the surf carried me ashore, I would recover, eventually. I would have remained in *langvarig sovn* some time longer, had you not awakened me." His hard mouth curved in a grimace. "I am sorry that I lied to you about it, Avril, but we normally do not tell new brides about this until they have been here long enough to adjust to Asgard, to accept their new lives—"

Keldan interrupted, speaking to Hauk in a tone that sounded urgent.

"*Ja, ja.*" Hauk gestured at him to be quiet. "Josette, Keldan did not mean to frighten you. He never intended to leave you here alone with him all afternoon. I had told him we would meet here at midday, so he believed I would be along momentarily to explain what was happening and reassure you."

Keldan nodded, saying something to Josette in

Norse, his dark eyes never leaving her. From the misery etched on his features, he was clearly begging for her forgiveness, as if he would—

Nay, not *die* without it, Avril corrected herself, clutching her hands in her lap to keep them from shaking. "But if you cannot die, then you . . . you are—"

"We are not immortal." Hauk shook his head. "There are some dangers even an *innfodt* cannot survive. Such as the wolves. Or falling from one of the cliffs. But as long as we avoid those and stay here on Asgard, we remain healthy." He paused. "And live a rather long time."

"H-how long?" Josette squeaked.

Hauk glanced at her. "Keldan here"—he nodded at his friend—"is a mere lad among us. He only celebrated his fiftieth year a few months ago."

Josette looked surprised, and a little relieved.

Avril could hardly believe it; Keldan did not look a day over thirty. "A-and what about you?" she asked Hauk, her heart thudding.

He met her gaze. "How old would you guess I am?" he asked quietly.

Avril studied Hauk's angular features and sun-colored hair. He appeared as youthful as his friend, barely touched by time. His face showed not one line or wrinkle, his smooth, tanned skin marked only by the stubble of burnished gold that skimmed his cheeks. With his strong jaw and those pale-blue eyes that matched the sky, he was more handsome than any—

She drew herself up short; she had been about to think *than any mere mortal had a right to be.*

But he was not a mere mortal.

"I . . . I cannot tell. You look no older than Keldan."

A fleeting smile brought out a dimple in his stubbled cheek. "Aye." He hesitated, and his expression became somber as he kept his gaze fixed on hers. "But I was born three hundred years ago."

Avril heard Josette inhale sharply. She herself could not make a sound. The evening sky seemed to whirl dizzily as Hauk's words echoed over and over in her mind, like the waves splashing onto the shore.

Three hundred. Three hundred.

Three.

Hundred.

All the air vanished from her lungs. She gasped, choked. An uncontrolled laugh bubbled up in her throat. "This is a jest. You cannot possibly be—this must all be some kind of *jest!* No one can live to be *three hundred*—"

"I am only in my middle years, compared to some among our people."

She shook her head in denial, but he was not teasing her. Clearly he was not. There was no amusement in his deep voice. And no happiness. He remained solemn, stating it all calmly.

As if he were relating simple, indisputable facts.

Trembling, she had to put out a hand to steady herself. Felt surprised to find solid earth beneath her. "You mean to tell me that all of those . . . those merchants and farmers and craftsmen in town are—"

"Older than they look. Some are *much* older than they look. We *innfodt* mature to the age of thirty, and then it is as if time . . ." He shrugged one bronzed shoulder. "Stops. In truth, we are not certain what the upper limit of our years may be. If there is one."

Josette looked at Keldan in astonishment and distress. "Do you mean you may live *forever?*"

"We do not know," Hauk told her. "For centuries, men have searched the world for the legendary key to eternal youth—what some have called the waters of life—and what they seek is here. On Asgard. Accidentally discovered more than six hundred years ago, by a small band of Norse explorers who were seeking a new sea route to the west." His mouth became a grim, bitter line. "And yet it remains a secret. A mystery—"

"You do not know how it is that the island affects you this way?" Avril guessed. "As you do not know how it heals."

"Aye." He nodded, his voice becoming harsh. "But whatever it is about Asgard that sustains us, it comes with a price. We cannot live without it. We have become connected to the island in some way—we are part of it and it is part of us. As long as we remain here, we may live forever." His eyes held hers again. "But in the outside world, in your world, we live no more than six days."

Avril felt her heart beat a strange, hard stroke that stole her breath. "You can never leave?" she asked softly. "You are"—she searched for a word, felt surprised when she found it—"captives here?"

He shook his head. "Most do not see it that way. Asgard is a pleasant place, after all. A paradise." He gestured at the sun-warmed beach, the lush forest. "The elders long ago made it a law that no one may venture out even for a short time, to protect Asgard and its secret. But it is almost unnecessary. Most *innfodt* are happy to stay."

"But not everyone," she said.

Not you. She could tell by his voice, had noticed it before—that trace of bitterness. Of yearning.

It occurred to her abruptly—jarringly—that she and Hauk had much more in common than she had ever suspected. She knew all too well how it felt for someone of independent, adventurous spirit to have that freedom curtailed.

How would it feel to live like that for three hundred years?

Something inside her knotted with pain as she remembered the books she had found in his *vaningshus*. Written in his youth, he had said. He must have longed to travel those distant lands. It must be torture for him, leaving now and then for a few days, enjoying a glimpse of the wider world, of freedom, only to be forced to return. She was amazed he left at all.

Then she remembered that he had told her he *had* to leave now and then, as part of his duty as *vokter*.

"Not everyone is happy to stay," he agreed quietly, glancing toward his boat moored in the cove. "We are Norsemen, after all. Exploration and wandering are in our blood." A muscle flexed in his lean jaw. "But those who have given in to temptation, who have tried to test the limit of six days, have paid with their lives."

The gruffness of his voice made her guess that included someone close to him.

Her throat closed. She had once assumed that Hauk lived alone in his clifftop *vaningshus* because he preferred it that way, because he was reserved and solitary by nature.

But that was not true. He had shown her this afternoon—and many times before—that that was not true.

And mayhap he had not always been so solitary.

So alone.

Josette's hesitant voice filled the momentary silence. "And what about us?" she whispered. "H-how long will we live?"

A shadow of discomfort passed over Hauk's features, as if he had dared hope that question would not arise. "Not long enough," he said, almost too faintly to be heard.

Avril could not speak. Dampness filled her eyes.

Hauk turned to face Josette and answered her quickly, stoically. "On Asgard, your lives will be longer than normal. You will reach mayhap seventy-five years, and you will retain your youth and health for much of that time."

"And after that?" Avril whispered.

He did not look at her, kept his gaze on Josette. "Only those who are conceived here and born here are *innfodt*, native-born. Anyone brought here later in life remains *utlending*. Foreign." After a moment, he added, "Mortal."

Josette looked at Keldan, who sat waiting, tense,

regarding her with hope and desperation in his eyes—
and another emotion that Avril recognized, though
she was not certain Josette could discern it.

Love.

"But why bring us here, if you will only outlive us?"
Josette demanded of him accusingly. "Why not marry
one of your *innfodt* women?"

"It is an ancient tradition," Hauk explained.
"When that first band of explorers—twenty men—
discovered the island's healing qualities, they did not
wish to spread word of this place, which would invite
the entire world to their doorstep. And since they
were a long way from home, they decided to follow
the Norse custom of the time and—"

"Go and steal themselves some brides," Avril said
dryly. "From somewhere closer at hand."

He nodded. "Unfortunately, Asgard's founders enjoyed only a normal, slightly longer life span. It was
the children of those couples, the first generation
born here, who were the first *innfodt*. They were the
first who did not die, and when they reached thirty,
they stopped aging." He paused, glancing out over the
sea. "But that generation found that unions between
two *innfodt* produce no children."

Avril felt her heart pounding, began to understand.

"Most Asgard men are content to remain here and
marry here," Hauk continued, his voice becoming
rough, "because to this day, if a man wants a family,
he must risk venturing into the outside world and
stealing himself an *utlending* bride. Few are willing to
take the risk anymore, because the outside world be-

comes a more crowded, more violent, more dangerous place every year."

Josette reached up to touch her mouth with her fingertips. "That is why you brought me here?" she asked Keldan with soft wonderment. "Because you want a family?"

"Aye, that is why he brought you here," Hauk replied, his expression gentle as he looked at her. "*Utlending* brides are considered special, Josette, and Keldan wanted to marry the most special one he could find. A woman who would touch his heart. A woman with 'sparks and liveliness,' he said. The moment he set eyes on you, he knew you were the one. All he wants is to live in that *vaningshus* he built in the meadow and make you happy all the days of your life. And raise a little carpenter or two."

Josette pressed her hand over her mouth, tears suddenly sliding down her cheeks. She left Avril's side without another word and walked over to Keldan, kneeling before him in the sand.

She touched his face, spoke to him in Norse.

Keldan uttered a shout of relief and joy, wrapping his arms around her in a fierce hug. He said something to Hauk, his tone one of gratitude, before burying his face in Josette's dark hair.

"*Ja, ja,*" Hauk replied hollowly, before he stood and walked toward Avril.

"I do not understand." She looked up at him in puzzlement as he drew near. "What did she say?"

"She told him she loves him." He glanced over his shoulder.

Keldan and Josette were now lost in a kiss, lost in

each other, oblivious to the world . . . and sinking onto the sand.

Hauk cleared his throat and reached down to help Avril up. "And I believe we should allow them some time alone."

18

"Avril," Hauk said after they had been walking along the shore for several minutes, "I find it difficult to believe that you have naught to say."

Avril did not look back at him, poking at a piece of seaweed with a long stick she had picked up as they wandered down the beach. Leaving Ildfast where he was, they had set off on foot, following the curving edge of the cove, which was so large it could almost be called a bay; it was shaped like a broad, elongated U, open at one end. As the lavender light of evening slowly gave way to darkness, she looked down at the icy water lapping around her bare toes. She had removed her boots, carrying them in her hand, and unbraided her hair after the wind made a complete mess of it

"You must forgive me if I do not know what to say," she finally managed to reply. "I have never before conversed with a man who is three hundred years old."

"It is not difficult. I am not hard of hearing," he said lightly, "despite my age."

She turned to face him in the gray, fading light. "Am I supposed to find that amusing?"

"I do not know." He crossed his arms over his broad chest. "You will have to tell me, which will require speaking to me. And you *have* conversed with a man who is three hundred years old—every day since we met in Antwerp."

Avril could only stare at him, mute, unable to sort out the jumbled thoughts splashing through her mind like the waves on the shoals. She brushed a wind-blown strand of hair out of her eyes, knew that what he said was true: This was Hauk, the same man who had abducted her, provoked her, fought with her . . . and saved her life, teased and aroused her. Comforted her. Cradled her tenderly in his arms.

And awakened longings and dreams and emotions in her heart she had thought she might never feel again.

Yet he was *three hundred* years old. Had been on this earth centuries before she was born.

And would be here long after she died.

"Avril," he said impatiently, moving closer, "there is no need to look at me as if I had just sprouted antlers. I am no different today than I was yester-day—"

"Aye, and apparently you will be the same tomorrow, and the day after that and the day after that—"

"How reassuring to see that your wit is still intact," he said dryly.

She dropped her boots and stabbed her walking stick into the sand. "You must pardon me if I am having a *somewhat* more difficult time adjusting to all of this than Josette. She is happily married to a man of fifty. I am . . ." She shook her head, looked down at her bare toes. "I do not know *what* I am anymore. Mayhap I am losing my mind."

"Do you doubt what I have told you? What you have seen with your own eyes? Do you think I have concocted an elaborate lie for some reason?"

"Nay." She swallowed hard and reluctantly met his gaze. "That is what frightens me the most. I believe you. I have seen enough of this strange place to believe you are telling the truth."

His expression softened. "Avril, I knew this would be difficult for you to accept." Reaching out, he caught a strand of her long hair in his fingertips. "That is why I did not wish to tell you so soon."

"And when *were* you going to tell me?" A spark of anger flared inside her. "After you had bedded me?" Another, awful thought struck her. "After I was carrying your child? Did you think that would—"

"After you had begun to have feelings for me."

The quiet way he said it startled her into silence.

His gaze held hers. "Which, after this afternoon, I thought might not be far in the future."

Her heart beat quickened. She looked away, afraid he would see in her eyes what she had barely begun to admit to herself.

What she dared not admit to him.

"You were mistaken," she said, trying to sound cool and remote when she was burning inside. Swallowing hard, she picked up her walking stick and boots and quickly changed to a safer subject. "Should we not go back and collect our friends, and return to town? I am still concerned about Josette. While she was babbling, she mentioned something about Thorolf—"

"Avril—"

"—But she was so upset about losing Keldan, I could not make sense of half of what she was saying. I want to make sure she is all right."

She started back the way they had come, noticing with a twinge in her heart how far apart the two sets of footprints were in the sand.

"Avril, she appeared well when we left her. You can check on her later. On the morrow." Hauk did not follow.

Avril stopped and turned. "We are not going?"

One corner of his mouth curved. "I do not think we should intrude upon them yet."

Avril felt warmth rise in her cheeks, realizing he was probably right; Josette and Keldan had barely noticed when she and Hauk left them. The young couple had been too busy celebrating their reunion.

Which might take the rest of the night.

And Avril did not wish to steal one moment of their happiness. Even if it meant being stranded out here with Hauk until morning.

That thought made her stomach do a nervous little flip. The last, tenuous glimmers of sunlight seemed to choose that very moment to vanish from the horizon, leaving the two of them cloaked in gray shadows and the tentative, silvery brightness of the moon.

"We should have thought to bring a torch," she said a bit uneasily.

"We will be perfectly safe out here, Avril. As long as you do not stray from my side." A husky note came into his voice. "Are you cold, milady?"

Since he was wearing no cloak, she could imagine

how he might offer to keep her warm—and the thought alone was enough to send a tingle of heat through her.

Trying to ignore it, to appear perfectly casual and unconcerned, she walked back toward him. "Nay, I am fine. Are you certain you do not have to return to town at once and see to Thorolf's punishment?"

He fell in step beside her as they continued wandering along the shore of the cove. "Not tonight. The men who rode with Keldan will take Thorolf to the council, then Josette and Keldan will have to appear before them on the morrow to tell what happened, and the elders will decide his punishment."

She slanted him a curious look. "How *do* you punish those who break your laws?"

He shrugged one shoulder. "Fortunately, it is rarely necessary. A person may be fined, or banished to a distant part of the island for a time, or even confined to solitary imprisonment. Thorolf's misdeeds over the years have earned him all of those penalties." Hauk's expression hardened. "But when he attacked Keldan, he broke the most sacred of our laws, and he will pay dearly for it."

"In France, he would be drawn and quartered," Avril said, still angry at the terrifying ordeal poor Josette had endured.

"Mayhap, milady. But violence of any kind, for any reason, is strictly forbidden among us. The sort of killing and mayhem that occur every day in your world are unknown on Asgard."

Avril looked at him in disbelief. "In all this time,

no *innfodt* has ever killed"—she caught her error—
"well, not killed, but—"

"Nay, no *innfodt* has purposely harmed another.
Not within my memory."

"All three hundred years of it?"

That comment earned her a frown.

"My apologies," she amended lightly. "I suppose I
should not tease you about being so old."

"Nay, feel free." A wicked gleam came into his
eyes. "I will be happy to prove to you that I possess all
the prowess and stamina of a man of thirty. Mayhap I
should demonstrate—"

"Mayhap not." She increased the distance between
them, waggling her stick in warning. His gaze roved
over the masculine garb she still wore, in a way that
stole her breath.

"I still do not understand," she persisted, trying to
keep his mind—and her own—on the subject at
hand. "Even if weapons and violence are forbidden,
there must still be disputes and quarrels and fights."

"Aye." He moved closer as they walked. "But the
first generation of *innfodt* decided that peace and co-
operation would be essential among our people, when
they realized none could leave Asgard and all would
be living here together a very long time." He reached
out and took her boots from her hand, gallantly carrying them for her. "Disagreements are brought before
the elders, they discuss the matter, and decide how to
settle it." He reached out and took her walking stick.
"Fortunately, troublemakers like Thorolf are rare."

Avril belatedly realized she had just been disarmed.
"I am surprised there are not more like him," she said,

turning around and walking backward, the better to keep an eye on Hauk's quick hands. "No matter where people live in the world, men are still men. Unless you have somehow managed to do away with rivalry and aggression and envy and greed—"

"There is little cause for any of that on Asgard. There is ample land and prosperity for all to enjoy, ample time to enjoy it, and all share in it equally. There are no lords here, no princes, no serfs." He regarded her with that hungry, possessive look again. "And as for the aggressive, physical side of man's nature, we channel that into sport." His smile flashed in the moonlight. "And other enjoyable pursuits."

She turned away and stopped walking, gazing out over the waters of the cove, glassy and black in the darkness. "You make Asgard sound like it truly is a paradise," she said softly, thinking of how different his world sounded from her own. France knew little else *but* war, as lords and kings battled for land and riches and power and revenge.

"Aye." His voice became serious. "Though in truth, I almost fear we have become too peaceful."

"How could it be possible to become *too* peaceful?"

"Because you *utlending* keep extending the boundaries of your world and coming closer to ours." He came to stand beside her, dropping her boots and walking stick in the sand. "For six hundred years we have been safe here. Few ships venture into these northern waters." He looked to where the silhouette of his *knorr* was just visible in the distance, the mast outlined by the moonlight. "But with each passing century, your people build bigger and stronger ships and explore farther into the unknown reaches of the world. Someday the outsiders will find us."

Avril felt a shiver go through her at the hollow certainty in his voice.

"And we have become so accustomed to peace rather than war," he continued, "that we may not be able to defend ourselves when that day finally comes."

Avril thought of the gentle, amiable people in town, of Josette and Keldan, and her heart clenched. She knew that the violent men of her world—the lords and princes and kings—would not hesitate to wage war to lay claim to this place.

"You have to do whatever you can to protect yourselves," she blurted. "You have to . . . to raise an army—"

"Build a fleet of warships? Give everyone weapons and teach them to kill? That would destroy the very way of life we are trying to protect." He glanced at her. "The time may come when I am forced to recommend that, but for now I have argued that we should change some of our traditions, such as the Claiming voyage. Because every time we venture out—"

"You risk having someone follow you home."

He nodded. "And in these times, with so many people crowding your world, we must be more cautious than ever about remaining hidden here. We must take greater care to protect Asgard's secret." A look of regret came into his eyes. "At all costs."

Avril held his gaze, understanding as she never had before why it was so vitally important to him that none of the captive brides leave Asgard.

Including her.

He had not kept her from returning to Giselle because he was unkind or uncaring; he cared a great deal.

But he also cared deeply for his people.

"So that is why you are the only one who leaves any more," she said quietly.

He nodded. "It is my duty to keep watch on the *utlending*, so that if necessary, we can take up arms. I observe their ports and their ships. Gather what news I can. Listen for word of explorers who might travel in this direction."

A chill chased down her spine. "But you said that you cannot survive away from Asgard—"

"Not for more than six days. My voyages are, by necessity, short. And I go only once or twice a year. But it is a risk I must take."

Her heart thudded at the danger he was placing himself in. "And if something were to happen to you while you were on one of these expeditions—"

"Away from the island, we do not have its healing protection. In Antwerp, two of our party were killed." He turned and moved away from her.

Avril followed him, the pain in his voice bringing a sharp ache to the center of her chest. "Hauk, I am sorry," she whispered. "It must be difficult to lose friends you have known so long."

He did not reply for a moment.

"They were young," he said gruffly. "Too young to listen when I told them what the dangers would be. Too eager. We only undertake the Claiming voyage every thirty years, when a new generation has come of age."

"Like Keldan."

"Aye." He looked back the way they had come. "Like Keldan." A rueful grin curved his mouth. "He wanted to go on the last voyage, but the elders refused because he was only twenty, barely more than a boy." Hauk's smile faded. "He has waited a long time for his bride."

Avril saw concern in his expression, and it troubled her. "Do you not think Keldan and Josette will be happy together?"

He turned forward and kept walking, shoulders hunched as if against the wind. "They will be fine. She will be very happy. As will their children."

"And Keldan?"

"Keldan is still . . ." He hesitated. "Too young to understand." Hauk moved on a few paces before he stopped again. He did not look back at her, his words almost lost on the wind. "What it will be like, when she is gone."

Avril heard the pain that laced his voice—and felt as if the moon had just fallen from the sky and knocked her to the ground. "You have been married before," she said, her voice shaking as she struggled to draw breath into her lungs, "to a woman like me, to an *utlending*."

For a moment, she was not sure he would answer her.

"Twice."

She gasped, suddenly trembling in the grip of a dozen different emotions. But of course. Of course he would have been married before. God's mercy, she could not believe she had not guessed sooner.

"You wanted children," she whispered. "A family."

He did not reply, standing there as still as one of the distant rocks that surrounded Asgard, pounded by the cold sea.

Only the unsteady rise and fall of his shoulders as he struggled for breath betrayed any emotion.

Avril shut her eyes, anguish tearing open some deep place in her heart. He had told her the only reason an *innfodt* married a mortal was to have a family. But he did not have a family.

And he had called it a foolish, senseless tradition.

Now she saw those words in a different, more painful light. Aching, wrapping her arms around her middle, she went to him. "Hauk, what happened?" she asked gently, tentatively reaching out to him.

He flinched when she touched his back but did not turn around. And did not speak for a moment.

Then the words started to come, haltingly.

"My first wife, Karolina"—his voice was strained, as if he had not said the name aloud in many years— "died in childbirth and our son with her, after we had been together a year. My second wife, Maeve . . ." He tilted his head back, looking up at the sky. "Died after we had been together more than fifty years. But in all that time, she never conceived."

Closing her eyes, she rested her forehead against his back. "Hauk, I am so sorry," she whispered.

She felt him shrug. "It happens to some couples. Large families are rare here. Most have only two or three children, which is mayhap for the best."

"That is not what I meant. I am sorry that you lost

them." She lifted her head. "I am surprised that you would marry again, after you lost your first wife."

He turned to look down at her, and their gazes met and held.

And a moment of understanding passed between them, too deep for words.

"We are not gods, Avril," he said softly. "Only men. Men who live and work and laugh . . . and want." His voice roughened. "And need."

She blinked hard, resisting the tears that blurred her vision. *And dream.* Hauk had dreamed, like any ordinary man. Dreams that had never come true.

And he had been left alone, to carry inside him all the pain and loss and sorrow of many lifetimes. She did not know how he could bear it.

"I had not planned to take another bride," he said tightly, grazing his thumb along her jaw. "Ever."

She leaned into him, reaching out to wrap her arms around him, unable to stay within the safe boundary she had drawn around her heart; she wanted too much to hold him, comfort him.

Slowly his arms came around her, drawing her in tight.

She pressed her cheek against his chest and listened to his heartbeat, steady and strong. "No wonder everyone has been besieging us with gifts." A strange, sad smile lifted one corner of her mouth. "They did not expect you to marry again."

His hands stroked her back, tangled in her hair. "I have been resisting my uncle's prodding on the matter for most of the past century."

"Your uncle? The man from the council of elders,

the one who looks like you?" she guessed. "I thought he was your brother."

"Nay, he is my uncle, Erik. My grandfather, Hakon Valbrand, was the leader of the group of explorers who discovered Asgard. Before he died, he had two sons—the eldest, my father, who was *vokter* before me, and Erik. They were part of the first generation of *innfodt*. The fourteen men who survived from that generation make up our council of elders."

"And the others," she asked hesitantly, "the ones who did not survive—"

"Were the ones who could not accept being made captive here. Could not accept what they were. What Asgard had made them. They persisted in trying to find some way to be free." He paused. "None were successful."

Her heart beat painfully hard in her chest. "And your father was one of them," she whispered. "Oh, Hauk, how old were you?"

"Eight." His chest rose and fell shallowly beneath her cheek.

She did not ask any more, simply holding him as he had held her before, sensing that he had already told her far more than he had told anyone in a long time.

But after a moment, he continued, unbidden.

"He loved my mother so deeply that he could not bear to lose her. He thought if he could discover Asgard's secret, find a way to give her the gift of being *innfodt* . . ." He exhaled sharply. "He thought he had succeeded. I do not know how. I was too young to understand. I only knew that the experiment killed her. And my father felt such remorse, he sailed away from the island, taking her body with him . . . and stayed away longer than six days, apurpose."

"Oh, Hauk." Avril could imagine how hurt and confused and angry a young boy of eight would have been, left behind. Alone.

"My uncle Erik was so angered, he burned my father's notes, his books, destroyed everything he had used in those accursed experiments." Hauk unwrapped himself from her embrace, turned away. "For years I hated my father for what he had done. It was not until much later," he said, his voice low, "that I understood him."

"After you lost Karolina," Avril said softly, remaining still as he paced.

"Aye." His voice became harsh. "My uncle was determined that I not make my father's mistake. He raised me to accept my place here and devote myself to training to be *vokter*. And I did, until I lost my wife and son. Then I neglected my duty, indulged in drink and danger and whatever willing women I could find and whatever *reason* I could find to open my eyes in the morn. That was when I . . ."

A look of unspeakable pain shadowed his features.

"When I understood why my father did what he did." Hauk raked a hand through his hair, hung his head. "Because everything and everyone around us, even those we bring here and care for and protect, *dies*. While no matter what we do, we go on. Unchanged."

Alone, Avril thought. Even after he had taken the risk of loving again, married a second time, he had been left alone. But no pleasure, no drink or sexual indulgence or risk could fill that part of his soul that ached for what he had lost. For what had lasted so briefly and been so sweet.

For love.

She walked over to him, silently, and took his hand in hers.

He drew her close, with a low sound of pain. "I did not want another wife, Avril. Do you not understand—"

"I understand," she said brokenly, even as she tilted her head up.

Even as his mouth covered hers.

It was a tender, startlingly gentle meeting of lips and breath and longing. Deep, warm.

Devastating.

And it made the last vestiges of her defenses against him, this golden-haired Norseman with a warrior's strength and a soft heart, crumble and vanish.

He drew her closer, deepening the kiss. "One day I will lose you," he said, his voice rough. "One day you will leave this world and I—"

"I do not want to leave you."

Her words made them both go still. Avril felt her heart fluttering as she realized what she had said.

What it meant.

She did not want to leave him.

He reached up to cup her face in his hands, looking down at her, his eyes darkened with emotion. "You wish to stay here with me, Avril?"

"I . . . I cannot stay here with you." She blinked hard, desperate not to cry. "I cannot abandon Giselle. Hauk, you know better than anyone how she is feeling. How alone and confused and frightened she must be."

He closed his eyes with a look of anguish, drew her close, buried his face in her hair. "Avril, I would set you free if I could. By all the gods, I would leave if I could. But I have learned to accept what I cannot change. I am what I was born to be. I have no choice in the matter. We have no choice in the matter."

She clung to him, holding on tight when she should be pushing him away. She could feel his heart pounding, as hard and fast as hers.

For a long moment, they held each other, silent.

"If I allowed you to return home and get her," Hauk said, his voice taut with strain, "would you come back?"

Avril could not find enough breath to speak, her thoughts whirling. *Would she come back? Accept her life here? Give up her freedom forever?*

Stay with him?

"You could . . . take me to the coast on your ship," she began shakily, trying to think of how they could accomplish it safely, "and return here, and then I could bring Giselle to the coast and you could come back for us."

He raised his head, pain and disbelief in his eyes. "You would bring her here to live all the rest of her life? Knowing she would never again be allowed to set foot in the outside world?"

Avril lowered her gaze, feeling her heart torn. Torn in two pieces that she could not seem to bring together. "Hauk—"

"And how would you explain to everyone where

you have been?" he asked roughly. "How would you persuade them simply to let you ride away with your daughter, with no explanation as to where you were going? How would you ensure that no one followed you when you left?"

She shook her head, uncertain, lost, her tears starting to fall.

"Avril, you said once that you did not want her made a captive here with you." Hauk tilted her head up, his voice hollow. "Has that changed? Would you willingly, happily give up your freedom—and hers?"

Her reluctant answer was wrenched from her, scarcely a whisper. "Nay."

19

Clouds had moved in, obscuring the moon, making the night as dark as Hauk's mood. Stretched out on his back, he stared up into the black sky, listening to the endless ebb and flow of the surf lapping against the sand. For more than an hour, he and Avril had lain in silence on the shore of the cove, side by side, not sleeping. Not speaking.

What more was there to be said? he thought bleakly.

I do not wish to leave you.

By Thor's hammer, he wished she had not uttered those words. If only she did not care for him, it would be easier to endure the idea that had begun to take shape in his mind.

An idea that could bring him more trouble than he had experienced in his entire life.

A pained, rueful smile curved his lips. He should have known his little Valkyrie would not make anything easy on him.

Turning his head, he looked over at her, lying so close to him. Even now, even as he fought the feeling, he could not deny how good and right it felt that she be here, beside him, with her tangled hair spread out over the sand, her eyes on the stars, her tunic and leggings still torn and muddied from this afternoon's adventure in the forest.

He did not want to think of what it would be like when she was gone.

But it would hurt less to lose her now, would it not, rather than after spending a lifetime . . . *her* lifetime . . . together?

I would set you free if I could. He kept turning the idea over in his mind. He did not know what the *eldrer* would do to him if he dared break the very laws he was sworn to uphold.

Ironically, it was Avril's feelings for him, and for Josette and the people of Asgard, that assured him it would be safe to let her leave.

He had no doubt she would protect them with the same fierce devotion she showed all her loved ones.

Yet how could he bear to let her go?

The wind blowing in across the cove made her shiver.

"Avril?" he asked quietly, reaching out to touch her arm, torn between the need to draw her close against the night's chill and the knowledge that holding her would never be enough. "Are you cold?"

She did not flinch away, but shook her head. "I was wondering if Giselle is looking up at the stars tonight. We like to—or rather, we used to . . ." She closed her eyes.

"Avril . . ."

"I never wanted her to grow up alone, as I did," she whispered. "I wanted to have many children."

Hauk rested the backs of his fingers against her cheek.

"God's breath." Her lashes lifted and she blinked rapidly. "I have not told that to anyone, not since I lost Gerard. I have tried so hard not to . . ."

"Not to want," he said gently, understanding in a way that brought an ache to the center of his chest. "Not to dream."

She turned toward him, her eyes brimming with tears. "I thought I would never do this again."

"Never dream?"

"Never love another man this way."

His throat tightened. *"Avril."* He slid one arm around her trembling body and drew her to his side.

She buried her face against his shoulder. "Why could you not be as arrogant and heartless and cruel as I always thought Vikings were?" she complained with a sniffle.

"My apologies," he whispered, caressing her hair.

"Why do you have to be understanding and brave and kind and caring and—"

"I shall try to be more demanding and tyrannical."

"Stop that. You are not allowed to have a sense of humor as well."

He chuckled, afraid to give in to any of the other emotions spilling through him.

She shivered again. "I did not think God could ever bring another man so special into my life," she said in a voice edged with wonder and sorrow. "I thought no one could ever take Gerard's place."

"No one ever will take his place," he assured her quietly. "You are only afraid—"

"I am not afraid." She looked up. "I am not—"

He pressed a finger to her lips. "You are not afraid of wolves, or sailing dangerous waters alone, or even rather large Norsemen who carry you off across the sea." He reached down to touch her hand. Her left hand. "But you are afraid to let him go."

Her dusky lashes swept downward. "That is not . . . I am not . . ." Her voice wavered, as if the possibility had never occurred to her. "It is only that . . . I never even had a chance to say farewell to him," she explained haltingly. "When he rode off that morn, I . . . I did not know it would be the last time I ever saw him."

Hauk gently kneaded the taut muscles of her shoulders, could tell from the tension in her that she needed to let the feelings out, had kept them inside too long. "Tell me, Avril," he urged softly.

"He and his father were going to a tournament." She said the word as if she hated it. "Only a tournament. I had not even told him yet that I thought I might be with child. It was too soon to be sure, and we had . . ." A low sound of hurt escaped her. "We had all the time in the world." Her voice choked out for a moment. "He never knew about the baby. He died without ever knowing that he was to become a father."

Hauk clenched his jaw, pained more than ever that he had taken the child's mother away from her. He held Avril tighter.

Knowing he would have to let her go.

"On the day he left," Avril whispered, "that morn, he had been hunting in the woods, and he came in covered in mud, and I chastised him for tracking dirt everywhere. Then that night, after his squire came to tell me . . ." She swallowed hard. "To tell me that he was dead, that both he and his father had been killed by an enemy's treachery, I ran to our room. I was on the floor, crying, and I looked up and saw a handprint, a muddy handprint on the wall beside the door. His handprint." A single tear slid down her cheek, dampening Hauk's chest. "For weeks I would not let the servants clean it away, because it was . . . as if he were still there with me."

Hauk shut his eyes, understanding at last. Thinking of the sketch of Maeve he had made in one of his journals. He had once believed that he could hold on to her by holding onto some part of her, some symbol, some memory.

"You do not need a handprint to remember him, Avril. Or a ring. You need not fear that you will forget him. You will never forget him."

She lifted her gaze to his, her eyes filled with emotion.

He brushed away her tears with his fingertips. "And you need not fear that letting another man into your heart means you must banish him. That you could not do. But you should not be alone, little Valkyrie. You were not meant to be alone." His voice became hoarse. "You need someone to share your life, and keep you safe, and tease you until you smile. And hold your hand."

But he would not be that man.

"You are wrong, Hauk Valbrand," she whispered as

she reached up to caress his cheek. "I do not need *someone*, I need—"

A movement in the cove made Hauk glance out over the water—and sit up in shock. Avril gasped as she saw what he did.

His ship, gliding straight past them toward the open end of the cove.

Hauk leaped to his feet with a curse. From here, in the scant moonlight, he could just make out a lone figure at the oars. A dark-haired man. "By Thor's chariot, what does Keldan think he is—"

"Why would he take your boat?" Avril cried.

The man aboard the ship stood up, reaching for a line that bound the tiller in place, and the size and shape of the silhouette made Hauk curse. "That is not Keldan," he growled, icy fury pouring through him. "It is Thorolf."

"Thorolf?" Avril gaped at the ship, her heart pounding. The single-masted vessel had to be more than twenty paces long, but with Thorolf at the oars, it cut swiftly through the waves. "But I thought the others were taking him to—"

"He must have escaped." Hauk swore. "And come straight back for the boat."

Avril glanced toward the distant end of the cove, near the forest, drenched by fear. "Sweet Mary, what if he hurt Josette and Keldan?"

"Go and check on them, Avril." Hauk was already taking off his boots.

"But what are you—"

"I have to stop him."

"Nay! Hauk, where could he possibly be going? If he can only survive for six days—"

"He is either insane, terrified of facing the elders, or angry enough to reveal our secret to the outside world. Mayhap all three. Whatever he is planning, I cannot let him leave."

Avril shook her head, alarmed at the idea of him going off to face Thorolf alone. "Hauk, you cannot—"

"It is my duty, Avril. He could endanger everyone on Asgard. If I run, I can cut him off before he reaches the mouth of the cove." He paused just long enough to give her a quick, hard kiss. "Do not argue with me. Go and see if Keldan and Josette are all right."

He turned and raced up the shoreline, into the darkness. Avril watched him, feeling helpless. If Thorolf was so determined to leave, he would be more dangerous than ever. And he might have weapons.

Hauk was armed only with the knife sheathed in his belt.

She glanced back the way they had come; they had wandered so far along the cove's edge, it would take her twenty minutes to reach Keldan and Josette. By then Hauk could be hurt. Or worse.

There are some things even an innfodt cannot survive, he had said.

Swallowing hard, she turned to look at the ship. It was nearing the mouth of the cove. She could just make out Hauk's silhouette as he reached the end of the shoreline and dove into the water, swimming straight for the boat. Terrifying memories of almost dying in those cold, night-black waters rushed over her.

But she could not leave Hauk alone when he needed help.

Gripping the hilt of her own knife, she ran after him.

Drenched and shuddering with cold, Hauk grabbed onto the ship's rudder, grateful for the concealing darkness and the noise of the surf. He treaded water as the light, shallow-keeled *knorr* bobbed up and down on the waves. He had to disable the ship. Quickly. His boat was meant to carry cargo in the space beneath its smooth deck; empty, it would sail over the waves as fast as a seabird.

With a fair wind, Thorolf could escape in a matter of minutes.

Hauk unsheathed his knife and placed it between his teeth. He could hear the scrape of wood against metal—the oars being pulled in through the oarlocks. Thorolf was preparing to unfurl the sail.

Gritting back a curse, Hauk took the knife and reached up to grab the low railing. Then he slashed through the leather thongs that held the rudder to the sternpost; it fell into the water, dangling uselessly by the ropes Thorolf had used to lash the tiller to the rail and keep the ship on course.

Almost at once, the boat began to drift. Gripping his knife, Hauk pulled himself up over the side, landing nimbly on the deck. "God *kveld*, Thorolf. Good evening," he said coolly as he helped himself to a sword Thorolf had left in the stern.

Standing amidships, Thorolf whirled with a startled oath. "Valbrand!"

"You have just lost your rudder," Hauk informed him. "I am afraid you will not be leaving Asgard."

Thorolf's gaze darted to the stern, and his face darkened with fury. "*Nei*, damn you!" He snarled. "You will not stop me, *vokter*. Not this time!"

"I already have." Not taking his gaze from Thorolf, Hauk crouched to pick up a length of rope. "I am taking you back to face the *eldrer*—"

"Never! I will never again set foot on that accursed rock. I am free now. And you will not keep me here." Thorolf yanked a line that dangled near his hand as he grabbed onto the railing.

The square sail unfurled with a sudden snap, caught the wind, and sent the ship heeling onto its side. Hauk lost his balance, tumbling to the deck, his weapons knocked from his grasp. Even as the ship righted itself, he scrambled to his feet—but could not dodge fast enough as Thorolf flung a dagger at him. Hauk dove sideways but the blade struck him in the right arm. Grunting in pain, he landed hard on the polished wooden planking.

Thorolf snatched up one of the discarded oars, lifting it over his head like a club.

But before he could strike, a knife came flying through the darkness from behind him, a silver flash in the moonlight that seemed to appear out of nowhere. It caught Thorolf in the shoulder and he stumbled, dropping the oar, roaring in surprise and pain.

Startled, Hauk looked past Thorolf—to see Avril

clinging to the railing at the bow of the ship, her eyes on Hauk's wounded arm. "Hauk—"

"Avril, nay!"

It was too late. Thorolf whirled toward her, sputtering curses of rage.

She screamed and started to drop back into the water, but Thorolf was faster. He lunged down and caught her, hauling her onto the deck. Yanking her in front of him, he turned to face Hauk. "Now, *vokter*"—he snarled—"let us talk about whether I am free to go."

Hauk jumped to his feet and grabbed the sword he had dropped, the pain in his arm forgotten.

"*Nei*, drop the weapon!" Thorolf demanded.

"Release her first—"

"Drop the weapon," Thorolf repeated, keeping one arm around Avril's throat and the other around her waist as she struggled and kicked. "And tell her not to try any tricks! Her friend taught me a lesson earlier. I will not be fooled—"

Avril—clearly unable to understand what Thorolf was saying in Norse—fastened her teeth on his arm and bit him.

Cursing, Thorolf snatched his arm from around her neck. But just long enough to reach behind him and yank her knife from his shoulder, gritting his teeth. He pressed the bloody edge against Avril's throat, and she gasped and went still.

"Tell her, Valbrand!" Thorolf's lips curled back from his teeth. "And put the sword down. They are pitifully fragile, these *utlending*. A single flick of this blade and she is dead."

Hauk met Avril's terrified gaze, his heart slamming against his ribs. He had no doubt Thorolf would do as he threatened.

"Avril, listen to me." He fought to keep his tone even, setting the weapon on the deck. "I want you to remain very still—"

"Hauk, I—"

"Do not try to get free," he ordered urgently. "If you try to use any tricks, he is going to hurt you."

She nodded and remained frozen. Hauk felt his gut clench at the way she was trembling in Thorolf's hold.

"Very good," Thorolf said more coolly in Norse, keeping the blade at her throat. "But I warn you, take one step toward me and she dies."

Hauk pressed his hand over the wound in his arm, trying to staunch the flow of blood, to ignore the searing pain. "Let her go." He fastened his gaze on Thorolf's black eyes. "Release her and you can have the boat. Go wherever you want and die and be damned."

"I do not think so. I have a much better plan in mind." Thorolf jerked his head toward the rudder. "First you will repair the damage you caused, *vokter*. And then you can sail this ship safely out of Asgard waters." He smiled. "In truth, I find this a most satisfying turn of events. You, who have always thwarted me, will now help set me free."

"You will only be free for six days—and then you will be dead."

"There you are wrong." Thorolf chuckled. "Fix the rudder and I will show you what I mean." He dug the knife into Avril's skin. "Or you can refuse—and lose another wife."

Hauk clenched his fists, fear and murderous rage and helpless frustration roiling inside him. He had no choice. Keeping his gaze on Thorolf, he moved back into the stern and dragged the trailing rudder up from the water, lashing it back into place.

"Very wise of you, *vokter*. Now take the tiller. You know the safest way through the rocks on this part of the coast better than I." Thorolf took up a position beside the mast, forcing Avril with him. "And I suggest you keep the ship steady. Any sudden movement and your pretty bride might be seriously damaged."

Hauk did as he said, his gaze on Avril. Her cheeks were pale, her eyes full of fear—and apology. He shook his head almost imperceptibly, both forgiving her and begging her not to make any move that Thorolf might find threatening.

Standing at the tiller, the deep cut in his arm throbbing painfully, Hauk guided the *knorr* through the moonlit darkness. He knew that he dared not give in to any of the dangerous ideas simmering in his head.

If he were alone with Thorolf, he would not hesitate to purposely slam the ship into one of the towering pillars of rock that loomed out of the fog.

But he would not endanger Avril.

He carefully navigated toward the safest passage he knew, between two of the ancient, massive stones. The *knorr* responded as he had known it would, gliding over the water as straight and fast as a sea bird.

The night wind quickly carried them beyond Asgard's boundary.

And into the open ocean.

"You have what you wanted," Hauk ground out. "Now release her. If you wish to commit suicide rather than face the *eldrer*—"

"The *eldrer* no longer hold any power over me." A grin split Thorolf's face. "Any more than you or those lackwits who tried to take me back to town earlier."

"What did you do to them?" Hauk demanded, his attention shifting back to Avril.

She was shivering as the cold wind cut through her wet garments. His heart pounding, Hauk struggled to think of some way to get her safely out of Thorolf's grasp.

"They should be awakening from *langvarig sovn* about now," Thorolf said scornfully. "The young fools are much better suited to being merchants and craftsmen than warriors. They are far too compassionate and soft-hearted. When they stopped to rest, I complained that they had made my bonds too painful. They loosened them to ease my suffering, and I rather quickly had my hands on a weapon."

Hauk grimaced. "And when you returned to the cove," he asked, not certain he wanted to hear the answer, "what did you do to Keldan and his wife?"

"I left them asleep on the shore," Thorolf bit out. "All I wanted is the boat. All I wanted was to leave. If you had not interfered, as you always do—" Anger darkened his expression for a moment, before he continued with a careless shrug. "In truth, I have done that whelp of a carpenter a favor. His wife is one of us now." He smiled. "I made her *innfodt*. She cannot die."

Hauk choked out a shocked, wordless exclamation. "You are insane."

"*Nei*, I am free. I have discovered the secret. Asgard's secret." Thorolf's smile widened.

Hauk stared at him in disbelief.

"Hauk," Avril called to him, reclaiming his attention. "I could pretend to faint, and then I might be able to—"

"Avril, nay," Hauk said in French, fixing her with a stern look. "Remain still. Do not even—"

"What are you saying to her?" Thorolf demanded, pressing the knife against her throat to silence her.

"I am only telling her not to move," Hauk insisted tightly, his heartbeat loud in his ears, his wounded arm stabbing with pain as his fingers gripped the tiller. He tried to think. Discarded one desperate plan after another. "What in the name of all the sons of Odin makes you believe *you* have discovered Asgard's secret? It cannot be done. For six hundred years our people have tried—"

"And your father almost succeeded. That is the tragedy, is it not? He came *so* close, only to fail." A satisfied expression stole across Thorolf's blunt features. "After your uncle so heedlessly destroyed your father's workshop, I sifted through what was left—and found enough remnants of his notes to start my own experiments. It has taken me *centuries* to re-create his work, to refine and distill various combinations of plants and minerals and water. To test my potions without arousing suspicion."

Hauk swore, horrified that his father's work had led to more suffering and death. "How many people have you killed?"

"Only a few *utlending* women." Thorolf shrugged. "I am afraid that none of my wives over the years met a natural end. And a few other carefully chosen females had to be sacrificed, as well. A missing *innfodt* would have attracted too much attention and a great many questions, but what is one *utlending* more or less?" He kept the blade at Avril's throat. "There are far too many of them in the world as it is. And they are inferior to us." He stroked his hand down her arm. "Fragile, pitiful creatures."

Avril cringed and Hauk ruthlessly subdued the rage that shot through him, the protective urge that made him want to stalk across the deck and fasten his hands around Thorolf's throat. "And what makes you think you have succeeded?" he challenged, trying to direct the whoreson's attention away from Avril.

"I know I have succeeded. I discovered your father's error—the elixir must not be stored in flasks of leather or wood or any material native to Asgard, for that renders it unstable. It must be kept in glass." Thorolf withdrew a small, crystalline flask from a pouch at his waist. "Like this."

Hauk stared at the ruby-colored liquid in the vial. It could be wine. He could be bluffing.

Or it might be true.

"If you are so confident," he said with a growl, "then drink it."

"I already have, hours ago. After I tested it on Keldan's bride. I choked her and she spent hours in *langvarig sovn*," Thorolf said triumphantly, clearly savoring the memory. "And then she awakened."

Astonishment stole Hauk's voice.

"I had more of the elixir, much more," Thorolf continued, his look of pleasure dissolving. "But it is lost to me now. This is all that remains."

"Hauk," Avril said quietly, "what are we going to—"

"Avril, it will be all right," he assured her in French. "I will think of something. Do not—"

"Cease." Thorolf snarled. "What are you saying to her?"

"Turn the ship into the wind," Avril suggested quickly.

He flashed her an anguished look. If the sail came around unexpectedly, it would knock Thorolf off his feet—but she might get her throat cut. "It will not work, little Valkyrie."

"Cease!" Thorolf demanded, his hold on Avril tightening.

"She is afraid," Hauk told him angrily. "I am trying to reassure her."

Thorolf chuckled. "You are a fool, Valbrand." He pressed the point of the blade against the tender underside of her chin, forcing her head up. "Why does she matter so much to you? I have never understood why so many of our kind care for these fragile, short-lived females."

Avril shut her eyes with a muted sound of distress, looking terrified. Hauk did not reply to Thorolf's jibes, pain wrenching through him, sharper than the agony in his arm.

Chuckling, Thorolf lifted the glass vial he held, examining the sparkling red liquid in the moonlight. "Mayhap you would like to have this for yourself, *vokter*?" he asked tauntingly, extending the crystalline flask toward Hauk. "Think of it. You would be free to live with her in the outside world. To go wherever you wish." He withdrew his hand, waving the vial in front of Avril's face. "Or, if I chose, I could make her one of us. Ah, you would like that, would you not? To keep your wife with you forever?"

Hauk bit back a curse. "Even if your potion worked to make Josette *innfodt*, you cannot be certain it will work on you. The *utlending* are different from us—"

"Indeed they are. And in truth, I was not certain." Thorolf looked back at the island, now barely visible in the distance, then he glanced over his shoulder and smiled.

He turned just enough to show Hauk. "But it does seem to be working, does it not?"

Hauk felt his heart slam against his ribs. The deep blade-cut in Thorolf's shoulder had already closed. And the mark where Avril had bitten his arm had vanished. Thorolf's wounds were healing.

Hauk's were not.

"*Ja*, Valbrand, it does seem to be working," Thorolf repeated with a smug expression. "I cannot tell you how pleased I am that you decided to try and stop me one last time. Now I shall not only be free, and a wealthy man—when I sell this elixir to whichever kings or princes are willing to pay my price—but I shall also have the pleasure of watching you die."

Hauk cursed him. "Six days is a long time, *hund feig*," he spat. "I will kill you before—"

"*Nei*, you will not. You cannot." Thorolf returned the vial to the pouch at his waist, chuckling. Fearless. "Mayhap, after you are dead, I will make your lovely bride immortal and keep her with me forever." He drew the knife slowly down Avril's throat, down the opening of her tunic, between her breasts. "Imagine it, *vokter*—your wife, in my bed. Night after night, for all eternity."

Hauk snarled an oath.

"*Ja*, it is a most pleasant thought," Thorolf mused. "Mayhap I will even take her *before* you die." He caught the front of Avril's tunic on the tip of the blade, slicing it open. "So that you may watch."

Avril uttered a strangled sound, eyes wide with terror. A white-hot fury descended on Hauk. He was not about to let Thorolf make good on his threats.

And the knife was at last away from her throat.

"Avril, get ready to break free of him."

"*Aye.*"

"What are you saying now?" Thorolf asked mockingly. "Telling her farewell already?"

"*Nei.*" Without warning, Hauk pushed the tiller all the way to starboard, turning the ship abruptly, sharply. Thorolf lost his balance and Avril pushed free of his grasp, diving toward the deck as the sail came around and knocked Thorolf off his feet.

Hauk launched himself forward. Thorolf was already getting up, bellowing with rage. Avril scrambled out of the way as Hauk slammed into him. He heard her frightened cry as they fell to the deck, grappling, landing brutal, pounding blows with their fists.

The *knorr* plunged over the waves at the mercy of the wind and current. With no one controlling the tiller, it pitched and rolled dangerously, threatening to tip onto its side.

"Avril, the tiller!" Hauk shouted.

He glimpsed her rushing toward the stern, out of harm's way, just as Thorolf struck him in his wounded arm. Pain exploded through his shoulder. His hand, his arm, tingled and went numb.

He rolled sideways to avoid a second hit to his injured limb and lurched to his feet, barely avoiding the ship's boom as it swung around. He looked for one of the blades they had used. Found none on the deck.

Thorolf closed in on him, black eyes glittering. Hauk managed to strike one blow with his good arm before Thorolf knocked him backward into the bulwark.

"You should have told her farewell when you could," Thorolf said with a look of triumph, his hands closing around Hauk's throat.

With his right arm weakened, Hauk could not break Thorolf's stranglehold. He heard Avril scream as Thorolf bent him backward over the railing, ready to throw him over the side. Could feel the icy splash of the sea spray, the dark waters ready to swallow him.

Then, for an instant, something distracted Thorolf and he looked aside. Hauk followed his gaze. Saw that Thorolf's legs had become tangled in a rope. Noticed what was attached to the other end at the same time Thorolf did.

The anchor stone.

In that single heartbeat of time, Hauk lunged from Thorolf's grasp. Choking on his own breath, he seized the rock and heaved it over the side.

Thorolf screamed in terror as the rope whipped over the edge of the boat. He grabbed the railing. But the weight of the anchor stone yanked him over.

Hauk dove toward him, tried to reach him in time, grabbed for his arm.

But his hand closed on empty air.

Thorolf was already gone, pulled beneath the waves.

20

"Hauk!" Her heart pounding, Avril lashed the tiller to keep it steady and ran toward him. He sank to the deck, one hand still outstretched, his expression stunned.

She dropped to her knees before him, throwing her arms around him, unable to stop shaking. "God's mercy, are you all right?"

He gathered her close, the wind and waves the only sound in the darkness. She held him fiercely, trembling with all the fear she had felt during the brief, violent, horrible combat. She had been so terrified for him. Felt such gratitude to God that he was safe.

Had come so close to losing another man she loved.

After a long moment, he set her back from him, his gaze searching her face. "Are you all right, Avril? He did not hurt you—"

"I am unharmed." She could not stop shivering, did not want to think about what Thorolf had *meant* to do to her, what would have happened if Hauk had not stopped him. "You are the one who is hurt." The deep gash in his arm was bleeding profusely. She untucked her tunic from the belted leggings she wore, and tore a strip off the hem, all the while trying not to look at the rip down the front, cut by Thorolf's blade.

Hauk did not flinch as she gingerly examined his wound; he barely seemed aware of the pain, turning his head to gaze out over the black surface of the moonlit ocean.

"I cannot believe I took a life," he said, his voice stark. "I cannot believe I killed him."

"Are"—she swallowed hard—"are you certain he is dead?"

"Aye," he choked out, his jaw hardening. "There are some things even an *innfodt* cannot survive." He shut his eyes. "I killed him."

"Hauk, *he* was trying to kill *you*," she reminded him, gently wrapping the cloth around his arm. "And I did not see any remorse in his face when he had you over the railing and was about to—" Her voice shook, and she left the sentence unfinished. She knotted the bandage in place. "And you saved me," she said softly. "Again."

He nodded, still looking stricken at what he had done.

She touched his cheek, aching inside, wishing she could ease the pain from his expression. Thorolf had shown no conscience, no hesitation in hurting Hauk, and Keldan and Josette, and mayhap others, but that fact could not ease Hauk's sense of guilt.

Though he was a warrior by training and by duty, in his heart Hauk was a man of peace. Even to save her, to save himself, to protect his people, he would not have taken a life by choice.

"Hauk, why *was* Thorolf so determined to leave

Asgard?" she asked quietly. "What was in that flask that seemed to please him so?"

"Thorolf claimed he had discovered Asgard's secret. Created a potion of eternal youth, based on my father's work." Hauk reached out to grip the railing. "He said he tested it on Josette after he kidnapped her."

"God's breath, he must have been mad."

"Mayhap, but I am not certain. His wounds were healing, Avril. Out here, beyond Asgard. And Josette . . ." He shook his head. "Thorolf said he had made her one of us. That she is now *innfodt*."

"But how is that possible?"

"I do not know. If in truth he discovered the secret, it died with him." Hauk clenched his jaw.

Avril leaned closer to him, resting her head on his shoulder. "Hauk, we have to go back to Asgard," she urged quietly after a moment. "Your arm needs to heal."

His hand buried in her hair, and he held her close, pressing his cheek to hers. She could feel his entire body rigid with tension, feared that his wound was causing him more pain than he was letting her know.

Then, slowly, he pulled out of her embrace and stood up. He moved toward the mast and trimmed the sails, knotting them in place. "We are not going back," he told her softly, firmly.

"W-what?" she asked, breathless. "What do you mean? We must go back. Unless you can experience your healing sleep here."

"Nay, outside of Asgard, we do not experience

langvarig sovn. For the moment, I am as mortal as you.
For six days. After that, I—"

"Then we have to return to Asgard at once!" Avril
looked over her shoulder. They had left Asgard so far
behind, she could no longer even see it in the moonlit
darkness.

"Avril, I am not taking you back with me," he said
in that same quiet, unyielding tone. He moved to the
stern, taking the tiller and turning the ship. Southeast. Away from the island. "It is two days to Antwerp
from here and two days back. I will return in ample
time to heal."

Her heart thudded hard against her ribs. "What are
you saying?" she exclaimed, stunned. She got to her
feet and went to him.

"I am taking you home." He met her gaze, his jaw
set. "I am setting you free, Avril. I cannot keep you
with me on Asgard any longer. You were meant to be
free and so is your daughter, and I will not keep you
from her any longer."

Avril felt a dizzying explosion of emotions all at
once. Surprise and disbelief and sorrow collided inside
her. He was setting her free. Was doing what she had
wanted from the beginning.

Then why did she feel only misery and pain?

"But why now? Hauk, you said you would never—
you would be breaking the laws!"

"You matter more to me than the laws, little Valkyrie," he said hoarsely. "And I know you will keep
our secret."

A sob escaped her as she wrapped her arms around
him, clung to him. And felt her heart torn in two.

He slid one arm around her, his voice a whisper almost lost in the wind. "And I have already broken a more serious law. When I return home, I will have to confess to the elders that I killed Thorolf." He hesitated. "And pay the price."

She lifted her head, alarm slicing through her. "But you were doing your duty. You risked your life to stop him from stealing your ship, from leaving, because of your *duty*. And you were fighting for your life. You had no choice—"

"I was not thinking of my duty when I attacked him, Avril. And what Thorolf did does not change what *I* did. I killed him. I broke the most sacred of our laws."

She felt a chill steal through her heart. "What will the elders do?"

"I do not know. In all my lifetime, no *innfodt* has killed another."

She buried her face against his chest, unable to speak, unable to bear thinking of what he might suffer. He drew her in close with one arm, keeping his other hand on the tiller.

"You are cold," he said gently. "I have a cloak and other garments, there beneath that plank amidships. And food and drinking water, as well."

Silent, numb, Avril went to where he indicated and found a hinged panel that opened to reveal a storage compartment beneath the deck; Hauk apparently kept his ship well stocked for his reconnaissance voyages. She took out a warm, fur-lined cloak, a flask of water, and some salve for his wounded arm.

She returned to stand next to him in the stern,

caring for his wound, still shivering in the wind's cold bite; it was hard to remember that it was autumn, here in the rest of the world, beyond the warm paradise that was Asgard Island.

She started to wrap the cloak around his broad shoulders when she finished, but he insisted she take it, tenderly enfolding her in its warmth. Trembling, she sank down beside him, not sure she would ever feel warm again, sitting at his feet as he guided the ship southeast.

The first hint of dawn slipped over the eastern edge of the world and turned the dark horizon to gray.

She should feel happy. She was going home to Giselle, at last.

Instead, she felt all shivery and brittle inside, as if she were about to splinter into pieces. She reached up and touched Hauk's hand. "I do not want to leave you."

"I know," he said quietly, his fingers closing around hers. "I do not want you to go. But this is how it must be."

They fell silent for a moment.

"You must remember never to tell anyone where you were, Avril, never whisper a word about Asgard."

She started to cry.

"And I . . ." His voice choked out for a moment, sounded thick when he spoke again. "I would ask one more promise of you." He drew her up to stand beside him.

She averted her gaze, trying to be brave and strong and failing utterly. "I will grant aught that you ask."

"Then find a husband who will love you, and take care of you, and give you more children to love."

Tears blurred her vision as she looked up. "But *you* are my husband," she whispered. "You are my husband, Hauk Valbrand."

He closed his eyes, his jaw tightening until deep lines bracketed his mouth. He hung his head. She reached up to touch his cheek.

And felt dampness there.

"It was not meant to be, little Valkyrie," he said, cursing softly. "The gods are too cruel."

She shook her head, unable to believe that. "God does not want us to live without love," she argued, caressing his cheek. "It is what makes life meaningful and precious, whether it lasts a lifetime or"—her voice dissolved in tears—"or only a handful of days."

His arm came around her shoulders, and he drew her against him. She clung to him desperately, buried her face against his shoulder, the thought too painful. *Only a handful of days*. It was not fair, that this would be all they would ever have—two final days, spent at sea, in the cold. This would be her last memory of him.

Nay, she did not want it to be her last memory of him. She could not say farewell to him forever when she had barely begun to know him. She could not look upon him for the last time, when she had not truly seen him, known him, loved him for the first time.

Her heart pounding, her decision was made, and it seemed so easy, so natural, to tilt her mouth up to his, to brush a kiss across his lips.

There were no words between them. Only his

mouth suddenly covering hers in a deep, infinite kiss. She could feel the tension within him, the way his muscles tightened beneath her fingertips when she slid her hands over his chest, down his ribs. A groan escaped him, a sound filled with deep pain and deeper need. Fumbling, quickly, he secured the tiller.

And then he was falling with her down to the deck, and there was only the ship's hard wood and the soft fur of the cloak beneath them, and the stars above giving way to the morning. And the yearning. The wildness. The love in her heart. She wanted to lose herself to him, to know what it was to be his. If only for a brief moment. One last, timeless moment.

His hands slipped beneath her garments, seeking and finding her softness, her body, and she could see his eyes darken with passion—the deep blue she had seen in her dreams.

A tear, unbidden, slipped from her lashes, and he caught it on his fingertip.

"Avril," he murmured hoarsely, nuzzling her cheek, "are you certain this is what you want?"

Gathering him close, she whispered her assent against his mouth, wanting to hold him and be held, to caress and feel cared for, wanting to give to him all she felt, all she was.

He slipped her tunic over her head, baring her to his gaze in light that might have come from moon or sun. Cold air, cold sea spray could not compete with hot kisses, the hot friction of skin against skin. She arched beneath him, felt his hands gliding over her. He aroused her so gently, with such tenderness, that she thought she could actually feel her heart breaking.

His fingers sought and found her feminine heat, brushing over her until need made her cry out softly. It seemed to take forever, a lifetime, before he finally became part of her, gathering her to him and possessing her fully as he already possessed her heart. The feel of him slowly becoming part of her, all heat and hardness and velvety steel, brought a moan from her lips, a soul-deep sound of longing and passion and exquisite, bittersweet pleasure.

Her hips arched to take him deeper and he began moving powerfully inside her, leaving her breathless. The rhythm of the ship and the sea became the rhythm of their bodies, flowing together, rising and falling. The sounds of the surf and the wind and their sighs filled the dawn as he filled her body.

And she clung to him, as she had once clung to the shattered pieces of her past, and she felt healed and whole and alive. More than alive. *Loved*. This gentle warrior had shown her how much love she still needed, how much love she could still feel. He had changed her life. Changed everything.

And soon she must lose him.

God, nay. Nay, please do not take him from me.

But not even heaven could keep them together. They could only cling to the present, this hour, this sweetest of moments. And try not to think of the morrow.

She surrendered herself to him, again and again, losing herself to the fierce power and passion of his lovemaking.

And when the sun rose, filling the sky with light, she felt agonizingly aware of the cold bite of autumn and a darkness descending inside her that even the sun could not pierce.

The docks of Antwerp bustled with traders and ships from every corner of the earth. All along the wharf, merchants haggled over prices in dozens of languages, inspecting goods and counting out coins, while sailors filled the air with lilting tunes in deep, salty voices as they unloaded their cargo and headed off to the taverns for the night.

There were so many people, Hauk thought. All of them foreign, *utlending*.

Her people.

The winds, curse them, had been favorable, carrying his *knorr* swiftly to Antwerp in just less than two days. He had wanted to slow down as the coast of Avril's homeland came into view. But he knew it would not help to prolong their parting.

And, though he tried not to let her know it, he was not feeling well. His wounded arm pained him, and fatigue made him light-headed. He knew he needed to return to Asgard at once.

To whatever fate awaited him.

After he had secured his ship to one of the crowded piers, Avril threw herself into his arms. He held her close, one last time, trying to memorize the feel of her as evening fell and stars lit the sky with shades of pearl gray and amethyst.

Then he helped her onto the dock and did not try to follow.

"I still say I should accompany you until you find this *beau-frère* of yours," he said.

Avril shook her head, blinking hard. "You have to return home. Do not worry about me. Gaston will have men searching for me everywhere, and since I disappeared from Antwerp, they will focus their efforts here. It should not be hard to find them."

Hauk tried to think of something more to say, and could not.

She stood there, wrapped in her borrowed cloak, so brave. So beautiful. He had never known a lady like her. And never would again.

From somewhere deep inside him, past the sorrow and the ache in his heart, the words came out on a shuddering breath. "I love you, little Valkyrie."

Her eyes seemed to shimmer with emerald brightness. "I love you, husband."

Those would be the last words he ever shared with her—those words, not *farewell*. His eyes burning, Hauk reluctantly took the rope from around the pier, and used one of the oars to push away from the dock, and began to row.

She did not move, watching him, as he watched her . . . until his ship was too far away . . . until she was naught but a distant silhouette in the fading light.

Until he could no longer see her at all.

21

 **M**oonlight poured in through the tall, arched window, bathing Avril in the glistening colors of stained glass; she sat on a tasseled pillow in the window seat, humming softly to Giselle, cherishing the sweet weight of her daughter in her arms. Though her little one had fallen asleep some time ago, Avril did not move, simply holding her, brushing her fingertips through Giselle's raven curls, caressing her round, rosy cheeks, so peaceful in sleep.

The ride from Antwerp had taken almost three days, even at a gallop. Since returning to Gaston and Celine's château this afternoon, Avril had offered a hundred prayers of thanksgiving for being reunited with her daughter . . . and yet her homecoming had not brought the happiness and contentment she had anticipated during her first days on Asgard.

Everything here was exactly the same. Exactly as she had left it.

Only she herself seemed different. Out of place, somehow.

Mayhap because she had left part of her heart and soul on that warm island in the center of a cold sea.

She hoped and prayed that Hauk had reached home safely.

She could not bear that she might never know what had become of him.

There was a knock at the door. Avril glanced up. "Come in," she whispered, careful not to wake her daughter.

Celine entered, wearing a dressing robe, her long red hair trailing down her back. "I thought I would find you in here." She smiled at finding Avril still cradling her little girl, came to sit beside her.

"I cannot bring myself to put her to bed," Avril explained softly. "I do not think I will ever let her go again."

"I don't blame you." Celine picked up a fabric doll Giselle had dropped, tucking it back into the little girl's hold with a mother's natural ease. "If I were away from Soren for a fortnight, I think I would go mad."

"I am so grateful to you and Gaston for taking care of her, Celine. And for not telling her that I was missing."

"We thought it best not to frighten her. Gaston was the one who decided we should simply tell her that you had been delayed in Antwerp for a few days."

A few days, Avril thought. It seemed she had been on Asgard much longer than that. How could her whole life have changed, in so short a time?

"But if you hadn't returned this week," Celine continued quietly, "I'm not sure how much longer she would've believed us."

Avril swallowed hard, preferring not to think of

that; she could only be grateful that the separation had proved to be much harder on herself than on Giselle. "Thank you."

"Avril," Celine said after a moment, "Gaston is still rather upset—"

"I know. I know he is angry with me."

"Not angry. Only concerned. We're both so relieved to have you back alive and unharmed, but you must understand . . ." Celine turned slightly in the window seat, facing her. "It *was* rather surprising to have you reappear in Antwerp so suddenly, saying only that you were taken hostage by mistake in a feud between two warring families. Why can you not tell us who these noblemen were, or where they took you? Gaston would like to—"

"I have tried to explain as best I can, Celine. There is no *need* for Gaston to go charging off to seek justice. They set us free as soon as they realized they had abducted the wrong women. And we were well treated. I was not harmed."

Celine regarded her with a puzzled look. "And Josette decided to stay with them."

Avril sighed. It pained her to have to be so secretive with her own family. "Sometimes, *ma soeur*, the heart makes choices that defy reason."

Celine reached out to touch her shoulder. "Avril," she said gently, "I know you may have been reluctant to speak freely in front of Gaston and his men, but . . ." She tilted her head, her eyes searching Avril's face. "Is there anything you want to tell me? I know you said that your abductors did not hurt you in any way, but you seem . . . troubled."

Avril blinked hard, forced a smile. "I am fine, Celine. Truly."

"You know you can tell me anything. I would keep it between the two of us."

Avril lowered her gaze. Celine was always so perceptive, especially when it came to matters of the heart. And Avril desperately *wanted* to pour out all that she was feeling. All the pain and loss and love and worry.

But she must never speak a word about Hauk, to anyone. Not even to Celine.

"I am sorry, *ma soeur*, but I must ask you to understand."

Celine nodded and dropped the subject. "I know that there are some secrets that simply can't be told," she said quietly. "But if you ever need to talk, I'm here. I'll always be here for you."

"Thank you. Thank you for understanding."

"Good night, Avril." Her *belle-soeur* stood, her expression soft, her skin aglow in the moonlight—that special glow of a beloved woman who had a child growing within her.

Avril felt a pang of jealousy so strong it made her hurt inside. "Good night, Celine."

Celine headed for the door. "I think I'd better go back to my bedchamber and try to soothe Gaston's ruffled feathers."

Avril smiled. If anyone could accomplish that, Celine could.

Celine paused one last time at the door, looking over her shoulder. "Welcome home."

Home, Avril thought, the word bringing a bittersweet ache to her heart as Celine closed the door behind her. Resisting the uncomfortable feeling, Avril stood and carried Giselle to her small bed, tucking the covers around her, dusting a kiss in her dark hair. Then she straightened and went to the window.

Looking out at the chapel in the forest, she closed her eyes.

And slipped the wedding band from her finger.

She held the circle of gold in her hand for a time, and then she walked to the hearth. Reaching up, she placed it in a lacquered box on the mantel that held Giselle's most precious belongings. "For you, my little one," she whispered.

Closing the box's lid, she felt a sense of peace steal through her, at least about her past. As she slipped out through the door that led to her own bedchamber, she did not want to think about her future.

Because she had no tears left to cry.

The sun and warmth and sea winds of Asgard had not made Hauk feel any better, though he had been home a full day now. His wounds had healed, but he still felt . . . numb. Empty. A bleak fog had descended on him, and only one ray of brightness managed to pierce it: the thought that Avril was home now, safe. With her little girl.

He held fast to that image, took strength from it as he prepared to face whatever punishment he was about to receive.

Josette and Keldan accompanied him as he approached the door of his Uncle Erik's *vaningshus*.

"Are you certain we cannot come with you?"

Keldan asked for the tenth time, his arm around Josette's shoulders as they walked. "I do not understand why the *eldrer* insist on seeing you alone. We all told them what Thorolf did—"

"*Ja*, and that does not change the fact that I broke our laws, just as he did. The punishments must apply to everyone equally, Kel, or they have no meaning at all. I thank you for standing by me, but I must face this alone." He turned to Josette, shifting to French. "Still feeling all right?"

She nodded. "I wish you and Keldan would cease hovering over me. I do not know if Thorolf's claims about that potion were true, but I feel perfectly well."

Hauk smiled at her, hoping that Thorolf's claims were true, that Keldan would never lose his beloved bride and they would be together forever.

But only time would tell. For whatever secret Thorolf had discovered had indeed died with him.

The three of them stopped before the door of Erik's remote dwelling. Hauk turned to tell his friends farewell, but emotion drew his throat tight, and he could not find the words.

He was not sure if this would be the last time he ever saw them.

"You have done a good thing," Josette said before he could speak, her eyes bright and earnest. "Setting Avril free was the only choice you could have made. As was killing Thorolf. Your council must understand that."

"I am not certain they will be as understanding as you, Josette." He looked at Keldan, held out his hand, tried to banish the leaden feeling in his stomach.

Only seeing the two of them so happy together made the parting bearable. "You are fortunate to have this bride of yours, Kel," he told his friend in Norse. "You were right in Antwerp. You chose wisely."

"*Ja*, as did you." Keldan gripped Hauk's outstretched arm, his voice hoarse. "I will take care of Ildfast until you return."

Hauk held his gaze; they both knew he might not be returning. "Take care of yourself, as well," he said gruffly. He pulled Kel into a quick, hard embrace. "Live a long and happy life, my friend."

"And you, Hauk."

Hauk stepped back, nodding in gratitude for his friend's good wishes. Though he did not believe they would come true.

Turning, he entered his uncle's *vaningshus*.

He stopped just inside the door, his heart thudding a single, hard stroke.

Only his uncle was there, standing before the hearth, the flames behind him casting his large shadow across the darkened chamber, his expression dire.

The other thirteen *eldrer* were missing.

"Have a seat, nephew."

Hauk shut the door, held himself rigid. "I would face this standing. Where are—"

"I believe you are going to want to sit down," his uncle told him somberly.

Hauk could not reply for a moment, cold dread spreading through him at his uncle's tone. "Where are the rest of the *eldrer*?"

"We finished our discussions an hour ago, and they

departed." His uncle grimaced. "I asked to be allowed to speak with you alone."

Hauk took a deep breath, sensing that his worst fears were about to be confirmed. "Then let us dispense with the prelude, Uncle," he said evenly. "I have naught to say in my defense. I killed Thorolf. I wish there had been another way, but there was not." Hauk came forward to stand in the center of the room. "I also set my wife free, and that I do not regret for a moment. Simply tell me what punishment you and the other *eldrer* have chosen for me."

"There can be only one punishment, even for the *vokter*. When you killed Thorolf, you sealed your own fate." A look of unmistakable sadness crossed Erik Valbrand's usually stoic face. "You are to be banished."

Hauk felt an icy tingle go straight down his back. "Death, then," he said, surprised at how calm he sounded upon saying it. "The sentence is to be death."

"I could not persuade them otherwise."

Hauk looked away, nodding. "I understand," he choked out, breathing unsteadily as he tried to absorb the idea, the word, the finality. *Death*. It was not easy after three hundred years on this earth. "I am grateful for your efforts, Uncle, but I understand the decision."

"And so do I. But that does not mean I accept it." Erik turned toward the hearth. "I did not tell the other *eldrer* the true reason I wished to meet with you alone."

Hauk glanced at him. "You cannot break with the

other *eldrer*," he said flatly. "I would not ask it of you. If I were to try to remain on Asgard, in hiding somewhere—"

"That is not what I meant." Erik picked up an object from the mantel. "The reason I wanted to meet with you alone was so that I could give you this."

Walking over to Hauk, he held it out: a small velvet pouch, like those Hauk and his mother used to use for collecting seashells, when he was a boy.

Hauk frowned in bewilderment. "Where did you—"

"Open it, nephew."

Hauk took the bag, pulled on the strings, and lifted out what was inside: a faceted bottle made of clear glass, the sort made to hold perfumed ointments. It held only a scant amount of whatever precious scent it had once contained, the green liquid just enough to cover the bottom of the flagon.

"It is the elixir your father created," Erik explained, "during his efforts to discover Asgard's secret."

Hauk's head came up sharply. "Elixir?" he choked out. "Are you saying it was this he used to try to make my mother *innfodt*? Was it this that killed her?"

"*Ja,*" Erik said quietly. "But your father was not trying to make her *innfodt*. You do not know the truth—I have never told you the truth," he amended, "about how your parents died."

"How they died," Hauk echoed, gripping the bottle in his hand. "What are you talking about? Why give this to me now? Are you offering me a chance to take my own life rather than choose banishment?"

"*Nei,* that is not my purpose at all. Hauk, your

father did not want to make your mother *innfodt*."
Erik shook his head. "He wanted to leave Asgard, to
live in the outside world with her. Hakon wanted his
freedom. He was trying to find a way to become mortal—*utlending*—not only for himself but for you. For
everyone on Asgard. So that we all might be free to
choose. Despite Thorolf's boasts, I do not think he re-
created your father's elixir, but rather stumbled onto
something different."

Hauk stared at him in shock. And when he studied
the bottle, he realized the green liquid it contained
was different from Thorolf's elixir, which had been a
clear, ruby red.

"Your father was about to test that potion on himself," Erik continued, gesturing to the bottle in Hauk's
hand. "But when your mother learned of it, she was
terrified for his life . . . so she went and took some
from his workshop. Secreted it in that perfume flask.
And tested it on herself."

Hauk whispered an oath, glaring down at the
flagon with revulsion. "*Why?* Why would she—"

"Mayhap she thought it might make her *innfodt*, I
do not know." A muscle worked in Erik's jaw as he
glanced at the floor. "I only know that she did not
want to be parted from him, wanted to stay here with
him—and with you—forever. But it took her life instead. And your father in his grief chose to take his
own life by leaving Asgard rather than live without
her."

Stunned, Hauk found the nearest chair and sank
down into it, the bottle still gripped in his fingers.
"Why did you never tell me, Uncle, in all this time?"

he grated out. "I thought he had been trying to make her *innfodt*, that he gambled with her life and killed her. I hated him for years. If I had known the truth—"

"You would have tried to continue your father's work," Erik pointed out gently. "I had lost the two of them, Hauk. I did not want to lose you, as well. I had to save their son."

Hauk returned his gaze, silent a moment, understanding his uncle as he never had before. "And that is why you destroyed his workshop—so that no one else would risk their lives by continuing his work."

Erik nodded. "And because I was so full of rage and grief. And guilt." He turned away. "Hakon had *told* me about his work. I knew it was dangerous. I should have stopped him . . . but I did not." He looked down at the fire on the hearth, his voice heavy with remorse. "Mayhap because I hoped it would work, almost as much as he did. I did not stop him, and they both lost their lives." He turned to face Hauk once more. "I could not forgive myself. And *ja*, I meant to make certain no one else ever took such a risk."

Hauk thought of Thorolf and the lives he had ruthlessly lost over the years in his quest, and knew his uncle had been right to be concerned. "And is that also the reason you were so determined," he asked hoarsely, "that I grow up to be satisfied with my life on Asgard?"

"I thought it was what your parents would have wanted, that you learn to be happy here, to accept what could not be changed." Erik held Hauk's gaze, that look of sadness coming into his eyes again. "But in truth, you are too much like your father, Hauk. Always dreaming of more, always longing to wander. It is in your blood."

Hauk swallowed past a lump in his throat and looked down at the flagon in his hand.

His father's dream, in a small glass bottle.

"It may kill you," Erik warned. "Or it may work as your father intended, on an *innfodt*. I do not know. After your mother's death, I did not want anyone to take the chance of testing it." Erik walked toward him. "I found it among her belongings, after she and your father were gone. Mayhap I should have destroyed it with all the rest." He sighed wearily, raking a hand through his hair. "But I did not. I suppose I thought that one day, if I came to find life on Asgard unbearable, I might wish to take the risk and test it myself. But that day has never come."

Hauk held the bottle up in the light. "Uncle, there is only a small amount—"

"*Ja,* enough for one. Or rather, I hope there is enough. If it works, you will become mortal, an *utlending*. Free to live in their world. But you will be vulnerable to injury and illness, as they are. You will begin to age as they do. And you will live only a short time," he said slowly, "as they do. Mayhap only another fifty or sixty years."

Hauk felt his heart pounding hard, not with fear this time, but with hope. *He would be free.* Free to leave.

Free to go to Avril.

He rose from the chair. "If I am thirty now, by their

counting, I would live to be eighty or ninety. That is a full lifetime, to an *utlending*."

"Hauk, if it does work," Erik told him solemnly, "you must never return here. Everyone on Asgard will have to believe that you were banished."

Hauk nodded, understanding his uncle's concern. His miraculous reappearance would only inspire his fellow *innfødt* to attempt a new round of dangerous experiments, in an effort to reproduce the elixir.

If it worked.

He felt an ache in the center of his chest for those he would leave behind. For the friends who would grieve for him.

For all who wanted to be free, and could not be.

"It is not fair, Uncle," he said gruffly, "that I be the only one to—"

"Your father would have wanted you to have it." Erik placed a hand on Hauk's shoulder. "And you have no other choice now."

Hauk met and held his gaze. "Thank you, Uncle." He reached out to clasp Erik's arm. "Whatever happens, know that I am grateful to you."

"I will miss you, Hauk."

Hauk felt his throat tighten. "And I you."

Cautiously, hesitantly, he lifted the bottle in the firelight.

And pulled out the stopper.

22

*L*ittle Valkyrie . . .

Avril stirred in her sleep, moaning a soft protest at the voice that disturbed her slumber. Sighing, she slipped back down into her dream. 'Twas a sweet, new dream: that Hauk had returned to her, that he was here with her, in France. In Brittany.

Avril . . . I need you . . .

She lifted her lashes, blinking drowsily, confused. And somehow she did not leave that voice—that familiar, beloved, deep voice—behind in her dreams. It sounded as if he were here, with her. Beside her.

. . . help me . . .

With a startled cry, she lurched upright, eyes wide. She was not dreaming. And yet she was alone. The last embers of the fire still glowed on the hearth in her bedchamber. She was home, in her family château in Brittany, as she had been for more than a sennight.

And she was fully awake.

Avril, please.

She gasped in astonishment, covered her heart with one hand, could feel it thundering. Hauk's voice was not coming from her dreams *but from inside her somehow*. Shaking, she rose from the bed and rushed toward the window, sensing that he *was* here.

Here, in France, in Brittany. Not far away.

And he was hurt.

She could see naught in the darkness outside though rain no longer pattered against the window pane—the storm that had lasted all day had abated. She did not stop to question how she knew he was here, or how it was even possible. She ran for the door, into the corridor beyond, and down the stairs. Below in the great hall, she paused only long enough to snatch up her cloak and throw it on over her shift as she raced outside.

It was late, most of the family servants asleep. She crossed the bailey with pounding steps, mud splashing her garments. Reaching the stables, she did not pause to saddle her horse, taking time only to bridle the stallion before she leaped onto his back, galloping through the château gates and into the surrounding trees.

Avril, I love you . . .

Her heart in her throat, she relied on her feelings to guide her, riding through the night until she found him, lying in a clearing.

He was stretched out on his back, a black horse nearby, its reins trailing on the ground.

"God's breath!" she cried, throwing herself from her stallion's back and rushing over to him. She sank down beside him in the drenched grass. He was garbed in a dark tunic and leggings and cloak, the garments soaked with rain.

He opened his eyes, a trace of a smile on his lips. "Heard . . . me," he said weakly.

"Hauk." She sobbed, leaning over him, touching his face. "How can you possibly be here—how long have you—"

"Seven . . ." he murmured, his lashes drifting closed. "Seven days."

"Do you mean you have been away from Asgard for *seven* days?"

He did not respond.

"Hauk—"

"Thought it worked . . ." he whispered. "Did not . . . kill me. But may have been . . . wrong."

Avril shook her head, unable to understand what he was talking about. She checked him for injuries, could not find any, save for a deep cut on his forehead. It seemed he had fallen from his horse.

She grasped his shoulders, felt anguished at how warm and solid and strong he felt, when she knew his life was ebbing from him. "Hauk, what can I do? There must be something I can *do*!"

"Saw you . . . one last time." He looked up at her, his eyes glassy. Lifting one hand, he brushed his fingers over her cheek. "Worth it."

"Hauk, nay—"

"Love you . . ." he whispered.

His arm fell back to the ground, limp, and his eyes closed.

"Nay!" she cried. Nay, she could not lose him, not again! *Mercy of God, not again.* She crumpled over him, wrapping her arms around him, wrenched with anguish. Her cheek pressed against his chest, she held

on tightly, as if by her will alone she could hold him here, with her.

And then she gasped in astonishment, in stunned relief.

His heart was still beating.

Even through the cloth of his tunic, she could hear it—steady and strong beneath her ear.

He was alive! She did not understand how it was possible, but he was not dead. Nor was he in the *langvarig sovn* trance he had said he could experience only on Asgard.

He was unconscious, his breathing even, his skin warm—too warm. Pressing a hand to his forehead, she realized he had a fever.

And an entirely different kind of fear shook her.

The first warm glimmers of sunset shimmered through the window, painting the bedchamber with shades of orange and gold, before his lashes finally lifted again. Avril exhaled shakily, felt as if she had been holding her breath all day. Sitting beside him on the bed, she brushed his damp hair back from his forehead, wanting to kiss him breathless, offer a prayer of thanks for his life, and besiege him with questions all at once.

She settled for leaning down to kiss his bronzed cheek, relieved to find his skin no longer hot. She set aside the damp cloth she had used to try and cool his fever.

"Hauk, are you all right?" she whispered brokenly, all the tension and fear of this awful day spilling out of her.

He blinked up at her for a moment, as if uncertain

she was real. Then he smiled. "Aye." His voice was a dry whisper. He tangled his fingers through the loose strands of her hair, caressing her cheek. "Tired . . . but well."

"You are not in any pain?"

"Nay." He sounded surprised.

"Thank God." Suddenly she was trembling. "Hauk, I cannot believe you are here. How is it possible? How long *have* you been away from Asgard? How is it that your—"

"Shhh, my little Valkyrie." Burying his fingers in her hair, he drew her down to him for a kiss. "I am sorry that I frightened you so. I am not in any danger—"

"But last night you said you had been away seven days," she sputtered. "*Seven*. And today makes eight."

"Aye," Hauk murmured, smiling as he tenderly kissed her tears away, a storm of emotions in his eyes. "It took time to find you. I first went to your *beau-frère's* keep in the Artois, only to learn that the *duc* and his wife had escorted you here, to your home in Brittany, with your daughter—"

"Hauk, I do not understand." She could not stop shaking. "How can you be here, with me, alive?"

"I am all right, Avril." He pressed a finger to her lips, his smile deepening to reveal his straight white teeth and the dimples in his stubbled cheeks. "More than all right. I am free. As free as you are. Let me explain."

Some time later, after he had told her everything, she sat staring at him through tear-filled eyes, too astonished and joyful and excited to speak.

"And that was when I fell from the saddle," Hauk finished, frowning as he admitted it. "I had been feeling unwell all afternoon—dizzy and hot—and I became light-headed and fell. I feared mayhap the elixir had not changed me after all."

"Hauk, I believe what you experienced is simply what we call the ague. It is what happens sometimes when one rides so long in a cold autumn rain." Relief bubbled through her as she smoothed his tangled hair back from his forehead, smiling down at him. "It is quite common among us mortals."

"I was eager to reach you, my love."

"And I am afraid you will have a mark to show for it," she told him reluctantly. "This cut on your forehead will take a while to heal, and it looks as if you may have a scar."

He reached up to touch it, an odd smile playing around his lips. "A scar?"

"Pray do not sound so pleased," she said. "I would greatly prefer that you not acquire any more."

He laughed. "I will try, my love."

"Hauk," she said more seriously, "there is . . . there is something else that puzzles me. When you were out in the forest, hurt, I-I *heard* you somehow, calling to me—"

"From inside you, as if I were in your mind, your heart."

"Aye," she said in soft wonder, holding his gaze.

"I am not certain myself how it is possible, only that it is said that some men of Asgard share such a bond with their brides. Does it frighten you, little Valkyrie?" he asked gently.

"Nay." Avril touched his face, her heart beating fast. "I . . . it only startled me. The way the dreams did. I—" She blushed, glancing down. "I had dreams of you, before we even met. Rather vivid dreams."

"And I have dreamed of you, as well," he said huskily, drawing her down onto the bed with him.

Their mouths met in a deep, lingering kiss.

"Hauk," she said with a sigh as he nuzzled her cheek, her hair. "I am afraid I cannot stay in here much longer, or they will become suspicious."

"They?"

"Celine and Gaston. They are waiting downstairs in the great hall."

"Avril, you did not explain to them—"

"Nay, of course not," she assured him. "I told them I happened upon an injured man—while I was out riding because I could not sleep—and like any good Samaritan, I brought you here to one of the guest bedchambers to heal."

"A pleasure to make your acquaintance, milady." He chuckled.

"And yours, sir," Avril returned with a grin. "But if I remain in here with you any longer, they will begin to realize I am much more to you than a concerned hostess." She started to get up. "I have been informing them of your condition every now and then."

"Tell them I will live—as long as you stay with me." Smiling, he pulled her back down to sit beside him. "Tell them we once saw each other from afar, and I have traveled a great distance to find you because I knew I would love you forever. But do not go yet, my love. First, I have something to ask of you." His expression became serious. "We must still keep Asgard a secret, to protect everyone there."

"Aye." She nodded, warmed by his words and his touch.

"And I am afraid I must retract the other promise I asked of you." He smoothed her hair back from her face, drew her down for another kiss, murmuring against her mouth, "I do not wish for you to find another husband."

"Oh?"

"Marry me again, Avril. In the tradition of your people. Let me love you, and take care of you and Giselle . . . and give you more children to love."

"Aye." Tears blurred her vision as she looked into his eyes, those pale-blue eyes like the sky lit by the sun's hottest rays. "Oh, aye, Hauk Valbrand. I will marry you. Again."

Another quick kiss gave way to long, slow kisses. And an embrace that made her body tingle in all its most sensitive places.

"Hauk," she murmured, even as she melted down onto the bed with him, "I really should go and speak to Celine and Gaston . . ."

"Five minutes," Hauk murmured hungrily, easing her onto her back, his hard body covering hers. "Only five minutes more."

"You are most impatient." She laughed, twining her arms around his neck. "For a man of three hundred."

"Thirty," he corrected lightly. "Here in your world, I am only thirty."

She pulled him closer, filled with wonder and joy. "I think you will be very handsome, all craggy and silver-haired one day."

"You will have a chance to find out, my love." He grinned. "Now then, I believe I was about to make your dream come true."

"You already have," she whispered happily. "You already have."

If you're looking for romance, adventure, excitement and suspense be sure to read these outstanding romances from Dell.

※

Antoinette Stockenberg
- ☐ **EMILY'S GHOST**   21002-X $5.50
- ☐ **BELOVED**   21330-4 $5.50
- ☐ **EMBERS**   21673-7 $4.99

Rebecca Paisley
- ☐ **HEARTSTRINGS**   21650-8 $4.99

Jill Gregory
- ☐ **CHERISHED**   20620-0 $5.99
- ☐ **DAISIES IN THE WIND**   21618-4 $5.99
- ☐ **FOREVER AFTER**   21512-9 $5.99
- ☐ **WHEN THE HEART BECKONS** 21857-8 $5.99
- ☐ **ALWAYS YOU**   22183-8 $5.99

Christina Skye
- ☐ **THE BLACK ROSE**   20929-3 $5.99
- ☐ **COME THE NIGHT**   21644-3 $4.99
- ☐ **COME THE DAWN**   21647-8 $5.50
- ☐ **DEFIANT CAPTIVE**   20626-X $5.50
- ☐ **EAST OF FOREVER**   20865-3 $4.99
- ☐ **THE RUBY**   20864-5 $5.99